DEVIL
IN
TEXAS

Lady Law & The Gunslinger Series
Book One

❖

Adrienne deWolfe

Book design by eBook Prep www.ebookprep.com

Cover by The Killion Group, Inc. www.thekilliongroupinc.com

First Edition
July, 2016
ISBN: 978-1-61417-839-2

ePublishing Works!
www.epublishingworks.com

CHAPTER 1

Galveston, Texas
August 1883

Death: the end of the line.

There was a certain poetic justice to the idea here, at the corner of Post Office and 26th streets, where The Wicked plied their trade in sin. Galveston's tenderloin district—better known as The Line—was doing a booming business. Drunkards whizzed on walls. Hooligans rolled dice in alleys. Prostitutes primped, flashing more than smiles in the ruddy light of brothel windows.

As far as the eye could see, no tin-star intruded on the scene, probably because payoff day occurred on the first of the month. Until then, the law never crossed The Line. That meant tonight, no one would interfere.

'No one will even notice,' mused the figure in the itchy, fake beard, who lurked across the street from the Satin Siren Casino and Saloon.

Asrael. The Regulator of God. That was how the figure thought of itself while disguised in the rumpled, linen sack suit that sodbusters favored in town. Like the Angel of Death, the mortal Asrael felt no remorse to orchestrate deeds ordained by the King of Heaven. The Satin Siren was a pestilential den of drunken savages and thieving whores. Behind its deceptively quaint, nautical doors, depravity raged unabated. More to the point, the casino was the lair of the She-devil and her spawn, who'd interfered in Asrael's plans.

For the last time.

Fueled by divine righteousness and a potent dose of contempt, Asrael felt no fear of The Line's shifty-eyed rabble, even as twilight faded over Post Office Street, and night stretched its tentacles toward the slutty redhead on the casino's sign. Asrael imagined the She-devil must look much like that garish, birdlimed mermaid.

Soon that mystery would be solved. At eight o'clock, the stage curtains were scheduled to rise. The "Mermaid Queen" would show her tits to morally bankrupt men for the last time.

As if on cue, the hired gun across the street checked his timepiece. When his eyes locked with Asrael's, the man grinned, tossed aside his smoke, and disappeared into the alley of the brothel.

Asrael's lips carved out a ghoulish smile.

Eight o'clock. Divine justice.

Death at the end of The Line.

Asrael couldn't wait for the show to begin.

Life was about to get good.

That's what William "Cass" Cassidy thought as he craned back his blond head to gawk at the mostly naked mermaid, who protruded in all the right places from the brothel's sign. When he spied the seagull roosting so happily between the nymph's pumpkin-sized breasts, Cass's grin turned lopsided.

"You see that, Collie?" Cass reined in beside his 17-year-old sidekick and jerked his thumb in the direction of the mermaid. "I'm gonna get me one of those."

Collie shoved back his hat, spilling sun-bleached hair to his shoulders. He frowned up at the mermaid's trident. "Looks like another way to get ventilated, if you ask me."

Cass chuckled. Dismounting, he let his buckskin forge a

place at the crowded hitching post. About 11 months ago, Collie had saved Cass's leg—and maybe his life—from the bite of a copperhead. Cass had rescued the Kentucky-born orphan from a life of small-time thievery in an even smaller Appalachian town. Somewhere between Louisville and Longview, they'd learned to tolerate each other. Sort of.

"I *told* you," Cass said, using his black Stetson to slap the trail dust from his all-black duds. "The Line is the safest place in Sin City for a fella on the run."

"You yak about a lot of things, Snake Bait," Collie grumbled, referring to the copperhead incident. He shooed his pet from his lap so he could swing from the saddle. "But what I really want to know is: why does a state senator want to meet you in a place like this?"

"'Cause Austin's crawling with Rangers."

"Well, *that* should have been your first clue."

"About what, Mary Sunshine?"

"That your old ranch boss is as crooked as a corkscrew."

"Says the kid who steals pies off windowsills."

"Hey! A fella's gotta eat!" Collie's lean, wolfish cheeks turned as red as his bandanna. "'Sides. I thought you wanted to *be* a Ranger, not piss one off."

"Depends on the Ranger."

The truth was, Cass was hoping to strike a deal with his old ranch boss. Now that James "Cattle Baron" Westerfield chaired the Senate's Criminal Justice Committee, he had the political clout to fix Cass's troubles with the law—troubles that had started back home, in Pilot Grove, when Cass learned the hard way that tin-stars took a dim view of Good Samaritans, who tried to clean up Texas with their guns.

Thanks to letters of commendation written on Cass's behalf by Kentucky lawmen, Baron learned that Cass wanted to return to Texas. Unfortunately, those same letters had fallen into the hands of Rexford Sterne, Cass's mortal enemy, who somehow got himself appointed Adjutant-General of Texas's elite law-fighting force.

Thanks to Sterne's Rangers, Cass and Collie had been forced to ride for three weeks through bayou country, where they'd seen more water moccasins, alligators, and mosquitoes than two men should have to see in their lives. Collie had wondered where the drought was. And the cattle. And why any sane person would settle in Texas.

Collie hadn't exactly fallen in love with the dive-bombing seagulls of Galveston, either.

Tethering his roan to the hitching post, the boy squinted across the street. "Don't look now," he warned in his gruff, backwoods manner, "but that fella on the porch has been watching you ever since we turned down Post Office."

Cass glanced over his shoulder.

"I told you not to look! It could be a *Ranger,* for crying out loud!"

"Wearing a bowler and sack suit?" Cass snorted. "You got sawdust for brains to think something so stupid."

"Stupid ain't *my* affliction," Collie retorted loftily. "I didn't travel a thousand miles to put my neck in a noose."

The kid had a point. Cass hated when that happened.

But Cass hadn't been able to stay in Kentucky any longer. Not the way tensions had been building up inside him over the fiancée of his best friend. After riding with Lynx for 11 years, leaving the Cherokee behind had been the hardest thing Cass had ever done. Even harder than watching Lynx put a ring on Sera's hand.

Cass squared his jaw. *Yeah. Leaving Kentucky was the right thing to do.*

"All right," he told Collie. "I'm going in."

"It's your funeral."

"And you're going in with me."

"No, thanks. I hear brain rot's contagious—*Hey!*"

Ignoring the growls of Collie's furry bodyguard, Cass dragged his sidekick through the fancy, nautical doors of the Satin Siren Casino and Saloon. His gunslinger's eyes only blinked once to adjust to the foyer's ambient lighting, which was relatively bright, even for a high-class house of sin.

Releasing Collie's arm, Cass halted on turquoise, shell-shaped tiles. As usual, his hands twitched above his .45s while his gaze hunted for threats. The gaming hall was crowded, despite the early hour. He had the fleeting impression of gilded frescos, crystal chandeliers, and liveried faro dealers.

Then he noticed the stage—or rather, its aqua curtain. Craning back his head, he couldn't help but grin as he drank in every detail of that panorama of lust. The central focus was a galleon, marooned in the middle of a tropical lagoon. Beneath the prow, the captain was wrestling a fantastical, whiskered tiger shark with a woman's breasts. An octopus with unmistakably female eyes was using her tentacles to make naked sailors succumb to lust.

But Cass's favorite part of the tapestry was the army of warrior mermaids, who were herding shackled swabbies into a coral cave. The captives didn't look all that alarmed by the dastardly things the Mermaid Queen was doing to their *compadres*. Who would have guessed fishtails could be used in such imaginative ways?

Suddenly, a whale-sized bully with anchor tattoos appeared to block Cass's educational view.

"What the hell is *that*?" the bouncer growled, fixing his good eyeball—the one without the patch—on the whiskered tub of lard at Collie's feet.

The boy bristled. He'd never been fond of authority. "Did ya go blind in both eyes? That's a *coon*, Blackbeard."

Cass coughed into his fist, mostly to hide his amusement. "Howdy, pard," he greeted the pirate. "Don't mind Coon Collie, here. Kentucky *dumbass* asylums don't get much sun. Our Texas drought must've fried his brain."

Blackbeard sneered at this assessment. He had only half his teeth, and most of them were chipped. "Coons ain't allowed. No dumbasses, neither."

"So who let you in?"

Blackbeard purpled at Collie's taunt. Cass had a vision of crunching bones and gushing blood—mostly Blackbeard's, if the bouncer dared to lay a hand on the raccoon's precious boy.

Fortunately for Blackbeard, a blonde in a flurry of gauzy

turquoise strolled into the fray. With her coral circlet and gilded trident, the bawd bore more than a passing resemblance to the nymphs on the stage's curtain.

"Welcome to the Satin Siren," she greeted, her silvery voice reminiscent of chimes. "I'm Randie."

Cass winked. "I'll bet you are."

Collie rolled his eyes.

"And who have we here?" Randie gushed, bending at the waist to let the coon sniff her manicured hand. The pose let Cass see clear to her navel.

"Why, that there's Vanderbilt," Cass drawled. "Vandy Vanderbilt Varmint. At least, that's how he's known on all the kitchen Wanted Posters. Vandy never met a sweetmeat he didn't like."

"Is that a fact?" Randie's rose-petal lips fairly dripped nectar. "Then we'll have to find your coon something yummy, won't we?"

"And my name's Collie," the boy interceded acidly. "Collier McAffee. Just in case you get around to wondering."

Randie's cool green eyes swept over the boy's buckskin shirt, which hid a deceptively lean, muscle-packed torso. Next, her eyes dropped to his package—or more likely, to the Levi pockets flanking his plain brass buckle and sturdy thighs. Spying no indication of wealth, the bawd dismissed Collie and lavished her honeyed smile on Cass.

"Baron's expecting you. In the private poker room. Tito, darling," she cooed to the bouncer, "let the nice raccoon pass."

Grudgingly, Tito stepped aside, and Vandy scurried past his boots. But even Randie's influence couldn't keep the bouncer from confiscating gun belts. Cass kept his peace, because like any self-respecting outlaw, he'd concealed all manner of weapons beneath his duster. Collie didn't fuss, because he only needed to bellow a two-syllable command to turn Vandy into a holy, freaking terror.

Thus, the male threesome trotted like lemmings after Randie's sweetly swaying hips. She led them to a side room, dominated by a mahogany poker table with five empty chairs and a well-stocked bar. Chewing the fat with the drink wrangler was a middle-aged man with a big-boned frame, much like a grizzly bear's. Despite the top hat that capped the gent's salt-and-pepper hair, and the elegantly waxed mustachios that hid the scar from an old sucker punch, Cass had no trouble recognizing the Burnett County ranch boss, who'd given him his first shot at earning an honest wage.

"Well, I'll be damned!" Baron boomed the moment Cass stepped across the threshold. "It's the Rebel Rutter! What's the matter, Cass? Run out of brothels in Dodge?"

"Aw, shucks. You'd think I was a voter, the way you sweet-talk me." Cass shook the old skirt-chaser's hand. "How ya doin,' Baron?"

"Still prodding, boy! That's what counts. You wearing a Ranger badge yet?"

"Not yet."

"Damned fools in Austin."

Puffing his stogie like a fiend, Baron squinted next at Collie and his ring-tailed charmer. "Looks like someone snookered his way out of becoming a hat," the senator observed drolly.

While Cass made the introductions, he couldn't help but notice that age, or maybe illness, had shaved at least twenty pounds off Baron's frame. His fancy swallowtails hung loosely around his middle section, and the whites of his coffee-colored eyes were faintly yellow.

But whatever was ailing the old bull hadn't dampened his libido. He patted Randie's shapely rump. "Give the boys what they want, Sweet Cakes. Put it on my tab."

Collie roused himself from his scowl. "You got Kentucky bourbon in this dive?"

"Collie's not used to Texas-friendly," Cass confided.

Baron chuckled. "The boy needs a teat, that's all. Randie, find Collie a heifer who knows how to treat a bull."

"Sure thing, Baron. You like blondes, don't you, Collie?"

"Now she notices me."

"Not her, kid." Baron's eyes danced. "A woman like Randie is champagne. After a steady diet of sarsaparilla, her kind of fizz is an acquired taste."

Randie lavished her nectar-dripping smile on Baron. He raised her knuckles to his lips.

Collie went back to scowling.

After the bawd made her graceful exit, Cass turned his attention to Baron. "So where's this high-stakes poker game you promised us?"

"Hell if I know. Me and the wife were attending a birthday social this afternoon, when my secretary brought me word that the poker game got cancelled. But the barkeep says the opening ante got moved to half-past-eight."

"So we're early?"

"Looks that way. Things used to run a whole lot smoother around here, before that Yankee cockroach won the joint last week. Aces high. Probably cheated." Baron tossed back a whiskey shot. "Damned Republican," he grumbled.

Cass ducked his head to hide his smirk.

"Anyhow, this Dietrich fella started making lots of changes. Busted Randie back to chorus. She's been headlining here nigh on eight years. Seems like a mean, low-down stunt to pull on a lady—even if that sweet little angelfish *is* getting long in the tooth."

The barkeep coughed into his fist. The mirth in his eyes betrayed his stoic demeanor. "Mr. Dietrich hired a new headliner, senator. A Miss Cassandra McGuire. She's a torch singer from San Francisco. And a natural born redhead—so I hear."

Baron's eyes warmed with interest. "Natural born, eh? Well, the Yankee's got taste in women, you gotta give him that. When does this new filly trot out on stage?"

"Eight o'clock, sir. Mr. Dietrich changed the program last-minute to feature Miss McGuire."

Baron harrumphed, checking his pocket watch. "Well, I reckon we got nothing better to do until the poker game starts. C'mon, boys. Let's find ourselves a stage-side table so we can take a look at the new gal's gams."

But an alarm went off in Cass's head as he surveyed Baron's destination. "Wait." He caught the senator's arm. "Those footlights will make us sitting ducks."

"You expecting trouble?"

"Maybe. I'm thinking all the schedule changes might not be a coincidence. You're an influential man in the legislature. Someone might not want you around."

The senator hiked a bushy eyebrow. "My arrival *did* cause a flurry in the dove cote. But I just figured the bawds were drawing lots to see who'd get first crack at my purse."

"Could be." Cass wasn't convinced. "To be safe, why don't you and Collie get acquainted, while I scout the premises."

Baron grunted. "You armed?"

"'Course."

The senator winked. Patting his own hidden shoulder holster, he waved Cass on his way.

Compared with the poker room, the gaming hall was a mob scene. Cass stepped into the guttural din of male voices, wheezing trombones, and raucous laughter, punctuated by occasional bellows of, "Snake eyes!"

After a leisurely stroll around the perimeter, he bellied up to the bar. Tossing down two bits, he ordered a shot of José Cuervo, then rested his elbows on the counter to survey the room. Near the stage, he spied the casino's duded-up new owner, Karl Dietrich, cracking his knuckles and ordering dancing girls around. Stocky, like a bouncer, Dietrich's darting eyes missed nothing. Cass took an instant dislike to him—and not just because the German was barking at women. Something about Dietrich wasn't quite right. He looked too young for gray hair and a silver goatee.

Next, Cass noticed the sodbuster, whom Collie had spotted earlier on Post Office Street. The granger sat in a dimly lit corner without friends, women, or even a deck of playing cards. His tankard was foaming with cherry sarsaparilla.

That country bumpkin traveled all the way to Sin City to drink fizzy pop?

Suddenly, the sodbuster stiffened. He leaned intently across his table. Cass followed the man's gaze and noticed the rippling stage curtains.

The auburn head of the mermaid queen split in two, replaced by a pile of upswept, flame-colored curls. A face that rivaled Aphrodite's hovered in that makeshift window for a moment, a bare fraction of time, but every nerve in Cass's body fired with recognition as a pair of tawny tiger eyes locked with his.

He sucked in his breath.

The face vanished.

Damn.

Cass's instincts had never failed him, and right now, they were screaming loud enough to rouse his pecker.

The devil's own daughter smoldered behind that curtain, and the firebrand's name wasn't Cassandra McGuire.

CHAPTER 2

⸻ ◆ ⸻

Sadie Michelson cursed under her breath as she dared to peer a second time through the stage curtains. Unfortunately, her eyes hadn't deceived her. The heartthrob with the sun-bronzed skin, sapphire eyes, and sinfully tight, leather chaps was none other than her cocky ex-lover.

Eros in Spurs. That's what William Cassidy was called in polite society, but Dodge City bawds had dubbed him the Rebel Rutter after he'd accepted a bet to seduce a bride on her wedding day. And succeeded.

There are 26 brothels on The Line, Cass. Why did you have to pick mine?

Sadie fumed, and not just because the inveterate skirt-chaser had waved Randie to his side. In less than two minutes, Sadie was supposed to sashay onto the stage, wearing a shameless, black satin gown that fit too tightly to allow a corset.

She was supposed to wiggle her hips, bounce her breasts, and tease the all-male crowd into a lusty lather during the first public performance of her *Ballad of Lucifire*.

She was *supposed* to use her seductive arts to cozy up to a corrupt state senator and entice him to spill his guts.

But how could she concentrate on making James "Baron" Westerfield confide all his loathsome secrets, when the real Lucifire lounged against the bar, sizzling hotter than the devil's pitchfork?

Damn you, Cass, you're going to blow my cover!

Panic threatened to drag her into its undertow. Four years ago, when Cass had ridden out of her life, she'd secretly died inside. Desperate to forget the soul-searing heat of his kisses, she'd clawed her way from the ashes, like a stubborn phoenix. She'd determined to prove to Allan Pinkerton that a cowtown whore had more useful talents than sex. Fighting her way into the Master Spy's secret circle of men, she'd gained credibility for her marksmanship, resourcefulness, and wit. She'd accomplished her directives in record time and more impressively, without bloodshed.

Now she faced the highest-profile assignment in her Pinkerton career. The whole agency was scrutinizing her. If she could pin a murder charge on Baron, after all her illustrious male colleagues had failed, she would finally gain the satisfaction of silencing her critics.

Determined to achieve that happy end, Sadie latched onto the first solution that presented itself: a busty blonde, who was hurrying past the curtains in her warrior-mermaid costume.

"You're on, Randie."

The older woman jerked her arm free. The glitter of frosty, green eyes challenged Sadie's right to order her around.

"Dietrich told me to change my costume for the Can-Can."

"Laryngitis," Sadie improvised in her hoarsest whisper. She patted her throat for emphasis. "Out of the blue."

"Not my problem."

Bristling, Sadie dug her fists into her hips. Miranda Reynolds had been a thorn in her side since Day One of this mission—not that Randie didn't have good reason. Only that morning, Pinkerton Agent Mace Ryker (alias, Karl Dietrich) had ordered the outraged soprano to give up the best bedroom in the brothel for his "new star performer."

"With an attitude like yours," Sadie said, "no wonder Dietrich busted you back to hoofer."

Well, *that* opened the proverbial can of worms.

"Listen here, you braying bitch! I can sing *circles* around your rusted pipes—"

Sadie grimaced as the 30-year-old diva aired her lungs. Only 20 feet of cigar smoke and a flimsy strip of velvet separated her from Cass. The whole reason she'd invented this laryngitis charade was so he wouldn't hear her.

"Yes, yes," she hissed at Randie. God knew, she'd been cursed by whores before. None of the women in the chorus liked her. Sadie didn't really care, except she had a job to do, and snooping for intelligence in a whorehouse would have been a whole lot easier if the bawds had accepted her.

Six days ago, Mace had snuffed out that pipedream after he'd "acquired the Siren in a wager" (Pinkertons had a way of getting what they wanted—fast.) Mace had cancelled Randie's solo performances to make room on the program for Sadie, who'd needed an entrée into Baron's close-knit circle of high-rollers.

"Got it," Sadie rasped. "I'm slime, and you're a doughty diva who can twist into a pretzel, naked. You want the solo or not?"

The spite in Randie's glare transmuted into a far more dangerous weapon: *cunning.*

"Your voice didn't sound so scratchy that time."

Sadie could have kicked herself.

"This sudden throat affliction wouldn't have something to do with Cass, would it…*Cassie?*"

Sadie groaned inwardly. *Why, oh why, did I choose that alias?* She spread her hands in a questioning gesture.

"Oh please." Randie snorted. "I had a chat with Mr. Long-Drink-of-Handsome by the bar. He told me you two go way back. He wanted directions to your dressing room. Frankly, I don't know what your problem is, trading a red-blooded charmer like Cass for a humorless prick like Dietrich. Stupid fever, maybe?"

Sadie reined in her notorious, Irish temper. She was sorely

tempted to point out that Cass hadn't earned his nickname because his talent was fidelity. However, laryngitis was supposed to be curbing her ability to mouth fight.

"Fine," she snapped. "I'll ask Mimi to sing my solo."

Randie blanched. "You can't," she protested, no doubt envisioning the triumph of her ambitious, 18-year-old understudy. "There isn't time. And besides, the show must go on."

How convenient.

"D-flat isn't exactly my key," Randie continued loftily, as if altos were a stink one scraped off one's shoe. "But I heard you caterwaul *Lucifire* enough times in rehearsal to commit the hokum to memory. Of course, by rights, a headliner should have a change of costume—"

Sadie yanked off her black boa and draped it over Randie's shoulders. "Here," she whispered, pushing the shorter woman toward the curtain. "The show must go on, remember?"

A smug smile curved Randie's lips. "Very well. I'll sing your stupid cowboy song. But you'll owe me. You'll owe me *big.*"

Attesting to the soprano's popularity, ear-piercing whoops and whistles accompanied the thunderous applause that greeted her unexpected return to the stage. Randie sauntered across the gleaming oakwood, all the way to front-and-center like a queen ascending her throne. A provocative little smile teased her lips as she turned her head from side to side, acknowledging the toasts of her admirers.

Taking the opportunity to peer over the soprano's shoulder, Sadie scanned the sun-blackened faces at the bar.

Uh-oh. Where's Cass?

Hastily, Sadie checked the gamblers, gathered around the faro, roulette, and craps tables. She couldn't see her ex-lover anywhere. Biting her lip, she dropped the curtain, allowing inky-blue shades to crowd around her.

Damn. Cass had already headed for her dressing room. That meant she'd have to retreat to her bedroom to retrieve a new costume—or better yet, a gun. Under a flood of stage lights, in skin-tight fishtails, she hadn't been able to disguise the bulge of a pistol on her thigh.

Sadie barely heard the strings bow the opening chords of *Lucifire*. Her mind was in a whirl as she weaved through hulking shadows cast by theatrical backdrops, shaped like pirate ships, Poseidon, and whales. It occurred to her she should warn Mace about the Cass problem before she reported to Baron's poker game.

Her feet faltered.

Suddenly, she was distracted by a tendril of tobacco smoke. She tensed. She would have recognized that signature blend of cinnamon and cloves anywhere. However, spying Cass amidst the prop clutter in the stage's dimly lit wing was going to be another matter entirely.

"The years have been good to you, Sadie."

Her heart skipped as that seductive, Texas baritone caressed her name. He was closer than she'd imagined, invisible except for his cigarette. The tip brightened, kindling orange flames in the sapphire mirrors of his eyes. When he exhaled, silvery, aromatic fingers reached out to her, beckoned her, enticing her as only the promise of secrets and sin can.

"You sound surprised," she rallied, reining in her galloping emotions. "What were you expecting? Wrinkles and warts?"

"And a pointy, black hat."

"Dog."

A flash of white hinted at his grin—a dimpled, darling grin that still had the power to sneak into her dreams.

He leaned a shoulder against the frame of a velvet swing. His new pose silhouetted him against the rising moon, peeking through the catwalk's window. Lunar light and star shine shimmered around his sun-streaked hair. Such a halo was incongruous for a man who looked like the devil in his thigh-hugging leather and denim.

As if on cue, Randie's voice soared like larksong through the house:

> *"Lucifire they called him,*
> *His draw was next to none;*
> *His smile was like an angel's;*
> *The devil ruled his gun.*
> *"The purdy gals in Texas*
> *Would sigh for him and swoon,*
> *When Lucifire went sparking—*
> *Sneaked thru windows to go sparking—*
> *Broke fair hearts when he went sparking—*
> *Each night beneath the moon."*

Cass chuckled, exhaling another stream of smoke. "Lucifire, huh? So that's how you're immortalizing my legend these days."

She cringed inside. She'd been hoping the scapegrace had forgotten how she'd once confessed, in the throes of sentimental lunacy, that she wrote all her love songs about him.

"You think *I* wrote those lyrics?"

"Wrote them and intended to sing them—until you spied me in the crowd."

"Nonsense."

"'Laryngitis,'" he mocked, pitching his voice higher and imitating the way she'd patted her throat. "'Out of the blue.'"

She kept smiling—barely. She remembered the other reason why Cass was so dangerous: he'd known her since puberty. They'd both come a long way since his thirteenth birthday, when he'd been forced to flee east Texas, charged with gunning down the Ku Klux Klansman, who'd murdered his older cousin. Still, Cass knew enough of her tricks and weaknesses to jeopardize her mission. Maybe even her life.

He cocked his head. Randie was singing again:

> *"The Devil in the darkness,*
> *His kisses burned like flame;*
> *Lawmen vowed to catch him;*
> *Fathers cursed his name."*

Sadie's face heated like a firecracker.

Cass chuckled, tapping ash from his cigarette. "Not that I'm criticizing, but you might add a verse about how Mothers adore me. And how little kiddies want to grow up to be like me. You know, to keep the record straight."

"Sure. And then I could add how pigs fly and buffaloes have wings."

"Naw." He winked with roguish charm. "No one would believe that part."

Randie launched into the next verse:

> *"Wanted by the Rangers,*
> *And fleeing Lady Love,*
> *Lucifire nursed a secret–*
> *An aching, soul-deep secret–*
> *Young Lucifire hid his secret—*
> *His heart yearned for a dove.*
>
> *"Her eyes were hot as cinders,*
> *Her heart burned like a brand,*
> *The outlaw's red-haired siren,*
> *Would never wed one man.*
>
> *"The fearsome Texas Rangers,*
> *Drove our hero from his love.*
> *But Lucifire vowed to have her–*
> *He'd trade his guns to have her–*
> *He'd wear a star to have her–*
> *The outlaw swore to God above."*

Cass's stare locked with hers. Sapphire flames blazed a path to her soul. In a heartbeat, she was transported back to her seedy sweatbox of a bedroom above Dodge City's infamous Long Branch Saloon. But she was laughing and snuggling, feeling safe, sated, and cherished in Cass's arms.

She tore her gaze from the primal calling in her lover's stare.

"So tell me," he said huskily, "how does Lucifire's ballad end?"

"You don't remember?" She couldn't quite keep the sting from her tone. "He rides away and never looks back. And neither does she."

A muscle ticked in Cass's jaw.

"Right."

He seemed to lose all interest in Randie's singing. Tossing aside his smoke, he rubbed out the tip with his boot. His fancy, Mexican-style spurs jingled above the poignant sighing of the violins.

"So." He hooked his thumbs over his waistband. "What do you know about Karl Dietrich and the shenanigans going on around this place?"

Alarm bells went off in Sadie's head. Cass's suspicions were way too close for comfort. "Care to be more specific?" she hedged.

"I hear Dietrich won the joint last week. And now he's making trouble for my friends."

"Friends like Randie? Or friends who hired your guns?"

"What difference does it make? Unless you're in cahoots with him."

"Honestly." She mustered a provocative tone—one of her best diversions. "You make love sound so…*illegal.*"

He snorted. "The only thing you're in love with is Dietrich's bank account."

"Sour grapes, darling?"

"Maybe." He folded his arms across his chest. "Or maybe you're too full of piss and vinegar to admit that throwing in your lot with Dietrich was a mistake. Half the whores in this establishment are gunning for him. The other half are gunning for you."

"Occupational hazard."

His brow furrowed. "C'mon, Sadie. This life isn't for you. You're 28 years old! How much longer do you think you can keep apes, like Dietrich, happy? Quit whoring around while you still can. Find yourself a decent husband. Settle down. Raise a passel of kids."

Her chest heaved at his presumption—and not just because he'd never committed himself to her.

"Because I can still turn a man's head?" she asked with deceptive pleasantness.

"Well sure. A fella would have to be dead not to notice you."

"Lucky me. So many Johns. So little time."

"I can't believe that's what you really want."

"No? Because the greatest thing a woman should aspire to in life is becoming the obedient thrall of a husband, who, by law, can do whatever he likes to her property, her body, and her children?"

"You know I never did cotton to the law."

"And yet you want to enforce it. As a Ranger."

His eyes flashed, a sure sign her barb had struck a nerve.

"Don't go putting Rangers in the same category as tyrant-husbands. Rangers aren't even allowed to get married."

"So now I'm supposed to believe you refuse to be roped into matrimony because you dream of a tin star?"

"I'm a wanted man."

"By every wedding-bell chaser in the West."

He had the audacity to smirk. "A renegade makes a worse husband than a Ranger. I'm doing womankind a favor."

She rolled her eyes. How many times had he used *that* cheesy line on some adoring belle?

"And now your roving has brought you full circle," she accused. "You've returned to Texas. To do what? Get yourself hanged?"

He arched a sun-gilded eyebrow. "If you keep talking sweet to me, I might get the notion you're still fond of this ol' red neck."

Redneck, indeed. Lawmen might call him Coyote Cass, but his brain was mostly weasel.

"You've taken a ridiculous risk by showing your face here, Cass. You need to leave Texas."

"Oh, I get it. You figure I should high-tail it to Mexico 'cause you got yourself a fella who packs a bratwurst and a big gun."

Smartass.

"Are you even *capable* of dragging your mind out of the gutter?"

"Sure. But what fun would that be?"

A creaking floorboard made her jump.

Like magic, a pistol materialized in Cass's black-gloved fist. The glint of that .38 was more than a little unnerving—and not just because he was notorious for a temper that fired as fast as his guns. At 25-years-old, Cass still didn't believe he was mortal.

Afraid to move, afraid to breathe, she waited, counting heartbeats. Eyes like blue steel raked the shadows for eavesdroppers—or maybe bounty hunters. Cass never had answered her question about why he'd returned to Texas.

Finally, reluctantly, he depressed the gun's hammer.

"Are you always so jumpy these days?" she demanded, her voice quavering with relief.

His glare didn't inspire confidence in his self-restraint. "If I have a reason."

She imagined what that reason might be, and her stomach clenched. "Then like I said, Cass. You need to leave. Before someone else finds you here."

Silence stretched as taut as any gallows' rope between them. She saw his chest rising and falling to the wild rhythm of applause. Tankards were thumping; boots were stomping; cries of, *"More!"* were shaking the oak planks of the floor. Randie's delighted laughter bubbled past the curtain. Apparently, Sadie's "stupid cowboy song" had been a smash with the sailors and conventioneers.

"Watch your back," Cass told her quietly.

He pinched his hat brim in farewell.

A moment later, he'd vanished, as if a drape of shadows had dropped between them, too thick and dark for even a moonbeam to pierce. For Randie's encore, fiddlers begun sawing out *The Night the Preacher Rang The Whorehouse Bell*. Sadie strained her ears, but she could hear nothing else above the whoops and whistles of the seamen: not Cass's spurs, not the echo of his boots, not even the squealing of the hall door when it swung closed behind him.

She swallowed hard.

Fool. She cursed her lapse into sentiment. How could she

have let him get under her skin, even now, when she finally had everything she wanted: the freedom to live her life as she pleased. The freedom to give her body to any man she wanted...

Baron! Crap! I almost forgot!

Anxious to spring her trap, she hurried toward the brothel stairs. She figured she had about 15 minutes to change her clothes before the private poker game started. Since Cass had spoiled her stage appearance, she needed to put Plan B into action: to make her first contact with Baron as a high-class beerjerker.

The senator had invested heavily in the western expansion of the Gulf, Colorado, and Santa Fe Railroad. The Pinkertons suspected he was using the drought and its resulting range wars as a cover to dispose of inconvenient sodbusters, who'd refused to give the railroad permission to lay tracks across their fields. The suspicion had risen when a disgruntled ranch hand, whom Baron's wife had fired for "drunken hooliganism," started complaining in capitol-area saloons that folks who made an enemy of Baron disappeared.

A week later, that same ranch hand, who'd trained horses for 22 years, got kicked in the head by his cowpony.

No one could pin that accidental death on Baron, of course. But accidental deaths seemed to pave the way to Baron's success. He'd been appointed to his first term in the Texas Senate because his duly elected rival got stampeded by steers. In business matters, Divine Providence had interceded at least six times on Baron's behalf, getting court cases dismissed because opposing witnesses hanged themselves, or got crushed by an overturning wagon, or fell through the rotted planks of a bridge. To make matters worse, Baron served as the chairman of the senate's Criminal Justice Committee. For two years, he'd had the power to appoint and remove Rangers. Texas's elite crime-fighting force practically worked for him!

No wonder Governor Ireland doesn't trust his own

Rangers, Sadie thought grimly.

As she began climbing the dimly lit stairwell, her scalp prickled. She couldn't have said why; no one was following her. Even so, she was relieved when she reached the comparative brightness of the second story. Over all but four bedrooms, a red lantern burned to signal the whore was working. Two of those empty rooms belonged to her and Randie. The other two were owned by shrilly laughing women, who were allowing their drunken, belching admirers a strategic grope in the hall to lure them over the threshold—if not for a rut, then for a roll to relieve them of their casino winnings.

Sadie had witnessed this scene a thousand times. She'd lived it for eleven years after her father's murder and her mother's suicide. She didn't judge bawds for what they had to do to survive. Most of them were under the age of 17, and the vast majority of those girls died before the age of 25. Every bawd she'd ever known had been orphaned, destitute, and one meal shy of starvation before they'd wound up on the steps of a brothel.

That's why Sadie nurtured the secret dream to help her former rival and friend, Wilma LeBeau, run a training center for "Pinkies," as female detectives were affectionately called. Sadie figured if she could save just one penniless girl from the streets, then God might relent and decide not to cast her into Satan's deepest dungeon for letting her twin sister drown.

Wracked by the usual self-loathing, Sadie forced her chin higher as she moved down the hall. Two pairs of kohl-lined eyes blinked resentfully at her as she passed the younger girls and their slobbering Johns without her own meal ticket in tow. Under the circumstances, the hall stretched on forever—at least, it seemed that way. Fishtail skirts didn't lend themselves to speed. Nor did spiky little heels.

But Sadie had learned at a tender age that clothing held only one value to a bawd: the degree to which it tantalized. That's why she wasn't wearing more than garters and stockings beneath her skin-tight satin.

Relieved to duck into her bedroom, she didn't waste any time kicking off her shoes and stripping off her fishtails.

Quick costume changes were a requisite skill for a stage performer. The orchestra had launched into a rousing version of *The Drunken Sailor* by the time Sadie finished strapping her holster to her thigh. She could feel the pulse of the music through her stockings.

But the pounding of boots and tankards, below, was accompanied by a fresh gust of goosebumps, this time down her spine.

Now what?

With the .32 gripped expertly in her fist, she looked beneath her bed. She wrenched open the doors of her stately, Louis XIV wardrobe. She poked the bombazine draperies that rippled from the sea breeze, blowing through her window. She imagined she should be hunting for a rat or a scorpion, since she'd exhausted all the places where a grown human could hide in her 9-foot by 12-foot box.

Then she spied a flash of light, hurtling out of an oleander bush near the building's foundation.

It all happened so fast.

One moment, she was peering out her window; the next moment, a smoking cylinder crashed open at her feet. Flames belched from the shattered crockery. The curtains ignited. The carpet caught fire. She stumbled backwards, choking on fumes.

Greek Fire! Water would be useless.

Her mind whirred into action. Wrenching a flimsy night wrapper from her wardrobe, she stomped on boots. She planned to sound a general alarm. But when she reached her door, it wouldn't budge.

Frantic, she rattled. She banged. She screamed. Her efforts were futile. Someone had taken the key, locking the door from the outside. Apparently, her window hadn't been an arbitrary target. Somebody wanted her dead!

Panic gnawed at her reason. *Urine*. Urine would buy her time.

She lunged for the sloshing bed pan and tossed its contents on the carpet, saturating the fibers between her and the racing wall of chemically-induced fire. She figured she had little more than two minutes to rip out the false back of her wardrobe and grab the box with her lock pick before her protective little barrier of urine was overcome.

Pinkertons prepare for assassination attempts. The words from her Field Agent Manual pounded in her head.

Ignoring the sparks that showered her arms, she wrenched aside the few gowns that hung in her wardrobe and ripped out the loosely nailed backboard. Frenzied groping located the hole she'd smashed into the plaster and the cracker tin she'd stuffed inside the wall. She burned her palms and fingers wrestling that metallic box from the hole, but she hardly noticed. She was too busy shoving her badge, cash, ammo, and train ticket into her trouser pockets.

Next, she grabbed a slouch hat, scarf, and duster from the hole. She knew when she did get to the other side of the door—and hopefully, the seawall—she mustn't be recognized. Otherwise, her brush with death could get a whole lot closer.

Gritting her teeth, she ignored the flames that roared ever closer. Perspiration made lock-picking tedious. Again and again, her slippery fingers lost their grip on the widdy. She wasted precious seconds, coughing from the smoke that burned her sinuses and stung her eyes.

Finally, the mechanism yielded. Nearly sobbing with relief, she wrenched open the door. A scene of mass hysteria greeted her. Shrieking whores, half-dressed Johns, and cursing waiters jostled each other, pushing and gouging in their efforts to escape the floor. Both stairwells were ablaze. Apparently, the murderer hadn't wanted any witnesses to survive.

Mace shoved his way to her side. "What the hell did you do? Light a cigarette?"

"You know damned well I don't smoke! Someone tossed Greek Fire through my window!"

The color drained from Mace's face. "You blew your cover," he growled, grabbing her arm and swinging her toward a darkened bedroom. "Follow evasion protocol, and get your tail out of here!"

She wrenched her elbow from the senior agent's grasp and dragged the scarf over her nose. A little sympathy from her colleague would have been appreciated, but then, Mace had never wanted her on "his" case. The only undercover work he did willingly with a Pinkie involved a bed.

As Sadie ducked into a street-side bedroom, Mace remained in the hall. He was shouting for folks to stay calm. To find an open window and take turns jumping into the flower bushes below. Wails of female protest greeted this suggestion, but Sadie didn't hesitate. The building was only two stories tall, and this bedroom, in particular, had a sturdy Mexican plum tree butting against its casement. She knew this fact because she'd cased every blessed inch of the casino to locate the best escape routes.

Pinkertons can't be too careful, the manual had instructed.

Ripping her burn-blistered palm, she nevertheless managed to shimmy down the trunk and stumble into the shadows of the privy before the first of the hurtling bodies crashed into the oleander bushes.

"Sadie! Has anyone seen Sadie?"

It was Cass's voice, adding to her cover problem. She shrank against the outhouse even as she recognized her ex-lover's pale gold hair in the casino's milling refugees on the lawn. He was turning his head every which way, shouting her name, searching the faces of the beerjerkers, who'd been ushered, along with the gamblers, from the building.

Surely, Cass wasn't part of the arson conspiracy.
Was he?

Suddenly, her casement blew out. Flames spewed triumphantly through the hole. Orange-red reflections flickered over Cass's face, illuminating his horror as the inferno devoured her bedroom. The building shuddered. The timbers groaned.

Cass was screaming for Cassandra McGuire now,
shaking off Baron and Randie and knocking some lanky
kid on his ass beside a raccoon. The Siren's bouncer entered
the fray. Fists started swinging. Cass's .38 glinted in the
firelight. Tito managed to wrestle the gun from Cass's fist
before he knocked Cass out cold.

Sadie exhaled a shaky breath. She forced herself to be
logical. To think like a Pinkerton, not a jilted lover. Cass
had coyote cunning; he survived in the world because he
was a consummate liar with a flair for the dramatic. If he'd
been part of the arson conspiracy, *of course* he would have
faked his concern for her, if he'd wanted her dead.

In any event, Tito had neutralized him. Now was her
chance to flee.

Flipping up her coat collar, she turned her back on the
soaring flames. She drove her leaden legs toward
Harborside Drive and the fishing wharves. Her plan was to
disappear while she still had time, while the brothel
refugees were too confused to notice the flight of a sloppily
dressed figure with a scarf-wrapped face. Let Cass—and
everyone else in that building—think Cassandra McGuire
had perished in the fire.

That way, Sadie Michelson could live to fight Baron
Westerfield another day.

CHAPTER 3

Six Weeks Later
Rocking W Ranch
Burnett County, Texas

"Good God. Is that gun loaded?"

"Who wants to know?" Cass growled, but the question was rhetorical. About a minute before he'd heard a mincing stride crunch gravel on the drive, a morning breeze had blown the scent of licorice hair tonic through the open doors of the carriage house.

"You know very well it's Pendleton!" snapped Baron's secretary.

Cass grimaced. Pendleton Prouse was the last man he wanted to deal with while sober.

After the brothel debacle, Cass had hired out his guns to Baron and started living in the Rocking W's bunkhouse with Collie and a passel of cowboys. Needless to say, this move had reignited his feud with Pendleton—or rather, Pendleton's feud with him.

A fussy little man, who nursed lifelong grudges, Pendleton preferred bowties to bolos and spats to spurs. He rarely ventured into the sun, as his milky complexion could attest, and he shunned any activity more rigorous than climbing a ladder to reach the top shelf in the library. Perhaps because he huddled over Baron's ledgers from sunrise to sunset, or perhaps because Baron paid him better than all his cowpokes combined, Pendleton thought himself exceedingly important.

"I demand an explanation, Mr. Cassidy!"

"All right." Cass didn't bother to turn. He was too busy focusing on his task. "I'm juggling."

"I can see that!"

"Then why'd you ask?"

Wisecracks. Hair-raising risks. Death-defying feats. These were Cass's salvation. Without them, he would have lost his mind—and not just because life as a regulator, with no bushwhackers to ventilate, was insanely boring. During the quieter moments on Baron's ranch, when Cass was watching the cattle graze or listening to a harmonica croon, memories of the brothel fire would inevitably creep in.

To distract himself from his latest bout of guilt, he'd started juggling an apple, a tequila bottle, and a .45. But he knew this reckless entertainment wouldn't spare him for long. He couldn't forget how he'd failed Sadie when she'd desperately needed someone to brave the inferno and carry her to safety. Self-loathing was like a burning blade, twisting in his gut.

Baron, Randie, and Collie had all assured him that running inside the Satin Siren would have been a suicide mission. But how was he supposed to live with himself? He'd let Tito knock him on his ass. He'd let Sadie *die.*

For days, Cass had camped out in the brothel's ruins. He'd worked as a volunteer beside the investigators, frantically combing the wreckage for some trace of Sadie's corpse, sweating out his terror that he might actually find it. After a week of fruitless searching, the Fire Marshal had pronounced Sadie missing and presumed dead. At that point, Cass had seriously considered killing someone. But who?

Dietrich?

Tito?

The Fire Marshal?

Who was responsible for Sadie's death?

"Mister Cassidy!"

Cass struggled with his latent rage. He kept tossing the .45 into the air.

"Yeah, Mr. Prouse?"

Pendleton made one of his fussy, clucking noises. "That is *quite* enough of your hooliganism."

"Naw." Cass pasted on a smile. Even Pendleton didn't deserve to tangle with the demon lurking inside him today. "I'm just getting started."

Collie snickered somewhere near the tack room. Cass could hear the boy buckling a harness onto Mrs. Westerfield's mare so the lady could drive to her Suffragette meeting. Pendleton was scheduled to accompany her, which was fitting, since tea-sipping would be part of the program. In the eight years that Cass had known Baron's secretary and sparred with him over inconsequential improprieties, like eating cheese slices from a knife, Cass had never seen Pendleton drink anything harder than jamoka.

"Save your sass for the good citizens of the jury," Pendleton blustered. "Assuming you don't shoot your brains out *before* Baron can get you exonerated for killing that Ku Klux Klansman."

"You been listening at doors again, Pendleton?"

"How dare you!"

"Now don't get all red and blotchy and bloat up like a puffer fish," Cass drawled. "Everyone knows you peek through keyholes."

"I most certainly do not you…you *troglodyte!"*

"What's a troglodyte?" Collie called.

"Beats me," Cass said cheerfully.

"I'm not surprised." Pendleton sniffed. "If it isn't a whiskey label, you haven't read it. Now holster that gun before you blow off somebody's head!"

"Quit being such a fuddy-duddy," Collie said. "The gun isn't even loaded. Right, Cass?"

"Reckon there's only one way to find out."

With the speed of a striking rattler, Cass snatched the .45

from the air, drilled a bullet through a knothole, spun the gun over his finger and holstered it. By comparison, the apple and bottle dropped like molasses into his hands.

"Nope." He took a bite of fruit. "No more beans in the wheel."

Pendleton was sputtering, his cheeks florid, his chest heaving. "Mr. Cassidy, you have an intellect rivaled only by doorknobs!"

Turning on his heel, Pendleton grabbed the mare's reins from Collie, booted Vandy out of the driver's seat, and "geed" the horse into the yard. Cass chuckled, watching the carriage round the corner of the Big House.

"What's the matter with you?" Collie growled, stomping across the straw like a rooster ready for a cock fight. "Pendleton was right! You could have blown off somebody's head!"

Cass took another bite of apple to swallow a fresh wave of guilt. "I was practicing a new trick shot. What's the big deal?"

"Me and Vandy don't have a hankering to meet the devil, that's what!"

Cass snorted. "As I recall, I had to wrestle a seven-foot gator to save your varmint from becoming a gulp and a memory."

"Oh, so now it's Vandy's fault Sadie's dead?"

"What does *Sadie* have to do with anything?"

"Everything, you lying sack of cow turds. 'Cause when you jumped into the bayou that day, and leaped onto that runaway stage coach a week later, and turned a cattle stampede all by your lonesome yesterday evening, you weren't doing it to save anybody's life. You were doing it to throw away your own!"

Cass scowled. Collie's insight was unsettling. It held a ring of truth.

"What would you know?"

"I know plenty!" Collie retorted. "You yak my ear off day and night. So if you don't quit bawling like a lost dogie and find yourself another redhead to fire up your pecker,

I'm gonna wire Sera and tell her to sic the Thunderbolt Angels on your ass!"

Amusement vied with Cass's irritation. Sera, who'd been named after the Seraphim, had a warm personal relationship with angels. It came in handy when she was cussing out her exploded jars of blackberry preserves or sneaking out her bedroom window to rendezvous with Lynx. Sera was a preacher's daughter, but she'd married the Cherokee half-breed in a secret Indian ceremony in the woods long before her folks could host the official one in a church. Cass was expecting to hear any day now he was a godfather.

"You made up those Thunderbolt Angels."

"Did not." Collie hiked his chin.

"Now who's the lyin' sack of cow turds?"

Cass tossed his half-eaten apple to Vandy. The coon gleefully chased it into the sunshine, until a callous black boot crushed it under his snout.

"Hey!" Collie cried as Tito thumped into the carriage house on oversized feet. "Watch where you're walking!"

"Coons ain't got no business here."

"Says who? At least Vandy was born in this country!"

Tito dismissed the threat of Collie's fist with a baleful blink of his one good eye. But then, Collie weighed 20 pounds less than Cass, and the pirate had already proved he could deck a gunslinger.

Thanks to Tito's red kerchief, which peeked out from his Stetson, and the gold ring in his earlobe, which winked amidst wisps of coal-black hair, he didn't look anything like a cowpoke. Outfitting the whale-sized, Italian sailor with a horse had proven an amusing challenge for Baron's trail boss, partly because of Tito's size, and partly because Tito knew as much about prodding cattle as Cass knew about netting tuna.

But then, Baron hadn't hired Tito for his cutting and roping skills.

"Baron wants you," Tito said with a grunt. Most of Tito's conversations were a series of grunts. "Now."

Cass bit his tongue, damming a flood of trash talk. He was still sore about Tito flattening him in front of Baron and the rest of The Line. Cass didn't share Baron's optimism that Tito's size and demeanor would scare off assassins. As far as Cass was concerned, Tito's bulk made him a bigger bullseye for any man who could handle a gun.

"What's Baron want with us?" Collie demanded.

"Not you," Tito said with his trademark sneer. "Cassidy."

Collie bristled. "Baron hired me as his regulator too!"

"This ain't regulator business."

"So what business is it?"

"It's none-of-your-business business."

"Yeah? Well, I'll ask Baron myself."

"He don't want you. Take a hike, Squirt."

"You're not the boss of me!"

Cass intervened, grabbing the kid's arm before Collie's tongue could dig his grave. "You sure you don't have a hankering to meet the devil? Go split some logs until you cool off."

Collie's chest heaved. He knew as well as Cass did that Tito could pulverize him. Maybe that's why the boy finally muzzled his mouth. Snapping his fingers at Vandy, he stomped off with his coon, ignoring the wood pile as he stalked past.

Cass shook his head. One of these days, Collie was going to sass the wrong bully.

Cass followed Tito across the rain-parched grasses, over the cedar wood veranda, and into the bacon-and-cinnamon-scented kitchen of the Big House. For what amounted to a two-story cabin made of logs, Baron's home was bright and airy. He'd built the sprawling structure with dozens of windows, every one of which had been thrown open to catch the morning breeze. Bees hummed in the rafters. An occasional fly buzzed by.

Mrs. Westerfield, a prickly socialite from Galveston, had decorated the parlors with the finest crystal chandeliers, the plushest Persian rugs, and the fanciest French furnishings. However, Poppy's influence ended at the door to her husband's study. Here, the stench of cigar smoke hung heavy in the air. Spur marks gouged the pine planks of the floor. Before a massive limestone fireplace, a pair of cowhide chairs, with antler frames, circled a puma pelt. On the opposite wall, a longhorn steer head, with seven-foot horns, guarded Baron's well-stocked liquor cabinet.

The center of this male sanctuary was dominated by a desk made from white oak trees that had once grown on the property. Behind it, Baron sat puffing a stogie. A swarm of official-looking papers littered the desktop.

As Tito and Cass cleaved the smoke, Baron tugged off his reading spectacles and hiked a bushy eyebrow. "You look like hell," he told Cass.

"Thanks."

"When's the last time you had a wink of shut-eye?"

"Church."

"So you're saying never?"

Cass shot his boss a withering glare. "If this place got any quieter, it'd be a graveyard."

"Things always get quiet before the storm." Baron waved him toward the liquor cabinet. "Pour yourself some O-Be-Joyful."

"I'll be joyful when I'm flushing out killers."

"How about tarnished tin-stars?"

Cass's ears pricked with interest. "Anyone I know?"

"Maybe." Baron darted a furtive glance at Tito. "So where's the kid?"

Cass shrugged. "I sent him to chop wood."

Baron gestured at Tito. "Go keep an eye on that kid."

The pirate nodded, lumbering out the door.

Repositioning the spectacles on his nose, Baron waved Cass to a seat. "Tell Collie no hard feelings. He's under age, is all. I need you to witness my will."

Cass hiked an eyebrow as Baron produced a freshly inked legal document. Ever since Galveston, Baron had gotten it into his head that somebody wanted him dead. Although he'd been a tad vague about the motive, he seemed to think vigilante sodbusters were gunning for him.

In any event, Baron believed that he'd been the intended victim at the Satin Siren.

Privately, Cass disagreed. As a murder weapon, arson was unreliable. As a *cover* for murder, it was perfect. But Cass wasn't one to look a gift horse in the mouth. Baron had offered him a job as bodyguard and the opportunity to clear his name. So nowadays, Cass—or Collie or Tito— rode with Baron wherever he went.

"A new will, huh?" Cass folded his arms across his chest. "So you've lost faith in me as your regulator?"

"If that were true, I'd have hired Hank."

"That's not very reassuring, considering how Hank's still incarcerated in Huntsville."

Cass recollected that Rexford Sterne had been the tin-star who finally put Henry "Hank" Sharpe in the state penitentiary. About eight years before Hank had earned his reputation as "The Ventilator," he'd worked for Baron as a ranch hand. However, the scum-sucking weasel had spent more time picking fights with the Rocking W's cowboys— especially Lynx—than he'd spent prodding steers. Eventually, Baron had sent Hank packing, but not before Lynx had been arrested for one of Hank's thefts, and Cass had been forced to bust his best friend out of jail.

"Buck up, grasshopper." Baron handed him a stylus. "I got bigger plans for you."

"Like what?"

"Like proving to the legislature that Rexford Sterne's as crooked as a dog's hind leg. You game?"

"Hell yeah." Cass glanced at the document he was supposed to sign. He hadn't meant to read it, but for some reason, his gaze was drawn to the name, Miss Reynolds. "You're including Randie in your will?"

A deep flush rolled up the senator's neck. "Don't make me gouge out your eyeballs, boy."

Cass shrugged, locating the signature line. He scrawled *William A. Cassidy* next to the bold "X" above the words, *Tito Salvatore Ferraro.*

"That's better." Baron winked. "By the way. No need to

alarm Poppy or Pendleton about my health. The will's a private matter."

"I gathered that," Cass said dryly. "What about Sterne?"

Baron sanded the document and folded it into an inner frockcoat pocket. "Poppy and Pendleton aren't due back from Burnet for a week. That should give us plenty of time to hatch our plan."

Baron flashed his horsey grin. "I figured it's high time you met my attorney—the man who's going to clear your name of murder and make Rexford Sterne a permanent resident of Huntsville."

CHAPTER 4

Lampasas, Texas
October, 1883

The whole town was abuzz. You couldn't walk through the business district of the so-called "Saratoga of the South" without getting your ears blistered by the news. It floated past the batwings of the Commercial Saloon; it poured through the windows of Hamon's Drug Store and Odd Fellow Hall. Heck, you couldn't sit in an outhouse as far west as Hancock Park without some jackanapes bellowing through a knothole:

"Did you hear? Baron's got his dander up! He went and challenged the General!"

The General, of course, was none other than local hero, Rexford Sterne. Sadie scratched her beard as she skimmed the front page of a dog-eared, tobacco-stained *Lampasas Dispatch.* Her copy had already been read by a traveling preacher, a one-eyed sheepherder, and the illustrious town marshal, Sid Wright, as the gents had parked their boots for a buff at Boomer's Barbershop. Sadie wasn't all that keen on getting her shoes shined—or her face shaved, for that matter—but the special edition was in short supply, so she'd chosen the lesser of two evils to get her hands on a *Dispatch.*

The article read:

"...When asked about his affiliation with the railroad, which has been covertly surveying farmland west of Lampasas, Senator Westerfield described himself as 'eager' to set the record straight during next week's assembly of the Southern Farmers Alliance."

I'll bet, Sadie thought snidely.

"'My record in Lampasas County speaks for itself,' Senator Westerfield said, 'and I don't take kindly to some bully with a Big Iron coming along to piss on it. Rexford Sterne has had a bad case of sour grapes, ever since he got himself winged and the Law Committee had to force him to take a desk job—for his own good, I might add. That mean-spirited campaign slogan of his ("Want Justice? Get Sterne.") just proves my point. And you can quote me on that, boy. You tell the citizens of Lampasas: Got a beef? Vote for Baron!'"

Sadie smirked.

My, my. The bull's on a rampage.

Despite this new opportunity to crack her case, Sadie had mixed feelings about the Farmers Alliance meeting at the Grand Park Hotel next week. Fence-cutting cattlemen were only half of the range-war story. Vigilante grangers were on the rise in Texas, and certain whispers in certain saloons placed the vengeance-minded ring-leaders in Lampasas.

As a Pinkerton, Sadie had been ordered to collaborate with her old ally, Rexford Sterne—mostly to prevent Baron from getting assassinated before she could get him to trial. Ever since the Satin Siren had burned to the ground, he'd been holed up on his 190,000-acre, Rocking W Ranch, where she couldn't touch him. His public announcement that he would address the farmers' meeting was the break she'd been waiting for.

And speaking of meetings...

Dragging a pocket watch from her vest, Sadie muttered an oath to see the hour was well past 10 a.m. She tossed a nickel to her shoeshine boy.

Joaquin couldn't have been more than 11 years old. He grinned, a flash of pearlescence in a sun-blackened face. *"Gracias, señor!* You will see Madam LeBeau now? And maybe under her skirts?" he added slyly, pointing to his reflection in Sadie's boots.

She coughed to hide her amusement. To wear a beard and a mustache had made her part of a previously inaccessible club, whose membership bandied all kinds of interesting dialogue that would never have been broached over embroidery hoops and baby cradles.

"Hope springs eternal, *niño,"* she said with a wink.

Abandoning the *Dispatch* to Joaquin's next customer, Sadie hopped a mule-drawn trolley and headed west on Third Street. Her destination was the "boardinghouse" that strategically straddled the boundary between the commercial district and Silk Stocking Row, where Lampasas's wealthiest residents had erected turrets on castle-sized homes.

From the outside, Wilhelmine "Wilma" LeBeau's brothel looked like any other charming, limestone cottage on Third Street. The three-story construction had a wrought iron gate, forest-green shutters, and a sprawling porch, whose pillars were festooned with drought-resistant climbers, like blue plumbago and sunny Lady Banks Roses. Thanks to the season, Wilma's porch also had enough leering jack-o-lanterns to qualify as a pumpkin patch.

Sadie rang the bell. Less than a minute passed before a railroad spike in black broadcloth opened the door.

"Bonjour, m'sieu," Cottonmouth greeted with aplomb. The twinkle in the Cajun's dark eyes betrayed his mirth to see her swimming in a brown linen sack suit. "And whom shall I say has called this morning?"

Sadie bowed, sweeping off her bowler and furtively checking her chestnut-colored sideburns in the window. The damned whiskers were constantly threatening to peel off.

"Dusty Dudman's my name; sodbusting's my game," she

announced in her brashest hick accent. "Madam Wilma is expecting me for brunch."

Cotton's lips twitched. Occasionally, her disguises fooled the big, bald lug, but not this morning.

Of course, there were only so many ways she could hide brandy-colored irises without being redundant. Her eyes had been her bane ever since she'd joined the Agency. Pinkerton had feared they would prove a liability in the field. In fact, he'd rejected her agent application on that basis. If Rex hadn't interceded, vouching for her street smarts and her cool head under fire...

She shuddered to think what her life might be like today.

"C'est bon," Cotton said gamely. "I shall show you to the solarium."

She followed his daunting six-feet, ten-inches past the parlor, with its orange dust covers and black-cat pillows; through the conservatory, where a massive arrangement of golden chrysanthemums topped a baby grand piano; to a lush jungle of potted palms. Above the frond spears, in the fluttering shadows of breeze-blown awnings, Sadie could just make out a shock of pewter hair, as thick as any wolf's pelt.

Rexford Sterne rose from the table as Cotton announced her. A handsome man in a harsh, sun-chiseled way, the Rangers' leader was lean, fit, and immaculately groomed in a suit of charcoal-colored pinstripes, complete with the obligatory Peacemaker and his beloved Justin boots.

Rex hiked a bristling eyebrow as she swaggered through the door. "You walk like a drunken sailor at sea."

"Nonsense," Wilma purred. "She walks like a cowpoke."

"I'm a *sodbuster,* for crying out loud."

Rex grunted. "Needs work."

Exasperated, Sadie elbowed Cotton, who was snickering because his twin brother, Gator, had schooled her for an hour in "the Cajun man strut."

"I suspect one must be born to the role," Wilma said diplomatically. "Tea?"

"Somehow, I don't think my new, sodbuster alias would

opt for rosehips," Sadie said drolly. "Jamoka. Black." She plopped into a chair like she'd been raised in a barn. "How'd I do that time?"

Rex sighed. Sadie grinned. There was something so endearing about a man who took exception to lewd conduct in a woman.

But Sadie knew from experience that the 50-year-old Ranger never let chivalry stand in the way of an arrest. When it came to his job, Rex couldn't be bribed by sex, money or power. Like the Alpha Wolf he so thoroughly resembled, he radiated command, even now, while engrossed in the most commonplace task, like slathering butter on jalapeno cornbread. The only woman whom Sadie had ever seen ruffle Rex's feathers was their wily hostess.

Dressed in an elegant, topaz-silk day dress, Wilma presided over a sumptuous table, set with crystal, sterling, and hand-painted china. The sloe-eyed, olive-skinned brunette was as mysterious as she was exotic, with a voluptuous torso and ageless face that rival bawds whispered was proof of dark magic. Only the identity of Wilma's grandmother, an octoroon Mambo, was a more closely guarded secret than Wilma's birth year.

Because Wilma used to manage a rival bordello in Dodge, Sadie knew the Mambo's richly embroidered gown and gracious manner disguised a barracuda's sense for business. Wilma's "business" was to ensure the success of her Pinkie protégés in a glittering circle of man-sharks. In fact, Sadie had been the one who'd convinced Pinkerton to recruit Wilma to train his up-and-coming agents in the finer points of seduction.

As Wilma waved Cotton from the solarium to fetch more coffee, Sadie wondered how three people were supposed to consume such a lavish, New Orleans-style feast. While Rex, the consummate Texican, poked suspiciously at a hush puppy with his fork, Sadie helped herself to a piping-hot square of gingerbread.

"Thanks to you, General Sterne," she chided with mock severity, "that poor editor at the *Dispatch* didn't sleep a wink again last night. He was too busy setting type." She smirked to imagine Baron's outrage as he'd spouted his tactless, front-page quote. "'*Want Justice? Get Sterne.*' That campaign slogan is priceless."

Rex's gun-metal gray eyes warmed with approval as they touched Wilma's face. "You can thank our anonymous tipster for luring Baron out of hiding with that slogan."

Wilma's cheeks turned pink with pleasure.

Sadie arched an eyebrow. Wilma never blushed.

"Mr. Perkins may have scooped the *Austin Statesman* with your campaign announcement," Wilma warned the Ranger, "but he's no man's fool. And neither is Baron. Few men who know you will believe you're content to retire from the force."

"I've been choking down injury pay for close to five months. I don't see why anyone would think there's much difference between pushing paper as a bureaucrat and a senator."

"The point, *mon ami,* is that you are unaccustomed to undercover work. You do not lie with great credibility."

Rex grimaced over his coffee cup. The dainty porcelain looked in dire peril from such a manly fist. "I like to think my reputation for *integrity* lent credibility to that cock-and-bull story in last week's *Dispatch.*

"In any event, my farewell speech—and Governor Ireland's trumped up response—were reprinted in some form by every newspaper in every major city. Most folks will believe anything they read."

"Baron sure did," Sadie said, relishing the beginning of the end of Senator Scum Bucket's political career.

"Hmm."

A forkful of gingerbread halted half way to Sadie's mouth. "*Hmm?*" she repeated archly.

Rex sipped his coffee. He didn't look like a man who was contemplating victory.

"What?" she demanded.

Wilma cleared her throat. "There have been…complications, *chere.*"

"Complications?" Sadie narrowed her eyes. "What kind of complications?"

Rex and Wilma locked stares.

Fidgeting, Wilma looked away first.

"I got word last night that Cassidy's murder warrant was cancelled," Rex said grimly. "Courtesy of Baron's attorney, who got him a trial and a not-guilty verdict in under three days. My hunch is, Cassidy's working for Baron now. And that means, he'll be accompanying Baron and Mrs. Westerfield to Lampasas. To keep vigilante grangers at bay."

Good God. Cass is Baron's regulator?

Rex was posing as bait for one of Baron's contract hits. But this plan had just taken a frightening turn. Cass was the only gunfighter still at-large in Texas, who could possibly draw faster than the Ranger.

Suddenly, Sadie didn't feel like eating. She lowered her fork to her plate.

An uncomfortable silence settled over the table, broken only by the trilling of a mockingbird. She could feel Rex's frank, assessing gaze on her face like the heat of the Texas sun. He clearly expected her loyalties to be torn, and the knowledge rankled.

Rex was more than her Ranger liaison. From the first night they'd met, four years ago in Dodge, he'd displayed a protective instinct toward her. She'd never understood why, and she'd resisted his friendship with a great deal of asperity at first, even though he'd known her mother.

Considering all her reasons to hate tin-stars, including the sex acts that Dodge City lawmen used to coerce her to perform for her "protection," the fact that she'd allowed Rex into her confidence said volumes about his character. Until she'd met him, she'd never believed she could trust a lawman. Never once during their acquaintance had Rex propositioned her. Sadie had sometimes wondered at her ally's restraint, but eventually, she'd come to accept his courtesies as an indelible trait of a southern gentleman's good breeding.

Squaring her jaw, she forced herself to withstand the lawman's probing stare. "Anything else I should know?"

Rex reached inside the breast pocket of his frockcoat and withdrew what, at first glance, appeared to be an unmarked envelope. When he slid it under her saucer, she spied the embossed insignia of the Gulf, Colorado, and Santa Fe Railroad on the flap.

"It's time you left town," he said gruffly. "Started working a new case."

She felt her temperature rise. She was a Pinkerton, by God, not some hare-brained ninny who swooned over studs in spurs!

Apparently, she still had to prove this fact where Cass was concerned. Rex had accused her of not being forthright about the young outlaw. He'd learned that Cass had entered the Satin Siren 20 minutes before it got torched. In Rex's estimation, that made Cass a prime suspect in her attempted murder.

But *lots* of people had entered the casino a half hour before it burned to the ground, Sadie thought. The Pinkertons had found no evidence to implicate Cass in the arson. In fact, he'd been playing faro (and griping about redheads) in a casino full of witnesses. His alibi was irrefutable.

Secretly relieved by this knowledge, she ignored Rex's train ticket and reached for her coffee cup. "You don't run at the first sign of trouble, and neither do I."

Rex drilled her with his no-nonsense glare. "The minute Cassidy learns you survived that fire, he'll come looking for you. He made a nuisance of himself with the arson investigators, and he spouted off so many times to *Galveston Daily News* reporters, they developed a keen interest in his allegations—namely, that Karl Dietrich was an insurance swindler. Do I have to remind you, Pinkerton was forced to reassign your colleague?"

And send him to Denver, Sadie thought smugly. *Cass did me a favor.*

"If Cass *is* working for Baron," she argued, "he'll be my best entrée into Baron's organization."

"Cassidy can't keep his mouth shut, drunk or sober."

"About what? He doesn't know I'm a Pinkerton."

"He sure as hell knows you're not Chantelle O'Leary!"

Sadie sipped coffee before replacing the cup in her saucer. "Give me some credit, Rex. Danger and death threats come with my badge. Cass knows singers take stage names. If he asks me why I'm so eager to know Baron, I'll tell him I'm looking for a wealthy patron. Cass has no claim on me. I made it clear in Galveston we're through. Now get that train ticket out of my face. I don't report to you."

A muscle ticked in Rex's jaw.

Wilma broke the tension with a chuckle. Reaching across the table, she retrieved the envelope. "I would say I hate to tell you so, *mon ami.* But then, I'd be lying." She winked at Rex. "I'll take this nuisance off your hands, and consider us even."

"Wait a minute." Sadie shot a withering glare at her old friend. "You two had a *wager*?"

As discreet as Wilma was, she'd never tried to hide the fact that Cass used to come to her bed in Dodge, during the days when he'd been green enough to learn something. Wilma had originated his Rebel Rutter legend. Her joke had spread like wildfire, mostly because Cass enjoyed living up to his fame.

"Did you bet against me or Cass?" Sadie demanded in wounded tones.

"My bet was against Baron."

Grinning like the Cheshire cat, Wilma slipped the ticket into her bodice. "Now then. Let us discuss more important matters, like a new paste for your chestnut sideburns. And the code name you will use, when you communicate with Rex…"

* * *

One Week Later
Lampasas, TX

"Well, if it isn't the sweetest little rosebud—"

"Shut-up."

Cass smirked. Hidden by silver sage bushes on the alley side of the swanky Globe Hotel, he craned back his head to watch Collie in a third story window. The kid's ludicrous widow weeds and four-foot mourning veil made him look like a grandma-lumberjack. He was pushing Sterne's darkened casement higher to lower a rope.

"Did you remember to shave?" Cass demanded, *sotto voce.* "'Cause when we make our getaway, folks in the lobby'll think—"

"Still yakking."

Cass snickered. After riding for a year with the Prince of Lock Picks, Cass was used to Collie's moods, but the boy was more surly than usual, thanks to his pet. Vandy had stolen a trout from the hotel's horrified, French chef and had broken $200 worth of crystal while fleeing out the window. Until Baron "fixed" matters with the manager, Collie was forbidden on the property. He'd been forced to concoct a disguise.

"What did you stuff inside your corset? Watermelons?"

"You gonna climb?" Collie countered in murderous tones.

"Well, I don't know. You gonna make it worth my while, sweetheart?"

"How 'bout I give you a shiner?"

Cass chuckled.

The rope finally swished within reach. He planted his boots on the limestone. To any insomniac, who happened to be peering through his shutters, Cass suspected his all-black attire would make him look like an enormous spider, crawling up the moon-splashed stone. To be caught in the night's cosmic spotlight would have strained the nerves of any self-respecting footpad.

But not Cass. Not anymore.

After Sadie had died, he'd started taking wilder, ever crazier risks. Cheating the devil, that had become Cass's way of coping with guilt. Tonight, he was actually hoping to run into Rexford Sterne. Ever since that pretentious, Scotch-drinking prick had stolen Sadie from his arms four years ago in Dodge, Cass had wanted revenge.

Now Baron had reason to believe Sterne's sudden retirement from the Ranger Force had been a cover up for misappropriation of funds. Everybody knew that Sterne, who'd grown up on a cotton plantation, had a soft spot for sodbusters. Since Ranger pay was notoriously poor, Baron suspected Sterne had been siphoning taxpayer money until he could get sufficient backing from the Farmers Alliance to fund his election campaign.

Cass's smile was smug. No one wanted more than he did to find evidence that Sterne had tarnished the Ranger badge.

Now I have something to live for.

Hauling himself over his enemy's window sill, Cass began to drag the rope back up the wall. "How much time do we have?"

"Tito's good at smashing, not yakking."

"That's why I sent Poppy as back up."

At the mention of Baron's wife, Collie screwed up his face like he'd choked down castor oil. "*She'll* make Sterne run for the nearest saloon, that's certain."

"Works for me."

Cass tugged the bandanna off his face. His eyes swept over oblong shapes, like a bed and a shaving stand, while his nose singled out lemon-balm hair tonic and something more ominous: *sulfur.* "You been burning powder?" he demanded, his right hand straying to his trigger guard.

"I didn't shoot nobody, if that's what you mean."

"Tarnation, boy! You're supposed to be a *girl*. Girls don't fire guns while they're wearing widow's weeds! You want to wake every dang body in this hotel?"

"A coyote was chasing my coon!"

Cass groaned, spying the hump-with-a-tail that had

nested on Sterne's pillow and was happily gnawing his badger-hair shaving brush. Sometimes, Cass didn't know which was the bigger liability: the kid or his coon.

They began ransacking the room, tossing chair cushions, dumping drawers, and turning the mattress. Cass rummaged through the campaign propaganda in Sterne's smaller traveling trunk, while Collie pawed through the change of clothing in the larger portmanteau. Vandy proved his worth by galloping merrily around the chaos with Sterne's underwear on his head.

"I hate politics," Collie grumbled, shaking out a box of red, white, and blue ribbons.

"You hate following orders," Cass corrected him.

"And you don't?"

"Listen here, smartass. I've been trying to keep you from screwing up the way I did and living your life on the run. 'Sides. A Ranger needs to care about folks. So he can protect them."

"Caring is your *problem,* Snake Bait. You got your head so messed up over that lying little snitch—"

"Don't be speaking ill of my Sadie!"

Collie sighed and shook his head. "Ten minutes before that brothel fire, all you could talk about was how she sold you out to the law."

"Yeah?" Cass squared his jaw. "Well, you shouldn't speak ill of the dead. Unless the corpse is Sterne's," he added darkly, rummaging through the trash. "Considering how he carried on with Sadie in Dodge, you'd think Sterne would have cared how she died. But as far as I can tell, the Rangers didn't lift a finger to stop Dietrich from fleeing town. He disappeared as thoroughly as a shadow at high noon."

Collie grunted. "I got one word for you: Pendleton."

"What about Pendleton?"

"The way I see it, Dietrich was just a goon, doing the heavy lifting. *Pendleton* was the brains behind the insurance swindle."

Cass snorted. "How do you figure that, Kid Detective?"

"Remember that nimrod sodbuster? The one we first saw on Post Office Street? He was drinking cherry fizzy pop. That's Pendleton's favorite."

"Wait a minute." Cass frowned. "You got a good look at that granger, and you're only saying so *now?*"

"Not a *good* look. Hell, he was wearing a *porcupine* on his face! But under all those bristly whiskers, he was the same size and weight as Pendleton. My guess is, Pendleton disguised himself so he could watch Dietrich and Randie carry out his plan."

"Aren't you forgetting something? Baron signed his name to an affidavit, giving Randie her alibi."

"Oh, right. Like Randie was *really* pouring Baron a drink in that back room."

"What Randie and Baron were doing at the time of the explosion is irrelevant. They gave each other alibis. And Pendleton was asleep in his hotel."

"So he says," Collie said snidely. "But that ain't much of an alibi."

"*Isn't* much of an alibi."

"That's what I said!"

Cass rolled his eyes, mostly at Collie's grammar.

Pendleton was a tad Puritanical, true, but Cass couldn't picture the fussbudget burning a cathouse to the ground just because he disapproved of lechery. Pendleton got paid plenty to manage Baron's books. Considering the way he pinched pennies, he'd probably accrued a small fortune in some bank account. With all that money, why would Pendleton risk a capital murder charge to burn an occupied building?

"Fess up, Collie. The only reason you suspect Pendleton of arson is because he accused Vandy of stealing his pocket watch last night."

"Shows you how much *you* know." Collie hiked his chin. "I've always suspected Pendleton. And coons like shiny things. Vandy was only doing what comes natural."

"You mean what comes natural in the *wild.*" Cass smirked, recalling the uproar at Baron's ranch. Vandy, masked rascal that he was, had dunked Pendleton's heirloom timepiece in Poppy's bathtub—while she was in it.

"Wanting Pendleton to be an insurance swindler doesn't mean he is one," Cass reminded the kid. "Pendleton has been managing Baron's business affairs for 20 years. His record's as lily-white as that milk potion he keeps rubbing into his hands."

"Big deal. He just hasn't been caught yet. I'll bet Baron's attorney is part of the conspiracy. Poppy too."

"Tarnation, boy! Do you trust *anybody?"*

"Nope."

Cass grabbed Sterne's fancy, silver flask. He'd intended to throw it at the kid until he realized the flask was a quarter full.

Well, damn.

Cass screwed off the lid.

So this is what prissy scotch smells like?

He gulped the imported, Irish whisky like the White Trash he was, smiled with perverse pleasure, then hurled the flask at the kid.

"Hey!" Collie caught the vessel with viper-fast reflexes. "You might have saved me some!"

Cass belched and grinned. "Naw. Wouldn't want to undermine all that good religion you got while living with Sera and Doc Jones."

"Bite me."

Vandy, meanwhile, was gleefully tracking cigar ash all over the hotel's plush, Aubusson carpet.

Cass muttered an oath. "Heel! Sit! Confound it. That varmint never listens to me."

"'Course he doesn't listen to you. You don't speak his language. *Candytuft,"* Collie barked at the coon.

Instantly contrite, Vandy retreated under the bed, dropping his snout to his paws and raising beseeching eyes to his boy.

"Stop being such a baby," Collie scolded.

Vandy growled.

"That's more like it," Collie growled back.

"Lord aw'mighty," Cass groused. "Why can't you just say, 'lie down,' or 'play dead,' like normal folks?"

"'Cause Vandy knows *candytuft* and *grubroot*."

"Well, sure! Those words sound like food!"

The commands Collie had invented to control Vandy were supposed to be Kentucky wildflowers, but half the time, Collie's "secret coon code" sounded like gibberish to Cass. The kid claimed he'd concocted the cipher so Vandy wouldn't get tricked into becoming a hat. The truth was, Collie was the jealous type, who didn't want Vandy loving anyone more than him. Cass had learned the hard way: Don't come between Collie and his coon, and don't talk flowers around Vandy. *Especially* pansies. Pansies earned you a whole lot of fangs in the face.

Planting his fists on his hips, Cass glowered at the coon's tracks, spreading out in all their circular paths of destruction. "Seems like you could've saved Vandy a whole lot of trouble if you'd just whitewashed the mirror with *'Cass and Collie were here.'*"

"You mean, *Collie* and Cass," the boy retorted, squatting to retrieve a mostly burned scrap of paper from Vandy's mouth. "Looks like he found something."

"Yeah. An ashtray."

"This isn't cig paper." Collie tilted the scrap to catch the moonlight. "There's a symbol here. Looks like a backwards seven with a boot. The words are mostly blacked out."

Cass joined him by the window. "Let's see."

Sure enough, a neatly lettered scrawl had been all but obliterated by Sterne's match. To Cass's mind, the remaining scrap looked like it had been part of the bottom, right-hand corner of the message: *'Trouble...arrived...meet here MN.'* The 'MN' was probably shorthand for midnight. But the backwards seven reminded Cass of a musical symbol that Sadie used to write.

"I think the seven is part of a signature," Cass said thoughtfully.

Collie grunted. "A code name?"

"Maybe. What time is it?"

Collie glanced out the window, calculating by the position of the moon. "Midnight, I reckon."

"Damn. If that rendezvous's tonight, Sterne's on his way to this room. We're out of time."

Cass cracked open the hall door. He wanted to make sure no one would witness two vandals and a varmint hotfooting it down the hall.

Gold velvet *fleurs-de-lis* decorated the rich, burgundy wallpaper, which shimmered in the flickers of the frosted sconces. The matching reds of the carpet amplified the illusion that he'd stepped inside the belly of a dragon. Or maybe a long furnace. The heat of Texas's ongoing drought was barely relieved by the languid breeze that stirred the draperies, framing the windows at each end of the corridor. It wasn't difficult for Cass to imagine himself headed down the road to Hell.

But then, a life like his didn't usually end with an invitation to join the saints.

"All right, the hall's clear," Cass said.

He stepped across the threshold while Collie rummaged between his watermelons, presumably to reposition his .38.

"Quit messing around in there!" Cass grabbed the boy's arm and dragged him toward the L-shaped bend that led to the stairs. "And hunch your shoulders. You're supposed to be a doddering old Mee-Maw. How come you're waddling like a pregnant duck?"

"I don't want to step on Vandy's tail!"

A whiskered snout was poking out from under Collie's hem.

"Honest to God, I can't take you any—"

A muffled thump reached Cass's ears. It was followed by a suspicious scuffling.

Collie cocked his head, a sure sign he was listening. *"Window,"* he mouthed silently.

Cass nodded, removing the trigger guards from his .45s. He'd learned to trust Collie's weasel ears. The kid's sense of hearing would have been downright legendary if he hadn't considered it one of his greatest weapons—and therefore, his biggest secret.

"Stay here," Cass whispered, edging along the wall.

When he poked his head around the corner, he spied a figure with chestnut sideburns. Dressed in a sodbuster's bowler and a brown linen sack suit, the man was emerging from the hardy camouflage of a live oak and swinging a leg over the window sill. A perverse sense of amusement curved Cass's lips. He'd caught a thief breaking into the hotel.

All his life, he'd wanted to be a Ranger. To fight for right. To make the world a safe place for little kiddies to play. That altruistic side couldn't let some desperado barge into the hotel and loot innocent folks.

Cass waited until the thief had committed himself, swinging his second leg over the sill and landing on catlike feet. Only then did Cass swagger around the corner.

"What's the matter, mister? Stairs aren't enough exercise?"

The thief caught his breath, his body going rigid. Cass had a revolver in his fist before the man could think about his own weapons.

"Hands," Cass barked.

Slowly, reluctantly, the thief spread his gloves in the universal sign of surrender. His demeanor was docile enough, but the rapid flutter of the linen draping his chest betrayed his agitation. The globe of an oil lamp burned behind his shoulders, so Cass couldn't see the intruder's eyes beneath the shadows of his hat.

"Not your lucky day, eh, *compadre?* I'm thinking your guardian angel up and skedaddled."

"I'll frisk him," Collie volunteered, lurching around the corner like Frankenstein's monster, thanks to the 50-pound coon cavorting between his boots.

Cass had half a mind to wallop them both. "Confound it, *Miss McAffee,* is that how your mama taught a lady to behave?"

The thief chuckled, a low, husky sound that reminded

Cass of whiskey, scarlet, and sin all rolled into one.

"Looks like McAffee found Admiral Farragut's lost torpedoes."

"Shut up," Collie said.

"Mind your manners, cockroach," Cass growled at the thief. "You're talking to a lady."

Straight white teeth flashed in that graying beard. "Somebody's got his facts all tangled."

Cass frowned. Something about the thief's voice wasn't right. For one thing, it wasn't scratchy enough to be old. For another, it was more contralto than tenor.

In fact, the more Cass studied his captive, the more things didn't add up. The thief's graying, auburn hair and sideburns suggested a man past his prime, yet the intruder's gloves and boots were far from man-sized; his shoulders were as slender as a girl's; and his baggy coat made the average sack suit look tailored.

Cass took a step forward. He couldn't tell from the drape of the linen if the thief wore a six-shooter strapped to his hip, but Cass wouldn't have bet against those odds. Besides, a .45 wasn't his only danger. Knives, blinding powders, knuckle dusters and all manner of other weapons could be hidden up a man's sleeve—including a one-shot derringer that was just as deadly as a Peacemaker at close range.

He glared at the thief. "So you're a wise guy, eh?"

"Just shoot him," Collie interjected, knowing full well Cass wouldn't.

"Junior's awful grumpy," the thief drawled. "Must've missed his baby nap."

"I'll plug you myself!"

"Settle down," Cass snapped at Collie, but he was only half listening to the boy's rant. Something about the thief kept niggling at the back of his mind. Cass thought it might have been the man's wit. It reminded him poignantly of Sadie.

He cursed himself. Now wasn't the time to let grief distract him. Sadie had made a fool of him more than once. She'd even betrayed him, telling Sterne about his murder warrant when the Ranger had ridden into Dodge City, bearing a Special Deputy U.S. Marshal's commission. After a hurt like that, Cass shouldn't have cared what happened to Sadie.

But no matter how he tried, Cass couldn't stop thinking about the first woman he'd ever kissed, about those long-lost days of star-gazing, berry-picking, and infatuated innocence back in their childhood home of Pilot Grove. A yawning emptiness consumed his soul. The nights had lost their thrill because he could never love, war, and make up again with the Devil's Red-Haired Daughter.

Dragging a ragged breath into his lungs, he forced himself to rein in such useless conjectures.

"What's under your coat?" he snapped at the thief.

The ghost of a dimple peeked from the shadows beneath the man's derby. "The usual."

"Want to be more specific?"

"See for yourself."

Cass's pulse quickened. This conversation was familiar—macabrely familiar. The only difference was, his memory had to do with a Dodge City brothel and a skimpy lace negligee that had all but stopped his heart.

"I'll make you want me, Sadie," he'd threatened, his loins hurting even worse than his pride.

She'd laughed up at him with those wicked, golden tiger's eyes. *"You'll always be that green-as-grass boy I taught how to rut."*

Cass forced himself to drag his wits about him. He glared at the thief. "Take off your hat."

"You want it?" Another saucy dimple peeked. "Come and get it, hotshot."

Cass's patience was rapidly unraveling. He stalked closer, defying popguns, blinding powder, and anything else the thief might throw. "Think you're something special, eh?"

"If you say so."

A breeze stirred the draperies. The masculine scents of leather and horse wafted to Cass, along with the feminine fragrance of rosehips.

Sadie's favorite tea.

Cass frowned.

Now he was close enough to notice anomalies beneath the man's derby: cheeks too smooth to be a graybeard's. A mustache that was just a hair off balance. Lips that were pink and kissably soft.

Cass halted, his heart slamming into his ribs. His brain told his senses they were liars, but his heart couldn't give up the hope. Sadie and Sterne were old flames. If she'd survived the Satin Siren, if she'd feared for her life, maybe she would have disguised herself to seek the Ranger for protection.

Cass reached a shaking hand. He knocked the derby off the thief's head.

Eyes as hot as golden brands burned into his. Cass sucked in his breath. In the next instant, a boot struck his forearm. His gun went flying. The second drop-kick plowed into his midsection like a battering ram.

"Son of a—" Cass stumbled to his knees, winded.

Sadie fled for the stairs, a snarling coon in hot pursuit. Desperately, Cass dug inside a trouser pocket and hurled pecans after Vandy's head. The eager moocher veered, scrabbling over the glint of gold that spilled from Sadie's neck. Collie muttered something about traitors and reached for the pistol in his bodice.

"No!" Cass tackled the boy's legs. They crashed to the carpet, rolling over Sadie's necklace in a tangle of limbs and lace.

"What the hell's the matter with you?" Collie struggled to free the gun arm Cass had pinned.

"That's Sadie!"

"Sadie's *dead!*"

She paused to look back, that wicked dimple flirting with her lips. One last smirk for his embarrassment. One last sigh for all that might have been. Then, with an audacious wink, she wrenched open the door to her freedom.

"You'll *wish* you were dead when I'm through with you!" Cass bellowed after that lusciously sweet ass.

Her husky laughter echoed in the stairwell.

Collie freed a fist and punched him in the head. "Get off me, lunatic!"

By this time, a dozen hotel guests in nightcaps were poking their heads into the hall, watching in horror as Cass and Collie flopped on the carpet like a couple of beached whales. Cass cursed vehemently, trying to free his legs from the strips of taffeta his spurs were shredding.

Just when he didn't think a man could get any more humiliated, the elevator bell dinged. Marshal Wright stepped into the hall, accompanied by none other than Rexford Sterne.

The cagey old wolf raised pewter eyebrows. "Well now. What have we here?"

Cass froze as gun hammers clicked above his head. His arch nemesis loomed over him, grinning like a small dog with a big bone.

"Why, if it isn't the Rebel Rutter. And Coon Collie, too. Doing it in public now, boys?" A rare levity lighted the ex-Ranger's steel-colored eyes. "Damn, kid. You sure make one ugly woman."

CHAPTER 5

For a man who wanted to wear a badge, Cass had seen the inside of way too many jail cells. Usually, he was arrested for misdemeanors, like dancing a drunken jig on a faro table, or taking potshots at some crabby old merchant's sign. Townsfolk with railroad spikes up their butts didn't like roostered cowboys causing mischief—which was fine by Cass. Arrest got him a free meal and a free bunk, where he could sleep off his busthead.

Needless to say, after spending so much idle time behind bars, Cass knew how to break out of jail. He carried three lock picks in his clothing. Most tin-stars, he was sorry to say, were dumber than fence posts. Finding Widdy #1, in his hatband, satisfied them. The rare few who kept searching never found Widdy #3, which Cass had stashed inside his boot heel.

Nevertheless, Cass didn't bust himself out of jail unless he had some emergency reason to reach the outside. Losing a prisoner was an ugly blemish on a lawman's career, and Cass figured that keeping friendly relations was good business. He knew his failings, and sure-as-shootin', he was going to get drunk and wind up in jail again. In fact, the first time he'd seen the inside of Sidney Wright's hoosegow was back in '78. At the time, Wright had been a deputy in Round Rock. He'd gotten promoted after Cass tipped him off about the whereabouts of notorious bank robber, Sam Bass. Needless to say, Sid had a soft spot for Cass. More importantly, he knew he could count on Cass's guns in a pinch, when serious outlaws were stealing payrolls or endangering honest folks.

Sid also knew his iron palace lacked certain creature comforts—like ventilation. So the marshal took pity on his only prisoners, hauling in a bucket of ice and some bottles of sarsaparilla (most of which Vandy guzzled, burping bubbles the rest of the night.) Breaking open a new deck of cards, Sid dealt rounds of Coon-Can while he commiserated with Cass about overbearing Rangers and conniving redheads. They chewed the fat about the drought, Lampasas's booming tourist trade, and Sid's vigilante-granger problem until 3 a.m., at which time Collie, with his usual flair for the cussid, hurled a boot at their heads and bellowed that he was trying to get some shut-eye.

Around 10 o'clock the next morning, Sid was rousing them with cups of java when the jail door crashed open. Poppy Westerfield stood on the threshold, disrupting the friendly, all-male atmosphere. Beneath a jaunty, peacock-colored bonnet and fashionably frizzed bangs, her emerald eyes glittered like ice.

"Marshal Wright, are you, or are you not, responsible for the safety of the dignitaries who visit your town?"

"Well, of course I'm responsible—"

"Good," Poppy snapped, sailing into Sid's office like a battleship at full steam. "Because when my husband gets gunned down by a vigilante granger, I shall see that your head rolls!"

Sid blinked.

Cass coughed to hide his amusement. He suspected no woman had ever talked to Sid in such a manner, especially in his office.

But Poppy's temerity was born from confidence. Petite and slender, with a mature beauty that could still turn men's heads, the 41-year-old social maven thrived in her role. As the wife of a rich and powerful senator, she didn't resort to eye-batting, tears, or swoons to control "lesser men"—which was the term she used to describe anyone who ranked lower than Baron in public office.

"In precisely one hour, my husband is due to give his speech at the sodbuster's convention," Poppy announced in an imperious manner. "Considering the way tempers are simmering in this town, Mr. Cassidy's guns may be the only things that stand between my dear, beloved Baron and a bushwhacker's bullet. I want you to release Cass this minute. *This minute,* do you hear me?"

Collie never missed a stroke with his whittling knife. "Don't put yourself out on my account, ma'am."

Cass nearly snorted java up his nose.

"Now see here, Mrs. Westerfield." Sid didn't look half as amused. "Cass and Collie got charged with vandalism and three separate counts of disturbing the peace by the Adjutant-General himself—"

"Rexford Sterne retired from the Ranger Force nearly a month ago," Poppy fired back, her eyes narrowing suspiciously. "To challenge my husband's re-election campaign, as you'll recall. Unless, of course, you've been apprised of some palm-greasing *skullduggery* that Baron should bring to Governor Ireland's attention?"

Sid's bearded, sun-weathered face grew as red as his suspenders, which strained across a beef-fed belly. Ranger or no, Sterne was a man to be reckoned with in Texas. Nowhere in the Lone Star State did the former Adjutant-General hold more sway than in his birthplace of Lampasas. Ever since Baron had gotten the notion to prove his clout by "taking the waters" and wooing Lampasas voters away from Sterne, Sid had been walking a tightrope between two looming shadows: the Ranger's and the senator's.

"Now Mrs. Westerfield, don't go putting words in my mouth," Sid backpedaled. "Retired or no, Rexford Sterne is still called general around these parts."

"Erroneously." Poppy sniffed. "It wouldn't surprise me

one bit if he was encouraging those granger assassins you're incapable of controlling in this town."

Sid looked like he wanted to knock her on her bustle. "Allow me to reassure you, Mrs. Westerfield. I hired six extra deputies to supervise the Texas Volunteer Guard as they patrol the convention and the hotels. You are perfectly safe in Lampasas. And so is Senator Westerfield."

"Forgive me if I don't share your faith in your pack of amateur tin-stars." Poppy wrestled a folded paper from her reticule and tossed the document, along with a $20 gold piece, on Sid's desk. "You're wasting my time. My husband and I are due at the luncheon. Release Mr. Cassidy."

Sid grunted when he read the letter. He even looked relieved. "Looks like you got yourself an attorney, Cass. *Mrs. Westerfield's* attorney," Sid added archly, turning an oversized key in Cass's cell door.

Cass darted a measuring glance at Poppy. She stood like an avenging angel, limned in her triumphant corona of sunbeams beneath the block-style letters that read, *Marshal's Office,* on Sid's window. When Cass's gaze collided with hers, her great bosom heaved. He was quick to notice the flush rising in her cheeks. A man like him didn't need much imagination to guess what a love-starved matron like Poppy wanted in exchange for her favor.

Next, Cass glanced furtively at Collie. Apparently, Poppy hadn't bothered to post the boy's bond. The kid sat cross-legged on the limestone floor of the adjacent cell with his half-whittled critter and his ring-tailed bunk mate.

"An attorney, huh?" Cass settled more comfortably on his cot with his legs stretched out, his back against the wall, and his coffee cup balanced on his lap. "Why, that's mighty fine, Sid." He took another sip of bellywash. "What'd the law wrangler say about springing my ward?"

"Ward, my ass," Collie muttered.

"Nuthin'," Sid said gamely.

"Nothing, huh? Now that can't be right. Why don't you read that high-falutin' paper again?"

"Mr. Cassidy," Poppy intervened impatiently, "my

husband is waiting for us outside the bank."

Cass's coyote instincts were on the alert: they'd noticed a peculiar phenomenon. Whenever Poppy mentioned "my husband" in an official capacity, she seemed to be referring to herself.

"Mrs. Westerfield," he drawled, "I'm beholding to you, ma'am. Really I am." He flashed his most ingratiating smile. "But you see, Collie's my charge. My responsibility. Surely a genteel lady like yourself, who cares about doing good Christian works and helping folks get out of jail, can understand why I can't leave an impressionable boy of 15—"

"Seventeen," Collie growled.

"—In the hoosegow by his lonesome," Cass finished smoothly. "Sid's likely to arrest some cutpurse or road agent! And then all those good Christian morals I've been trying to instill in the boy would get snuffed out like a candle in a hurricane."

Cass couldn't say who looked more annoyed by his speech, Collie the Thief or Poppy the Barracuda. But civility—or at least the appearance of civility—was more important to a senator's wife than to an authority-hating youth.

"Of course, Mr. Cassidy," Poppy said briskly. "I quite see your point. I shall have my attorney correct the oversight. Release the boy, marshal."

"But is that legal, Mrs. Westerfield?" Cass gushed in his best greenhorn's voice.

"My husband will *make* it legal," she retorted, tossing another double eagle on Sid's desk. "I trust that will cover the expense."

Collie shot him a warning look, and Cass winked. Why, any fella with eyes could see Poppy was eating out of the palm of his hand!

Sid unlocked the kid's door. Collie gathered his hat and boots. As he reached for his knapsack, he leaned his blond head close enough to the cells' shared bars for Cass to whisper:

"Find Sadie."

Collie nodded, donning his poker face beneath his curtain of shaggy hair. Most of the time, Collie eyed women the way he eyed rattlers. Cass figured Sadie's loins-stirring smiles and seductive shimmies would be wasted on the kid—which would be a well-deserved comeuppance for the Devil's Red-haired Daughter. After the way she'd kicked him in the gut, Cass wanted nothing better than to tie his born-again lover to a bedpost and paddle the stuffing out of her.

Too bad Sadie would like it so much.

Grunting farewell to Sid, Collie stomped past Poppy with callous indifference. Vandy flashed his fangs at the senator's wife before scampering into Fourth Street.

Now it was Cass's turn. Unfolding his long legs, he settled his Stetson on his head and reached for the gun belt Sid was extending to him.

"Much obliged."

"I certainly hope so," Poppy breathed.

Cass hid his amusement. He'd been speaking to Sid.

As Poppy hustled him into the bright, cloudless morning, heat waves were already undulating off the sun-bleached planks of the boardwalk. *Dia de los Muertos*—the Day of the Dead—was only a few days away, and Gringo curiosity-seekers were entertaining themselves in the Public Square by inspecting *Tejano* handcarts piled high with sugar skulls and ritual toys. As Cass passed street vendors, he could hear haggling in broken English.

Lampasas was a railroad boomtown, thanks to the Gulf, Colorado, and Santa Fe, which had completed its feeder line out of Belton only months ago. The result had been to end cattle droving in central Texas and populate nearby hills with tents.

Lampasas, with its famed mineral springs, was perfectly positioned as a vacation resort, since the governor was talking about calling a special session of the legislature in January, to discuss the state's problem with fence-cutting gunnysackers.

The state's other problem was a covert organization of vigilante grangers, who'd given honest, hard-working sodbusters a bad name. The Southern Farmers Alliance had denounced the guerilla tactics of the anonymous radicals, who festered in their ranks and lynched suspected gunnysackers. But a proclamation from a lobbyist group wasn't going to stop the murderers from attending the convention.

Or assassinating Baron.

"Lampasas is such a barbaric place," Poppy said, as if guessing Cass's thoughts. She shuddered. "I can't wait for this convention to be over. Sid Wright is worse than useless. Yesterday, I approached him with my private concerns about that floating poker game at Aquacia Bathhouse. Contrary to what all the sodbusters think, their wives are *perfectly aware* that their husbands are sneaking out of the convention to lose their shirts. But when I asked Wright to disband the game, he told me his hands are tied! Can you imagine? *Assassins* are running amuck, and Wright claims he can't send deputies two miles down the road to arrest them!"

Cass cleared his throat. Baron, himself, had staked that poker game as part of his strategy to undermine Sterne's popularity with voters. Apparently, Wright had been too much of a gentleman to acquaint Poppy with the truth.

"The bathhouse *is* located outside of town," Cass reminded her politely. "Sid's jurisdiction is limited to Lampasas."

"What a lot of rubbish. A crime is a crime. Who cares if a sheriff, a marshal, or a Ranger makes the arrest? It's a lawman's *sworn duty* to protect decent folks from outlaws!"

"Well...it *is* true lawmen need a little help now and then. That's why Baron hired me and Collie."

"Oh, Cass. Don't you see? My husband hired private security to protect us from that overbearing tyrant, Rexford Sterne. You're the only gunfighter in this town with the nerve—*and* the skill—to stand up to his badge-wearing bullies."

Cass averted his eyes. As much as he wanted to think that Sterne was an unholy bastard, he wanted to cling even more to his ideal that Rangers were noble. All his life, Cass had wanted to be someone whom other men respected. The kind of person whom women loved and little kiddies admired. He knew he could never go back and fix the mistake he'd made at the age of 13, when he'd gone vigilante, drawing too fast and plugging Abel Ainsworth before the Ku Klux Klansman could turn all the way around to face his doom. That split second of adolescent rage, of wanting to avenge Cousin Bobby's brutal murder, had forced Cass to spend his life running from the law, rather than enforcing it.

Still, in his heart, he tried to be worthy of Rangerhood: to fight for right. To protect the innocent. To defend the weak. That's what being a Ranger meant to him.

"You needn't worry about Baron, ma'am," Cass said gruffly. "Tito knows how to handle ruffians. He'll look after Baron when I'm off duty. Besides, most chuckleheads who strap on guns do it for show. They're slow to draw."

"I suspect that's how Marshal Wright got his job," Poppy said disdainfully. "Frankly, I don't think that man would recognize a crime unless he stumbled over a corpse!"

Slowing her steps, she peered into the milliner's window, with its tuxedo-wearing scarecrow and cheerful jack-o-lanterns. Each pumpkin was topped with a witch's hat that sported multi-patterned orange bows. Poppy worried her bottom lip as she stared at the display—or perhaps at the wall clock.

"Cass, you were good to me once, when I needed a friend." She turned to face him again, her expression troubled. "I haven't forgotten how you tried to comfort me that day in the calving barn."

Uh-oh. Cass's insides squirmed. He hadn't been expecting her to revisit *that* topic.

"You were only 17," she murmured. "Remember?"

Yeah, he remembered, all right. He'd found Poppy crying her eyes out after her second miscarriage and trying to slit her wrists with a whittling knife.

"That kind of sensitivity is so rare in a youth..." Her eyes filled with tears. "And now look at you. A full-grown man, putting your life on the line for my husband. I can't let you get hurt, Cass. It wouldn't be just."

"Uh...thanks, Mrs. Westerfield. But it's my job to make sure you and Baron stay safe. It's what I'm good at. That's why Baron hired me."

She nodded reluctantly, giving a watery sniff and tightening her hold on his arm. "I'm so glad my husband found you."

There it is again. That, 'My Husband,' thing.

They continued their stroll toward the half-constructed, limestone courthouse at the center of the Square. The gothic structure was already imposing, even without its clock tower, which the *Tejano* laborers would eventually erect above the red-slate tiles of the mansard roof.

Poppy grimaced at the Spanish-speaking workers, many of whom were swearing and whipping their mules. Playing the damsel-in-distress, she dragged Cass closer—so close, he couldn't fail to see her flushed skin, dilated eyes, and fluttering pulse. The scent of violets rolled off her breasts like an invisible fog. He was a little surprised by all these sexual signals. Poppy had always seemed too distant for a flirtation.

The truth was, Cass had never been opposed to affairs with married women—or older women, for that matter. Sadie was three years his senior, and when she licked her lips, smiling at his crotch, she could damned near pop the buttons of his fly.

Wilma could shrug off a skimpy lace nightdress in a downright dastardly way—one that never failed to make him salivate, even if she was old enough to be his mother.

But Poppy?

Cass winced to imagine his boss's weepy wife, mourning the ghosts of dead babies and lying like a sack of potatoes in his bed.

Poppy wouldn't be much fun.

Suddenly, she halted between the Commercial Saloon and a driverless wagon, piled high with beer kegs. Cass braced himself, expecting a temperance tirade. To his surprise, she ignored the liquor.

"That footpad at the Globe Hotel got me thinking," she confessed. Tears glimmered on her lashes as she raised beseeching eyes to his. "Baron has so many night meetings. So many *mistresses.* What if some burglar comes to *my* hotel room when I'm all alone and defenseless?"

Cass fidgeted. Her reasoning wasn't outside the realm of possibilities. A senator's wife was as much of a target as her husband.

"No one's going to hurt you on *my* watch, Mrs. Westerfield."

As if to prove him wrong, a gunshot shattered the morning air. The saloon window behind Poppy's head exploded into a thousand pieces.

"Sniper!" she shrieked, flinging herself into his arms.

Cass muttered an oath, dragging her down behind the buckboard to avoid the shower of glass.

The boardwalk had turned into a chaotic jumble of screaming petticoats and jostling sack suits. Above the sound of a bawling toddler, a *Tejano's* handcart crashed to the street. Sugar skulls rolled; marigolds got trampled. Cass recognized the second and third reports of a Winchester rifle; he smelled the taint of black powder on the breeze.

Struggling to free his arms from Poppy's clutches, he drew his Colts and squinted to the east. The shooter was strategically positioned across the Public Square on Third Street, his back to the morning sun, his vital organs shielded by the false façade of the grocer's roof. A fire-limned derby was all Cass could clearly discern of the man's appearance.

But derbys are favored by sodbusters.

"Stay down!" Cass barked as Poppy tried to rise from her knees.

She locked her arms around his middle section. "Don't leave me!"

"Let me go!"

"You'll be killed!"

"Cass!" It was Baron's voice, booming from a mess of toppled handcarts, several doors up the street. "Tito was hit!"

Cass cursed at this news. "Take cover!" he shouted at his boss.

But Baron, being as stubborn as his prized longhorn bull, ignored this advice. He was returning the fire, trying to protect Tito. The pirate sprawled on his butt amidst smashed pumpkin rinds, while Pendleton cowered in his boss's shadow, wielding an utterly useless derringer. Baron's .45 wasn't much more effective under the circumstances. A Peacemaker's range was only 50 yards, while a Winchester could strike a target at 400.

Cass broke free of Poppy's frantic hold and tried to draw the sniper's fire. His strategy succeeded a little too well. Cartridges plowed into the kegs; wood chips exploded around his hat; beer foamed around his boots. Half blinded by sawdust and sun, he nevertheless heard a pinging sound. One of his own bullets had struck sparks from the brass receiver of the sniper's Winchester.

That deadly close-call must have enraged the assassin. He turned his rifle on the beer wagon's horse. The frightened animal neighed and bolted. Cass cursed as his cover began galloping away. To complicate matters, Poppy chose that exact moment to faint. He had to get the confounded woman inside the saloon before the dust settled!

"Cass! Take cover!"

A lanky youth with blond hair was trying to draw the sniper's fire. Collie had entrenched himself with his rifle and coon behind a stack of slate tiles on the courthouse's construction site. The boy's fire blew the sniper's derby off his head. In retaliation, the sniper sheared off the top few layers of slate. Cass could hear the boy cursing like a muleskinner as sharp, red shards rained down around him.

"Take him out, boys!" bellowed an authoritative voice from the south side of the Square. Shielded from the sniper's view, Sid Wright ducked into Third Street. He was sprinting beneath porch roofs with his deputies.

As the tin-stars opened fire, the grocer's sign quickly turned into the wooden equivalent of Swiss cheese. Outgunned and out of cartridges, the sniper fled, ducking behind façades as he headed west. Cass finally had the diversion he needed to drag Poppy through the batwings of the saloon. He emerged a heartbeat later with both guns and a vengeance.

"Baron!"

The senator waved. He appeared to be all right. He was squatting beside the pasty-faced Pendleton, who looked like he might spew his breakfast as he tied a neckerchief around Tito's bloody arm.

Cass muttered an oath when he realized Sid's panting, pot-bellied deputies had become less concerned with apprehending the sniper than a passel of looting adolescents. The Public Square was in chaos. Matrons were shrieking; toddlers were wailing; and sodbusters were raging against "the depraved morality of city folk." If Cass wanted the sniper caught, he'd have to do it himself.

Squinting against the sun, he scanned the eastern skyline until his watering eyes spied a two-legged shadow, sprinting through the undulating heat waves.

Found you, you bastard!

Charging into the middle of the Square, Cass nearly got flattened by a rearing horse and its surrey before he reached his destination: the grocer's porch. Ignoring the red-faced merchant's threat to press charges, Cass vaulted for the rain spout and scrambled onto the roof.

"What the hell are you doing, Cass?" Baron yelled. "You're not deputized!"

Sid yelled something similar, but Cass was burning with vigilante vengeance. The sniper had made him look like a gun-waving bumpkin. Worse, the renegade had nearly plugged Baron and Poppy, who were counting on him for protection. No way was Cass going to let that gunman escape!

The sniper was four stores ahead, bounding toward Live Oak Street like a suicidal jackrabbit. Gritting his teeth, Cass did the same, clawing for purchase at chimneys, ripping shingles from roofs with his spurs. Collie was sprinting across the construction site, firing his Winchester, because Cass's .45 was out of range.

"Hey, kid!" Cass yelled when Collie's cartridge pinged off Boomer's barber pole. "Who taught you how to aim?"

"You did!"

"Then you didn't learn squat! Toss the rifle here!"

Collie obliged, and Cass caught it on the run, snapping the breechblock.

"It's only got one cartridge left!" Collie shouted, his voice fading as he fell behind.

Never warn the enemy, kid.

Cass slid to a halt on the building's edge. He had seconds—fractions of seconds—to steady his stance and take aim before the sniper jumped down to the hay wagon parked conveniently outside the livery. Cass could see a saddled bay, waiting patiently in the shadow of the iron horse sign that wobbled in the wind.

A numbing calm swept over him.

"That's bully, Pa," he remembered his 10-year-old self praising the 12-point buck his father had felled. "Caught him on the run, too! Not even a Ranger could shoot so good! You *could* be a Ranger, Pa. Why don't you wear a badge?"

"Cause I got family, Billy. A Ranger would never risk the people he loves. Too many vengeance-minded outlaws prey on a lawman's kin. 'Sides. It takes more than fancy shooting to be a Ranger."

"It does? Like what?"

"Like respect for life, boy. Like knowing right from

wrong. A Ranger keeps the peace. He doesn't take the law into his own hands."

Not long after that, Matthew Cassidy had been caught in the crossfire as feuding neighbors did the very thing that he'd warned his son not to do.

And Pa wasn't the only Cassidy who got murdered by a menace the law was too chicken-livered to punish.

Hardening his jaw at the bitter memories, Cass squinted through the rifle sight. Shooting a man in the back was a death sentence. He'd learned that the hard way. Since the fleeing sniper wasn't likely to turn around and make the shot defensible in court, Cass had to devise another plan. And fast. The bastard was getting ready to jump. Cass didn't have the protection of a badge if he missed.

So it's a good thing I never miss.

With a feral snarl, he pulled the trigger. Sparks flew as the cartridge ripped the iron horse from its mooring. The swinging sign slammed into the sniper with a clang. He yiked, dropping his Winchester. The rifle clattered down the shingles and plunged into a watering trough. A heartbeat later, both the sniper and the sign went crashing through the damaged timbers of the roof.

"Cassidy!" It was Sid's voice. "So help me God, I'll throw away the key to your cell this time!"

Cass gave the lawman a cheeky salute. "He's all yours, marshal. Wrapped up nice and pretty with a bow."

Lumbering into the livery yard with a deputy, Sid warned Collie and Vandy to stay out of harm's way, a warning which they obeyed for roughly 90 seconds.

In the meantime, Cass shimmied down a porch pillar. When he caught up with Collie inside the stable, he was dumbfounded to see Sid and his deputy wading through straw, poking their rifles into hay bales, and generally looking perplexed.

"He got *away?*" Cass said incredulously. "What the hell happened?"

Collie rolled his eyes. "Your lawman friend moves

slower than a three-legged tortoise. My guess is, the sniper was disguised. He threw off his granger clothes and disappeared through the tack room into the crowd."

About two minutes later, Vandy proved Collie right by sniffing out a ratty brown wig and sack coat, stashed under the straw.

But by that time, the sniper was long gone.

CHAPTER 6

Cass had two things on his mind the rest of that day: identifying the sniper and tracking down Sadie.

In Cass's opinion, the sniper had been a professional. He'd positioned himself so anyone returning his fire would be sunblind. He'd even pre-planned his escape. So why had the bastard been such a lousy shot?

That question plagued Cass for hours. Baron hypothesized that his would-be assassin had hit Tito because the big man was in the way, but Cass wasn't so sure. The sniper had taken numerous potshots at Tito, while Baron, who'd been returning fire, only dodged two bullets.

In any event, Baron was too canny not to milk the incident for every ounce of publicity he could get. He awarded Tito a medal. Poppy all but smothered the big man with her maternal fussing. She dressed his wounds and vowed she would only have a *hero* as her bodyguard.

Thus, while Cass was relegated to Baron Duty, he kept his ears pricked—and not just for sniper news. He figured he owed Sadie a colossal comeuppance.

Cass couldn't forgive the Devil's Daughter for kicking him in the gut, and worse, for laughing at him while he'd flailed like an oaf on the hotel carpet. He imagined how the hellcat must have hidden in the stairwell, watching in delight as Rexford Sterne slapped him with cuffs.

But Cass's good humor was restored around dinnertime, when Collie returned from his Sadie Hunt. Apparently while whittling critters and trading quips with Joaquin, the shoeshine boy from Boomer's Barbershop, Collie had heard some juicy gossip:

A sodbuster with "cat's eyes and goat whiskers" liked to play poker at a boardinghouse near Silk Stocking Row. The granger wasn't much good at cards, which got him lots of invitations, and his losses were something of a joke in that establishment, since he never seemed able to afford a rut. As a result, he often got served "consolation shots" by the proprietess, a spooky Cajun with red and blue snakes crawling on her hands.

Cass had no trouble recognizing the description of his old friend, Wilma LeBeau. Apparently, Wilma was sheltering Sadie. The question was, why would a money shark like Wilma let Sadie freeload in the casino, instead of earning her keep upstairs?

To learn the answer, Cass left Tito to guard the sleeping Westerfields and reported to Wilma's boarding house around 2 a.m. He could hear piano music and husky laughter behind the secret, sliding door of the pantry. That's where Wilma's long-time bouncer, Cotton, had bid him and Collie to wait. At any hour of the day or night, a man could drink, gamble, and rut to his heart's content at Wilma's place.

The exception, of course, was a man who'd been saddled with a sullen 17-year-old and a felonious coon.

"I still don't see why we had to stop at a *bathhouse* first," Collie groused, folding his arms in a huff. "I dunked my head in a stream last week, when Vandy caught us a trout."

Cass rolled his eyes, not bothering to dignify the kid's objection.

Scrubbed down, combed back, and sporting his cleanest duds, Collie frowned. He was glaring up at pantry shelves lined with spice tins and bottles. "What kind of brothel is this, anyway? They have a pond in the kitchen, but no liquor in the cupboard?"

"That *pond* is a basin swarming with mudbugs," Cass retorted, slapping Collie's hand away from a bottle labeled, *Cooking Sherry.* "Vandy's lucky he didn't get his tail snipped when he tried to fish one out."

The coon whined from the knapsack slung over Collie's shoulders. After the mudbug incident, Cotton had ordered the boy to stuff his pet in this leather prison.

Collie snorted. "Vandy's not afraid of a few foreign crawly fish."

"The term's *crawfish,* pal. And a crawfish is the least of your worries if you steal that Voodoo woman's liquor. Wilma will roast your balls. Then she'll sic her ghosts on you!"

"Bring 'em on," Collie retorted loftily. "I got more dead kin than most, and my spooks would make *you* look like an altar boy, Snake Bait."

At long last, the secret panel whispered open and Cotton waved them into a lavish, red-velvet parlor. According to the gossip at Boomer's Barbershop, Wilma's girls were the finest in Lampasas—which had come as a surprise to Cass. The last time he'd visited Wilma, her Dodge City brothel had been a watering hole for common cowboys and buffalo hunters.

But now, as Cass surveyed the room, he had to admit that Wilma had moved up in the world. Her bevy of high-class bawds lounged in skimpy silks in various come-hither poses on elegant sofas and chaise lounges. Some girls smoked cigarettes from long, black holders. Others sipped crystal glasses with sparkling champagne. Not a one of them would have suffered a man who chewed tobacco, stank of sweat, or scratched his balls. In fact, those yahoos never made it past Cotton.

The whisper of taffeta, followed by a murmur from the men, heralded Wilma's appearance on the second-story landing. Smoldering like a coal in her sheath of shimmering scarlet, she stood above the cigar smoke, surveying the crowd with cagey eyes that were nearly as dark as the blue-black corkscrews piled so elegantly on top of her head. No man had ever claimed Wilma for his own; Cass suspected even her most ardent admirers were slightly afraid of her reputation as a Mambo. Just mention "mojo" or "gris-gris" to any man who claimed to be head-over-heels in love with her, and that gentleman would toss back a shot and change the subject.

At last, Wilma's eyes rested on Cass. She flashed a sultry smile that would have made the limpest pecker stand up and salute. Graceful to the point of hypnotic, she descended the staircase, sauntering around a curve. The slit of her gown rose practically to the apex of her thighs. Grangers, ranchers, politicians, and merchants gawked with lust-glazed eyes, hoping to glimpse private parts that could cost a cowboy a year's worth of wages—and that was on a night when Wilma was feeling philanthropic.

Cass grinned, viscerally aware that her enticing sashay was raising the temperature of every man in the parlor. He crossed to the foot of the stairs.

"Cass," she drawled in her molasses-thick accent. She halted one step above him, playacting the Queen of the Sex Vixens to the hilt. "It has been too long, *cher.*" She extended a hand.

Cass gallantly raised it to his lips.

"Ah, you have brought new friends for me to love. Who is this handsome devil?"

Collie reddened to the roots of his lanky blond hair.

"The *handsome* one's the furry bandit with the mask," Cass said drolly.

Amusement warmed Wilma's eyes. She lavished her loins-stirring smile on Collie. "I hold a special place in my heart for beasts," she murmured—which might have been a double entendre. With Wilma, it was hard to tell. Everything that came out of the woman's mouth sounded like sex. Her husky, Louisiana alto could say something as innocuous as, *"I like buttered toast,"* and the wickedest images would plague a man's mind.

Cass adored her.

Collie, however, was out of his league. When Wilma's

bold, measuring gaze fastened on his fly, he got so flustered, he nearly spilled Vandy to the carpet. Mumbling something that sounded like, *"Bourbon,"* he fled for the nearest, liveried waiter.

Wilma's chuckle was low and husky. "Surely the boy's not a virgin. Not in *your* care."

"You'd have that effect on Casanova."

"True." Wilma's dimples peeked as she placed a bejeweled hand on his sleeve.

They strolled across the gold-and-crimson geometrics of the Aubusson carpet, making small talk, chatting amicably about Dodge, Lampasas, and mutual acquaintances. The latter topic inevitably led to Sadie.

But Cass knew better than to ask where his Texas Tiger had holed up. He hadn't earned the nickname, Coyote Cass, because he was in the habit of letting a woman make a cat's paw of him. His job was to distract and to decoy, while his secret weapon, Collie, prowled the premises with his weasel ears.

Since Wilma's secret parlor had no windows or balcony for romancing, Cass escorted her to a red-velvet settee behind potted palms.

"And now I can give you your present," he teased affectionately, drawing a small pouch from his vest pocket.

Her eyes lit up, as he knew they would. "But your company is present enough, *cher,"* she cooed gamely.

"Aw. You always know how to make a fella feel special."

As a point of pride, Cass never paid for a bawd's services. Wilma never gave away a rut for free. After haggling like fishwives a couple of times back in Dodge, they'd finally agreed on a wager. If he could get her to scream his name just once in ecstasy, he could have his pick of the bawds in her house if—and that was a big "if"—the lady was agreeable.

That "wager romp" with Wilma had nearly killed him. He'd had to work for six unholy hours at his task, which had rendered him incapable of sitting astride a saddle, much less walking without a limp, for two days. However, he'd learned things about pleasure that he, in his 18-year-old arrogance, had never dreamed might happen between a man and a woman.

After that night, Cass had started a tradition. Each new droving season, when he would show up at Wilma's house for the first time, he would bring her a present—not because he had to, but because he liked to give pleasure to women.

He flashed a wicked grin. "You know me. Always trying to be a better man." He offered her the pouch. "Consider these a token of my esteem. I saw them, and I thought of your eyes," he added gallantly.

Curiosity sneaked across her features. When she tipped the bag, a perfectly matched pair of tiger eye earrings spilled into her palm.

"My eyes?" she repeated archly.

He adopted his best hang-dog expression. "You don't like them."

"They are lovely, *cher*. And yet, I cannot help but think you had some other tiger in mind."

He widened his baby-blues. "Whoever could you mean?"

Indulging in a showboater's gene, he dropped the other object hiding in his palm. "Oh, darn," he drawled, taking great pains to make sure Sadie's necklace spilled across his boot. "There I go with my butter fingers."

Anybody who knew Sadie knew that necklace meant the world to her. The pendant was actually a brass button from her daddy's Confederate uniform. Crossed sabers dominated the design, with '8' centered above, and 'TX' below. The etchings signified the Eighth Texas Cavalry—more commonly known as Terry's Texas Rangers. Sadie had once confided to Cass that other than an old Henry repeater rifle, the battered button was the only memento she still possessed of Roarke Michelson.

Cass stooped, retrieving his prize. "Say, Wilma. Do you know where I might find a poker game with a freckled sodbuster? I could use this necklace as my opening stake. I figure it must be worth a couple of dollars, at least."

Wilma looked torn between amusement and agitation. "Since when did you become interested in freckled sodbusters?"

"Since one kicked me in the gut last night."

"Poor darling. You didn't happen to be holding your gun at point-blank range?"

"What mean-spirited busy-body started that rumor?"

She chuckled as his show of indignation. "Wait here. I'll see what I can do."

CHAPTER 7

Chewing the fat with a discontented group of grangers, Sadie sprawled man-like in her chair with a circle of empty shot glasses cluttering her side of the poker table. The four of clubs was showing in her Stud draw, and a stack of chips was rapidly depleting at her elbow. She was losing on purpose. She was also slurring her words and laughing louder than necessary. God knew, she'd observed enough rednecks in Western saloons to know how to mimic one.

According to Cotton, Cass had arrived, hunting for her. Sadie wasn't surprised. In fact, she'd prepared. That's why she'd donned a dingy linen sack suit (which was the ugliest thing she'd ever worn); blue-tinted railroad spectacles (to turn her amber eyes a shade of green;) flesh-toned putty to hide the freckles on her nose, and auburn facial hair. Knowing Cass as she did, she figured she was due for a monumental showdown.

Her mind flashed back to a torrid night in Dodge, when she'd insisted she was a business woman who would never give her heart to any man. He'd taken offense at the idea. When she'd refused to make an exception, even for him, he'd used his lariat to bind her to the posts of her bed. She could still hear his provocative drawl above her ripping breaths as he'd tantalized her feverish, sensitized nakedness. She could still remember melting into a sparking puddle of nerves when he'd plied his considerable talents at sin, tormenting her with whipping cream and his wickedly mobile tongue. Unable to resist a moment longer, she'd begged him to take her, and he'd plunged triumphantly inside her until she'd exploded like a freaking supernova.

A lusty little smile curved her lips.

'Stop that!' her ever-practical brain railed at her nether region. What the Rebel Rutter knew about love could probably be poured into a thimble.

As if on cue, the parlor door opened, and Wilma crossed to Sadie's table with a serving tray. As the madam flashed her secretive smile and leaned over Sadie's shoulder, Sadie could smell the oddly pleasant combination of dried peony and rosemary, which the Mambo regularly replenished in her *gris-gris,* the protection pouch swinging from a leather cord around her neck. Wilma ardently believed in banishing evil—as well she might. A whore, and especially a whore of mixed blood, often saw the darkest side of men.

"Are you sure you're up to meeting with him, *chere?"* the Mambo whispered, placing a shot of whiskey-colored sugar water by Sadie's elbow.

Sadie nodded curtly. She didn't see how fleeing through Wilma's secret tunnel would help her dig up dirt on a senator. Besides, the only way to determine if Cass could be turned into a trustworthy informant was to figure out how loyal he was to Baron.

"C'est bon," Wilma murmured. "I shall send him to the poker room. Let us see how long your disguise fools our Rebel Rutter."

Wilma waved; Cotton nodded; and within minutes, Cass and Collie were stepping through the sliding panel that separated the gaming hall from the parlor. A great deal of grinning and giggling arose from the two female beerjerkers in the room. Sadie couldn't tell whether they were admiring Cass's rugged good looks or Collie's. If she hadn't known better, she would have thought the kid's silvery-blond hair, sun-chiseled features, and rangy torso made him Cass's younger brother.

Pushing her spectacles up her nose, she pretended to focus on shuffling. The hayseeds in her game were well on their way to having their crops freighted, so to speak. In fact, they were more interested in gawking at "big city titties" than shelling out money for a rut. Sadie figured her Bubbas were the best part of her disguise to fool Cass.

But she hadn't considered the raccoon. Cass let the varmint sniff something that looked suspiciously like Daddy's button. The next thing she knew, the roly-poly nuisance was galloping across the carpet in a silvery ripple of fur, sniffing his way past boots and spittoons before clambering triumphantly into her lap. She glowered at the creature.

"Tarnation!" cried Bubba One, blinking blearily across the table at the furry game-crasher. "I'm seeing coons!"

"Dag-nabbit." This from Bubba Two. "I gave the bouncer my squirrel gun!"

"Don't make no never mind," said the heroic Bubba Three, who was trying—rather clumsily—to impale the coon with a walking stick. "I'll barbecue the varmint!"

The coon swiped a paw, flashing ferocious fangs. A heartbeat later, Cass and Collie stood scowling on either side of her chair.

"You barbecue my coon, and I'll barbecue your ass," Collie threatened in a gruff, Kentucky accent.

The coon grabbed her shot glass and began guzzling the sugar water.

Honestly. How does Cass keep a straight face around these clowns?

"Scram," the gunfighter growled, drilling his iced baby-blues into the rednecks.

The grangers gulped and fled, their chairs toppling backwards onto the carpet.

So much for the safety of numbers.

But Sadie had been playing games with Cass—both in and out of bed—long enough to recognize a real threat when she saw one. Right now, his anger was under control.

"Looks like we're one short in our foursome," she drawled, continuing to shuffle her cards. "Should I be dealing a hand for the coon?"

Collie arched an eyebrow at Cass. "You put up with that mouth?"

"With a gag."

Sadie snorted. "So you'll be kissing my ass, then."

Reluctant amusement sneaked across the steely planes of Cass's face.

The kid shook his head. "You're a goner, Snake Bait." Hoisting Vandy to his shoulder, Collie reached for a Bubba's half-empty bottle of Wild Turkey. "I'm getting drunk over yonder. So if you need rescuing, you'll have to give Vandy a holler."

Cass nodded.

For a long moment, he continued to stand there, flexing his hands over his missing Colts as if he wanted to draw— or maybe to shake her. Eyes the color of a wind-swept Texas sky raked over her wig, facial hair, and voluminous coat, possibly checking for weapons. God knew, she was about as alluring as a potato sack in all this baggy linen.

But Cass...Well, he would have made her mouth water with an apple barrel suspended from his shoulders. As usual, he wore black. All black. Since his gun belt was in Cotton's capable hands, only the winking of his fancy, Mexican-style rowels detracted from the sleek, feral lines of his six-foot length.

She decided to break the stalemate.

"Where'd you get that pendant?" she demanded, hiking an eyebrow at the battered brass. It was Daddy's button, all right. Cass had let it flop onto his bandanna to make sure she saw it. She'd been hunting for that pendant all damned day!

Cass flashed his Coyote grin and tucked the makeshift, leather cord beneath his collar. "What, this old thing?"

"Play you for it," she challenged.

"Don't know if you can afford the stakes."

Smartass. He knew precisely how much that button

meant to her.

Sadie shrugged and riffled the deck of cards. "Sounds like you're scared you'll lose."

"Them's fighting words, Four Eyes."

"I'm shaking in my boots, cowboy."

It was the old banter, with a delicious new twist: the unknown element of Cass's loyalty.

He picked up a chair and straddled it. As he settled close beside her, Sadie struggled to ignore the captivating shower of sparks that danced along her nerves. The crackle of current between her and Cass had always been like some hungry, growling thing. Never had it been more dangerous than tonight, when she had to keep her head cool and her heart hard to discern the truth from his lies.

He doffed his Stetson and set it on the table. "The name's Cassidy," he said in ironic tones. "William. Most folks call me Cass."

"Uh-huh."

"You got a name?"

"Depends on what I'm wearing."

The twitch in his lips betrayed his mirth. He'd maneuvered his chair close enough for her to catch the faint whiff of sandalwood soap. So few men bothered to sponge off the stink of sweat and steer before they came to solicit a rut. But Cass knew how to please a woman. More accurately, he knew how to make a woman melt into a sparking puddle at his boots—and that was before he flashed all those dazzling teeth.

"Seems like we've met before," he drawled.

"Must've been a past life."

"As I recollect, you weren't so fond of wearing a beard back then."

"A wretched nuisance," she confided. "It itches like hell."

"I like it."

"You would."

Never missing a beat, she dealt the first hand for Stud Poker. The Queen of Hearts showed on her side of the table, the Knave of Hearts on his.

"How fitting." His baritone was velvety, nearly a croon. Picking up chips, he tossed them to the center of the table. He'd staked 100 dollars.

Showboater.

But she'd expected no less. From day to day, Cass was either as rich as a bank or as poor as a migrant orchard picker. When she'd reunited with him four years ago in Dodge, he'd bragged that he'd just won every stitch of clothing in a game of chance. Money meant nothing to Cass. If his guns earned him thousands by noon, he gambled away his winnings by sundown. He'd always been of the opinion that he could live off the land, and life's other necessities—like ammo, whiskey, and riding tack—could be won in some contest he dreamed up on the spot. Knife-throwing and target-shooting were the areas in which he excelled, although he pitched a mean game of horseshoes, and she'd seen him crush rival marble-shooters, mainly because he threw off their aim with his banter.

Peeking at her cards, Sadie was hard-pressed not to sigh. They were crap, of course. Having lived above a saloon most of her life, she'd been playing high-stakes card games since the age of 13. She knew the value of a Poker Face, so she was careful to keep hers firmly in place. Besides, no one liked competition more than Cass.

"I'll see your hundred, and raise you a hundred," she said, tossing her chips into the kitty. She'd be damned if she lost to him. The Pinkertons gave her an allowance for gambling. Rarely was she called upon to spend it, but when she did, her bluffing skills usually earned the agency money.

"Harvest must've been good this year, granger." He met her stakes and demanded two cards.

Thinks he has a decent hand, does he?

She dealt herself two cards and prayed for queens. "Some things ripen with age."

"Like women?"

"Like cheese."

He chuckled. The leading bet was his again, so he tossed another hundred dollars into the pot. "Don't know too many men who wear sun-shades in a poker game."

"You calling me a cheat?"

"You wanna wrassle over it?"

"You'd only get whupped."

He flashed all those pretty teeth. "That's why I brought an extra lariat."

Oh, he really was a cut-up.

Doing her best to ignore the delicious tingles skipping down her spine, she drilled him with her best no-nonsense glare. "I call. Show your hand, cowpoke."

"Poke being the operative word." With a deft finger he flipped his cards. "Full house."

Damn.

"Double or nothing?" he taunted in provocative tones.

Ever-conscious of her cover, she shot him a withering glare. "Only if you watch your manners. I have a reputation to keep."

"You should've thought of that before you grew a beard." He poured her a drink then scooped up the cards. He handled the pasteboards like a professional, letting them fly between his hands in a rippling arc of red and white.

"Impressive. Who taught you how to shuffle like a sharper? Doc?"

"You mean, Holliday?" Cass chuckled. "Naw. Collie did."

She nearly snorted whiskey up her nose. "That kid scares me."

"Not so loud. He'll only gloat."

She laughed, tossing back her shot. Cass dealt. The cards flicked so fast across the table, they blurred. This time when she peeked, she had a shot at a full house or a three-pair. The Ace of Spades was showing on Cass's side of the table.

She bet one hundred.

"I'll see you, and raise you two hundred," he said.

She rolled her eyes. *Of course you do.*

"Two cards," she said, and he dealt again. She got her third ten.

"Dealer takes one." He slapped down the deck. "So, Granger. About this red-headed sister of yours—"

"We were talking about sisters?" She tossed her stake into the pot.

"We were talking about women."

"I thought we were talking about cardsharps."

"That's 'cause you hear only what you want to hear," he retorted.

Donkey butt. How many times have I accused you of the same thing over the years?

"So what happened to the girl?" he demanded.

"What girl?"

"Your firebrand of a sister."

She shook her head. "Sad story."

"I'm listening."

"You *know* what happened to Maisy."

He had the good grace to redden. Back in Dodge, he'd gone snooping through her bedroom and found the untitled ballad she'd written as a catharsis about her drowned twin. After reading lyrics like, *"Secret angel of my heart, I hate that we are parted,"* Cass had leaped to the conclusion she'd been writing love songs about Rex. The blow-up that night had been cataclysmic, and the beginning of the end of their affair.

"Not *that* sister," he persisted, tossing another two-hundred dollars into the pot. "I'm talking about the sister who's too ornery to die. The sister who wouldn't pay the devil his due."

"I like her already."

"I couldn't help but notice a certain family resemblance."

"What sharp little eyes you have."

"Just wait 'til you feel my teeth."

She ducked her head to hide her smirk. "I'll see your two hundred, and raise you two more."

But he ignored her bet. He was leaning closer now. The air between them shimmered with heat. *Sparks and cinders,* she thought a trifle breathlessly. Lucifire was lurking in the blazing blue depths of those eyes.

"Is your sister in trouble?" he demanded quietly.

The fire in that stare was making her grow hotter by the second—partly from guilt, and partly from the insane urge to grab a fistful of his sun-streaked hair and kiss him. She had to remind herself Cass was dangerous. That he worked for the enemy. That she was wearing a beard.

"Trouble's my sister's middle name," she rallied.

"Can't argue with you there, Match Head."

"Now you're pissing me off."

"Good. I haven't lost my touch." His dimples peeked, but his eyes fairly smoked. "If we're being watched—" he lowered his voice "—all I need's a simple answer: Yes or no?"

She squirmed. Now she felt like she was sitting on a furnace. If she answered, "No," she'd have to explain why she'd been climbing through a hotel window last night to avoid Tito, who'd been blocking the stairs. If she answered, "Yes," she'd have to deal with the unmitigated mess of Cass snooping around and learning things he shouldn't. She could never let him get that close again, even if he sincerely wanted to protect her.

Gulping a breath, she opted for the coward's way out: Diversion. "Quit stalling, hotshot. Place your bet."

"I bet your sister's in way over her saucy red head."

"Only when you're around, Romeo."

"You don't say?"

"I just did."

But he wouldn't back down. "So what kind of trouble are we talking about?"

She waved a vague hand. "You know women."

"I like to think I do."

"You're too modest by far."

"You can't believe everything you hear."

"Except in your case."

"Aw. That's sweet." Once again, he refused to be sidetracked. "Maybe you could put in a good word for me. Tell your sister I have friends. Friends who could fix any trouble she's in."

"Are you referring to Big Iron and the Peacemaker?" She arched a suggestive eyebrow. "Or the pistol in between?"

His chuckle was wolfish. "Now there's a thought. But I was thinking more along the lines of the law."

"You know the law?"

"I know folks who *make* the laws."

"Well, I'll be dinged."

He drove his point home. "My folks could help your folks go a long way."

She was glad for the spectacles because the tint disguised her uneasiness. She'd been hoping Cass didn't know how Baron conspired to kill off his rivals. But Cass was talking like a confidence man now.

"All the way to Ranger headquarters?" she demanded. She couldn't quite keep the accusation from her voice.

A blue norther rolled between them.

It wasn't hard to guess what Baron was using to exploit Cass's loyalty. From the first day she'd met 12-year-old William "Billy" Cassidy, trotting after her like a puppy on a string, leaving wildflowers on her brothel windowsill, naming the sky's brightest stars after her, Billy had talked her ears off about three things: sex, guns, and his dream to become a Texas Ranger.

Recalling the idealistic youth Cass had been, Sadie supposed it had been inevitable that he'd turn vigilante. That he'd feel responsible, as the last surviving member of his clan, to take on the patriarch's nickname—and the patriarch's duty of hunting down the man who'd murdered his 18-year-old cousin. When Cass had plugged Abel Ainsworth, he'd not only made an enemy of prominent Ku Klux Klansmen in northeast Texas, he'd shattered his dream of becoming a Ranger.

Now Baron was preying on Cass's childhood dream, dangling a Ranger badge like a carrot under his nose. If

Baron learned Rex was trying to pin a murder charge on him, Baron would do more than remove Rex from the Force. He'd have Rex silenced—by Cass!

"You got a problem with Rangers?" Cass demanded.

"I never have a problem with Rangers," she said grimly. "As long as they haven't tarnished the badge.*"

"Then wake up and smell the java."

"What's *that* supposed to mean?"

"It means your Ranger friend's a big phony."

"Forgive me if I question the word of a man who's been holding a grudge for four years."

"And with good reason."

She rolled her eyes. "Time to change your tune, cowpoke. You're like a rusty old gate, swinging in the wind."

"Maybe if you *listened* for a spell, you'd finally hear the truth."

"All right. I'll bite. What truth?"

"Do I have to spell it out for you? Your Ranger's got greased palms."

"That's ridiculous! Rex would never take a bribe! He's the most honorable, upstanding man in all of Texas!"

Cass snorted. "You'd have to have sawdust for brains to believe a whopper like that. Find yourself a new protector. Sterne's days are numbered."

Sadie's heart stuttered. Was that a threat? Was Cass *threatening* Rex?

"Just so we're clear—" she had to force the words from her constricting throat "—if you mess with him, you mess with me."

Cass shoved back his chair. Anger punctuated that economical movement. All his neat little piles of red, white, and green chips toppled, scattering with a flimsy *chinking* sound.

"Glad we cleared the air," he said pleasantly—too pleasantly. He set the Stetson on his head.

"Cass, wait!"

He paused in mid-stride, his broad back like a wall, his

features chiseled by shadow. When he locked stares with her over his shoulder, an arctic blast came from that ice-blue glare.

"I don't want our friendship to end this way," she pleaded.

"That's been your problem since the beginning, darlin'. The loyalty you show your friends."

Hard-lipped and diamond-eyed, he tipped his hat before striding away.

She muttered an oath and shoved her cards across the table. A crushing sense of frustration weighted her chest as she watched him slam out the door. Cass *wanted* to believe Baron's lies.

Her coyote had been thoroughly snared.

CHAPTER 8

The next morning, Sadie was in disguise again: this time, as a frumpy, gray-haired maid with a pillow for a paunch.

Doing her best not to think about Cass, and how she might be forced to arrest him, she shuffled around the lobby of the Grand Park Hotel in her white mobcap, ruffled apron, and navy-colored uniform. Occasionally, as conventioneers hurried past, she would swipe her feather duster with great exuberance over a Tiffany lamp shade or the eight-foot rack of a stuffed, longhorn steer. Her goal was to keep an eye on the stairwell. She figured Poppy Westerfield would have to descend from the second story eventually.

The Grand Park Hotel was one of the crowning, architectural achievements of Lampasas. It's only flaw appeared to be its lack of an elevator. Built by the railroad as a mecca for conventioneers, vacationers, and convalescents, the hotel looked like an enormous mansion with wrap-around porches and banner-bedecked turrets. Boasting 200 guest rooms and at least a dozen cabins, it sprawled across the southwestern corner of the city with a first-class dining room, ballroom, and recreational area, which offered boating, horseracing, shooting contests, and music recitals. As if these entertainments weren't enough, a guest could travel via boardwalk or mule-drawn trolley to one of the many mineral springs that had given rise to the city's reputation as a health resort.

Sadie had heard the rumor that Baron was ailing. Then again, he might have gone on his morning pilgrimage to Aquacia Bathhouse because a "secret" poker game was attracting conventioneers. About an hour ago, she'd watched the senator stride through the lobby with his gangly, bespectacled secretary. Pendleton had scurried to keep up, looking every inch like an underling, from his thinning, greased-back hair, to his starched chin-high collar, notebook, and stylus.

According to rumor, Baron treated Pendleton like family. The secretary had none of his own, probably because Pendleton spent every waking moment, managing Baron's business accounts. He was wholly devoted to the senator, and frankly, Sadie wouldn't have been surprised to learn that Pendleton covered up Baron's crimes.

She strained to hear what the prune-faced clerk was telling his boss, but she only heard intermittent phrases— something about an upcoming luncheon with railroad financiers. Apparently, Poppy had accepted the invitation on behalf of the senator, but he was refusing to cancel his javelina hunt with his cowboy cronies.

Cass trailed behind Baron and Pendleton, keeping an eye peeled for suspicious characters. As hard as she tried not to care, Sadie wasn't able to ignore how the heartthrob's dimpled grin quickened more than one fluttering hand-fan as ladies of all ages sighed in his wake. The knowledge that she, herself, looked like an apple barrel with a gray mop for hair didn't improve her mood.

Baron and his retinue had left the hotel 30 minutes ago. Now Sadie was waiting futilely for Collie to exit the building. She still wasn't sure where the hooligan was. Gritting her teeth, she imagined him ransacking her bedroom. She couldn't help but recall the shambles in which he and Cass had left Rex's room at the Globe Hotel. After grimly wading through what resembled a torpedo strike, the Ranger had retrieved one of the few personal indulgences he allowed himself: a silver flask. Finding his imported, Glenmorangie Scotch completely drained, Rex had raged: "*It'll be a cold day in hell, before Cassidy wears a Ranger badge!*"

Sadie couldn't blame Rex. Especially since Vandy had taken a crap on his pillow.

A heavy boot thumped behind her, interrupting her reverie. Ducking her head, Sadie pushed her spectacles up her nose and looked busy. Tito was exiting the stairwell with Poppy Westerfield on his arm.

For the first time, Sadie was able to lay her eyes on Baron's flesh-and-blood wife, rather than a sienna–toned daguerreotype. Sadie had to admit, Poppy was stunning, possessing all the traits Baron was rumored to covet in a woman.

Sadie studied the Galveston native. Aside from her bodice, Poppy was petite, with strawberry curls, meadow-green eyes, and an enviable waistline for a woman of 41 years—but then, Poppy had never borne children, according to her Pinkerton dossier. The senator's wife walked with an air of privilege in her elegant day dress. A shameless array of matching emeralds adorned her ears, wrists, and fingers. However, nothing more than a silver heart pendant graced her neck. She kept sliding the bauble along its chain, as if she were agitated.

Sadie thought back to a conversation she'd once had with Rex, when she'd been plying him with questions about the type of woman she needed to "portray" to attract Baron's attention.

"But what's Poppy *really* like?" she'd asked Rex. "You come from the same circle of privilege; I've never been to a political rally, much less a debutante's ball."

Rex had fidgeted, a sure sign his southern chivalry was vying with his lawman's code.

"Poppy grew up as the only child of a widowed attorney. She used to scribe legal documents for her father when she was a school girl, during the days when he couldn't afford the wages of a full-time clerk. Eventually, he built a prosperous legal practice and became renowned for manipulating tax laws in favor of shipping interests. However, the wealthy clientele whom he served never truly accepted him into their circle. Poppy got jilted by her first steady beau—a young sugar planter, who had political ambitions. He started courting a gal with Old Money—a textiles heiress, I believe.

"Poppy took it hard. She left Galveston to live with friends in Austin. She met Baron at some capitol shindig. Back then, he was little more than a cowboy with a dream, but he did manage to get himself elected to the Burnet City Council. He doted on Poppy. Fact is, he never did like competition, and he wound up punching out one of her suitors. Eventually, Baron won her hand. The same week he whisked her off on their honeymoon, her ex-beau and his fiancé had a tragic boating accident."

Sadie nodded. She'd read Baron's biography in a dossier. "Yes, yes," she said impatiently, "but what kind of *woman* is Poppy? Prudish? Flirtatious? Maternal? Absent-minded?"

"She can be charming," Rex hedged.

"Can be?" Sadie hiked an eyebrow. "And when she's not being charming, what then?"

Rex hardened his jaw. "Cold. Ice-water cold."

Recalling that conversation now, Sadie looked for signs of that chilly social maven in the agitated woman, who was toying with the heart-shaped religious relic around her throat. Sadie wondered if Poppy was merely misunderstood. Losing three children in childbirth couldn't have been easy for a wife, who watched her husband choose progressively younger mistresses every year that she aged.

Thoughtfully, Sadie watched Tito hand his boss's wife into a private surrey. Only after the two of them trotted off into the sunshine did Sadie loose a ragged breath and hurry for the stairwell.

The Westerfields' suite was located on the hotel's top floor, where Baron had reserved five rooms in the west wing. Sadie had been forced to bribe a maid to learn Cass and Collie shared the room, flanking Poppy's side of the suite. Tito's room flanked Baron's, and Pendleton's quarters were closest to the stairs. Normally, Sadie would have saved herself the fee for palm-greasing by snooping through the hotel ledger; however, the page with Cass's, Baron's, and Tito's signatures had been missing.

Half expecting to be attacked by a snarling raccoon at any moment, Sadie glanced warily over both shoulders before withdrawing a widdy from her apron pocket and unlocking the Westerfields' door. She'd already searched every desk drawer, file cabinet, wall hanging and floor plank in the Spartan campaign office that Pendleton ran for his boss in the Public Square. Unless one considered a backroom with a mattress suspicious, she could find only one other questionable thing. Pendleton had hidden two ledgers. One had contained the names of campaign donors, all meticulously entered and perfectly legal, as far as she could tell. The other ledger, oddly enough, had been blank.

Sadie sighed. Detective work wasn't quite as romantic as she'd first expected. When she'd signed on as a Pinkerton, she'd imagined posing as some exotic celebrity with a foreign accent so she could save her country. In reality, she spent most of her time skulking around in drab disguises so she could blend into a crowd. If she wasn't on a stakeout, she was searching some suspect's room. Digging through a lowlife's personal belongings was pure, nerve-wracking tedium.

Gritting her teeth, she rummaged through the dingy unmentionables in Baron's underwear drawer. It was hard not to be creeped out by the notion she might have to peel a pair of these nasty-looking shorts off the scum-bucket's erection.

Damn! What's he hiding, and where is it?

The chiffonier had been her last resort. She'd searched the entire suite for false panels in walls, fake bottoms in drawers, cleverly repaired seams in cushions, and loose floorboards under the two beds—because, apparently, Baron no longer slept with his wife.

Now what?

Frustrated by her failure to find evidence to incriminate him, Sadie stood with her hands on her hips, sweating bullets under her cotton shift and scowling at the furniture. Poppy's starched, white night cap lay on top of her neatly folded bed gown at the foot of a tightly tucked quilt of baby-blues and bonbon-pinks. The coverlet was embroidered with adorable yellow ducklings that reminded Sadie of a baby blanket.

She cocked her head, inhaling violet perfume, licorice hair tonic, stale Cleopatra Federal cigars, and a citrusy-frankincense aroma that suggested copal. The smell of incense made her glance toward the writing desk, which Poppy had turned into an altar by draping half of it with white linen. The usual prayer book, rosary, and saint images adorned the cloth, along with satin hair ribbons of every hue, apples and pecans, two vases of yellow marigolds, and three intricately painted sugar skulls.

Considering that *Día de los Muertos* was only four days away, Sadie didn't think the contents of the altar were unusual. Even "Gringos" couldn't walk down the streets of Lampasas without a Spanish-speaking vendor shoving colorful altar decorations into their hands.

She turned her back on Poppy's room and studied Baron's side of the suite. Boxes of red-white-and-blue campaign propaganda were stacked as high as Sadie's chin beside a cherry wood wardrobe. In a brass pot by the window, peace lilies were wilting; she figured they were parched for water, like the rest of Texas. Green bottles half-filled with medicine nestled between pricey liquors, brandy snifters, and shot glasses on the pink-marble of the vanity.

Sadie frowned. Besides Poppy's duckling quilt, the only thing that Sadie saw out of the ordinary was the fireplace. It was full of ashes. Unless the maid hadn't shoveled out the hearth since January—when Central Texas had suffered a freezing rain—the ash was probably the result of burned papers. However, none of the documents could be sufficiently identified. If Baron was plotting to blow up a west Texas farm or assassinate a rival candidate for the senate, he'd obliterated the evidence.

Damn that blood-sucking weasel. Sadie really had hoped she could avoid the revolting act of touching him, especially since some poor deluded, Christian woman had agreed to be his wife. Now she feared she would have to crawl into Baron's bed to accomplish her mission.

And that posed the unavoidable complication of Cass.

Suddenly, a floorboard creaked outside the door. Choking back an oath, Sadie glanced at the clock on the mantel. She'd been searching the room for two-and-a-half hours.

Damn! I let time get away from me! And I still have to search Pendleton's bedroom.

A key scraped in the lock. Frantically, Sadie grabbed for her feather duster and began an industrious cleaning of Baron's liquor bottles. The door creaked open. The intruder gasped.

Poppy Westerfield stood on the threshold, minus her bodyguard.

"Where's Sofia?" the senator's wife snapped, hastily hiding her clinking reticule behind her back. "Who the devil are you?"

Sadie's eyes narrowed. So Poppy didn't want her to see her purse, eh?

Cupping her hand over her ear, Sadie acted like the world's dumbest deaf woman. "The sofa, you say?"

"Sofia! Our maid!"

"Slow down there, missy," Sadie croaked in her best crone's voice. "My hearin' ain't so good. You say you want the sofa made?"

Poppy made an exasperated sound. "Out!" She pointed an imperious, red-lacquered fingernail at the door. "I don't have patience for fools."

Adopting a subservient manner, Sadie shuffled forward. Her eyes were focused on Poppy's protruding elbow, the one connected to the arm with the reticule. She had to find out what Poppy was hiding.

Thinking fast, she tripped, slamming into the older woman's arm. Poppy cried out, dropping the bag, and a half-dozen tins of *Serenata's Soothing Throat Pastilles* spilled across the carpet.

Sadie frowned. *Lemon lozenges?*

Poppy went apoplectic. "Stupid oaf! Look what you've done! I'll have your head for this!"

She ripped off her gloves, fell to her knees, and raked up the scattered pastilles with her hands. Sheepishly, Sadie tried to help—until their heads butted. Poppy recoiled, hissing an oath. When she looked directly into Sadie's eyes, suspicion furrowed her brow.

Sadie cursed her stupidity.

"Er…looks like you'll need a broom, missy," she blathered, leaping to her feet and fleeing for the door. "You won't want to fall *kersplat* on your bustle—"

"Hold."

The cold edge of Poppy's voice froze Sadie's feet two paces from the door.

"I will have your name."

Sadie figured a real maid would have been terrified of a senator's wife. She hung her head and wrung her hands. "Mrs. Dalrymple, ma'am. I'm real sorry about the lozenges, ma'am. I don't want to lose my job—"

"Shut up. Get out. And close the door behind you."

Bitch.

Sadie held onto her temper long enough to bob a curtsey and obey. Turning with a vengeance, she ducked into Pendleton's room.

As the sun sank behind the mansions of Silk Stocking Row, Cass shared a smoke with Gator on the steps of Wilma's back porch, where he was secretly hoping to catch a glimpse of Sadie.

Fraternizing with the enemy. That's what Pa would have

called it. Not that Gator was an enemy, exactly. Cass had spent many an enjoyable evening in Dodge, helping Gator and Cottonmouth beat the stuffing out of reprobates, who'd tried to stiff Wilma's girls. Cass had never cared about the color of a man's skin; his best friend was half Cherokee, after all. Cass considered the Mulattos his *compadres,* too, even though they came from the Bayou, spoke a different language, and exasperated the bejabbers out of him every time they lied to cover up for Sadie.

But Cass could charm the rattle off a rattler. Biding his time, he blew smoke, flicked ash, and yakked about things of importance to Gator: barbecued armadillo, Cajun snake fry, and alligator wrestling.

"I thought I counted a few more fangs on that string around your neck," Cass observed when Gator finished spinning his yarn.

"Gators are good eating," the Mulatto drawled in his thick, bayou-bred accent. "Like coons. Where's your little buddy? I'm hungry."

Cass chuckled, shaking his head. Cotton was the prim and prickly twin. Gator was the cut-up. If one could believe Gator, he'd just won his 12th consecutive alligator wrestling tournament. Cass secretly wondered if there really was a contest. Over the years, he'd begun to suspect that Gator just liked to dive into swamps and beat the tar out of unsuspecting alligators, who'd been minding their own business, snoozing in the sun.

"Collie's guarding Baron, if he knows what's good for him," Cass said. "A sniper took potshots at us in the Square yesterday. But I reckon you read all about that in the *Dispatch.*"

Gator grunted, sucking his smoke. Wilma had taught the twins to read—and how to shoot, come to think of it. After she'd found the desperately hungry, 8-year-old orphans lying unconscious on her compost pile, she'd nursed them back to health from their bout with yellow fever. Nowadays, at the wise old age of 27, they were ardent believers in *gris-gris,* dream messages, and Ancestral curses.

"I know you hear things," Cass prompted.

"Moi?" Gator grinned, flashing startling, white teeth. "I am deaf and mute."

"Then you see things," Cass said dryly.

"I see and know nothing," Gator assured him merrily.

Cass sighed. At this rate, they'd be trading windies all night. "Look, Gator. I know Wilma keeps her clientele confidential. I'm not asking you to betray her trust. All I'm asking is, have you heard anything that might help me identify this vigilante granger before he tries to kill again?"

Gator's coffee-colored eyes were turned toward the horizon. He seemed to be considering the question. "Many newcomers arrive with the railroad," he said carefully.

"Lampasas's vigilante granger problem started long before the railroad boom."

Gator shrugged. "Not all newcomers are devoted to the sod."

Cass frowned. So Gator *had* heard something!

"Texas Jack? Pink Higgins? Clay Allison?" Cass rattled off the names of gunfighters who were supposed to be at-large in Texas.

"Not in *this* establishment," Gator said flatly. "But snakes tend to go underground. A wise coyote might lie in wait at a watering hole. Even vipers need to drink."

Cass wasn't surprised by this answer. "You got an address?"

"Look where the sun sets."

Western Avenue. Cass nodded grimly. "Anything else I should know?"

The ghost of a smile touched Gator's lips. "You may find your viper isn't as hungry for beef as you think."

That was news. Cass cocked his head. "Care to explain?"

"Just a hunch, *mon ami.*"

"I'll settle for a hunch."

Gator blew a long, leisurely spiral of smoke. It drifted toward the scarlet sage bush at the side of the porch.

"Beached whales make easy prey," he advised finally.

Now Cass was getting impatient. He was about to tell

Gator he was done playing guessing games, when the last, lingering rays of the sun glanced off something black and shiny under the sage.

A shoe!

Cass narrowed his gaze. He was preparing to drop his .38 from his wrist to his fist, but a tiny gasp stayed his hand. Cornflower-blue eyes blinked anxiously at him through the explosion of red flowers. He could just barely make out a nose full of freckles, yellow sausage curls, and a rag doll. Then the child ducked beneath the rustling leaves.

"Mice," Gator said drolly. "They are such curious creatures."

Cass's dimples peeked. No wonder Gator was talking in riddles! He'd been aware of the wide-eyed innocent, who probably lived somewhere in the neighborhood.

"No doubt the mice are attracted by all the corn in your tall tales," Cass retorted, rubbing out his cigarette.

Since Gator had said all he was going to say, Cass rose, slapping the dust from his backside. That's when the hairs on the nape of his neck prickled like his coyote namesake's. He glanced up, spying a busty redhead peeking at him through the lace of a third-story window.

Sadie?

He sucked in his breath. His heart thumped against his ribs.

Suddenly, a traitorous memory sneaked inside his head— a memory of another twilight. Another westward-looking window…

She'd been freckled, auburn, and fiery, like the setting sun. The ivory silk of her nigh transparent night wrapper had done little to disguise the taut nipples on her pert young breasts. At 12 years old, he had never laid eyes on a half-naked girl. She was exotic. Dangerous.

He guessed her to be about 15 years old. She perched on the brothel window sill, sucking cream off of strawberries and smiling lusciously down at him as he craned back his head to gawk at her from the gutter. In his ratty straw hat, patched overalls, and dusty bare feet, he couldn't believe this golden-eyed goddess had noticed him at all. He looked over his shoulder to make sure some other fella wasn't waving at her from Pilot Grove's saloon.

"What's your name?" she called in her husky, older-than-her-years voice.

"Billy." He doffed his hat and held it over his racing heart. Pretty girls never talked to him, least of all, *older* pretty girls. A sharecropper's son was too poor to get noticed by the persnickety, fairer sex. "What's your name?"

Her dimples peeked in the most tantalizing way. "I'll give you three guesses. If you guess right, you can sample my berries."

In his innocence, he hadn't known her real meaning. But he *had* known he wanted to please her. For some reason, pleasing this red-haired Aphrodite had become even more important than scrambling up a tree trunk or diving into a root cellar.

So he ignored the baying of Farmer Hinckley's hounds. He could hear them tracking his scent from the cornfield that he'd just raided. The dogs were old and fat. He was young and smitten.

"*Lucera* is my guess," he improvised grandly. "In Spanish, the name means heavenly body."

She looked pleased. "Close enough," she purred. "You win the berries."

"I do?" His face burned like a firecracker—and not just because he'd sprinted a quarter mile under a blazing, summer sun to outrun Hinckley's shotgun.

That's when he remembered his bedraggled appearance. Dismayed, he glanced down his length at his fraying hand-me-downs. His sun-blackened forearms were coated with scratches and dusty rivulets of sweat. He'd spent the afternoon stealing his dinner—the first dinner he'd had in three days. Corn silk trailed from the satchel on his back and the bib pocket of his overalls. His mama, God rest her soul, had taught him never to accept a dinner invitation from a lady without bringing the hostess a gift. But all he had to give Lucera were some ratty old ears of maize that the crows had found too tough to gnaw.

Suddenly, he remembered the marble in his pocket. His prized shooter had won him a fishing pole yesterday, but the trout had refused to bite. He dug the milky quartz out of his trousers. In the long rays of the setting sun, the marble's pearlescent center flashed with rainbows.

"I have something for you too," he said shyly. "See? A shooting star that fell to earth."

"How lovely." Amusement warmed those golden tiger eyes. "But I can see that prize is special to you, Billy. Are you sure you want to give it away? To someone like me?"

He opened his mouth, but a man's shrill, outraged bellow cut off his answer.

"Cassidy!" The sounds of baying had grown perilously closer. "I'll skin you alive and feed your carcass to my hounds, you thieving White Trash!"

Mortified, Cass turned his gaze back to Lucera, his lovely Lucera, who'd overheard the ugly truth about him: he was worthless. *Less* than worthless. He expected her to wrinkle her pert, freckled nose in revulsion. He expected her to slam the shutters and send him away, like all the other pretty girls in town would have done.

But to his utter mystification, she came to his rescue. She waved him urgently toward the rear of the brothel. "Hurry, Billy! I know a place where you can hide…"

Cass's heart was still racing as his awareness spiraled back to the present. He turned his eyes toward Wilma's third story. His red-headed voyeur hadn't moved from the window. He tried to identify the face, veiled behind the lace curtain. She was dressed in nothing more than a corset. The prominent mounds of her breasts were milky white.

Cass hid his disappointment. Sadie's breasts were freckled.

Tipping his Stetson, he pasted on a roguish grin and winked at his voyeur.

She hastily grabbed the cord and drew the heavier curtains.

Strange. Bawds were usually more flirtatious.

"I see Wilma has a new redhead," he drawled.

"But not for you," Gator retorted pleasantly.

"Says who?"

The Cajun chuckled, standing and rubbing out his smoke. "Ah, *l'amour.* It tangles the tongue and muddies the mind."

"You're so full of crap."

Gator winked. *"Bon chance, mon ami.* I hope you catch your snake in the grass."

I will, Cass thought darkly, watching Gator retreat inside the house. He didn't usually go looking for showdowns, but he wasn't afraid of a challenge. He was confident in his gun-fighting skill. He would have pitted his quickdraw against any killer in Texas.

Any *renegade* killer, he corrected himself grimly. John Wesley Hardin and Hank Sharpe were safely in jail. With any luck, they'd rot there.

Reluctantly, Cass raised his eyes once more to the brothel's third story. Like a naughty smile, the golden sickle of a harvest moon was rising behind the chimney. He couldn't help but wonder if Sadie really was in one of those dimly lit rooms. The hour was just after 7 p.m. The grangers' dinner was over at the Grand Park Hotel. That meant Sadie was free to do what she did best after the sun went down: smolder like the devil's daughter in some other man's bed.

Against his will, Cass found himself recalling the slow, predatory approach of his lover as she prowled through moonlight and shadow. Sadie liked to wear sinfully transparent temptations that were strung together with fewer stitches than a buttonhole. When she moved, ebony-silk rosettes would flutter in a hide-and-seek pattern across her more fascinating freckled places.

God. The things they used to do in that Dodge City brothel four years ago. His loins throbbed at the memory. Sadie had come a long way since their first lusty romp in Pilot Grove. She'd learned how to flash those tawny eyes, curve those blood-red lips, and rumble deep in her throat, reducing a civilized man to his most primitive urges. And that was *before* she stroked a perfectly lacquered finger across his burning flesh.

Cass drew a shuddering breath. He forced himself to turn his back on the window, to gather his horse's reins and spur Pancake away from Sadie's memory.

Damn her, anyway. She'd betrayed him to the Rangers. She couldn't be trusted. She'd made that painfully clear last night—again. They were finished. *He* was finished. So why was he torturing himself? Hell, there were other redheads in the world!

As if to torment him, a vision of Poppy Westerfield sneaked inside his mind.

Cass grimaced. He wasn't looking forward to facing his boss's wife when he reached the hotel. In fact, he took the long way to Hancock Park, uncertain how to deliver his bad news: the maid whom Poppy had sent him to investigate had vanished as thoroughly as yesterday's sniper.

To tell the truth, Cass wasn't sure Mrs. Dalrymple even existed. Poppy had described golden eyes, which weren't common. When she'd added blue spectacles to the maid's list of accessories, Cass had begun to suspect that a certain freckled redhead, who'd begun to favor disguises, had been snooping through Baron's room. The question was, why? Had Sterne sent Sadie as his campaign spy?

Or was Sadie sleeping with Baron?

Cass's heart twisted at the thought.

As much as Cass cared about the randy old skirt-chaser, he didn't know how long he could pretend indifference if Baron was humping Sadie. In fact, he didn't know if he could stop himself from punching out Baron's lights. Or worse.

Baron's skirt-chasing was a problem for other reasons too. As his bodyguard, Cass was supposed to be on the lookout for assassins, and Baron wasn't helping matters by letting beerjerkers do a bump-and-grind in his lap.

As if that wasn't bad enough, the senator was practically

inviting that granger vigilante to take another potshot at him. Baron liked to claim he headed to Aquacia Bathhouse each morning to make peace with the sodbusters, but the truth was, Baron was ailing. His trousers were growing too big in the waist, and the whites of his eyes were a jaundiced yellow.

In public, of course, Baron remained his charming, baby-kissing self—most of the time. An exception to the norm had occurred at the pool that afternoon, when Pendleton had rushed in the door with a private message. After a quick but agitated conference with his secretary, Baron ignited the paper with a few puffs of his cigar and waved Pendleton back to the campaign office.

Nevertheless, the secretary's news must have upset Baron, because he promptly lost a $10,000 poker pot. Although Baron never did volunteer the contents of the message, he confided that Poppy was going to be on the rampage.

Sure enough, Poppy was. The minute Baron walked through the door of their hotel suite, his wife accused him of entertaining his mistress in their bedroom. No one was more surprised than Baron at this accusation. He blinked blankly at her when she produced a strand of dark, auburn hair as evidence. In Cass's private opinion, that hair looked suspiciously like Sadie's.

"I found it in your drawer of *unmentionables,*" Poppy spat, her cheeks nearly as red as her own strawberry curls.

"Why the devil were you snooping through my underwear?"

"I wasn't snooping! The drawer was shut crooked, so I…" Her chest heaved. *"You were fornicating!"*

Baron snorted. "As if this damned wasting sickness has left me the balls to do it."

"Don't you *dare* change the subject, James Westerfield!"

Baron rolled his eyes. "I've been making nice with sodbusters since nine o'clock this morning. A dozen witnesses can vouch for me at Aquacia Bathhouse."

"All men, I suppose."

"Hell, yeah! Men have better things to do than nag!"

Cass winced at the memory. He owed his loyalty to Baron, so he'd forced himself to keep quiet about his suspicions: namely, that Baron had been rutting with Sadie.

What did the hellcat hope to gain by seducing Baron? At least her affair with Sterne made sense. The former Ranger was fit and single. Since Sterne's retirement allowed him to take a wife, he represented the *possibility* of a better life for Sadie.

Not that marriage guaranteed happiness. Baron and Poppy were living proof of that.

Cass thought back to his childhood. He couldn't remember his parents cuss-fighting the way Poppy and Baron did. In fact, Cass liked to think that Pa had really loved Ma, the way fairytale couples loved each other. If Cass hadn't screwed up his life, getting his face plastered on Wanted Posters all around the West, he would have wanted to love a woman that way and start a family.

Working for an important man like Baron, a man who had the power to make sweeping changes for good, was how Cass hoped he might finally earn his redemption, at least in the eyes of the law.

He just wished Baron would treat women better.

As Cass rode up the Grand Park's drive, he spied his philandering boss sneaking out of the hotel's lobby. Baron was dressed in his best swallowtails. His freshly shaved chin looked softer than a baby's bottom, and he reeked of lemongrass soap. Cass didn't need to see an engraved invitation to know his boss was headed for a tryst, minus the inconvenience of a bodyguard.

"Hell," Baron boomed as Cass threw his reins to a waiting stableboy, "no wonder you took so long to run Poppy's errand. You're still riding Flea-Bait."

"Pancake," Cass corrected him.

"Yeah. Same thing."

A muscle ticked in Cass's jaw. Baron didn't think the buckskin could measure up as a Ranger's horse. Cass secretly agreed; however, he was just ornery enough to defy this logic because Pancake was the one subject both Collie and Baron could agree upon, and he needed Baron to accept Collie.

Besides, Cass was supposed to be a law-abiding citizen now. He couldn't indulge in his favorite tradition: rustling his mount from a town with an odd name. Last July, he'd been tickled by the notion of retiring Jelli, from Jellico, Tennessee, so he could "borrow" a buckskin from Pancake, Texas.

Being a law-abiding citizen sure isn't much fun.

"Uh-oh." Baron's canny gaze darted from Cass's scowl to the trigger guards of his holsters. "Who'd you plug this time? That smart-mouthed kid?"

Cass folded his arms across his chest.

"Pleading the 5th, eh?" Baron boomed jovially. "Can't say I blame you. But it *would* be a shame to shoot the coon. Especially after Vandy crapped on Sterne's pillow."

Cass wasn't amused. "Where are you going?"

"To church." Baron rolled his eyes. "Don't wait up, Ma."

Cass refused to budge.

"I distinctly recall giving you the *whole* night off," Baron said archly. "Collie too."

"Yeah? Well, I recall your promise to stay in. *With Poppy.*"

Baron flashed his horsey grin. "Change of plans. The ol' gal had a headache. Took a sedative and fell asleep."

"So Tito's with her?"

"You mean Pantywaist the Pirate?" Baron snorted. "Tito wrote a note. Said he was done letting snipers use him for target practice. He headed home to Galveston."

Cass hiked an eyebrow. "Tito knows his letters?"

"Surprised the stuffing out of me too. I reckon he had someone write it on his behalf. In any event, he quit."

Cass frowned, digesting this news. "If Tito isn't upstairs, and neither is Collie, then who's protecting Poppy?"

"Uh…Pendleton?"

Cass had half a mind to slug his boss. Pendleton would

pee his pants at the first sign of a masked man with a gun.

"What's the matter with you? After convincing your wife that a *burglar* was rummaging through your underwear drawer, Poppy's scared out of her mind."

"You're half right," Baron said dryly. Then he turned sheepish. "Aw, hell, Cass. Don't look at me that way. A man's got needs. You know that better than anyone. I told the hotel detective to pass by the room on his rounds. She'll be all right. If Poppy wakes, tell her I'm playing poker. *Comprende?"*

Ignoring Cass's sputtered objection, Baron saluted with his walking stick and breezed past him on the stairs. Cass watched through narrowed eyes as the senator reached the boardwalk and strolled beneath the orange and yellow lanterns, bobbing in the languid breeze that riffled the live oak trees. Every now and then, Baron would tip his hat to passing ladies. The boardwalk was moderately crowded with well-heeled couples, who were enjoying the autumn stars and the romantic strains of a stringed quartet.

But as Baron drew abreast of the musicians' pavilion, a voluptuous redhead in a slinky, black gown materialized at his side and slipped an arm through his.

The woman looked an awful lot like Sadie.

Damn her anyway!

Sickened by the visions dancing in his head, Cass decided Baron could, indeed, protect himself from bushwhackers tonight. The last thing Cass needed was to sit outside Baron's campaign office, listening to him and Sadie rut on the mattress in the back room.

Slamming through the lobby doors, Cass stalked past brass planters of prickly pear cacti and a fountain that spouted garlands of autumn leaves, in lieu of precious water. When he finally climbed the stairwell to his floor, he found Pendleton snoozing on a chair outside Poppy's room. A newspaper was spread over the secretary's face to shut out the flickering light of wall sconces.

How can a book-learned man be so stupid?

Cass had half a mind to kick the chair out from under Poppy's "guard." Gritting his teeth, he snatched the *Lampasas Dispatch* off the secretary's head. The rustling news print—or maybe the sudden flash of light—caused the older man to snort awake.

"Cassidy! I was just—"

"Snoring. Yeah, I heard."

Pendleton had the decency to redden. Leaping to his feet, he straightened his rumpled suit coat and shoved his wire-rimmed spectacles up his nose. "I tried to tell Baron he was making a mistake."

"You mean about making you a bodyguard?"

Pendleton hiked his chin. He had a crab-apple face from squinting at numbers all day and a stooped frame from hunching over ledgers. With his pasty complexion, extra thick lenses, and thinning hair, he looked ten years older than Baron.

Ironically, he was ten years younger.

"I have no trouble conceding I'm not the sharpshooter you are," Pendleton said testily. "However, every man has talents. You might be able to brand a steer, but I can make it turn a profit—even in a drought. I assure you, men with my talent are far rarer than men with yours."

Cass hiked an eyebrow. He hadn't been aware he and Pendleton were competing for the designation of Best Hired Hand.

"No one's questioning your loyalty, Pendleton. Or your work ethic. Just your choice to take a nap."

Fiercely brown eyes raked Cass from hat to toe. If he'd been a misplaced decimal point, he would have tucked his tail and headed for the hills.

"Watching Baron play poker all day is easy work," Pendleton accused. "Try discussing water issues with Bo Bodine. That nitwit can't even convert miles to acres on a map!"

Cass hiked an eyebrow. *"You* met with the Chairman of the Senate's Agriculture Committee?"

Pendleton bristled. "Not that it's any of your business, but yes. Yes, I did. We crossed paths in the lobby around dinnertime. Baron's always saying, 'Seize the day,' so I did. Mrs. Westerfield was carrying our maps, so I pleaded Baron's case.

"Bodine's a real piece of work," Pendleton continued grimly. "I don't think he can even *read* the Texas Constitution, much less uphold it as an elected official. The sodbuster said some pretty vulgar things about Baron's reelection hopes too. Mrs. Westerfield was so upset, she retired with a headache."

Cass frowned. "Shouldn't you be leaving the discussion of water rights to Baron's attorney?"

Pendleton stiffened. "For your information, Mr. Cassidy, Baron bought that parcel of land from my father, after Pa fell on hard times. *No* law wrangler knows that acreage better—or cares about it more—than I do. I shall continue to advocate for its improvement during the drought. By this time next year, I should have all the money I need to buy it back."

With a terse nod, Pendleton turned on his heel and marched toward his suite. He'd only taken three steps, however, when he halted.

"A word of advice, Mr. Cassidy," he called over his shoulder. "Mrs. Westerfield is not as hardy as she seems. Despite appearances to the contrary, Baron has grave concerns about her."

"You got a point, Pendleton?"

The secretary's thin lips twitched in a mocking smile. "In certain circles, you are hailed as Eros in Spurs, are you not? I think you know my point, Mr. Cassidy. Good evening."

Cass scowled.

Pencil-necked fussbudget.

Resigned to the tedium of babysitting a sedated woman, Cass decided to splash water on his face. He stripped off his hat, spurs, and boots. Then he tugged a bottle of tequila from his saddlebag. Only when he was settling down on the edge of the bed to toss back his first shot did he hear the unmistakable creak of a floorboard in the hall.

A moment later, a tentative knock sounded on his door.

"Cass?" Poppy's plaintive voice quavered as she called out his name. "Is…is Baron with you?"

Just my luck. The sedative wore off.

Stuffing his tequila under a pillow, Cass forced a smile for his boss's wife and tugged open the door. He found Poppy standing barefoot and tear-streaked, her perfumed cloud of auburn hair spilling over a flimsy, peacock-blue negligee that left little to his imagination.

Despite being 16 years his senior, Poppy was undeniably attractive. She had lush breasts, voluptuous hips, and legs that went on for miles. She also had a tendency to weep, rail, and swoon—behaviors that seemed more frequent now than they had in '78, the last year Cass had prodded Baron's steers along the Western Cattle Trail to Dodge.

Poppy's big, misty green eyes peered eagerly past him to the bed. "Are you alone?"

"'Fraid so, ma'am."

She blinked, squeezing out a tear. "That bastard! He's with *her* again, isn't he?"

Before Cass could utter a single, credible excuse for his boss, Poppy started wailing like a banshee and threw herself into his arms. He staggered backwards, biting off an oath as the door swung closed behind her. In the next instant, 120 pounds of buxom, blubbering femininity were sliding down his ribcage toward his nether region. Cass wasn't any saint, but even he was horrified by the way his pecker was responding to his boss's wife.

However, this wasn't his first rodeo with Poppy's "episodes," as Baron liked to call them. Eight years ago, when Cass had found Poppy threatening to slash her wrists, she'd claimed life wasn't worth living because she'd miscarried another baby.

Baron had been grieving his lost heir, too, but since Poppy had frozen him out of their bed, he'd started turning his wolf loose on younger, doe-eyed prey. Cass supposed that womanizing had been Baron's way of feeling manly.

Or maybe extra marital affairs had been Baron's way of proving his seed wasn't "poison," as Poppy had once shouted loudly enough for every cowboy in the bunkhouse to hear.

How Baron and Poppy managed to stay married was anybody's guess. Cass suspected that Baron must still love his wife, deep down, because any other man would have lost patience with her erratic moods. Baron had even hired a Mexican missionary to keep Poppy company while he was away from the ranch. That missionary had suggested that Poppy wear a *relicario,* to commemorate her lost children, and that she begin observing October 31st as *Día de los Muertos*, when the souls of babies returned to the earth.

"I can't go on this way!" Poppy wailed, clinging to Cass's shirt front. "I might as well be dead!"

"Now Mrs. Westerfield, you don't mean—"

"Baron doesn't love me, and he won't let me have babies!"

"I'm sure if you just talked—"

"I have no reason to live!"

"Here now. That's not true." Cass was struggling to drag his bandanna from his throat with one hand and to keep her hips hoisted safely above his traitorous pecker with the other.

"I want to be a mother!" she hiccupped into his pectorals.

"Of course you do."

He wanted to shove his bandanna into her hand, but she seemed more intent on mopping her tears with his shirtfront—especially where the placards gaped and tufts of tawny hair peeked through.

"You've always been so kind to me."

"You deserve kindness, Mrs. Westerfield."

"You'd make a good father," she whispered between sniffles.

"Uh...thanks."

"You do want babies, don't you, Cass?"

She was rubbing her cheek on his shirt, her breaths

steaming through the linen. His nipples pebbled.

He told himself she was distraught. He told himself he was lower than a snake's belly to think some poor, bereaved woman was pawing him like an inept lover. Sadie had been right. His mind was in the gutter. He should be flogged— and not in a good way.

Confound it. There I go again!

Burning with embarrassment, Cass tried to swing Poppy's slippery, satin-sheathed hips toward a chair.

That's when another knock rattled his door.

"Oh no!" Poppy cried, throwing her arms around his neck and flattening every inch of fevered femininity against his flesh. "It's Baron!"

Blood surged to Cass's forbidden places. He bit the inside of his mouth hard. He didn't often have to rein in his carnal urges, and he discovered, to his aggravation, that restraint wasn't as easy as preachers and virgins made it look.

"I'll handle this," he hissed, grateful for any excuse to detach Poppy the Cockleburr from his crotch. "Sit here. And stay out of sight."

He drilled her with a commanding stare and pressed his fingers to his lips. She nodded meekly, but her eyes were hungry as they feasted on the bulge in his trousers. At that point, he almost hoped his visitor *was* Baron.

Gritting his teeth, Cass reached for a Colt, checked the beans in its wheel, and crossed to the door. He was expecting to see a drunken Collie sliding down the wall and a desperado coon toting one of the hotel's koi between his teeth.

Imagine his shock when he found the Devil's Red-haired Daughter, smoldering like a brand on his doorstep.

CHAPTER 9

Sadie waited nervously outside Cass's door, her reticule clutched in a sticky, damp fist.

Her search of Pendleton's room had yielded nothing to incriminate Baron for killing sodbusters—or anyone else, for that matter. The convention of the Farmers Alliance would be over in three days. She was running out of time. She needed to crack this case before Baron holed up again on his ranch. That's why she'd decided to choke down her pride and strike a truce with Cass.

Of course, the sentimental side of her had other, ulterior motives for knocking on his door. She couldn't bear to think he was beyond saving. She was desperately hoping she could convince him not to throw away his last hope of Rangerhood by doing dirty deeds for Baron.

But turning Cass into an informant wouldn't be easy—at least, not as easy as seducing him. Cass and Baron went back a long way, even longer than he and Wilma did. As fond as Wilma was of her Rebel Rutter, she hadn't held out much hope for Cass's conversion.

"You aren't just talking about a romp in the sheets, *chere*," Wilma had warned. "You're asking Cass to turn state's evidence against one of the most powerful men in Texas. A man who could make his career or crush it—and that's only if Baron lets Cass survive the initial act of betrayal."

Rex had been even less encouraging, if that was possible.

"It will take more than reckless courage to fight Westerfield," the Ranger had said in dire tones. "It will take a man who believes in doing the right thing. A man who loves justice more than he loves comfort, money, or privilege. Can you really tell me Cassidy is that man?"

Sadie swallowed hard to recall Rex's question. The truthful answer was…no. No, she couldn't.

But she *wanted* Cass to be that man.

William Cassidy was a dyed-in-the-wool rascal. He'd robbed stages, smuggled moonshine, rustled livestock, and seduced virgins. Sadie had no illusions about Cass.

However, knowing him since adolescence had given her insights into his character that neither Rex nor Wilma possessed. For instance, Sadie knew that Cass had grown up too poor to wear shoes. He'd watched every man in his family get gunned down in the bloody Lee-Peacock Feud of northeast Texas. She knew he'd carried his mother's grave marker on his own aching back for five miles. And he was deathly allergic to bee stings.

At the age of 12, Cass had been the only person in all of Pilot Grove who'd had the courage to stop the Ku Klux Klan from torturing Lynx, a Cherokee half-breed, who'd eventually become his best friend. Cass was willing to give the benefit of the doubt to anyone at least once, and this idealism could sometimes be sniffed out by older, cannier coyotes with less integrity.

Like Baron.

'I have to try,' Sadie told herself. *'For the sake of that idealistic boy who used to blanket my windowsill with bluebonnets, I have to turn Cass.'*

Drawing a shuddering breath, she mustered her courage and rapped her knuckles on Cass's door. A muffled oath ensued, followed by the creak of a chair and the unmistakable click of a well-oiled Colt cylinder. A heartbeat passed. Then another. Finally, her wary lover cracked open the door. She caught a whiff of tobacco and spicy musk as he arched a pale gold eyebrow at her titian curls and jade evening gown.

She wasn't reassured when he scowled, but at least he holstered his gun.

"You lost?" he challenged in gravelly tones.

Cass hadn't been expecting company; that much was certain. His hair was rumpled. His shirttails were hanging. His feet were shod in stockings—black ones, of course. But even when he was disheveled, the rapscallion made her mouth water with those flame-blue eyes, chiseled cheeks, and tawny chin hairs.

God is so unfair, she thought uncharitably. She'd had to work for an hour to curl, paint, perfume, and powder—not to mention her trials with a corset, bustle, and garters—just so she could achieve the right appearance for seduction.

All Cass had to do was run his fingers through his hair.

Hell. He doesn't even have to do that, *apparently.*

She pasted on a luscious smile. "This is the lair of Lucifire, isn't it? The notorious heartbreaker, whose kisses burn like flame?"

He snorted. "Depends on who's doing the asking...*Mrs. Sterne.*"

She ignored his dig. "You were most persuasive at Wilma's place last night."

"How's that?"

"Well, for one thing, you weren't packing a pistol."

"I'm always packing, sweetheart."

"Mmm." She let her eyes trail lower. "Why don't you show me?"

He leaned his shoulder against the jamb and folded his arms across his chest. "What's the matter? Some sodbuster get a putter in his pecker?"

"Let's just say...I like my stud ponies to run the long race."

A reluctant mirth flickered in his glare. Nevertheless, he continued to bar her entry.

Cass was a game-player. Nothing excited his inner Coyote more than giving chase—except, perhaps, getting snared by the Tigress in her den. So Sadie let her shawl gape to advantage. The ploy revealed the bulging tops of freckled, patchouli-scented breasts.

"A lady could freeze out here, waiting to be invited inside," she said huskily.

"Good thing it's hotter 'n the devil's frying pan, huh?"

Smartass.

"But darling, I brought your favorite dessert. And I made my own whip—er, whipping cream."

"I'm flattered."

"You're *tempted.*"

"Hmm." He rubbed his stubbled jaw. "So what's the pleasure of this visit gonna cost me? Daddy's button?"

"Pendant."

"That's what I figured."

"I could never fool you." Her smile dripped honey.

He tossed a suspicious look at her handbag. "Got anything else to declare in there? A scorpion? Or a rattler, maybe?"

"Nothing that bites as good as you."

"Aw. That's sweet."

He still wouldn't budge.

"You aren't still mad at me for dying, are you?" she asked with a pretty pout.

Something dark and dangerous flitted through the sapphire depths of his eyes. But the emotion fled so quickly, she couldn't put a name to it.

"Refresh my memory. Weren't you planning to visit *Sterne* the night you sneaked into the Globe Hotel, wearing trousers and a beard?"

She wrestled with her annoyance. She'd told Cass a dozen times—no, *two* dozen—she'd never had an affair with Rex. Why couldn't he simply believe her and drop the subject?

"I thought you liked my beard," she rallied with a naughty grin.

"Sure. Why don't you mosey on back to Wilma's place and put it on for me?"

She blinked. In all her years of game-playing with Cass, she couldn't remember a single other night when he'd turned down her offer of sex.

"We'd just be wasting time," she countered in provocative tones. "And my berries would wilt."

"Worse things could happen."

"You mean...*your* berries could wilt?"

He smirked. "As a gentleman, I plead the 5th."

"Not to worry, darling. I know the cure for berries—*and* for gentlemanly inclinations."

She sidled closer. He kept barring the door.

Her eyes narrowed.

She remembered how he'd answered her rap carrying a gun. But that wasn't so disturbing. Always ready for a showdown, that was her Lucifire.

What *was* disturbing—at least to her womanly intuition—was the way Cass continued to shield the door. He wasn't just trying to drive her away, he was preventing her from seeing past his shoulders to the dimly lit interior.

"Well?" she demanded.

"A deep subject."

Hilarious.

"Are you going to let me in?"

"How bad do you want that button?"

"Enough to come. Here," she added provocatively.

His chuckle was wolfish. "That could be arranged."

"Promises, promises."

The smoking sapphire of his gaze trailed leisurely over her bodice, her belly, her hips. By the time he was staring at the apex between her thighs, she was licking her lips.

"You know," he drawled, "that kick of yours left a dent in my gut."

"You're a big boy." She fought fire with fire, training a lusty stare at his crotch. "I figured you could handle it."

She was gratified to see his buttons strain.

"Would it have been so hard to say, 'Howdy, Cass. It's me under the beard?'"

"A woman likes to play hard to get."

"This is playing hard to get?"

She was sorely tempted to kick him again. "You want me to beg for forgiveness? Is that it?"

"It couldn't hurt."

Donkey butt.

She struggled with her notoriously short temper. "All right, fine. Cass, I'm sorry. I need you. I want you. I can't live without you."

"Aw, you didn't say pretty please. With cherries on top."

She gritted her teeth. "Pretty please. With cherries."

Those wicked, blue eyes danced. "Now say—"

"Impossible man." She grabbed his shirt front and kissed him.

He chuckled into her mouth, stepping into the hall and letting the door slam behind him. As their tongues wrestled for dominance, fire rushed through her blood. Sparks showered her nerves. Enjoying the sensations, she wasn't shy about demanding pleasure. She shimmied until the taut nubs of her breasts jutted into his shirt; he dragged her hips closer, tantalizing her with the hot, throbbing promise of his arousal.

Cass wasn't called "Eros in Spurs" for nothing. His erotic enticements were soon melting the rational part of her brain. She began to forget why she'd knocked on his door. She began to lose sight of her starry-eyed ambitions to topple a corrupt senator.

The heat of Cass, the taste of Cass, the scent of tobacco, sandalwood, and leather, were heady aphrodisiacs. They called to mind other nights, other seductions. Cass wasn't just some informant whom she could trick into helping her solve her case. He was the only man whom she'd ever yearned for in the secret, lonely chambers of her heart. He was the one lover who could set her nights on fire.

She dragged his hips closer and rubbed against them. In the next moment, she wasn't sure who was growling, who was panting, and who was needier for release. She tugged at his shirt buttons; he hiked her skirt. She squirmed, her breaths sawing when he shoved his free hand down the front of her bloomers. Within seconds, he proved that he knew precisely how to make her body beg. His uncompromising mastery had her shaking with craving. And that was before he found her spot.

"You will *never,*" he snarled in her ear, "pretend to die on me again! You put me through hell!"

His name tore from her throat; he silenced her with a wild, untamed kiss. She tried to retaliate, but he seized her hand, backing her into the wall.

Her knees threatened to buckle from the cyclone of pleasure coiling between her thighs. She thought she heard the seams of her bloomers rip. She tried to care, but her senses were reeling, and her mind was white noise. She clawed at the drawstrings, making it easier for him to plunder his prize.

He rewarded her submission with plunging, serpentine thrusts that soon grew maddening. He took her to the brink again and again, punishing her with the sweetest of tortures. Relentless in his expertise, he milked her liquid fire but refused to let her come.

"I promised myself I'd make you sorry…" He caught her earlobe between sharp teeth.

She tried to jerk away, but he tangled a hand in her hair, holding her head captive, tormenting the tender inner space of her ear with his tongue. Chills chased the sparks that danced over her flesh.

"…*Really* sorry for toying with me," he added huskily.

Shuddering with the effort to stand, she clung to his shoulders, silently cursing the slippery fabric of her gown. It kept interfering when she tried to hook her ankle over his buttocks to sweeten the pleasure. She began to fear she really would come in the middle of the hall—and worse, that Baron would arrive in time to see the show.

"Cass, please," she whimpered, hating that he'd reduced her to begging.

"What, no cherries on top?"

She was close…*so damned close.* "Take me inside!"

"Aw. But then I'd have to stop."

She squirmed, stretching desperately. "I can almost reach the doorknob—"

He abruptly released her. If a sturdy wall sconce hadn't been within reach, she would have stumbled to her knees on jellified legs. Uncomprehending, she blinked as he took three steps back, barring the entry to his room once more.

"Th-that's it?" she demanded.

"Yep."

"The best you can do?"

"For tonight."

"But what about the payback you promised me?"

"Some other time, sweets."

Her eyes narrowed. She remembered the creaking chair, and realization dawned. "Get rid of her!"

"Naw. I kinda like this one."

Sadie's heart kicked hard at this confession.

"You kinda like *all* of them, until the sun comes up," she accused.

Before he could respond, the door cracked open two inches. Sadie had the fleeting impression of green eyes and bare arms behind Cass's brawny shoulder. The woman was still clothed—barely—in a blue silk negligee, but then, she might have draped her private parts so she could step into the hall.

Auburn hair. Big breasts. Cass would, indeed, like this one.

In a volcanic eruption that shook Sadie's world, her heart spewed ash and flame.

The grief was catastrophic.

"Cass?" her redheaded rival whispered. "A-are you still out there?"

"He's with me, bitch! Get over it!"

The woman gasped and ducked back inside the room.

Cass cleared his throat. At least he'd had the decency to redden.

"Now Sadie, that wasn't very nice."

"Screw you, Cass!" Her eyes burned in their efforts to dam tears.

"I tried to tell you, didn't I?"

She snatched her reticule from the rug. Flipping him the bird, she turned on her heel.

Cass muttered an oath. He couldn't very well admit Baron's wife was in his bedroom. Nor was he at liberty to announce that Poppy had come to him, crying her eyes out, because Baron was a cheat.

Could this night get any worse?

Cass caught Sadie's arm. She wrenched free, rounding on him. He saw the blaze of fury in those jungle-cat eyes, and he gulped a restraining breath.

Yep. The night could definitely *get worse.*

"Don't try getting friendly with me now," she flared. "I don't do threesomes, remember?"

"Keep your voice down," he retorted in a low, urgent tone.

"What's the matter? Afraid Mrs. Westerfield will hear?"

He winced. "Sadie—"

She sneered. "I don't know why I bothered to come here."

"Why are you so spitting mad? You're the one who tossed me aside for Sterne, remember?"

She choked, turning even redder, if that was possible. "That's right. Blame the whole, damned Dodge fiasco on me. Never mind that you had a three-day orgy at Wilma's place."

His chest heaved. "I asked you to ride away with me! You turned me down flat!"

"They would have killed you!"

"By *they*, are you referring to Wyatt Earp and Bat Masterson? Or some other tin-star whom you told about my murder bounty?"

"That's a lie!"

Is it?

Cass struggled with the old, painful suspicion.

She might have forgotten what she'd said one fateful night, four years ago, but he could still remember their argument, like it had happened yesterday. He'd found her secret love song—the one she'd *claimed* she'd penned to some made-up, dead twin. When he'd torn the music to shreds, she'd been incensed. She'd threatened to tell the law he was wanted for murder back in Texas. And then who had she gone running to?

A Ranger named Sterne!

Sadie flared, "If you believe that rubbish, for a single, solitary second, then we were never meant to be together!"

"Sorry, sweets. But I'm of the mind actions speak louder than words."

She looked considerably paler now. Even her knuckles had whitened over the handle of her bag. "So that's it then? We're history? Old news? Water under the bridge?"

He crossed his arms across his stricken heart. "I reckon."

She drew a shuddering breath.

"Well then." Her smile was bitter. "I'm sorry I disturbed you."

Turning on her heel, she swept down the corridor in a rustling swath of jade silk. When footsteps sounded in the stairwell, she ducked her head and made a beeline for the north wing.

In that nerve-jangling moment, Cass didn't know what made him sicker, the thought of Sadie walking out of his life forever, or the notion that the hotel detective might step out of the stairwell and find Baron's disheveled wife in his bedroom.

Fortunately, Collie and Vandy shoved open the stairwell door, not the tin-star.

As if on cue, Poppy poked her head back into the hall. "Is that harlot still plying her trade out here? A hotel has *rules* about that sort of thing, you know."

Collie's jaw dropped to see Baron's wife leaning out Cass's door in her flimsy silk night gown. He shot Cass a blistering look that screamed, *"Idiot!"*

Cass cursed under his breath.

He hated when the kid was right.

CHAPTER 10

Loose ends. Incompetent minions.

Asrael couldn't abide either.

If the devil was in the details, then Satan was having a field day at Asrael's expense. Thanks to a colossal case of mistaken identity, the She-devil from the Satin Siren had escaped divine retribution and was continuing to wreck havoc on Asrael's life.

Yes, sometime within the last two months, the bitch had come out of hiding long enough to achieve her most diabolical feat yet. She'd arranged for her freckled spawn to inherit everything Asrael had worked so hard to build. *Everything!*

Nevermind that James Westerfield would be nothing but a stinking cattle prodder today, if Asrael hadn't worked so diligently—so *invisibly*—as his avenging angel, greasing palms, negotiating behind closed doors, and hiring regulators to dispose of certain business threats. All Asrael had ever requested in return for this tireless service was loyalty.

But apparently, the insufferable clod couldn't even manage that.

Seething with hatred beneath a mask of glacial calm, Asrael sipped cherry sarsaparilla and waited in the Grand Park casino for the arrival of an ally, a soul of sufficient darkness to eliminate the double plague of the She-devil and her demon spawn.

Much like that fateful night in Galveston, the hotel's sumptuous green gaming hall festered with sin. Many of the characters from the Satin Siren's last chapter were gathered here, tempting the patience of angels. Most noticeable among those characters was the Siren's mermaid queen, a big-busted, red-haired alto with a whiskey voice.

Asrael's smoldering glare followed the strumpet as she strutted through the crowd with two brandies on a tray. The Siren's star performer had apparently changed her name. Tonight, she was Chantelle O'Leary, a slut in a skin-tight witch's costume with spiky black heels. The strumpet's gown was criss-crossed with silver threads, like cobwebs, and looked in danger of disintegrating with a sneeze. All that held the fabric together over that shameless visa of freckles were a few strategic knots.

Whoops and whistles erupted from Chantelle's drunken admirers as she maneuvered her tray over their heads without spilling a drop. Within minutes, the recipient of Chantelle's expensive liquor became clear. She sidled up to the chair of Senator Baron Westerfield and thrust her tits into his face.

"Cherry fizzy-pop? Seriously?" taunted an oily, Midwestern accent from the crimson drapes behind Asrael's shoulder. A medium-built man emerged from the booth's curtain and slid behind the table. "Are you trying to ruin my reputation?"

Asrael's fist whitened over the tankard of blood-red suds. "I didn't have you paroled for your lip."

"Comes with the package. Get used to it."

Even in his disguise as an aging, bearded sodbuster, everything about Henry "Hank" Sharpe was average: his height; his weight; his balding pate and brown eyes. He was the type of man whom people didn't notice in a room, especially if those people were female.

Nevertheless, in certain circles, Hank had earned a reputation for standing head-and-shoulders above the crowd. To his clientele, who preferred that their business transactions remained anonymous, Hank was known as The Ventilator.

"So the gang's all here from Galveston," Hank drawled.

Asrael tossed him a withering glare. "I had hoped a man of your reputation would be eager to rectify his error, not gloat about it."

"You mean *your* error, pard," Hank retorted, tugging a pouch of tobacco from his duster pocket. "You picked the window."

"And what, pray tell, was your excuse on the grocer's roof?"

"Get off your high-horse." Hank began rolling his quirley. "You said to throw suspicion on the sodbusters and make Baron look like the target. That's what I did."

"Except, of course, nobody *died,*" Asrael sniped in a low, exasperated tone. "I had to get rid of the Neanderthal myself."

"Serves you right for changing the plan at the last second."

"I'm the reason you're still alive! You should be *thanking* me!"

Hank snorted. "You mean 'cause you kept getting in the way?"

A muscle ticked in Asrael's jaw.

Hank struck a match with his thumb. When he bent his head to puff his smoke, a ruddy glow illuminated his harsh and grizzled features beneath the brim of his chocolate-brown Stetson. He was watching a blond gunfighter in black duds. Cassidy was shooting tequila shots at the bar and glaring daggers at Chantelle, who was diligently trying to entice Baron away from the craps table.

A muscle ticked in Asrael's jaw. "Must I remind you, Cassidy has never lost a gunfight?"

"It only takes one."

"Don't be obtuse. I've kept Cassidy from learning you're in town and hunting you down. In case you've forgotten, you're the reason that Injun pal of his can never show his face again in Burnett County. Lynx would have been lynched for that church offering you stole, if Cassidy hadn't busted him out of jail. Cassidy's young, but he's not stupid. You'd be wise not to underestimate him."

Hank exhaled a perfect smoke ring. "He'd be wise not to underestimate me."

Asrael's chest heaved. The Ventilator was entitled to his boast. Hank had never lost a gunfight, either. But the vermin's real value lay in his ability to make murder look like an accident: a hoof to the head. A stampede. A drowning. An avalanche. A broken axle wheel. Hank was particularly crafty at rigging backfiring pistols—which would be the end of Rexford Sterne if the ex-Ranger became a serious threat to Asrael's ambitions.

"Since you're obviously feeling your oats," Asrael said irritably, "find a way to exercise your creativity. Bodine has become a nuisance."

"What's the deadline?"

"The end of the conference."

Hank smirked. "Oh, goodie. Rush jobs cost double."

Loath to be baited by such lowbrow humor, Asrael moved briskly to the next topic on the meeting agenda. "Have you found where she's hiding her spawn?"

"Not yet." Hank exhaled again with great gusto.

Asrael waved away the stench of cheap tobacco. "How hard can it be? There are only five hotels in town."

"They're crammed full of sodbusters. Even if she registered under an alias, no clerk has seen hide nor tail of a big-busted blonde, traveling with a kid."

"Try the brothels."

Hank hiked an eyebrow. "What kind of mother—"

"Exactly," Asrael interrupted in a low, venomous undertone. "A whore like that doesn't deserve to live."

Hank chuckled, flashing yellow, mongrel teeth. "Sounds like one more reason to enjoy my work."

"Glad to hear it." Palming a small, clanking tin, Asrael slid it across the table to Hank.

"What's this?"

"A little treat for the brat."

"Perfected the formula, did you?"

"Let's just say I had to bury a lot of dogs."

Hank grunted, pocketing the tin. "And the will?"

Asrael stiffened. The will was a particularly sore topic. It was the main reason why Hank had agreed to kill Ferraro and Cassidy in the first place. Asrael had entertained second thoughts about silencing Cassidy, mostly because Hank was as trustworthy as a viper. Cassidy, on the other hand, possessed a glimmer of conscience that could work to Asrael's advantage. Especially if Hank strayed too far out of line.

"I'm working on it," Asrael hedged.

Hank's eyes narrowed, coldly accusing. "That's what you said last time."

"These things can't be rushed."

"Hell, all you have to do is name yourself the executor."

Asrael tamped down a surge of resentment. Few people knew Hank was kin, and worse, that he hailed from the wrong side of the blanket. Theirs was a symbiotic relationship. Asrael sent attorneys to rescue The Ventilator from the law, while Hank discretely eliminated sodbusters, politicians, lawmen, ranch hands—in short, anyone who stood in the way of Asrael's ambition to live in the governor's mansion.

And maybe even the White House.

Hank's name could never be associated with Asrael's, of course. Fortunately, they shared a common interest—the estate—because the only other thing that kept Hank under control these days was the staggering payoff the vermin earned each time he successfully carried out Asrael's bidding.

"The document must be copied precisely," Asrael said tartly. "One tiny mistake could throw the estate into probate for years. I see no reason to tempt fate, and certainly not with haste."

Hank made a derisive noise. "Have you taken a good

look at Baron lately? The man's got one foot in the grave."

Asrael shot the regulator a daggerlike glare. Baron's ailment wasn't all it appeared to be. That carefully guarded secret was another Ace up Asrael's sleeve. One that needn't be played tonight.

"I promise you: Baron *is* going to win this election."

"Because you're nothing if he doesn't?"

Asrael stiffened at this insult—an insult that had struck much too close to the truth.

"Just for the record, dear boy, if I die before the age of 100—for any reason—you get nothing from my estate. Furthermore, should I die of unnatural causes, my Last Will and Testament instructs my attorney to deliver to the U.S. Marshal's Office a catalogue of your less publicized crimes, the ones that I've worked so diligently to keep out of court, lest they send you to the gallows."

"Is that a threat?" Hank's face had turned florid. He leaned across the table and stabbed the air with his cigarette. "Are you *threatening* me?"

"Don't be absurd." Asrael was careful to hide a smirk behind the mug of sarsaparilla. "I've always been of the mind that blood is thicker than water."

Careful what you wish for.

That's what Sadie told herself as she pasted on a luscious smile and ramped up her flirtation with Baron. She hadn't tried this hard to be agreeable to a man since the night when Madam Snake-Eye had threatened to beat the living crap out of her if she didn't spread her legs to relieve some foul-smelling carpetbagger of his purse.

Just like that night in Pilot Grove, more than 12 years ago, Sadie was mystified by her intended John's disinterest. In Baron's case, she'd gone to great lengths to perfect her costume, especially her witch's hat, which she'd hoped would be a conversation-starter. She'd embroidered the cone with the cheerful greeting, *"I kiss toads."*

If Baron had found the jest amusing, he didn't say. In truth, he'd barely glanced her way. The best she'd earned for her hours of labor with a needle and thread was a grunt, which he'd directed at the general vicinity of her breasts. She had half a mind to dump an ashtray in his lap just to see if she could get a rise out of the man.

Her mind raced for something to say. Something provocative. Something intellectual. Something that would elevate her above a common beerjerker in a senator's mind. Why the devil was she having so much trouble enticing him? Had Cass said something about last night's hallway feud?

Louse.

Sadie forced herself to keep smiling. The part of Cass that wasn't Coyote was mostly Magpie—with some Mother Hen thrown in. For the first time in days, he wasn't hovering over his boss, scaring all the big, bad sodbusters away with his double-holstered rig. She suspected he was visiting the water closet.

In any event, he'd be returning soon, and she was scheduled for a costume change in under ten minutes. This might be the only chance she got to convince Baron that Chantelle O'Leary's bed would be more interesting than whatever private poker game he'd been invited to this evening.

Edging closer, she dropped her hand to Baron's thigh. "I brought you something," she murmured in his ear.

Baron placed a bet before finally deigning to turn his head her way. Through his cloud of cigar smoke, he looked a tad peaked for a man who was rumored to ride the range when he wasn't stumping for votes.

Suddenly, she remembered a piece of advice Madam Snake-Eye had confided between benders:

"There are only two times in life when a John isn't receptive to a rut: When he's on his deathbed, and when he's sick with love. During those times, you'll just have to work a little harder for your pay."

Letting a provocative dimple peek, Sadie offered Baron one of the two snifters on her tray.

"For me?"

"For us," she purred.

His smile was polite but discouraging as he scooped up the glass. "Much obliged, Sweet Pea. But you should know, my wife can sniff out my assignations like a bloodhound."

Sadie's smile never wavered. "Then perhaps we should go to a place where she can't find us—like my hotel room."

Baron chuckled. "Don't think I'm not flattered. But Poppy would gut a sweet little thing like you like a fish. No offense, Sugar Plum."

Sadie blinked. She wasn't sure how Baron had gotten the idea she was sweet. Or that a woman who swooned at the sound of gunfire could pose a threat to a street-smart bawd like her. In any event, Sadie's mind was racing for some appropriate way to prove herself equal to the Poppy Challenge, when a velvety baritone crooned in her ear:

"Oh look. You found that pointy hat."

She stiffened at Cass's taunt.

He'd sneaked up behind her in the din. She shot him a get-lost glare, but he didn't take the hint. Instead, he made a nuisance of himself, staking out his territory by her side—or maybe by Baron's. It was hard to tell, since the craps players had wedged themselves so tightly around the table, they had to turn sideways just to raise a glass. Shouts of "Snake eyes!" were making her head pound.

But Cass didn't flinch. He stood before her with his thumbs hooked over his gun belt. Considering how close they were, she wondered how she could have failed to miss his scent: an alluring blend of cloves, cinnamon, and sandalwood.

As if he knew the devastating effect he was having on her senses, he flashed his devilish grin. She was sorely tempted to punch out all those pretty teeth—especially when he scooped the second cognac from her tray and tossed it down his gullet like sugar water.

"That *Cordon Rouge* will cost you $20 dollars," she said pleasantly.

He winked. "Put it on my tab, Cassie. Or is it Chantelle tonight?"

Baron arched a salt-and-pepper eyebrow. "You two know each other?"

"It was a long time ago," she said with practiced indifference.

"Sometimes it feels like yesterday," Cass quipped.

She turned her shoulder on the pest and lavished her most stunning smile on Baron. "I've always admired a man who knows what he wants. And how to make it his."

"Can't fault a lady for that," Baron said, rolling his stogie to the other side of his mouth and raking in his winnings.

"Or Chantelle," Cass chimed in.

"Tell me," Sadie purred, mustering the will to ignore Cass completely. "Are you enjoying our fair city? And all it has to offer?"

"The view isn't bad," Baron admitted, glancing once more at her breasts.

"I could show you more."

"Chantelle prides herself on her hospitality," Cass said drolly.

Baron snorted with mirth.

Sadie wanted to scratch out both their eyes.

Resolutely tamping down her anger, Sadie tried again. "It's a pity women can't vote, senator. A charming *gentleman*—" she emphasized the word for Cass's benefit "—such as yourself, should be in the Governor's Mansion. Maybe even the White House."

That earned her a grin of appreciation. "I always did believe in looking after the ladies. Are you a suffragette, Miss O'Leary?"

"I admit to doing my part to support my man. And you're a man whom a lady would definitely like to see on top," she said suggestively.

"Of a pike," Cass added.

Baron guffawed. "Tarnation, boy. Should I be renting a room for you two?"

Sadie shot Cass a withering glare. He had the decency to redden.

At that inopportune moment, the craps dealer roared for

bets, and the orchestra started playing the cue for her costume change. Choking down her frustration, Sadie was forced to settle for Baron's promise—and a distracted one, at that—to watch her performance.

Seething at Cass's sabotage, she stalked off through the crowd, plotting all manner of paybacks. She hadn't walked more than 20 feet, however, when strong, callused fingers wrapped her wrist and tugged her to a halt.

She rounded on her bushwhacker. "How *dare*—"

"I'm sorry," Cass murmured. "About last night."

Her chest heaved. They were surrounded by spectators: leering craps shooters, gawking beerjerkers, liveried black-jack dealers.

Even more dangerous to her cover were the orchestra and it's hoity-toity conductor. Maestro Lundgren was an import from the vaunted New York Academy of Music and resented how Rex had called in a favor to get her the Grand Park gig. Lundgren had no idea she was a Pinkerton. After hearing her solo for the first time, the Maestro had complained she wailed like a banshee in heat.

Then, of course, there was Baron, his eyes hooded in speculation as he watched her and Cass through a cloud of blue cigar smoke. As much as Cass deserved to have his head chewed off, Sadie steeled herself against the temptation. She wasn't going to blow her cover because her showboater of an ex-lover got his jollies by making scenes.

"It's forgotten," she said, trying to jerk her wrist free.

"Just like that?" he countered warily.

"What does it matter? I'm due backstage for a costume change."

"I kind of like the costume you have on," he cajoled.

The smolder was unmistakable in those sapphire eyes. Her traitorous heart kicked.

Damn you, Cass, I'm not a fiddle to be played whenever you get nostalgic for the old tune!

She pasted on a smile for their audience and tried again to twist her arm free. "I don't have time for this. I have to sing."

"About me?"

"Sure." She rolled her eyes. "Whatever."

Actually, *Wager with the Devil* had been inspired by their poker game at Wilma's place. But he didn't need to know that. Hell, he didn't *deserve* to know that!

"I can't wait to hear it." He cocked his head in a winsome manner. "Do you take requests?"

"That depends on the request," she said warily.

"I'm kind of partial to *Lucifire.* "

"You and all the ladies."

"Aw. Don't be that way. Meet me afterward?"

"We burned that bridge, remember?"

He flinched.

Remorse needled her.

"Look," she said grudgingly, "I know what you are, *who* you are. I don't expect you to change for my sake. If she makes you happy, then be happy. Life's too short to hold grudges."

His throat worked, and his hand tightened over her wrist.

"Sadie, it's not like that—"

A trumpet fanfare sounded.

She bit back an oath. Her snooty bastard of a conductor was cuing the opening bars of her solo. *On purpose!*

"Cass, I really have to go!"

He must have read the desperation on her face, because reluctantly, he released her. Another trumpet blast shook the rafters.

Their stares locked.

Cinders and smoke. Hunger and hurt.

"Watch your back," she whispered earnestly.

Amidst the laughter and applause, she hiked her hem and fled for the steps of the stage.

Another night, another failure.

Sadie wondered how she could possibly file her next Pinkerton report without getting booted off the case. The convention would be over in two days—*two days!*—and she still hadn't found a scrap of evidence to incriminate Baron for capital murder. Hell, she hadn't even been able to seduce him! If a room full of whistling, stomping sodbusters hadn't deafened her after her performance, she might have worried she was losing her appeal.

Unable to face herself in the mirror, Sadie threw on trousers, a hat, and a beard. She wanted to avoid Cass and sneak out of the casino. She was furious with herself for letting him work his Coyote Charm on her. No one knew better than she the danger Cass posed with those bottomless baby-blues, adorable dimples, and well-rehearsed lines.

'He's the Rebel Rutter, you sap! Of course, he made you feel like he sincerely cared! That's how he gets sweet little maids to spread their legs!'

Damn Cass. She had to get him out of her system. But how could she end her attraction to him overnight, when four years of separation had failed to snuff out the spark?

That was the question plaguing her mind as she trudged through the park, to the woods, and finally located the secret tunnel which led to Wilma's boardinghouse. The brothel had been built over a cave, carved by a defunct river. Two decades earlier, Confederate engineers had altered the riverbed, so a mule could haul war-time supplies along a mine-cart track to a distant farm. Allan Pinkerton had secretly bought that farm on behalf of his operatives, and when construction of certain covert facilities was complete, Sadie hoped to help Wilma establish her training center there for Pinkies.

In the meantime, Wilma's cave was the perfect hiding place for Sadie to stash trunks bearing her more elaborate disguises—or so she'd thought. When she arrived at the secret chamber and unbolted its door, she surprised a two-legged mouse in a sea of light.

The child couldn't have been more than nine years old. She'd wedged herself between towering kegs of moonshine in the hopes she wouldn't be noticed. Clearly, the urchin had been rummaging through forbidden treasures. Blonde and sheepish, she huddled in the black lace of Sadie's favorite old negligee, accessorized with a string of Sadie's pearls and beaded slippers. Streaks of azure powder accented cornflower-blue eyes; great circles of rouge decorated the child's gaunt cheeks; and cherry-red paint had been smeared—crookedly—over bowlike lips.

To complete this comical picture, wilted daisies jutted from Sadie's most matronly beaver hat (for the days when only an old-woman disguise would do), and the kid's sausage-style ringlets bobbed beneath the net veil.

Sadie cleared her throat, keenly aware that the child wasn't the only one playing dress-up. She tugged her hat brim lower.

"Are you lost, little mouse?" she asked in her best imitation of a man's voice.

The child cocked her head, drawing tawny eyebrows together. "What's the matter? You got a frog in your throat?"

Just my luck. An urchin with attitude.

"Nothing's wrong with my throat," Sadie retorted.

The child giggled. "You sound like a burro with a head cold!"

Sadie choked at this assessment. "Does your mother know where you are?"

"I hope not." The kid grinned, crawling out of her hideout and dragging the negligee's hem through an eon's worth of filth. "Where'd you get your beard? Can I wear one?"

Sadie groaned to see the kid stumble into the lamplight, cobwebs sparkling all over the once pristine beaver fur. The child had a Cajun accent, much like Wilma's, and was wearing a *gris-gris* from her neck. The amulet could only mean one thing: Wilma was trying to protect the little beanpole.

"I don't think a beard would go with the pearls," Sadie said dryly, watching her negligee spill off the kid's scrawny shoulders. "Or with the dust." She arched an eyebrow at the knees of the gown.

"Oops! Sorry." Hastily, the child knocked the worst of

the grime from the silk, coughing behind her hand as dust rose up around her. "There. As good as new. Almost." The little charmer beamed, crowding her freckles together. "I'm Jazi. Well, actually I'm Jazlyn. Mama couldn't decide between Jasmine and Jocelyn, so she invented an even better name!"

"Does Grandma Wilma call you Jazlyn?" Sadie probed slyly.

Illuminated by the radiance of six kerosene lamps, Jazi traipsed over to the rickety vanity that Wilma had nagged Gator and Cotton to drag into the cave—along with Sadie's costume trunk, an accordion-like wheeler's cot, a no-frills wash stand, and a copper bath tub. The rest of the chamber was stacked head-high with kegs of liquor, crates of cigars, and various sundry items needed by bawds.

"Wilma's not my Nannan," Jazi supplied absently, studying her reflection as she tilted the beaver hat at varying angles beneath her daisies. "She's Mama's madam. Or at least, she used to be on Bourbon Street. Wilma calls me Boo."

The mystery deepens.

"Aren't you going to tell me *your* name?" Jazi asked over her shoulder.

"Well, I don't know. How good are you at keeping secrets?"

Jazi's thin chest puffed out with pride. "The *best.*"

"How can I be sure?"

"Well…" Jazi seemed to consider this question. "I never told anyone who really paid for my medicine when I was sick."

"Is that a fact?" Sadie edged closer, setting her lantern on the vanity table. She tugged a drooping sleeve back to the child's shoulder, releasing the sweet scent of strawberries. "Someone with plenty of money, huh?"

"If I told you *that,* it wouldn't be a secret!" Jazi countered triumphantly.

Their eyes met in the mirror. Sadie smiled.

"You got me there."

Jazi giggled and reached for a powder puff.

"You can call me Maisy."

"Maisy?" the child repeated uncertainly, the powder puff pausing half way to her nose. "You sure?"

"Uh-huh."

Jazi shrugged, making space so Sadie could fit on the bench beside her. "*Mais* well." Now she really did sound like Wilma. "Freckles are the *worst,* aren't they?" She was gazing wistfully at her reflection again. "Mama doesn't have freckles," she confided. "Not a single one! So she doesn't know how to hide them."

Removing the hat shadowing her face, Sadie let Jazi gaze fully at her complexion. "Now why would you want to hide something that makes you so beautiful?"

Jazi's mouth formed a perfect "O" as she craned back her head to stare at the pesky red dots on Sadie's nose. Naturally, the beaver hat slipped, plunking down to block her view.

"Hey!" She shoved the beaver back to her brow, leaving powdery fingerprints on the fur.

To her amazement, Sadie realized she didn't care about her soiled hat. She wasn't sure why, since her headgear and ruined gown had cost a small fortune, and she had to justify the purchase of every new gewgaw to Pinkerton.

Maybe the part of her that mourned her drowned twin, Maisy, liked the idea of playing dress-up with Jazi.

Or maybe a desperate, lonely side of her wanted to relive the innocence she'd lost after Daddy had been lynched as a Yankee spy.

Of course, Sadie hadn't known about Roarke Michelson's secret work as a Pinkerton at the time. Back in '68, all she'd known was that she and Mama had become pariahs in a very small town. Tossed into the gutter—presumably for lack of coin—13-year-old Sadie had tried to find lodging for her bereaved mother. Trudging the streets during a torrential rain, she'd been rejected at boardinghouse after boardinghouse, until she'd plowed headlong into Pilot

Grove's new marshal.

The tin-star had seemed like a friend, despite his northern sympathies. He'd offered her and Mama shelter in his hayloft, mainly because he'd liked the sight of Sadie's shivering curves beneath her sodden gown.

But the grunting pig had soon grown bored with humping a child who hadn't known the first thing about pleasing a man. Within the week, he'd abandoned Sadie and her grief-shattered mother on a brothel doorstep. Two days later, unable to face the shame, Mama had thrown herself out a third-story window.

Sadie hardened her jaw at the memory.

Now as she sat looking at the freckle-faced innocent sitting beside her, a child who'd been borne to a whore, and who'd probably wind up becoming a whore, Sadie's inner Tigress roared. She wanted to protect this impish cub from the desperate life prostitutes were forced to live. She couldn't help but wonder if the *gris-gris* Wilma had fashioned for Jazi was to keep away men who preyed on children for sex.

As if on cue, a light bloomed overhead, and the wooden stairs shuddered, sloughing off dust. Sadie spied the curly dark hair of Wilma as the brothel's proprietess descended, holding her lantern overhead and illuminating the sweating limestone of the cave's walls.

"Boo! Where you at? What did I tell you happens to *petite gagas*, eh?"

Jazi squirmed at Wilma's scolding.

A rapid-fire discussion ensued. Thanks to Sadie's study of arias written by Bizet, Offenbach, and Berlioz, she was able to follow bits and pieces of the argument. But Cajun French, as it turned out, was virtually unrecognizable as a by-product of the European language that Sadie's music tutor had taught her.

"Allons!" Wilma ordered in a tone that would not be disobeyed.

A sheepish Jazi hastily shed Sadie's clothes, kicking off the slippers and thrusting the hat into her hands.

Wilma was tapping her toe under the scandalously high slit of her tangerine taffeta. "And the gewgaws. Or you'll be making *do-do* without supper."

Sadie hid her smile. To make *do-do* was a term she did understand. In Cajun, it meant to go to sleep.

Sulking, Jazi surrendered the pearl necklace, a matching bracelet, and (to Sadie's amusement) a red satin garter. Then she scampered up the stairs in her own faded, thrice-turned calico, ducking Wilma's lantern and fleeing for the upper stories.

Affection crept across the Mambo's exotic features as she watched Jazi's petticoats flounce out of sight. "Even a house as fancy as this one is no place for the *chirens,*" Wilma said wistfully. "I told Mira to leave Jazi with the nuns. But she dotes on the child. Wouldn't hear of being separated."

"And Mira would be—?"

"A *protégé*. She arrived yesterday afternoon. Between the tourists, the convalescents, and the Farmers Alliance, the hotels have no vacancy. I could not turn her away. Not with a sick child."

Sadie frowned. "Jazi looked healthy to me."

"And yet her cough lingers. From a bout with swamp fever last spring. She does not yet have the stamina to run and play, like other children. I fear her lungs are scarred. But she makes up for it in other ways. Jazi is wiser than her years. She has the sight."

"That would explain how she bypassed the lock," Sadie said dryly.

"*Ça va.* I shall speak to her. Boo understands the importance of secrets. You need not worry. Mira won't be staying here for long.

"Now then, *chere.*" Wilma's cagey brown eyes locked with hers. "Why are you here? Were you not planning a seduction tonight?"

Sadie grimaced. Admitting Cass had foiled her plans would only prove to Rex and Wilma that she couldn't handle her ex-lover. Sadie didn't need that headache.

"Change of plans," she answered breezily.

"Oh?"

Wilma crossed the uneven limestone in a graceful strut, one which Sadie knew took hours to master, even though Wilma made it look as natural as breathing. When the Cajun finally halted beside the vanity, she arched a finely brushed eyebrow at Sadie's reflection. "Did you lose something?"

Sadie's neck heated at the reminder. Wrenching open the top drawer, she displayed her tiny, leather pouch of reeking herbs. "I…uh, just took off the *gris-gris*. There it is. See? Evil Spirits don't stand a chance around me."

"You are a pitiful liar."

"Wilma, be reasonable. I can't seduce Baron smelling like garlic!"

"Rosemary," she retorted testily. "And unless your snake senator has started rutting with bearded grangers, you've been nowhere near his bed tonight. You know the rules of my house. Put on the *gris-gris*, or it's back to the hotel with you."

Sadie scowled, draping the leather cord over her head. "What I need is a *gris-gris* full of echinacea," she grumbled. "And maybe some chamomile. That way, I'll have the ingredients of a nice tea to ward off a cold."

"You bear a death mark. How can you jest?"

"Humor keeps me sane."

The truth was, Sadie had damned near peed her pants the night she'd fled Galveston and arrived in Lampasas. Wilma had greeted her at the boardinghouse door with a shriek, lots of arcane gestures, and entreaties to Loa Eshu to protect her and the girls in her care. Apparently, Wilma had glimpsed the personification of Asrael, the Angel of Death, peering over Sadie's shoulder.

"Can we change the topic to something else?" Sadie said irritably. *"Anything* else?"

"Oui." Wilma propped her derriere on the vanity top. "How goes the battle for the button?"

Sadie shot her friend an exasperated look. "Any topic except *him."*

Wilma chuckled. "You always were a sore loser.*"*

Sadie scowled. Letting Cass win at poker was another reason to be pissed at herself. "A *temporary* setback, I assure you. Cass won the battle, not the war."

"Spoken like Aphrodite in Ares's arms."

"Don't start."

"Cass is dynamite. You are fire. Attraction is natural."

"Attraction is *stupid.*" Sadie began the unpleasant task of gluing putty on her nose.

"*Mais well.*" Wilma's lips twitched. "Take Cass to *gogo*, and the sizzle will fizzle. In time. Maybe."

Gogo, as the Cajun called it, was the last thing Sadie should be doing with Cass. "And when Baron finally takes the bait, how do I explain I'm too busy for a rut, because his bodyguard is in my bed?"

"You say, 'You have competition, Pig Senator. Please me if you can.'"

It was Sadie's turn to fight a smile. "Now I see why you are the illustrious Madam, and I am merely the bawd."

"Not so mere, *chere.*" The Cajun's dark eyes were much too insightful for Sadie's peace of mind. "Since you plan to sleep here tonight, I can only assume your stage shimmies failed to entice the right man?"

"Abysmally."

"It is said, the old bull is ailing."

"I'm starting to think the old bull's a *steer.* No wonder his wife doesn't sleep with him."

"Mrs. Westerfield has turned shrew. She blames Baron for her miscarriages. What man could desire such a woman?"

Sadie frowned. "You're *defending* that butcher?"

"Non. But one must understand one's enemy in order to defeat him."

"Has he ever walked through your door since coming to Lampasas?"

Wilma shook her head. "And yet, he is getting his satisfaction somewhere. Only a monk can go without—and sometimes, not even then."

Thoughtfully, Sadie drummed her fingers on the vanity. "So what you're saying is, I have competition."

"A secret lover, perhaps. A mistress he hides from his wife."

"Great. Just what I need. Another complication."

Wilma tapped her lips, a far-away look stealing into her eyes. "To compete with such a rival, you will need a new weapon in your arsenal of love."

Sadie gazed critically at her reflection, trying to guess what Wilma meant. The woman had an uncanny way of intuiting future events. It was downright spooky. "Another wig?"

"No, *chere.* It is time to introduce a new player to the game. A worthy opponent. One who makes our pig of a senator rise to the challenge."

Sadie arched an eyebrow. "I'm listening."

"Senator Swine does not see you as you wish to be seen, so during your gala performance on Devil's Eve, let us show him what he's missing. Through the eyes of his political nemesis."

Sadie's breath hitched. "You mean Rex?"

"Mais oui. Cass already believes you and Rex are lovers. He'll give the lie credence, should Baron become skeptical."

Sadie's heart kicked at this idea. It was brilliant, like all of Wilma's ideas. But was the cost too high?

Cass would never forgive her for "finally admitting," after all these years, that she'd been having an affair with Rex. More to the point, matters between Cass and Rex could escalate to lethal proportions.

As if guessing her concern, Wilma fixed her with a stern stare. "Do you or do you not want to see Baron pay for his crimes?"

"I do, but—"

"Then you must remember why you took this assignment. Baron must be stopped. He hides behind the trappings of his office, ordering the murder of innocent farmers, while other men—like your Cass—go to the gallows in his stead."

Sadie fidgeted. Everything Wilma had said was true.

"I just can't bear the thought of a high-noon showdown, that's all. Especially over me."

Wilma patted her shoulder. "If anyone can handle Cass's guns, it's *mon po po*."

"Your *po po?*" Sadie hiked an eyebrow.

Wilma blushed prettily. "Uh…policeman."

"Right." Sadie cleared her throat. Like Rex, Wilma was scrupulously discrete about her private life. But a body would have to be blind not to see how Wilma's eyes sparkled whenever Rex entered the room—and vice versa. Sadie was delighted they'd found each other. She just hoped their affair survived this mission.

"What if Rex doesn't…can't…well, *you* know." Sadie blew out her breath. "Wilma, he just doesn't *think* of me that way!"

Wilma looked amused. "You are capable of holding the man's hand, are you not? And stroking his cheek?"

"I'm not worried about *my* theatrics. Rex is the straight-laced son of virtue."

Wilma chuckled, as if at a private joke. "Have faith, *chere*. A mistress knows all her lover's secrets. Baron will want to know about Rex's campaign. He'll take the bait. You'll see."

Sadie bit her lip, envisioning an enraged Lucifire with blazing six-shooters.

That's exactly what I'm afraid of.

As if the matter was settled, Wilma rose from her perch and reached for her lantern. "I must return to my sodbusters, *chere*. They are clamoring for more liquor. Shall I arrange your invitation to a poker game?"

Sadie sighed, inspecting her pesky sideburns for signs of peeling. "You might as well. *Some* sodbuster in this town must know who took potshots at Baron. I'm hoping the sniper can lead us to a farmer with a big enough grudge, that he'll testify against Baron."

"Bien. I shall have Gator watch over you."

Wilma turned to go. A moment later, the madam's spiky heels stopped clicking on the limestone. *"Qui c'est q'ca?"*

Sadie glanced over her shoulder. Wilma had raised her lantern and was frowning at her stacks of contraband.

"What's the matter?"

"Perhaps nothing. It is just that I thought this crate of bourbon was under the Glenmorangie. To make the scotch easier to access when *mon po po* is in the house."

Wilma set her lamp on a pickle barrel and lifted the crate's lid. It was stamped with black block letters that read, *Ripy Brothers Distillery. Tyrone, Kentucky.*

Sadie crossed to Wilma's side. "You're worried. Should I be?"

"I do not think so..." But the madam's brow remained furrowed. "Perhaps I did not tally the bourbon correctly. I shall have Cotton re-inventory the Wild Turkey in the morning."

CHAPTER 11

As inky indigo spread across a cloudless sky, Cass grimaced. A hoity-toity gala wasn't the way he'd envisioned spending Devil's Eve.

Violins and woodwinds were making a high-falutin' noise in the gaily lit musicians' pavilion at Hancock Park. Everybody who was anybody in Lampasas had congregated here to raise money for the hospital's new wing. To Cass's way of thinking, this charity fandango was really just an excuse for a lot of rich folks to sip champagne, munch on snails, and show off gold watch fobs and diamond earbobs.

Oh. And to watch Sadie perform.

Apparently, his social-climbing ex-lover had become quite the darling of the Grand Park regulars. Even *he* had to concede that the way she'd filled out her skin-tight, black satin gown last night should have been grounds for a public indecency charge. He'd been sorely tempted to punch out Baron's lights when the randy old skirt-chaser kept ogling her breasts. Cass was almost relieved to know that Poppy had accompanied her husband to Sadie's recital tonight.

Almost.

The truth was, Poppy was getting on Cass's nerves. She kept finding reasons to stand beside him, brush against him, stroke his arm. Cass didn't like the way his body responded to her attentions—and especially when his brain didn't want the complication. In truth, he was more than a little insulted. Poppy thought nothing of risking his job, his friendship with Baron, and maybe even his freedom from a penitentiary, because she'd decided he'd make a suitable stud pony.

But Poppy was wrong to think he was free with his seed just because he was a womanizer. To think he might have slipped up somewhere, leaving his baby in some long-forgotten lover's belly, had the power to give him nightmares. No child should have to grow up without a father. He, Collie, and Sadie could all attest to that fact.

Besides, a Ranger, who roamed the state risking bullets every day, had no business siring rugrats when he couldn't be home, protecting the ones he loved.

Cass drew a ragged breath at the notion. Tonight was as close as he had ever come to being a real Ranger. He didn't want anything to go wrong on his watch. He had a lot to prove, now that he'd been exonerated and was working for a senator.

That's why he'd taken extra care at dinnertime, when he'd visited the Barleycorn Saloon on Western Avenue. He'd acted as civil and cordial as a fella in chaps could be while visiting a taproom full of cowboy-hating sodbusters. He'd even bought the house a round of drinks to loosen tongues and win allies.

But charm only went so far when roostered rednecks were itching for a cockfight. He'd no sooner coaxed a sweet, young Mexican girl, named Marisol, to confide how her brother, Joaquin, had shined the shoes of a mean-spirited *homre* with notches on his six-shooter, when a brute in a sack coat grabbed her arm and yanked her away from Cass's table.

"I don't like my ruts to stink of cow," the redneck announced with a sneer.

"I am a dancing girl, *Señor* O'Shaunessy!" Marisol protested, trying to wrench her arm free of her captor's ham-sized fist. "Let me go!"

Cass smiled pleasantly, rising with his whiskey bottle. *"Señorita* Marisol asked you kindly, *amigo.* Don't make her ask again."

O'Shaunessy curled his lip at Cass's pale gold hair and honey-colored tan. "I don't take orders from Greasers. Especially albino ones."

"Good thing I'm Irish then." Cass winked.

O'Shaunessy roared, taking a swing. Cass ducked, grabbing the bully's arm, twisting it behind his back, and using O'Shaunessy's momentum to slam his face into the table. Cass didn't need much strength to pin O'Shaunessy there, not after smashing the whiskey bottle for a weapon. He let the amber glass scratch blood from the redneck's throat.

"Now then," Cass instructed in that same pleasant tone. "I believe you owe *Señorita* Marisol an apology. Let's hear it, *amigo,* lest I remember where I hid my Peacemaker."

"You mustn't trust him, *señor,"* Marisol whispered urgently, pointing at a suspicious lump under O'Shaunessy's sack coat. "He has a six-shooter!"

"Well, lookie there." Cass relieved the redneck of the .45 poking from his waistband. "Little notches. And they look like steers."

"It ain't even loaded!" O'Shaunessy wailed.

"Yeah? Well, mine is. Start talking if you don't want your ass used as target practice."

Cass sighed at the memory. Like he'd assured Poppy earlier in the week, most gun-toting chuckleheads strapped on firearms for show. O'Shaunessy fell into that category. The redneck had practically peed his pants at Cass's threat. That's why Cass believed O'Shaunessy's claim that he knew no other "mean-spirited *hombre"* with a notched six-shooter.

Marisol had tried to help by describing a brown-eyed, brown-haired, brown-bearded customer of Joaquin's. The features she'd listed could have belonged to any one of hundreds of men in Lampasas. But when she'd described how the *hombre* had rendezvoused with a gaunt, stoop-shouldered man with a crab-apple face, Cass had suspected Pendleton. Marisol swore up and down that Pendleton had passed the *hombre* a sack of money.

Maybe Collie's suspicions about Pendleton aren't so far-fetched, after all.

Cass's jaw hardened as he remembered how the *hombre*—or rather, the sniper—had escaped from the livery. He couldn't let the bastard elude him again. But recognizing an assassin at a public gala in Hancock Park wouldn't be easy. Little more than starlight and paper lanterns were available to illuminate the faces of the crowd.

Cass scanned the white folding chairs, marching like well-heeled soldiers across the sun-beaten grasses that surrounded the pavilion. A dozen suffragettes with wildly waving fans had taken refuge in the shade with their perspiring beaux, but most of the highbrow couples were congregating under hardy live oak trees or golden cedar elms, rather than strolling through the field of wilting, yellow daisies near the boardwalk. Unfortunately, a dry heat couldn't be eluded anywhere during a Texas drought, even after dusk.

The conductor of the Grand Park's orchestra was swinging his arms with great gusto, and his blue-liveried musicians were fervently playing the kind of ruckus mostly heard in opera houses. Cass didn't know Mozart from Bach—or Bach from Stephen Foster, for that matter. But he did know a two-bit killer could clean up as good as any dude in a top hat.

And Sadie should know that too.

That's why Cass had half a mind to walk over to that stage, tear down the handbill with her golden-eyed portrait, and cry fraud. Or thief. Or *something* that would make Sid lock her up out of harm's way.

Yes, Collie was right. Caring makes me a fool.

But Cass couldn't shake his worry that Sadie was in danger. Why else would she go to such lengths to disappear, creating a multitude of identities with beards, spectacles, and wigs?

Did the sun fry her brain? What can she possibly be thinking, to let her face get plastered all over Hancock Park for some stupid music recital?!

"You got cotton in your ears, boy?"

Cass's neck heated. Apparently, Baron had asked him a question.

"Uh…reckon I was scanning the crowd for snipers, sir."

Baron laughed good-naturedly, clapping Cass's shoulder. Despite his show of good spirits, the senator was having trouble disguising his affliction. His swallowtails looked more like a sack suit on his diminishing frame. According to his doctors, who'd posed a variety of uncertain diagnoses, Baron's weight loss was probably due to a faulty liver.

Poppy claimed that sex, whiskey, and tobacco were the real culprits.

At any rate, Lampasas's famed mineral baths didn't appear to be leeching the poison from Baron's blood. And that could be bad news for cattlemen, especially if Baron withdrew from the election.

"Fess up, boy," Baron ribbed him, twirling his handlebar mustachios. "You were scanning the crowd for pretty faces."

"Naw." Cass grinned at Baron's lampoon. "I wouldn't stand a chance against Coon Collie, here."

The boy shot him a withering look. As usual, Vandy was frisking at Collie's heels, acting adorable, and earning coos from eyelash-batting belles. Vandy was a skirt magnet. Cass didn't understand why Collie didn't have at least one female trotting after him like a puppy on a string.

As if on cue, Collie growled in his usual, surly manner, "That churnhead of a clerk refused to give me the tickets. He claimed the front row is sold out."

Cass arched an eyebrow at the stretch of seats in question. Huddled beneath long ropes of orange and yellow lanterns, in honor of the Halloween season, the chairs were pinned with paper signs, each scrawled with the word, *Reserved.*

"I'm sure Mr. MacAffee did his best," Poppy said to her husband, her tone suggesting that Collie's best would never be good enough. "But you can hardly blame the clerk for refusing to believe that a youth of his…er, proclivities was running an errand for a senator. The chef at the Globe Hotel made such a ruckus over that stolen-trout incident, Mr. MacAffee's coon made the headlines—which is more than I can say for your campaign, dear. Perhaps *you* should get a coon to steal a trout."

"Cranky already?" Baron hiked an eyebrow at his wife, whose elegantly piled curls barely came up to his chin. "Did you remember to take your medicine?"

"Did *you?*" she fired back.

Cass winced. Baron wasn't fond of highbrow music recitals, but he was forever looking for opportunities to win votes. According to a rumor on the street, Rexford Sterne and his "plus one" had RSVP'd for this charity event, so naturally, Baron had bought tickets.

The senator reached for a pair of champagne glasses on the tray of a passing waiter. "Here," he said, handing one to his wife. "Drink. You need it more than I do."

"What I need is relief from this heat."

"Say the word, Sugar Plum, and I'll send you back to the hotel."

Poppy's chest heaved.

Baron smirked.

Cocking his head, the wily senator trained his gaze in the direction of the big-eared hick at the Will Call table.

"Tarnation, Collie. Is *that* the fella who's making my precious Popsicle melt? Good thing he sassed you instead of me, 'cause I would've plugged that hayseed on sight."

The air around Poppy crackled with chill. "Yes, by all means. Let us rid our lives of inconveniences, starting with marauding raccoons, that like to cannonball into bath—*ow!* Baron, for heaven's sake, watch where you're walking!"

Apparently, Baron had stepped on her toe. Cass wasn't

surprised, since Baron had been looking at every woman in the park, except her. Now he was gawking at a particularly curvaceous Cajun whom they both knew. Clinging to Wilma's hand was a girl—approximately nine years in age—who was pointing with great excitement at a shooting star. The child was dressed in blue calico with a crisply pressed pinafore, white cotton stockings, and highly polished, black Mary Jane shoes. Her head was ringed by yellow sausage curls.

Cass arched an eyebrow—first at Wilma, since she was the last person on earth whom he'd expected to see entertaining a child—and second at Baron, who swung his wife so quickly in the direction of the Will Call booth that she stepped on Vandy's paw.

The coon yiked.

"Hey!" Collie barked at his boss's wife.

"Serves the varmint right! He's always underfoot."

"Don't mind the missus, boys," Baron counseled with his horsey smile, but irritation roughened his tone as he herded them away from Wilma. "Poppy wouldn't know what to do with herself if the good Lord made nagging a sin."

Poppy's eyes flashed green lightning. "Allow me to remind you, *dear,* that I agreed to risk my *life* in this trigger-happy boomtown, only because you promised to start taking your medicine."

Baron rolled his eyes. "Nasty stuff," he muttered to Cass. "Tastes like ashes mixed with turpentine."

"Honestly." As usual when Poppy was upset, she started fondling her *relicario*, the heart-shaped pendant bearing a drop of blood from each of her miscarriages. "You're worse than a child. I mix in molasses for you, don't I? What good is there in winning an election if you're too sick to do the job once you reach Austin?"

"No squirmy little liver bug is gonna keep *me* out of Austin," Baron flared, hiking his breeches and snorting the way an angry bull does before its charge. "I won over Lampasas County voters once, and I'll do it again!"

The Westerfields' bickering attracted the notice of a grim-faced Sid by the refreshment stand. The marshal had been conferring with a heavily veiled woman, who kept wringing a handkerchief. Sid directed his glare first at Baron, then at Cass's double-holstered rig.

The next thing Cass knew, the tin-star was headed their way.

"Howdy, Sid." Ever the politician, Baron pasted on a grin and pumped the marshal's hand. "Any news about that sniper?"

"'Fraid not," Sid admitted gruffly. For this hoity-toity affair, he'd traded his usual dungarees for fancy, black broadcloth and a silver bullet on a rawhide bollo. Standing well over six feet, Sid's balding head and barrel-sized chest were easily as imposing as Baron's.

"Perhaps you should question your friend, Rexford Sterne," Poppy told Sid snidely. "I daresay the *Rangers* already know who was crouching on that rooftop—and probably what he ate for breakfast. In fact, I'm tempted to wire the Rangers myself to find the elusive Mrs. Dalrymple. Clearly, she was a *fraud.* And probably a thief."

Cass stiffened as Poppy waved Sadie's handbill under Sid's nose. Poppy could be a bulldog when she sank her teeth into any scrap of evidence that might lead to Baron's paramours.

But Sid had bigger fish to fry. "Begging your pardon, ma'am," he said grimly, "but I did wire the Rangers—to help with another manhunt that has to take precedence. Seems like we've got a killer on the loose. Refresh my memory. When's the last time you saw Tito Ferraro?"

Poppy blinked. Two spots of color bloomed on her powdered cheeks. "M-Mr. Ferraro?"

"Now see here, Sid," Baron interceded testily. "Tito was in *my* employ, guarding *my* missus. Are you saying Tito is wanted for murder?"

"Tito's dead," Sid said flatly. "What the coyotes left of him was found this afternoon in a cedar brake, about two miles south of town. Doc says it was the bullet that killed him. But bullets don't make a man's tongue turn black or his eyes go yellow and buggy."

Poppy gasped, pressing a gloved hand to her mouth.

"Collie," Baron barked, "escort my wife to a proper seat. A lady's ears shouldn't suffer such tales."

For once, Poppy didn't argue, but Collie looked madder than a wet hornet to be missing this juicy bit of gossip. He dragged his feet as he herded her away.

"What the hell's the matter with you?" Baron growled at the lawman. "You know better than to talk business in front of a woman."

Sid's flinty gaze was openly speculative as he glanced between Baron and Cass—searching for an incriminating reaction, perhaps? But Baron looked as stunned as Cass felt by the news of Tito's death.

"Tito left a note," Cass volunteered. "He was heading home. He wasn't familiar with these hills. Maybe he was bitten by a copperhead, became feverish, and got lost," he added, recalling how snake venom had nearly snuffed out his own life last year.

Sid grunted, turning to Baron. "You still have this note?"

"Hell, Sid, if I kept every scrap of paper that ever crossed my desk, I'd have to build another barn."

"Uh-huh." Sid didn't look convinced. "I heard Collie had words with Tito. I heard they argued lots of times."

Cass tensed. "Says who?"

"Says a witness, that's who."

Baron was frowning. "Collie's just a kid."

"Age don't make no nevermind. I was riding posse on my thirteenth birthday. Shot my first bank robber that year, too. And I'm not the only one who took to guns young," Sid added, drilling Cass with a dire glare.

Cass's jaw hardened. So much for his assumption that he and Sid were friends. "That hurts my feelings, marshal."

"Cut the crap, Cassidy. Don't you think I contacted a few Kentucky tin-stars? According to the Whitley County sheriff's office, Collie was arrested on murder charges in Blue Thunder Valley about two years ago. Seems like he was stealing coons from a taxidermist, who took exception to the thefts—and wound up dead."

Cass clenched a fist. No one knew better than he did how a youthful crime could ruin a boy's life. "If you wrote to Sheriff Truitt," Cass said acidly, "then he should have told you those murder charges didn't stick. Collie was released for lack of evidence, and the real murderer was shot by a bounty hunter."

"Whom *you* plugged," Sid accused.

"The bastard had just murdered a man! And he was fixing to plug Sera, Lynx, and Collie, whom he was holding hostage!"

Baron clapped a restraining hand over Cass's shoulder. "That bounty hunter had a stack of murder warrants against him, and Cass was exonerated in a court of law," the senator said in crisp, businesslike tones.

Sid's eyes glanced narrowly from Baron to Cass.

"Just so we're clear, Cassidy," the marshal ground out. "I'll be watching you. And that smart-mouthed kid, too."

With a terse nod, Sid turned on his heel and strode into the night.

Cass was so angry, his limbs were shaking.

Baron's beefy hand squeezed his shoulder, half in sympathy, half in reproach. "Simmer town, hotshot. That tongue of yours is going to dig your grave."

"Collie's a good kid!"

"I know, son. But somewhere in town, the boy made an enemy. Maybe even Sterne."

"Sterne?"

"Sure. Everyone knows Sid's in Sterne's back pocket. Sid even admitted it. After he found the corpse, he called in the Rangers. When a body's found outside the city limits, the *proper* procedure is to call in the county sheriff." Grimly, Baron shook his head. "Looks like Sterne found a new way to make things personal between you and him."

Cass was seeing red at that point.

The crowd rippled and parted near the pavilion. Applause swept through the seated members of the audience, who quickly climbed to their feet. Whoops and hollers erupted as the clapping grew louder, rushing like wildfire from couple to couple. Sterne strolled onto the grounds with a stunning, brandy-eyed redhead on his arm.

Sadie.

Cass's heart kicked hard.

Her luscious figure was sheathed in a sleeveless evening gown of breezy, ivory silk. A daring scoop revealed the abundance of freckles on her back, and a golden bow rode flirtatiously above her bustle. A gauzy shawl of matching gold drooped from her shoulders and fluttered over her elbow-length gloves.

Cass was pretty sure he ground his teeth hard enough to crack one.

Baron also noticed the couple. He hiked a bushy eyebrow as Sterne bowed formally, kissing Sadie's knuckles. She laughed at something the ex-Ranger said before she finally—and much too slowly, in Cass's opinion—withdrew her hand from his fist. Patting his craggy cheek, she raised her skirts above velvet shoes and sauntered behind the scarlet curtains of the stage.

Some tenderfoot in swallowtails approached Sterne, slapped his back, and raised his champagne toward Sadie's ass.

By that time, Cass was ready to shoot something.

"Easy, son." Baron handed him a glass. "No need to rush things." An unpleasant little smile curved the senator's lips. "There are plenty of ways to skin a cat."

Behind the curtains of the stage, Sadie paced like a caged tiger in the early evening shadows, waiting for her musical cue. Beyond the Grecian columns from which the velvet had been strung, she could see the evening star rising against the backdrop of purple-blue dusk.

Unfortunately, no breeze found its way between the columns. The dust of a parched, Texas landscape had invaded everything, including her sinuses. Despite the cooling plunge of her gown's back, her skin glistened with perspiration.

Or maybe it was the charade of being Rex's lover that had her sweating out this performance. Even the thought of Wilma and Jazi in the audience, cheering her on for moral support, couldn't ground the butterflies in Sadie's stomach.

Her breath hitched as a stringed quartet began playing the first, yearning strains of her introduction. The tender sighing of the cello haunted her. Cellos were considered the instrument most like the human voice, and *Destiny* was a lament. The lyrics had been inspired four years ago by her estrangement from Cass. Sadie had never intended to sing *Destiny* for an audience. However, she had suffered a sentimental bout of lunacy last night, and she'd dragged out the sheet music, reviewing it over a shot of tequila.

All right, over *four* shots of tequila.

Maybe that was why the song had somehow found its way into her music folder. She'd been none the wiser until dress rehearsal that afternoon, when she'd handed her folder to her accompanist. Curious about the title, the pianist had tugged *Destiny* from her stack of compositions. The next thing she'd known, Maestro Lundgren had directed her to "sing the love song."

"But it still needs work," she'd protested in rising panic. She'd been planning to sing *Habanera,* which, in part, compared love to a gypsy child, who had never known the law. Sadie had always related to that message. "I prepared a selection from *Carmen. Habanera* is better suited—"

"I shall decide which music is suitable for tonight's event," the Yankee had interrupted in his testy tenor. "Bizet is passé. Every mezzo-soprano in every two-bit musicale screeches *Habanera. Fresh.* That's what's needed if a singer of your caliber is expected to pull off a gala performance."

Sadie supposed she should be flattered that a conductor from New York's vaunted Academy of Music had arranged her simple tune for stringed accompaniment.

But *Destiny* had been torn from her heart, a catharsis for an old flame that was dying. She quailed to think of parading her pain before dozens of snooty matrons and their bored husbands, who would sit in judgment, sneering up at her through the footlights as she struggled to sing through tears.

"You *will* sing tonight," Wilma had counseled her firmly, "because your love is for music. You will take the stage, because that is your *mission.* The performance will cost three minutes of your life. That is a small price, *chere,* for ending the career of a monster."

The cellist began bowing her musical cue. Sadie squeezed her eyes closed, seeking comfort by reaching for Daddy's button. But of course, the familiar warmth of that battered brass wasn't resting over her heart.

That's another payback I owe you, Cass.

She gulped a fortifying breath. She couldn't remember the last time her stomach had churned before a performance. Hell, she'd jumped out of a burning building, hadn't she? Stage fright should be nothing compared with that.

It's now or never.

She muttered a prayer and forced her feet forward. Pasting on a luscious smile, she sauntered into the blinding haze of gaslights at the front of the stage. The crowd hushed. She dragged her gaze from Cass, sitting arms akimbo at Baron's side in the front row. Rex was standing in the aisle, stage right, as they'd planned. She let her smile drip honey and begged God with all her heart that the vocal seduction she was about to perform wouldn't destroy her friendship with Rex—or worse, get him killed.

Taking the conductor's cue, she began to sing:

> *"Leave your cares, far from sight.*
> *Heat the chill; burn the night.*
> *Hold me close, let love start;*
> *Touch my soul, free my heart.*
>
> *"Deep in dreams, every night,*
> *Yearn for you; feels so right.*
> *Don't you know? Can't you see?*

Why you're mine, destined be?

"Suns may rise, stars may fail.
Worlds collide; love prevails.
Through all time, you and me,
Heart to heart, destiny.

"Never doubt, you're my man,
Through God's vast, Master Plan.
Always yours, I shall be.
Born for you, destiny."

Cass could scarcely breathe as the last, haunting strains of Sadie's song faded beneath the stars. Wildflowers started sailing over the footlights. Tear-streaked matrons and whiskered Old Farts surged to their feet. In tribute to Sadie's performance, hotel promoters were hurling yellow-rose bouquets onto the impressive little garden growing at her ankles.

But the only roses Sadie deigned to catch were the dozen blood-red blossoms thrown by Sterne.

The applause was deafening.

"Cass?" Poppy was watching him speculatively from Baron's other side. "Are you all right?"

Cass barely heard her as he watched Sadie blow kisses to the grinning Sterne. A crushing weight had settled over his heart. Her lyrics kept reverberating in his skull: *"Never doubt you're my man, through God's vast master plan..."*

No! Sadie wrote those lyrics about me, by God. She always writes her love songs about me!

Poppy sidled closer, linking her arm through his. "There now, Cass. Everything's going to be all right. What's this Miss O'Leary to you?"

"Trouble," Collie said harshly.

Baron chuckled at the worried expression on the boy's face. "Redheads. They're the ones you have to watch out for. Right, Collie?"

"You're not helping," Poppy snapped at her husband. Her tone softened as she patted Cass's arm. "Come, Cass. Walk with me. You need a change of scenery."

"You might as well go, son," Baron said with an expansive wave of his champagne glass. "Mother won't quit whining till you do. Me and Collie can hold down the fort. We'll find out what Chantelle finds so jo-fired fascinating about Sterne."

"Chantelle?" Poppy repeated suspiciously.

"That's her name, ain't it?" Baron boomed jovially. "Collie, go on over and introduce yourself to Miss O'Leary. Tell her I have a request."

"It had better be a singing request," Poppy sniped.

Baron rolled his eyes. "Of course it's a singing request," he lied.

"I'll go," Cass insisted hoarsely, some vague plan forming in his mind that he would drag Sadie off the stage and remind her why he was called the Rebel Rutter.

But Collie had grown more cussid than usual. He shoved Cass back with a force that put the spurs to his already straining temper.

"Your name ain't Collie," the boy snapped.

Cass clenched his fists.

Vandy growled.

"Something wrong with your hearing, boy?" Baron grabbed Cass's closest gun arm in restraint. "My wife asked you to walk with her. Start walking, lest I have to cool that hot head of yours by busting it open."

By that point, Cass was ready to punch out Baron.

Seething like a firestorm, he stalked away from his boss, the festive paper lanterns, the sparkling champagne, and the tinkling laughter. His mood was as dark as the path that kept twisting somewhere into the night. He had no real memory of jewel-colored evening gowns, scattering before him, or black swallowtails, stepping hastily out of his way. He'd even forgotten Poppy—probably because he'd turned a deaf ear to the sound of spiky little heels trying to keep pace.

"Ow! For heaven's sake, Cass, stop! I-I think I've twisted my ankle."

He halted, his chest heaving, his mind spinning with

shadows and shades. He'd gone so deep into his own, personal darkness, that for a moment, he couldn't remember where he was.

He forced his vision to focus on the green-eyed redhead, whose freckled face bobbed near his shoulder.

"Help me," Poppy whimpered.

He scowled, not liking how that single phrase could exhume nobility from the dark side of his soul. Apparently, his demons couldn't stave off an attack of conscience where a damsel-in-distress was concerned.

Reaching unceremoniously for Poppy's waist, he swung her around and propped her spine against a tree.

"Y-you're so strong," she gasped.

He grunted. He could be described as a lot of things. But strong? After he'd let Sadie under his skin again?

He started to turn away.

As if on cue, Poppy teetered and flailed, throwing her arms around his neck. "Don't leave me!"

He scowled.

Cass knew women. Most of the time, he liked them— especially redheads. What he didn't like was being played for a fool. Clearly, that's what Poppy was trying to do with all the flailing and the limping.

He glared a warning into the misty green eyes of his boss's wife. But Poppy didn't wise up and take the hint. He wondered if that made her fair game. Panting, trembling, she looked like a wild doe caught in his sights. Her breasts reeked of violets as they heaved, grazing his chest. Her lips trembled open, moist, plump and ripe. Musky heat rolled off her hips.

The predator inside him smelled sex.

"T-Thank you. I'm so grateful you caught me," she murmured. "You're always so gallant and kind. Such a good friend. And you need a good friend, too, don't you? To take away your pain…"

She stroked his chest. The fruity scent of champagne lingered on her breath. His nostrils flared. Her eyelashes fanned lower.

"Let me be that friend, Cass..." Barely audible, the words hovered between them, more invitation than plea.

He was tempted.

The part of him that wanted to punish Sadie for her treachery was darkly, dangerously tempted. Steamy little waves of femininity brazed the buttons of his crotch. The brass grew warmer. Tighter.

Poppy swayed, swoonlike, and their chests collided in earnest.

Oh, he could have had his boss's wife, all right. She'd been making that evident for days: her coy touches. Her kittenish mews. Her ridiculous eyelash-flapping. She thought herself so worldly; she lorded her sophistication over women who weren't as privileged to be a senator's wife. But in bedroom matters, Poppy was clearly a schoolgirl.

Cass decided a crude dose of reality was needed to put an end to Poppy's infatuation.

"You need to mount a horse, Mrs. Westerfield?"

She shrank back at his clipped tone. "I-I'm not sure..."

"Then maybe you should think on it a spell."

Confusion vied with the indignation on her face. Apparently, she couldn't decide if he'd meant "horse" in the conventional sense.

"Are you *angry* with me?"

Her bottom lip quivered, and a spark of humanity bloomed in his chest. It reminded him his quarrel wasn't with Poppy. Sadie was the redhead he wanted to punish.

"No," he said gruffly, tugging off his bandanna and shoving it into her hand. "Wipe your eyes. The second half of the program will start soon."

She dabbed her tears as instructed, but she refused to put a respectable distance between their loins.

"My poor, sweet Cass," she crooned. "Always so thoughtful. Always so sensitive to my needs. But you're hurting too, aren't you? First the news about Tito. Then the proof that faithless woman spurned you."

Cass reined in his demons. Poppy was too naïve to know

how he spared her. A conventional, missionary romp wouldn't have satisfied a man of his appetites. In truth, he'd already grown bored with Poppy's adolescent wiles and tentative groping. Baron was the man who needed to be instructing his bride in the art of pleasure-giving.

"Let me help you, Cass." She sidled closer, dropping a fluttery hand to his thigh. "Let me take away your pain."

He caught her wrist in an uncompromising fist. "I have a better idea. I'll take you back to your husband."

She blinked. She looked like an owl caught in the light of a hunter's lantern. "But you like me. I can see the proof in your pants."

"I like a lot of women," he said harshly.

"But we could make such beautiful babies together!"

"No doubt Senator Westerfield will be thrilled to know you're feeling affectionate for a change."

Her cheeks mottled. "How dare you!"

"Blame it on my upbringing, ma'am. You're a fine lady, and I'm…well, just a trashy kind of horse."

At last, his strategy worked. She recoiled in outrage, her chest heaving, her fists clenched.

"Insufferable baboon! You'll regret your conceit! Someday, you'll rue the way you mocked me. And on that day, your guns will be cold company!"

Shoving past him with surprising strength, she marched into the night on spiky little heels that didn't wobble or limp.

Well, lookie there. The lady's ankle made a miraculous recovery.

Cass snorted to have his suspicions confirmed.

Pushing Poppy from his mind, he headed in the opposite direction, away from the lights and the milling crowd. He had a score to settle with the Devil's Red-haired Daughter. He figured the best way to do that was to surprise the hellcat in her lair.

The musicians were filing from their chairs for intermission. Sadie stood at the top of the stage steps. Like a queen, she cuddled Rex's roses and daintily offered her hand to her other admirers.

She hoped all this posturing made her appear in her glory after her "triumphant love song," as the stagehands were crowing about it. God knew, she didn't feel triumphant. When she'd blown a kiss to Rex, accusation had rolled off Cass in waves. She'd cringed, her insides shriveling before the blast of heat in Lucifire's glare.

Throughout her performance, Rex had staunchly played the doting beau. He'd stood in the aisle, just beyond the orchestra's seats, so every gossip in the crowd could watch their ruse. Although Wilma had orchestrated tonight's charade, Rex had improvised. He'd surprised Sadie by throwing that big, flashy bouquet of roses. Who would have guessed Rex possessed a theatrical bone in his body?

Now he stood watching her possessively, his arms crossed over his crisp white vest and linen shirt. He looked every inch the dashing Alpha Wolf, with his slicked back hair, immaculate swallowtails, and gleaming Justin boots. (Even Wilma hadn't been able to coax Rex into wearing opera pumps.) At the appropriate moment, one of Rex's campaign staff was supposed to appear with an urgent message to lure him away, leaving Sadie an unguarded little lamb, ripe for Baron to slaughter, so to speak.

Apparently, that moment was now. A plump clerk waddled over to his boss. Rex made a credible show of looking grave and bowing his head toward the shorter man. The campaign manager gestured urgently— *melodramatically* might have been a better description. Rex tossed her a look of disappointment that would have been flattering if he hadn't been acting out a role. Then he turned, and his commanding presence parted the mob of sycophants as cleanly as Moses had parted the Red Sea.

Baron continued to ogle her, but his expression was openly calculating. Sadie tried to be glad Wilma's plan was working. She forced herself to ramp up her flirtations. She was *so close* to luring the weasel from his lair! But pretending was hard—damned hard—when she had to lavish loins-stirring smiles on balding, pot-bellied admirers with tobacco-stained teeth. The only man whom she could have possibly wanted in that crowd had stalked out of the garden with his boss's wife on his arm.

"Outta the way," growled a male with a rough, Kentucky accent.

A roly-poly ripple of silver—equipped with flashing fangs—bounded up the stairs, causing her suitors to stumble backwards and mutter oaths. However, none of her erstwhile beaux dared to openly challenge the double threat of a 50-pound raccoon and the Colt .45 that was strapped under Collie's buckskin coat. The older men scattered to a resentful distance.

Cass's rangy sidekick halted two steps below her, a tactic that still allowed the crown of the 17-year-old's Stetson to tower over her by an inch. Sadie found herself staring into a sun-blackened face and flint-colored eyes, which were uncommonly hard for a youth. She imagined she was staring into iced steel.

Finally, Collie's lips interrupted their sneer long enough to speak.

"Baron wants to meet for a screw. Name your terms."

Sadie winced. In her whoring days, she'd been accustomed to uncouth propositions from drunken cowboys, buffalo hunters, and wolfers. But for some reason, Collie's lack of sentimentality made her stomach clench.

And then she understood why. Hatred burned in the black centers of the boy's eyes.

"Baron?" she repeated hoarsely. Her mouth had gone dryer than Death Valley. "Are you referring to Senator Westerfield?"

Somehow, she forced the lump from her throat. She pasted on a coy smile.

Collie snorted at her attempt at flirtation. "Save it, woman. I'm not Cass. That means I'm not gonna put up with your games. You in or out?"

Sadie drew a shuddering breath. She didn't dare glance at

Baron. She suspected Collie was deliberately sabotaging the senator's proposition.

"You're loyal to Cass." She kept her voice low and even. "He's lucky to have a friend like you. You're not the kind to give trust easily."

"Don't change the subject." The boy's voice had a razor's edge. "This ain't about me."

"If you're *really* Cass's friend," she insisted in that same urgent undertone, "you'll get him the hell out of Baron's organization. Before it's too late. Before Cass gets himself *hanged.*"

Collie's eyes narrowed. At the age of 17, he already had a gunfighter's stare. The proof was unnerving. "What's it to you?"

"Everything."

She drew herself up to her full five-foot-eight-inches. She didn't give a damn what Collie thought of her, as long as he looked out for Cass.

"Now go tell your boss a lady doesn't like to be ignored," she said with as much temerity as she could muster. Tonight, at least, she had to behave every bit like the whore Collie thought her to be. "Baron had his chance with me. So he'll have to do a lot better than a slap and a tickle if he wants me to spy for him on Rexford Sterne."

CHAPTER 12

Later that night, Cass stood in the woods across from Wilma's back fence, dodging moonlight and resisting the urge to light a smoke. Shadow sheathed him from his Stetson to his boots. He'd stuffed his pale gold hair beneath his hat; he'd readied his bandanna for the mission to come; and he'd discarded all reflective silver, including his buckle and spurs.

He was planning to ransack another bedroom.

When Collie had caught up with him, minutes before Act II, Cass ordered the boy to babysit Baron for the rest of the evening. But Collie hadn't been fooled by Cass's excuse—namely, that he had a sniper to catch. The boy guessed Cass was planning a showdown with Sadie.

That's when Collie surprised him by blurting out the news: "Sadie said if I was really your friend, I'd get you out of Baron's organization before you get yourself hanged."

"Oh, did she now?"

"Why would she say a thing like that?"

"Beats me."

"Don't you think you should find out?" Collie demanded, looking troubled.

"Don't you think you should mind your own business?"

"Hell, you're such a pain in my ass, you *are* my business," Collie retorted. "'Sides. I'm tired of getting you off of murder charges, Snake Bait."

"You're *what?!*"

"You heard me," Collie said loftily. "I didn't ride all the way to Texas for a suntan. You promised me a Ranger badge. But the way I figure it, you screwed up so bad with Sterne, he's got us both blackballed for life."

"Baron's going to fix that."

"I don't trust Baron."

"You don't trust anybody."

"That's what helps me survive," Collie said flatly. "And speaking of surviving, Sadie offered to spy on Sterne—for a price. Maybe she's playing Baron and Sterne against each other. You're the only body in this town, who can see through that woman's lies. You need to find out what she's really up to, before she gets herself plugged."

Cass blew out his breath. He hated when Collie was right.

In any event, Cass had decided to search through Sadie's trunks. The ones Collie had found in the Confederate munitions cave beneath Wilma's kitchen.

As autumn leaves eddied above the ten-foot cedar planks that circled Wilma's tool shed, Cass waited impatiently for a friendly cloud to gobble up the moon. It was Devil's Eve, so he figured a party was underway at the brothel. No doubt every bouncer on the property was on alert for pranksters. He'd already seen a pair of Sid's deputies trot down the street, shotguns in hand, scanning the shadows for mischief-minded youths.

As the sky finally dimmed and the moon disappeared, Cass dragged his bandanna over his nose.

Time to make my own mischief.

With the stealth of his coyote namesake, he passed through cedar needles and thorn scrub, crossed the crackling grasses of the thirsty yard, and skirted the parlor window, where Cotton entertained himself by sharpening a 10-inch blade. No doubt the spinning whetstone was the Cajun's way of discouraging vandals.

By the time the racing cloud had thinned, allowing a few silver moonbeams to poke through the night, Cass had picked the lock on Wilma's gate and slipped inside the protective darkness of her tool shed. The smell of compost, chiefly potato skins and pumpkin guts, made his nose wrinkle. He let his eyes adjust to the moonlight, stabbing through the chinks in the roof.

Careful not to cause a resounding crash, he avoided the clutter of shovels and axes as he tiptoed across straw to reach the trap door in the northwest corner. Just as Collie had described, the tunnel's entrance was cannily disguised beneath the long, brown drape of a gardener's table, piled high with flower pots, muddy gloves, herb bundles, and a handy lantern.

A satisfied smile curved Cass's lips as he turned up the sputtering wick, raised the door, and poked his head into the blast of air that assailed his face.

Stairs. With little, woman-sized shoe prints. If he sucked down a deep enough breath, he could detect a lingering trace of patchouli, Sadie's favorite perfume.

Drawing a gun, he crept down the steps. The subterranean air was damp and refreshingly cool. He was almost sorry when, 50 paces later, he encountered another door. A rectangular peep hole was cut into the oak portal and set at the height of a man's eyes. Cass figured the hole had been used by the Confederates to identify friend from foe. Right now, yellow lantern light was pouring through the hole into the tunnel.

Cass doused his own lamp to avoid discovery. He'd staked out the house long enough to know Gator was manning the brothel's backdoor, and Cotton was stationed at the front entrance. Nevertheless, things could have changed in the six minutes he'd walked through the tunnel. God only knew who might be stationed in the cave. The smell of bourbon was strong—either from a recent spill, a leaking keg, or a bawd secretly bent on a bender.

Cass flattened himself against the wall to peer furtively through the hole. He couldn't see any humans among the crates and barrels. The space where Sadie had set up a rustic, folding bed and vanity was also clear.

Relieved by the observation, Cass tugged the bandanna off his chin and starting wielding his lock pick.

But when he shoved back the door on well-oiled hinges, he found himself tripping over a kid-sized broom, twined with black and red ribbons.

"Careful, clumsy. I'm warding off witches."

He nearly jumped out of his skin to hear that pipsqueak soprano with the Cajun accent. Only then did he spy sausage-style curls and smell the sweet scent of strawberry cologne. He cursed himself for being an idiot. How could he have missed the kid? She was sitting in plain sight on a barrel!

He glanced tensely at baskets of potatoes, crates of apples, kegs of liquor, and crates of cosmetics, but he couldn't see any other pint-sized spies. Of course, that didn't mean this kid wouldn't start screaming for Cotton and his pigsticker.

"Don't worry," the child said. "I don't want witches to know I'm here, either. That's why I was hiding."

She sat cross-legged on her throne, dressed in a beaver hat, strings of pearls, gobs of bracelets, and a dusty silk chemise that looked suspiciously like a ruined version of Sadie's old, rose-patterned negligee. Cass tamped down a flare of irritation. There was no helping the fact that the kid had seen his face. That meant he'd have to waste time, making friends. *And fast.*

Pasting on his Coyote grin, he mustered his notorious charm. "Well, you're doing a fine job, hoodwinking those witches, sugar."

She giggled. "I'm not Sugar. Sugar has dark hair. My name's Jazi."

"I reckon I owe you an apology, then."

"Naw. That's okay." She shrugged. "I come here when I can't sleep. It's a lot cooler than the attic. 'Sides. It's Devil's Eve. Who can sleep?" She held out her paper sack, with its caramelized pecans. "Want a praline, Cass?"

He choked down an oath to learn the kid knew his name. He wondered if she was the "neighbor child," who'd been eavesdropping on him and Gator.

"Wilma said you wear guns to stop bad men."

"She did, eh?" Cass frowned, still pondering the mystery of Jazi's origins. Why would Wilma take a neighbor's child to the Gala? Maybe the kid was related to one of Wilma's girls.

"Can you stop the witch too?" Jazi blinked big, hopeful eyes at him.

"Well, sure." Crossing the uneven limestone, he accepted her caramelized peace-offering. Mostly, he was stalling for time, since he had to invent some plausible excuse for being in the cave.

She loosed a gusty sigh of relief. "That's good. I told Mama we shouldn't come to this town. On the day she got the letter, I told her the evil witch wrote it to trick her. Why don't grown-ups listen to kids?"

"Hmm." He shot her a sideways glance. "I reckon they don't understand the dangers of witches, like you do."

She nodded, looking sad. "Mama doesn't even believe what *Wilma* says about witches."

Suddenly, Jazi started coughing. She seemed to have trouble catching her breath. Faintly alarmed, Cass patted her back until she recovered enough sensibility to retrieve the tin of Serenata's lemon pastilles under her thigh. She popped a couple of lozenges into her mouth and began sucking with great gusto.

"Better?" Cass demanded.

She nodded, but a few more moments passed before her labored breathing slowed, and she was able to speak again.

"Can I tell you a secret?" she rasped.

"Sure."

She fidgeted. She seemed to be mustering her courage. "The real reason I can't sleep is because…Well, because I keep dreaming about the witch. Mama said I can hide in Wilma's attic until after the farmers convention is over. But that means we'll be here for Halloween! And Halloween is the most powerful time for witches! I'm scared she'll find me and do something *awful!"*

Cass frowned. He didn't like anything to inspire so much fear in a child. Lowering to one knee before Jazi's barrel, he doffed his hat and took her hand. "Who's this witch that's got you so scared?"

She worried her bottom lip. "I...I don't know. But I can see her in my nightmares. Her head's on fire, and she's got bloody claws. She eats souls, and she makes folks sick with bad medicine."

"That sounds like a terrible nightmare, all right," Cass commiserated. "But honey, nightmares aren't real."

"I know what I saw!" Jazi snatched her hand away. "Just because you can't see it, doesn't mean it's not real!"

"I meant no offense," he soothed, chagrinned by the tears glistening in her eyes. "So this witch was doing bad things, huh? Was she hurting people you know?"

She nodded vigorously, the beaver hat plunking to the bridge of her nose. "She hurts you, and Collie, and maybe even Vandy!"

"Hmm." He darted her a sideways look. He wasn't terribly concerned about witches. To his way of thinking, they were women, and he'd been wrapping women around his little finger ever since he'd hit puberty.

He decided to change the subject. "So you know Collie, huh? How'd that happen?"

Sneezing now, thanks to the dust billowing off the critter on her head, she wiped the back of her hand across her nose. Cass solemnly offered her his neckerchief.

"He comes here at night—" she stopped talking long enough to blow her nose "—and other times when he's thirsty."

"Is that a fact?"

"Yep. I like to meet him with sandwiches and apples, and pralines for Vandy. Kind of like a picnic. I don't think Collie gets to eat much during the day. You know, 'cause Vandy beats him to all the food."

Cass did a masterful job of keeping a straight face.

"Anyhow, me and Collie swore a pact. I told him I wouldn't rat him out for stealing Wilma's liquor if he tells me a bedtime story. So last night, he told me about moonshining. And the night before that, he told me how to pick a lock."

Cass cleared his throat to disguise laughter. "So let me get this straight. Collie sneaks in here, steals Wilma's Wild Turkey, and tells you things that would raise every hair on your mama's head?"

"Uh-huh." Beaming, Jazi returned Cass's soiled bandanna. "And someday, we're going to get married."

Cass's grin turned lopsided as he imagined Collie ragged out in a bowtie and swallowtails. "Does Collie know about your wedding plans?"

"Of course, silly! He said we'd walk down the aisle when ducks whistle. Won't that be a lovely wedding march?"

Choking back laughter, Cass shoved his bandanna into his back pocket. "That sounds mighty fine, all right. But maybe I should talk to the rascal for you. Get him to speed things along. Otherwise, you might be waiting at the altar for a good, long spell."

"Naw." Jazi popped another praline into her mouth. "Collie still needs some training around womenfolk. I figure I'll let you do the hard work while I'm growing up. After all, I've got my hands full with Mama. She thinks I should marry a banker. Or maybe a grocer." Jazi stuck out her tongue and made an unladylike sound. "Wouldn't that be the most boring life ever? Pinching pennies and squeezing melons?"

Cass was trying so hard not to laugh, his eyes were swimming with tears. "You have a point."

"But you can't tell Mama about my wedding plans! Promise?"

"Cross my heart. We can swear a pinky oath to make it official."

Jazi looked confused. "You can't swear a Pinkie oath. You're a boy."

"Sure I can! Boys swear pinky oaths all the time."

"But boys can't be Pinkies."

He raised his eyebrows.

"*Lady Pinkerton agents,*" she emphasized, as if he were as dense as a slug of lead. "Why else would a woman own four sets of whiskers and a broach that sprays ink?"

Cass was pretty sure he was gaping like a guppy. "You mean…"

No. He shook his head, laughing a little at the notion. *That's not possible. Womenfolk don't sign up to be undercover tin-stars!*

So why did Sadie's behavior suddenly make a whole lot of sense?

Suddenly, Jazi jumped, as if a bee had stung her. "Uh-oh. I hear Mama calling. I have to go!"

Launching into a frenzy of activity, she hopped off the crate, tore off her hat and gew-gaws, shrugged out of the silk remnant that had once been Sadie's nightgown, and shoved all this grown-up plunder inside her throne. Then she gathered her patched, blue calico above her knees and dashed for the kitchen stairs.

"Be sure to blow out the lanterns, Cass," she called down in an urgent undertone. "Nobody wants another fire."

Jazi blew him a kiss. A flash of impish dimples was his last glimpse of the child before she lowered the trapdoor and latched it over his head.

For a long moment, he stood alone in that cavernous storage chamber, his mind spinning, his heart pounding hard enough to crack a rib. He couldn't believe he was seriously considering this lamebrain idea. But if Sadie really was a Pinkerton, then she had to have something that gave her immunity from prosecution. Something that would keep her safe from arrest if she fired a gun in the line of duty. No lawman worked without one.

His sniper's eyes probed every shadow, corner, and cobweb before his gaze alighted once more on the vanity. Standing on toothpick-style legs, it was constructed of whitewashed pine and painted with pink and yellow butterflies. Gingerbread frou-frou framed its beveled mirror, and the drawers were dominated by daisy-shaped knobs. The contraption looked like something out of a wealthy schoolgirl's nursery. It was the antithesis of anything Sadie had ever owned and was ever likely to own, if given a choice.

Acting on a hunch, he ripped off his gloves, grabbed a lantern, and crawled beneath the vanity's belly. Supple fingers, well-practiced in palming cards, picking locks, and other thieving skills, probed for concealed seams. The work was painstaking in such cramped quarters, but eventually, he was rewarded. He heard the click of metal and the rasp of sliding wood. Warily, he felt inside the secret compartment until he withdrew a thick and cumbersome envelope.

Cass's hands shook as he opened what proved to be a letter of commission. Air whistled past his teeth as he rubbed the pad of his thumb over the crisp, white vellum. There was no mistaking the embossed insignia of the famous Chicago-based detective agency. It matched the polished, brass badge that accompanied the letter. Both were imprinted with the words, Sarah Jane Michelson—Sadie's given name.

CHAPTER 13

Cass knew.

Sadie's heart beat a nervous little tattoo as she stood in the cave, staring at her outlaw lover's calling card.

A 10-inch pigsticker, with an elk-handled grip, was buried in the frame of her vanity's mirror. The blade pierced one of her casino handbills—through the nose, no less—and the following ransom note was scrawled in red lip paint across her face:

Want to see your daddy's button again, tin-star? Then get your freckled hiney to Aquacia Bathhouse at midnight. Come alone, or you'll be sorry. P.S.

She was forced to wrestle Cass's Bowie knife from the wood before she could turn the page and read his post script:

You owe me $800. Don't make me come and get it.

"You mean $400, swindler," she muttered, referencing their poker game. "And you owe me a new vanity!"

She flung the knife and message into a drawer and slammed it closed. How Cass had learned about the cave wasn't clear, but he'd obviously searched the vanity. And since he'd been the one who'd taught her how to create a trick latch in the first place...

Panic welled inside her. Dropping to her knees, she dove under the counter to inspect the sealing wax she'd affixed to a seam in the hidden drawer. It was broken, all right. After some frenzied pawing, she was able to unlatch the compartment and search its contents. To her relief, the badge and letter of commission were still in place.

Reprobate. Now she knew how Cass had been spending his time since intermission!

But Cass wasn't the only one who'd left the event early. Baron and Collie had, too. She couldn't help but wonder if the boy had relayed her message to the senator. She'd waited futilely for Baron to wade through the sea of admirers, mobbing her dressing room. Finally, after shooing the lovelorn from her quarters, she'd dragged on trousers and sneaked out the backstage door to update Wilma about Baron.

Not that there's anything to tell, she thought irritably.

The furtive creak of stairs made her jump. Like a gun-slinging veteran, she grabbed for her pocket pistol.

Another heartbeat passed before her eyes discerned the shadowy, female figure with bottled red hair. The bawd was standing on the third step beneath the kitchen landing, her voluptuous length sheathed in a slinky, black negligee.

"Poor Cassie." Her voyeur *tsked.* "Talking to herself. That's the first sign of madness, you know."

Sadie scowled. She would have recognized Randie's silvery, sniping soprano anywhere, even with the new, Cajun accent.

"Shouldn't you be humping a shark or something?" Sadie retorted acidly.

"Sorry to disappoint you, *chere,"* Randie taunted, continuing her descent. "I gave up sharks for bigger fish."

A memory of the shadowy redhead in Cass's doorway flashed through Sadie's mind. Her lip curled, and she cocked her gun hammer. "That's far enough."

Randie halted, arching a finely plucked eyebrow.

"What are you doing here?" Sadie demanded in iron tones.

"Talking to a ghost, it seems. So you're the Maisy my Boo has been sneaking off to visit."

Randie was Jazi's mother?

Mira. Miranda. The names made sense now. *Ballsy bitch.*

Randie had yet to bat an eyelash at the pistol, pointing with such unwavering accuracy at her chest. Her Cajun accent was even more believable than her Texas one, which made Sadie wonder if the bawd was really a native of New Orleans—or *N'awlins*, as Wilma liked to pronounce it.

"I must say," Randie drawled, "you're not being very hospitable. With manners like yours, one might think you were born in...well, a cave."

Hilarious.

Sadie refused to take her thumb off the gun hammer. Never mind that Wilma had vouched for this "Mira." Never mind that one of Wilma's *gris-gris* hung from Randie's neck. Sadie didn't trust Randie. As far as Sadie was concerned, Randie had plenty of motive to want her dead, and she had lots of shady admirers. Any one of them could have locked Sadie's door from the outside or hurled Greek Fire through her window at the Satin Siren.

"Intruders don't deserve hospitality," Sadie fired back.

"Well, if it isn't the pot calling the kettle black. Now you know how I felt after you and Dietrich destroyed everything I worked for."

"I nearly got crispy-fried because of you!"

"Me?" Indignation stained Randie's porcelain cheeks. "If my prayers had that kind of power, my husband would never have died. My Boo would never have suffered malaria. And I sure as hell would never have set foot inside the Satin Siren!"

Sadie's eyes narrowed.

"Now Tito is dead," Randie continued grimly. "His body was found in the woods. According to Marshal Wright, Tito's death wasn't an accident. I think whoever was gunning for me back in Galveston followed me here."

"You?"

Her chin raised a notch. "What, you think you're the only diva who ever made an enemy? Not everything's about *you*, Cassie. The bomb was tossed through my bedroom window.

Or at least, it *was* my bedroom window, up until the morning of the fire. You were in the wrong place at the wrong time, that's all."

Sadie frowned. Randie could be suffering from delusions of grandeur.

Then again...

"Why would your enemy want to kill Tito?" Sadie demanded. "You think he knew something about the fire? Something he didn't say to the arson investigators?"

"Maybe." Randie's eyebrows knitted. "Tito wasn't incredibly bright. But he always looked out for me. He was infatuated with me, in truth. It was a sticky situation. I just didn't feel the same way. Things got especially tense when..."

Her voice trailed off.

"When what?" Sadie pressed.

Randie's chin raised a notch. "When Boo got sick," she said tartly. "Tito wanted to look out for her too. And be a family."

Sadie eyed Randie speculatively. She suspected the older woman wasn't telling the whole truth. "Have you told Wilma any of this?"

"Good God, no. You know how she is, always fretting about evil spirits. It's bad enough she made me and Boo wear these herbal talismans," Randie added, sniffing her *gris-gris*. She wrinkled her nose and let the pouch flop back between her breasts.

"Besides, it's not like Wilma can do anything—except worry. That's why I paid a call on Marshal Wright tonight. I told him everything I know about Tito, the Satin Siren, and you. So don't be surprised if he comes calling, wanting your side of the story. He'll be trying to piece together any information you can tell him about Tito. If Tito really was murdered here, and his death had something to do with that Galveston fire, then the local law should be looking out for us."

Sadie wasn't moved by this peace overture. She was too

busy wondering why so many of the Galveston survivors had found their way to Lampasas. *Almost by design.*

"Why did you come to Lampasas?" she demanded.

Randie stiffened. Pink bloomed in her cheeks. "Why does anyone come to Lampasas? I thought the mineral springs might do Boo good. I suppose my timing could have been better. I didn't know the convention had gobbled up all the hotel rooms. As much as I adore Wilma, her house isn't the place for an impressionable child. We'll be leaving for New Orleans just as soon as Halloween is over.

"Mais well," she added briskly, squaring her shoulders and erecting a façade of aloofness once more. "As lovely as this reunion has been, I have to attend to my daughter. Boo needs her medicine. I can see she didn't leave her tin of pastilles on the crate. So unless you're still planning to shoot me for a crime I didn't commit, I'll continue my search upstairs."

Narrowly, Sadie watched Randie turn and climb the steps. Frustration flurried through her gut as the trap door banged closed.

Sass, class, and the protective instincts of a mother tigress.

No wonder Cass liked Miranda Reynolds.

Unlike Hancock Pool, with its mule-drawn trolley to the Grand Park Hotel, Aquacia was off the beaten track, about two miles north of town. It was also privately owned, which allowed wealthy patrons to rent the bathhouse after hours.

Remembering the adage, *"Pinkertons can't be too careful,"* Sadie tethered her horse about a tenth of a mile from the building. Beams from a round, amber moon filtered through the tree canopy, lighting her way, but her insistence on stealth made the walk tedious. She was glad she'd tugged one of her oldest, rattiest pair of dungarees from her trunk, because she encountered thistle bushes more than once as she forged a path toward her destination.

Finally, she reached a clearing. The spa was nestled in a park-like setting of golden cedar elms, fiery maples, and broadleaved evergreens called live oaks. Blood-red tiles capped white stucco that made the Spanish-styled structure fairly glow in the moonlight.

The tinkling splash of the courtyard's fountain reached her ears. Tugging her slouch hat low over her bearded face, she flitted past a charming walkway of terra cotta tiles to the moon-drenched sun porch, which was attached to the main pool. No windows had been built into the bathing chamber, just an enormous, stained-glass bubble dome. Nevertheless, if she strained her ears, she could detect a rhythmic flutter-kick beyond the door, which Cass had propped open.

He was inviting her to be seduced.

Thinking of Randie in his hotel bedroom, she scowled.

Two can play the conquest game, Rutter.

For a long moment, Sadie stood in the doorway, cicada song swelling behind her in the woods. Moonbeams spilled through the skylight, illuminating dust motes that danced like fairy magic over verdant waters. A long, lean swimmer's body was power-stroking through the pool. Completely naked, Cass's exquisite length glimmered like a torpedo-shaped pearl.

She told herself she should arrest him for breaking-and-entering. Unfortunately, *she* was arrested—even mesmerized—by the view: emerald waters sliding over alabaster flesh; corded limbs surging through frothy bubbles; the breadth and power of rippling shoulders, rising above the wave. Most endearing of all was the sight of his own dimpled moons, winking at the celestial orb that peeked slyly through the skylight.

Seeing him so appealingly undressed, Sadie had a hard time repressing a little growl. Cass's exquisite musculature was a sculptor's dream—and a woman's wet fantasy. But then, he'd always been an athlete, taking care to keep his reflexes as sharp as his mind.

Her man-shark hadn't noticed her arrival yet. That gave her time to plot her strategy. She raced him along the pool's longest edge, beating him to the shallows, where she waited triumphantly with a scowl. She was loath to let him know just how much she enjoyed watching his shameless virility cleave her ominous, black silhouette on the water.

When he pretended not to notice her, looming over him like an angry volcano goddess, she tugged his Bowie knife from her belt and flung it. The blade struck the deck's wooden planks above his head with a resounding *thunk.*

That got his attention.

He reared up out of the water, tossing back his hair in a gleaming arc of spray that looked like a moonbow around his golden head.

"I stopped by Wilma's place," she announced. Planting her fists on her hips, she straddled that erect and quivering hilt. "What the hell is *this?"*

Cass grinned. He trailed his wicked gaze from the knob on the hilt to the apex of her spreading thighs. "I'm not sure. But it looks illegal."

"You're illegal."

"That's why you like me."

She snorted. "As far as I'm concerned, Wright should have locked you in the calaboose and thrown away the key."

"Aw. Whose fluffy, white pillow did Vandy *really* soil? Yours or loverboy's?"

"You think vandalism's a game?"

"Life's a game, sweetheart. I just play by different rules."

"This from the man who wants to be a Ranger."

"I'm starting to have second thoughts about Rangerhood," he said drolly. "Women aren't allowed on the force."

"Oh, so now you're all about equality."

He winked. "Mostly, I'm about undercover work."

She didn't dare let her lips twitch.

"So tell me," he drawled. "How does a woman who couldn't bear to breathe the same air as a tin-star wind up becoming one?"

He was probing. Her guard raised a notch.

"If you can't fight 'em, join 'em," she answered breezily.

"Now that doesn't sound like you."

"Let's just say I liked the perks."

His eyes narrowed with speculation. "Care to be more specific?"

"Oh, you know. Steady pay. Lots of travel."

"And a tyrant boss to take the place of a husband?"

With a sudden flash of insight, she guessed where his questions were leading. The scapegrace was actually concerned about her! The notion warmed her heart in a dangerously romantic way.

"Does putting up with *tyrants* sound like me?"

He cocked his head, studying her. "No. But tyranny does sound like Sterne's style."

She rolled her eyes. "Right. I forgot who I was talking to."

"'Course, if you *like* being bossed around these days…." He flashed his Coyote grin.

"My, aren't you the considerate villain."

"Just doing my part to keep womankind sated and happy."

Dog.

Plotting his comeuppance, she let her gaze roam over the chamber. Tiled with colorful, Mexican-style images of suns, moons, and stars, it was the perfect backdrop for a heavenly body, like Cass's. Great earthen pots of yellow lantana, silver sages with lavender flowers, bushy dwarf palms and other drought-resistant flora had been cleverly arranged on limestone tiers to form a grotto, beneath which the spring's source bubbled forth. White colonnades, painted with fanciful sunflowers marched along the pool's eastern side, closest to the vaulted doorway that led to a pitch-black corridor and parts unknown.

Finally, Sadie spied what she'd been searching for: the glint of silver. Cass had stashed his all-black wardrobe in the shadows, under one of the grotto's slabs. Beside his boots and spurs sat his Stetson. He loved that hat almost as much as he loved breathing. Once, after he'd lost everything except his guns during a particularly bad craps shoot, she'd watched him bet his horse for the return of his hat—not for the knife that had made him a mumblety-peg champion. Not for his award-winning rodeo buckle. Not even for the hand-tooled Justin boots that he lovingly polished each morning until he could glimpse his stubbled mug on the toes.

The fact that he had stolen back his gear and his gelding hours later was beside the point.

"I don't suppose you *paid* to enter this bathhouse after hours," she accused.

"Why rent a pool when you own a lock pick?"

"Is that a *confession*, hooligan?"

"Are you going to arrest me?" he countered hopefully.

"Not if you're going to like it."

"Then I confess. I hate to swim. Especially when I'm butt-naked and all alone."

"Isn't that a shame?" Her smile was smug. "'Cause all I came for was the button."

She turned on her heel and headed for his trousers. She was intent on ransacking his pockets—maybe even tossing his hat into the pool.

"You mean this button?" he challenged, opening his fist. Brass flashed from the chain that slid through his fingers.

She sucked in her breath.

"Take another step toward that hat, Tin-Star, and the button gets it." He was wading backwards into the pool's center, her keepsake dangling precariously above murky waters.

"If you don't want to walk out of this bathhouse in your birthday suit," she retorted, annoyed that he'd out-coyoted her, "you'd better get your butt *and* my button up on this pool deck!"

He flashed all his pretty teeth. "I got plenty of duds stashed in Baron's private locker. You only got one button."

Baron has a private locker?

She filed that information away for future reference. Then she shot a vengeful glance at the Stetson.

Retaliating, he let the chain slide lower.

"You wouldn't dare!"

"Try me."

She fumed. The water was lapping around his pectorals now. If he dropped Daddy's button, even by accident, she wasn't sure she could ever find it in the pool's dark, green depths—at least, not by moonlight.

"If you lose Daddy's button, I swear to God, I'll skin you alive!"

"Be my guest. 'Course, you'll have to dive in first."

Donkey butt.

She eyed the water dubiously. In this part of Texas, spring-fed pools could be colder than a witch's tit—and that was in the sunshine.

"Truce?" she offered grudgingly.

"Spoken like a loser."

"A loser who pocketed four-hundred of *your* dollars, sucker."

He snorted at this dig. "Where'd you learn to count poker chips, cheater?"

"Cheater!?"

"Why, sure. If it looks like a duck, and waddles like a duck—"

"You are *so* dead, Cassidy." She ripped off the first boot.

He twirled the chain around his fingers, quacking like a mallard.

She ripped off the second boot. "You're fowl, all right!"

He winked, dunking the button like a teabag.

Her hat, trousers, shirt, and breast bindings flew off at his threat. Gritting her teeth, she took the plunge, leaping feet first into the shallows. The shock of that icy water ripped a shriek from her throat, especially when it slapped the undersides of her breasts and puckered her nipples. Sputtering curses against him and all his ancestors, she planned to drown him the moment her blood thawed.

Meanwhile, her man-shark was knifing through the water

on a collision course with her. She glimpsed taut buttocks, gleaming like snow-capped hillocks in the lunar light. She was almost sorry when the show ended. He surfaced before her, a cascade of liquid emerald rolling off moon-chiseled shoulders, biceps, and pectorals and an abdomen that might have been cut from white granite. Tossing back his hair, he revealed starlit eyes that twinkled with mirth.

"Aren't you forgetting something?"

Uncertain what he meant, she shot her sea monster a warning glare. It didn't stop him from wading closer.

"Where's my button, felon?"

"Reckon you'll have to search me for it, detective."

His head lowered, and his tongue slid along her bottom lip.

That's when she remembered, to her utter mortification, she was wearing whiskers.

But Cass, being Cass, was thoroughly amused by the sheer wrongness of kissing a bearded woman. He rubbed his chin against her chin. He nibbled the bristly end of her mustache. From the corner of her eye, she glimpsed his dimples. Darling. Devilish. Dangerous to any female with a functioning brain.

So what did that say about her?

"The glue tastes like honey." His murmur throbbed with sin. He reached for her waist.

"Don't you dare get my face wet!" She reared back, shoving a hand between their chests. "I'm wearing my favorite beard, and it has to look presentable after you ravish me!"

His chuckle was wolfish. The next thing she knew, he'd kicked her feet out from under her. She squealed in protest, but it was already too late. Cold, dark waters were closing over her head. She came up blind and sputtering, her sodden curls plastered over her nose, her whiskers floating somewhere in a sea of bubbles.

"Ducks don't have beards," he said cheerfully. "'Course, now you look more like a drowned rat."

"I hate you."

He whooped and splashed her in the face.

"All right. That does it, slug-head."

She pounced, but he fended off her headlock, and they had a rollicking wrestling match in the shallows. As her legs grappled with his, she felt the small pouch that he'd strapped above his right knee. But it was hard to plunder pouches when his wicked fingers kept dancing across her flesh, stroking and tickling. She tried to dunk his cocky head, but the water worked against her, slowing the Judo moves she'd learned in Pinkie training.

"Is that the best you can do?" he taunted.

She grabbed a fistful of his hair, yanked his head lower, and thrust her tongue into his mouth. He growled. The rumble vibrated deep into her belly, awakening her smoldering volcano, shooting sparks of lightning along her nerves. When she locked her thighs around his waist, he turned predator. He kneaded her buttocks with powerful hands. He slanted his mouth across hers, demanding more of his feast.

Now she was panting, but he was too. His arousal was hot, like velvet-sheathed steel sliding against her belly. She rubbed his swollen head, delighting in his throttled groan. Knowing his weakness, she clamped her teeth over his earlobe and tormented the ticklish inner space. He staggered, and she smiled wickedly, enjoying the way his nipples pebbled against her chest.

But Cass had tricks of his own that could drive her wild. Most had to do with his mouth and her cleft, but with the water in the way, he shifted tactics. He arched her back over an arm, suckling a ripe, rosy breast while circling his thumb in an insidious pattern of pressures over her pleasure bud. She bit back a moan, nearly crawling out of her skin when his forefinger finally, slyly probed her. She hiked her hips in shameless wanting, and he obliged, taking his time to please her, to tease her, to milk her restless yearning to a fever pitch.

"Take me Tiger," he murmured, "make me yours."

So you can leave me again?

For an embarrassing moment, her eyes filled with tears. She was aghast at her traitorous rise of sentiment. A woman like her couldn't afford to feel. If caring for Cass had been unwise as a whore, it was sheer lunacy as a Pinkerton. Cass excelled at many things, but fidelity wasn't one of them. He was the minstrel of charm, the sensei of seduction...

And the wizard of pleasure. An exquisite, aching kind of pleasure that could leave her shattered in a jumbled heap of emotions she didn't dare explore. His expert caress fanned her inner fires in a way that no other man's could. Friend and foe, lover and rival, student and master—that was Cass. When the stars faded and daylight bloomed, she could count on him to ride away. Because that's what the Rebel Rutter *always* did.

She squeezed her eyes closed.

She blocked out the hurtful memories.

Hugging his shoulders tighter, she locked her ankles over his buttocks. He shuddered as her hips sank, driving his sleek, slick length into her smoking core. She delighted in the erotic sensation of rubbing bellies and the sinful indulgence of sensitized nipples, dragging through silky man fur. His heart beat a wild, ecstatic cadence against her breasts; her blood thrilled to the surge of his pleasure.

With each rhythmic pump of her hips, she reveled in the corded strength of his thighs and the primal power of his thrusts. He was like her mountain, her Gibraltar. On the outside, icy green tidal waves buffeted her body; on the inside, a firestorm crashed and flashed, raining stars and comets on her senses.

And then came the explosion. Crackling, sizzling, her awareness rocketed through a heavenly storm.

Cass staggered, gasping her name. He clutched her heart fiercely to his, burying his face in her hair. Only a desperate act of will could silence the rapture that wanted to rip from her throat in wild, fearless song:

Always yours, I shall be,
    Born for you...

He must never know, she warned herself sternly. *He must never, ever know...*

"Sadie." He was panting. "How could you not tell me you were a Pinkerton?"

Emotionally drained, physically spent, she slid from his hips. She hadn't expected her knees to buckle. He caught her waist from behind, and for one precious moment longer, she leaned against him, serenaded by the thrumming of his heart.

"Here," he murmured.

The button swung before her tear-glazed eyes. She swept aside her sopping hair, and he fastened the chain around her neck.

Then he turned her shoulders to face him. His fingers, warm and tender, steadied the bauble where it nestled among her freckles, just above her cleavage. She gazed down at his big, sun-bronzed hand, and another forbidden frisson of feeling threatened her composure.

He'd bought her a gold chain.

"Sadie," he murmured, cupping her cheek with his palm. His eyes were like velvet midnight, soft, luminous and full of stars. "I know how lawmen can throw their weight around. I know how they can bully folks, making it seem like you don't have a choice, except to do their bidding."

"Cass—"

"Listen to me." He was holding her face between both hands now and staring into her eyes with an intensity that sent shockwaves to her soul. "Sterne got you into this mess with assassins and arsonists. But you don't have to be afraid any more. I can help you. *Baron* can help you. All you have to do is tell me—"

A rifle blast shattered the night, echoing like an explosion in the room.

CHAPTER 14

Cass cursed, bowling her off her feet. They went down with a frenzied splash. Sadie tried to break free of his arms, but he was shoving her into deeper waters. *Safer* waters.

For a long moment, she was too busy retrieving her footing and trying to swipe hair out of her eyes to surface. Through the bubble fizz above her head, she glimpsed Cass looming over her, like the marble bust of some Grecian warrior-god. His head was cocked to the west. He appeared to be listening.

By the time she'd breached the surface and gulped down air, he'd become Lucifire, minus his guns.

"Head down," he snapped.

She obeyed reluctantly, straining to peer past his hips and over the edge of the pool. As far as she could tell, no assassin was threatening from the deck or the sun porch beyond. Since the skylight wasn't shattered, Sadie concluded that neither she nor Cass had been targets.

That's when the second shot rang out.

"Damnation," Cass muttered, splashing for the deck. "Who's shooting out here after midnight?"

She gave chase. "Maybe Collie's just bored and treeing varmints—"

"Collie's in town. Guarding Baron."

Cass was throwing on his clothes, buckling on his guns.

She quailed to think how much this scene resembled their last night together in Dodge: gunfire blazing outside her bedroom window, Cass punching his legs into trousers and pumping bullets into his Colts. That night, she'd feared she would never see him alive again.

The same worry plagued her now.

"I'm coming with you!" she insisted, hauling herself out of the pool.

"You're staying here. Out of sight."

"Dammit, Cass, I know how to fire a—"

"Stay put, woman!" He blasted her with the heat of his glare. "I won't let you die on me again!" Snatching up his pigsticker, he sped down the hall like a black knife, cleaving even darker shadows.

Sadie hurled an oath after his domineering head and grabbed for her trousers. A heartbeat later, she was cursing her denim. It kept sticking to her wet skin. By the time she'd shimmied her dungarees up over her buttocks, the glint of Cass's pale hair had vanished. She couldn't hear the echo of his boots. Only the usual night sounds reigned: katydids, tree frogs, cicadas, owls.

She blew out her breath. Between her shivers and her adrenaline, she despaired that her shaking fingers would ever get her shirt buttoned. Since no one in their right mind would think she was a man without her breast bindings, she didn't bother attaching her suspenders or tucking in her shirttails. She simply stomped on her boots and plunked on her hat.

After the relative brilliance of the pool room, the hall was blacker than Satan's heart. Sadie found herself stumbling blindly into picture frames, potted plants, and towel tables. No wonder Cass had charged down the center of the corridor, instead of edging along the walls.

She braved the yawning void of the hall's center, but she was loath to trot, much less charge into that gloom, since she couldn't see her hand in front of her face. When she came to a four-way intersection, capped by another bubble dome, she didn't have a clue which way he'd turned.

She was just thinking Cass's wisdom to stay put might have been a good idea, when suddenly, her ears caught the rumble of voices, rolling out of the southern corridor where the men's dressing rooms were located.

"...When I heard you got paroled." Baron's resonant baritone carried through a deep, thick silence as unnerving as any tomb's.

"No thanks to you," the outlaw growled in a surly, midwestern accent.

"My attorney kept you from getting hanged in an open-and-shut case. Use the smarts God gave you, Hank. You're finished here. Get the hell out of Lampasas."

"And buy a train ticket with what? My good looks?"

"I'll make the arrangements. Just stay away from Poppy, you hear?"

"Aw, you've gone and hurt my feelings," Hank taunted. "'Course, you being up for reelection and all, I can see how you'd be a bit antsy, not wanting certain things to leak to the press. Say! Maybe we could rendezvous at the ranch. I could take care of your rustlers, like old times."

"I already got a regulator," Baron said curtly.

"You mean that pretty blond with the flashy rig?" Hank snorted. "Hell, Cassidy's as green as split pea soup. I'm not even sure he shaves."

"Do yourself a favor, Hank. Stay off my land."

"Ooh. Now I'm shaking in my boots. You don't think I can take Pretty Boy."

"I don't think you can keep your ass out of jail long enough for me to worry about it. But just so we're clear: if you take on Cass, you're on your own."

"And if your Golden Boy takes me on, what then? A man's gotta right to self-defense."

"Nothing you ever do is self-defense."

Hank chuckled. "That reminds me, boss. You owe me my hard-earned wage, with interest, since I couldn't collect my usual fee in jail."

Sadie's heart was fluttering like a hummingbird's wings. Recalling that Baron kept a private locker in the building, she wasn't surprised when she heard the unmistakable clicks of a combination lock, followed by the squeal of rusted hinges.

Next, she heard a thump. The noise could have come from anything being tossed onto the floor: a heap of dirty towels. Greenbacks in a sack. Baron's rolling head. Sadie's imagination was going wild. She had to get close enough to see this Hank.

"Much obliged," Hank grunted.

Hank didn't sound "obliged" at all. In fact, he sounded like a greedy, barn-sized pig, except Sadie had too much respect for swine to include Hank among them.

"Wait a minute," Hank growled in ominous tones. "This ain't my usual fee."

"You'll get your usual fee when you get your ass out of Texas. Like we agreed."

"I don't like being stiffed."

"I don't like being blackmailed."

Chills scuttled down Sadie's spine. So Baron had hired Hank at some point to "take care of rustlers." Sadie didn't need much imagination to think that murder was involved, or that Hank had killed for Baron many times in the past. Now Hank was threatening to talk. But who would believe the vermin? Hank must be able to produce some really damaging evidence—evidence that would convince the courts to take an outlaw's word over a senator's!

Excited by her discovery, Sadie had visions of closing her case. She couldn't let the men walk out of hearing now, not when one of them might say something concrete that would let her send Baron to a hanging judge!

As their voices moved down the hall, she eased her pistol from its holster and began the nerve-wracking process of feeling her way along the walls. Her eyes were slightly more useful now, thanks to moonbeams from the skylight behind her. She passed closed doors, which she suspected were massage chambers, dressing rooms, and assembly parlors. She also tiptoed past a set of stairs, where she could hear the gurgle of water—most likely the spring's tufa chamber. When she came to the next intersection, she eased her head around the corner.

The first thing she realized was she'd been walking in a circle. Baron and Hank had halted several feet from the entry to the pool. With the glimmers of moon-dappled water dancing over their forms, Sadie could discern vague details, like Baron's walking stick and Hank's pointed boot toes. The assassin proved to be a man of average height, average build, and average hair color. He was the perfect, nondescript nobody most folks wouldn't notice in a crowd—until he started firing his gun.

She squinted to get a clear view of his face, but his Stetson shadowed the parts that weren't covered by scruffy whiskers and lank, shoulder-length hair. His most recognizable feature proved to be his voice: cold. Guttural. Sneering.

"So how's the missus? Still crazier than a loon?"

"Runs in the family—so I'm told," Baron added snidely.

Hank barked with laughter. "You know, a love like that can be a poison."

"Prison taught you about love, eh?"

"I learned a lot of things in prison," Hank drawled. "I also met a couple acquaintances of yours—and some cronies of your railroad pals, too. Maybe I'll swing by the hotel. Introduce myself proper to your rich friends."

"Be my guest. The Grand Park is crawling with tin-stars. And speaking of tin-stars, remember the Ranger who got you locked up in state prison? You can pay your respects to him at the Globe Hotel."

Sadie's hackles rose. *I have to warn Rex!*

They'd turned their backs on her and started walking again. Suddenly, Hank's boots slid out from under him. He sputtered a blood-curdling oath but recovered his balance with the agility of a rattler. Squatting with a vengeance, he swiped his fingers across the terra cotta tiles leading to the pool's vaulted entry.

"Some bastard was bathing here tonight! These drip-drops lead down yonder—"

Sadie was so busy backing around the corner, she never saw the attendant's station. Her hip slammed into it, causing a loud thump and a metallic crash.

Holy freaking crap!

Hank charged after her. She could hear his boots pounding like sledge hammers above the crashing of her heart. She fled past the first room and ducked inside the second, only to learn, to her horror, that she'd entered a billiards parlor with no window and no bolt for the door. She was trapped!

Suddenly, a familiar, Kentucky drawl groused in the hall: "Dang crazy varmint. You want to wake the dead? C'mere! Gimme that! I told you to stop washing my gloves in that green stinkin' pool."

Collie!

God bless his quick thinking.

Muffled growls reverberated through the corridor, as if the boy was wrestling Vandy for his supposedly sopping glove. Under the cover of this cacophony, Sadie heard Hank's furtive retreat and what sounded like the squealing of the sun porch door.

Collie raised his laconic baritone above Vandy's ferocious snarls. "Baron! You down this way?"

Sadie held her breath, counting five heartbeats before Baron's irritated voice boomed:

"I told you to wait outside, boy!"

"Well, dang. Blame a body for doing his job. You've been holed up in here for a coon's age. How was I supposed to know you weren't drowned?"

The scrabble of claws on terra cotta was accompanied by the steady thumping of a long, rangy stride. Tense and quivering, Sadie tightened her grip on her pistol as the boy strolled past her door. She had no doubt Collie knew she was hiding. The question was: Did Baron?

A deep grunt and the faint clinking of what might have been a belt buckle reached Sadie's straining ears.

"Hell, kid. Can't a man crap in peace?"

"Sure, Baron. But Cass told me to watch over you."

"While I'm taking a *dump?*"

"Aw, don't be that way. Cass thinks of you like his own Pa. He'd plug me himself if something happened to you on my watch."

"Where *is* Cass?" Baron demanded in grudging tones. "He's been missing ever since the recital."

"Last I saw, he was paying a call on Dr. Cuervo. And asking ol' José to cure him of redhead fever."

Their voices were fading now, along with the echo of boots in the corridor.

Silently, shakily, Sadie slumped against the door.

Kid, I owe you a lot more than a new pair of gloves.

Worried Hank might be lingering in the woods outside Aquacia, Sadie didn't dare exit the bathhouse through a door. Instead, she sneaked out the window of an assembly room, trusting a hardy live oak and a bristling row of forsythia bushes to cover her escape.

Fortunately, Cass was the one to find her, not Hank. When she threw herself into his arms, he dragged her back into the brush, a night predator intent on devouring his prey. His demanding kisses rained fire on her senses. Heat coiled in the furnace below her belly, threatening to incinerate her wiser half. She had to tear her mouth free.

"Baron will see us!"

"Baron's long gone," Cass growled, gripping her buttocks with a possessive hand and tilting her hips against his. "You could have broken your fool neck crawling through that window. Didn't I tell you to wait for me?"

"But Hank's getting away!" she gasped.

"Who?" he mumbled against her throat.

"Baron's regulator!"

Cass stiffened, raising his head to lock stares. "Come again?"

She bit her lip. Despite the thunderheads racing past the moon, and the patterns of shadow they cast across his face,

Cass's upset was unmistakable.

"Didn't Collie tell you what happened?"

"No," Cass said slowly, taking a step back. "Collie and I didn't get a chance to talk. At least, not since I found him rubbing out Pancake's hoof prints. He told me Baron came here to fetch something out of his locker. When Collie saw my horse, he hid Pancake and fired shots as warning. He figured Baron would be pissed to know I wasn't watching Poppy."

"But didn't you see a man fleeing through the sun porch?"

"I was on the other side of the building," Cass said in gravelly tones. "Tell me about Hank."

Grimly, Sadie explained that Hank was a killer, whom Baron had hired in the past, and that he was itching to prove he was faster on the draw than Cass. She recounted how Hank was blackmailing Baron for some sordid deed. Then she extrapolated a bit. She added her opinion that Baron was going to expect Cass to kill people too—and maybe even face off with Hank, to end the blackmail.

Collie hadn't been exaggerating when he'd said that Cass loved Baron like a father. The only thing that Cass heard in this whole, damning tale was Baron was in danger from a hired gun.

Sadie shot her lover an exasperated look. "Baron wouldn't be in this mess if he didn't murder inconvenient sodbusters."

"That's ridiculous. Baron isn't the type you want to cross in a business deal, but that doesn't mean he murders folks."

"Baron might not pull the trigger with his own finger, but in the eyes of the law, he's just as guilty as the man who does! What if you fall out of favor with him, Cass? What if he tries to pin Hank's crimes on you? Who do you think the courts will believe? A gunslinger, who ran from a murder charge for 12 years? Or a Texas Senator?"

Cass squared his jaw and shook his head. "And if I walk through a lightning storm, I might get zapped. That doesn't mean it's going to happen."

"My God, do you need to see *blood* to accept the truth?"

"I'm telling you, woman, Baron didn't hire Hank! Someone else did—to kill Baron!"

"Haven't you heard a word I've said?" Sadie countered impatiently. "Hank's not going to kill his golden goose!"

"Hank was the sniper on the roof!"

"Then Hank's extorting Baron for *putting* him on that roof!"

"Can't you hear how crazy that sounds?"

Sadie wanted to shake him. "You weren't in the bathhouse. You didn't hear their argument. You're going to have to trust my judgment."

"Your *judgment?* Hell, you've been gunning for Baron ever since Galveston! You're so deep in Sterne's back pocket, you don't know which way is up. You'd do anything to save Sterne from a senate investigation— including seducing Baron right under his wife's nose! Wasn't that the original plan? Until I came along and threw a wrench in the works?"

She sucked in her breath.

His laughter was hollow. "You used to be a lot smarter, darlin'," he said bitterly. "A whole lot smarter than this."

"What's *that* supposed to mean?"

"It means you haven't left the whorehouse as far behind as you think."

Her hand lashed out. He caught it before it could strike his cheek.

For a long moment, they stood quivering, sucking down air, two predators ready to pounce. Thunder rumbled in the distance; lightning spat behind the crown of Cass's hat.

Finally, she yanked her wrist from his grasp.

The moon had dipped below the tree canopy. As much as Sadie would have liked to track Hank, she figured the task would be impossible now. If a storm really did unleash itself—rather than dumping the usual dry rain—then Hank would head back to town. It was only two miles away. On a night like Devil's Eve, he'd find plenty of mischief to entertain himself.

"Collie was in the bathhouse too," she bit out. "He can

settle this argument."

"I'll be real interested to hear what Collie has to say."

Why would you take the word of some beardless whelp over mine!?

Cass whistled for Pancake, but she had no intention of getting cozy with her lover in his saddle. She turned on her heel and set a course for her mare.

CHAPTER 15

Sadie didn't speak a word during their eight-minute jog back to town. But that was fine by Cass. If she'd accused Baron of hiring contract killers another second longer, he might have stuffed his handkerchief in her mouth. Baron was the *victim* here! Hank Sharpe had broken out of jail—or he'd been miraculously paroled.

In either event, Cass didn't need much imagination to guess why Hank was in Lampasas: to seek revenge. Baron had kicked him off the ranch, and he'd stopped paying Hank in jail. So *of course* Hank was blackmailing Baron. Hank liked to torture folks right before he watched the light go out in their eyes. Extortion was just the beginning.

But Cass wasn't the only man familiar with Hank's history as Baron's hired hand. In fact, he was willing to wager that Pendleton knew more than he did. Recalling his conversation with Marisol, Cass wondered if Pendleton had been following Baron's order to pay Hank's extortion fee.

Or did Pendleton use his own money to hire Hank?

The latter possibility chilled Cass's blood. Baron trusted few men as thoroughly as he did Pendleton. The secretary knew every detail of Baron's ranching business, political funding, and campaign schedule. Pendleton could be as dangerous as Hank was. And if the two men were conspiring against Baron…

Cass's stomach roiled. He honestly didn't know if he could stop The Ventilator.

Eight years ago, on Baron's ranch, Cass had suspected Hank of pinning a theft on Lynx. When matters escalated, Cass had lost control of his tongue. Hank had demanded a high-noon showdown to "repair his honor."

Lynx had been horrified by the news. He'd threatened to confront Hank first—*knowing* he wouldn't survive the shootout—if Cass refused to flee Burnet County with him. So grudgingly, Cass had left the Rocking W. At the time, he'd blamed the Cherokee for making him look like a coward. But secretly, Cass had been afraid. He'd known Hank possessed the faster quickdraw and the steelier nerve. At 17, Cass hadn't been able to compete with The Ventilator.

At 25, Cass still didn't know if he was fast enough.

But he kept his tongue firmly between his teeth. He didn't confide his worries to Sadie. Nor did he confess his private vow to stop Hank or get killed trying.

At Western Avenue, when she wheeled her horse and left him choking on her dust, Cass figured she was heading for Sterne's hotel so she could warn him about Hank. Cass followed discreetly, until he was certain she got safely inside the Globe.

Then Cass spurred Pancake toward the Grand Park, one mile further west. He figured no matter what he asked Pendleton, the secretary would lie. So Cass's strategy was to question Collie. The boy might know where Hank had gone after leaving the bathhouse. With nothing but suspicion and circumstantial evidence to pin on Pendleton, Cass was disadvantaged. If he wanted Baron to believe his allegations, he'd have to find concrete proof. However, a fussbudget like Pendleton would have buried the evidence, and Cass didn't have time to search for it.

That's why Cass figured that neutralizing Hank was the quickest way to guarantee Baron's safety—at least for the night.

So Cass set off to question Collie. He expected to find the

boy sucking down Wild Turkey outside the Westerfield's suite and grousing about having bodyguard duty on Devil's Eve. But Collie wasn't in the hotel's hall. Nor was he in the bedroom.

Cass frowned. No light spilled from the crack under the Westerfields' suite. Maybe Baron had dragged Collie off to one of the hotel's myriad gaming rooms. Considering the size of the grounds, Cass could have spent more than an hour, searching fruitlessly for Collie.

Feeling pressured for time, Cass abandoned his plan to confer with his sidekick. Mounting up again, he cantered the half-mile back to Third Street and Wilma's boarding house. He hoped Cotton or Gator would have news about The Ventilator.

But Cass's strategy changed again when he led Pancake into the brothel's livery. Sterne's dappled-gray Quarter Horse was snoozing in a stall. Like its rider, the gelding was legendary in these parts. Steel could run down any four-legged renegade in Texas. He had the spirit of a Comanche warrior and the stamina of a locomotive. He suffered no one to sit on his back except Sterne.

By comparison, Pancake was a big lovable moocher who didn't care who rode him, as long as a bag of oats was at the end of the journey.

Wistfully, Cass ran his hand over Steel's rump and received a snort for his impertinence. Collie and Baron were right: Cass needed to be more choosey about his horseflesh if he wanted to be a tin-star, whom outlaws feared.

That notion put the spurs to his already straining temper.

So Ranger Holier-Than-Thou is cheating on Sadie and dandying Wilma's bawds on his knee? Why doesn't that surprise me?

Cass's intent wasn't clear when he decided to confront Sterne. On the one hand, he was pragmatic enough to want Sterne's cool head, seasoned tracking skills, and legendary quickdraw on his side during a manhunt for The Ventilator. On the other hand, Cass was so full of piss and vinegar, he couldn't pass up this opportunity for his long-awaited reckoning with the man who'd ruined his life. The trouble was, Wilma prided herself on protecting her clientele. Nothing short of a crowbar could have pried Sterne's room number from Cotton's or Gator's mouth.

So Cass decided to sneak through a second-story window.

Breaking and entering was child's play for an outlaw of Cass's accomplishments. Tracking Sterne to the appropriate bedroom proved more challenging, but Cass eventually arrived at the ornately carved cherry wood of Wilma's boudoir door. When Sterne's laughter floated into the hall, Cass's hackles rose.

Stooping, he peeked through the keyhole. The room was well-lighted with tapers and gas lamps; even so, he couldn't see much from his angle, just that Sterne and Wilma were still clothed and Sterne had shed his gun belt. For what Cass had in mind, he didn't need to know more.

He rapped once and pushed inside.

Shock registered on Wilma's face. Her eyes flew from his scowl to his tethered .45s. When she leaped to her feet, tangerine chiffon billowed around her olive skin like a tropical storm.

"Cass! What—"

"I have business with Sterne."

"How *dare* you come bursting through my—"

Cass yanked his buckle. His cartridge belt swung off his hips. He tossed it across a plump, wingback chair, and Wilma's sputtering paused. She darted anxious eyes toward Sterne.

The old Wolf stood beside a small table, littered with the remnants of a late-night repast. To his right could be glimpsed Wilma's towering, half-tester bed. Behind him was a silk dressing screen, depicting naked lovers, entangled in the throes of lust. The subject was fitting, considering how Sterne had stolen Sadie from his arms in Dodge.

Cass had never hidden the fact that he hated Sterne; what he did keep secret was how he envied him. The specter of Cass's dirt-poor, share-cropper heritage rose now to haunt him as he glowered at his rival. If the Yankees hadn't confiscated all Confederate holdings during the war, Cass figured that tonight, Sterne would be sipping Glenmorangie in a gilded parlor beneath a crystal chandelier and smoking a Cleopatra Federal cigar, infused with cognac.

Maybe there is such a thing as Divine Justice.

Sterne had shed his swallowtails, but not his satin vest, frilled shirt, or bowtie. Only his plain brown, Justin boots hinted that he'd once walked among Texicans with the power of a god and the badge of a Ranger.

A no-good, *lying* Ranger, Cass thought darkly when he spied Sterne's gun belt hanging from a brass peg beside Wilma's door. Sterne was embezzling money from the good citizens of Texas. He was a bigger crook than Cass had ever been!

"You know I forbid weapons in my house," Wilma scolded. She was shielding Sterne with her body. "And *I* know you pack a lot more than six-shooters."

"You also know I never miss," Cass snapped. "If I'd come here to ventilate him, you wouldn't even get creased in the crossfire."

"And I suspect Cassidy wouldn't have knocked on the door," Sterne said dryly. "It's all right, Wilma. You can leave."

"Absolutely not! I'm not letting you two smash furniture and bust heads."

"We'll settle our differences like civilized barbarians." Sterne reached behind her hip. "Over scotch."

"Keep your hands where I can see them," Cass warned. "I know she packs a derringer on her thigh."

Sterne hiked a graying eyebrow at this confession, but he didn't challenge it. Instead, he retrieved two glasses and a crystal decanter from Wilma's liquor cabinet.

Wilma glanced uneasily toward Cass's hips. Only then

did he realize his hands were flexing over the holsters he no longer wore.

"Pour me a dram too," she told Sterne.

The Ranger's flinty stare locked with Cass's. "Does the lady need to share our whisky to keep you from firing that popgun up your sleeve?"

"I *said* I didn't come to ventilate you, old man."

Grunting, Sterne poured two fingers' worth of Glenmorangie into the clean glass. With his free hand, he waved Wilma toward the door.

"Go on. You've got Cassidy's word."

Wilma's chest heaved. She shot Cass a glare that promised all kinds of hell and retribution. "If you harm a *splinter* in this room, you'll rue your decision to burst through my door."

Cass didn't doubt Wilma's word. As a Mambo, she could make his life a waking nightmare. However, his quarrel wasn't with Wilma, so he nodded his consent.

The door whispered closed behind her.

Sterne was pouring another dram. "You don't like me, and I don't like you."

Cass sneered. "I can drink to that."

"Good." Sterne thumped a glass on the table.

Taking a seat, the Ranger sniffed his own scotch; put his palm over the glass rim; and swirled the contents around the bottom. Cass watched this hoity-toity drinking ritual with unabashed contempt.

"We're agreed on one other point," Sterne said, sipping his whisky.

"What's that?"

"We both want Sadie safe."

"So you let her become a *Pinkerton*?"

To his credit, Sterne managed his surprise without choking on his scotch. "So she confided in you."

"Hell no. I had to sniff, like a weasel, through every scrap of frippery she owns! Sadie's too damned stubborn to admit when she needs help. I found her badge."

Sterne looked troubled. "Then you know that brand of

stubbornness can't be dissuaded. Sadie was determined to leave the whorehouse. She didn't think she was suited for marriage. She didn't believe she had the temperament to be a schoolmarm or a seamstress."

"There are *plenty* of other ways to leave the whorehouse! Jumping in front of bullets didn't have to make the list."

"Don't you think I tried to tell her that?" Sterne retorted. "Sadie wanted to prove her mettle. She wanted the opportunity to be respected, like Kate Warne."

"Who?"

"Outside the Pinkerton Agency, few folks know who Kate is," Sterne admitted. "She stopped an assassination attempt on President Lincoln before the war. She was an invaluable asset to the Union and one of Pinkerton's most resourceful agents. Unfortunately, she died of pneumonia a few years after General Lee surrendered at Appomattox."

Cass didn't know whether to scoff at this intelligence or be alarmed by it. Pinkerton had sent a woman into *war?* What the hell kind of monster was Sadie working for?!

Stalking closer, Cass planted his palms on the table and shoved his face into Sterne's. "Sadie doesn't need to prove her worth to me," he growled. "You think I don't know her story? She was robbed of her maidenhead by a tin-star. She got thrown in a whorehouse by a tin-star. Wyatt Earp, Bat Masterson and others of their ilk extorted her for protection money in Dodge. Now you're trying to convince me she wants to *be* a tin-star? Hell, you aren't fit to wipe the muck off her shoes!"

Sterne's color was on the rise. He released a long, shuddering breath.

"I'm not arguing with you," he said quietly.

This easy victory was like a splash of kerosene on fire. Cass couldn't have reined in his tongue if he'd tried. "What kind of man lets his woman face killers to cover his lies? Or deludes her into thinking dodging bullets is romantic? What the hell kind of man are *you,* Sterne?"

The Ranger was uncommonly quiet. So quiet, Cass could hear the surging of his blood, the ticking of the wall-clock, the soughing of wind-blown branches beyond Wilma's shuttered windows.

"You love her," Sterne said.

"Of course I love her! She's the fire in my blood, the light in my soul! If I thought for a moment you were born for her, and she for you, then I'd step aside so you could marry her, and she'd be happy! But you're not the right man—"

"I agree."

The breath whistled past Cass's teeth. He'd been so pumped up to point out Sterne's failings, he couldn't let the argument rest so easily.

"You *agree?* Since when?"

Sterne stared at Cass's chest for a long moment, as if he were peering into his heart.

"Sit down, William."

"I'll sit when I'm good and ready!"

Sterne's smile was mirthless. "Am I to understand from all this caterwauling, you think Sadie's my lover?"

"Don't tell me you're going to deny it after that little performance at Hancock Park!"

"It was a performance. Nothing more."

"So you *admit* you've been coercing Sadie to do your dirty work—"

"Sadie has worn a badge for Allan Pinkerton for four years. If I thought she was working against her will, I would have put an end to the arrangement long before this."

Sterne's gaze didn't waver. No prevarication lurked in the lawman's manner. But Cass didn't want to believe him. Four years of hatred egged him on.

"Well, you and Sadie weren't *performing* back in Dodge. How many times did she sneak off to meet you at the Harvey House, eh?"

"I assure you, William. It would be quite impossible for me to have a sexual liaison with Sadie."

Cass sneered. "Bawds talk. The way I hear it, your equipment works just fine."

"That's reassuring," Sterne said dryly. "But the fact

remains. Sadie is not my lover. Nor has she ever been."

Cass shook his head. Why Sterne would deny carrying on with Sadie, especially now, after his Ranger career was over and he was free to marry her, didn't make much sense. But Cass didn't let that fleeting doubt muzzle his mouth.

"You high-and-mighty Rangers think you rule the world. You think you can ride into any town, take any woman you want—"

"William," Sterne interrupted flatly, "Sadie's my daughter."

Cass wheezed. He couldn't have been more stunned than if Sterne had pulled a rattlesnake out of his holster. For an endless moment, Cass just stood there, gawking. Then his Coyote brain finally kicked into gear.

"No. That's not possible. Roarke Michelson—"

"—Was married to Sadie's mother at the time of our affair. I thought Meg was a widow."

Cass frowned. He was dangerously moved by Sterne's story, not because of anything the lawman had said, but because he'd allowed Cass an unexpected glimpse into his pain. Sterne's throat worked. His lips pursed. He averted his eyes and tossed back the rest of his scotch like any old White Trash. Faced with the proof of such anguish, Cass had trouble believing the notion he wanted to cherish most: that Sterne was a no-good rat-fink and a liar.

"Then Sadie should have told me—"

"Sadie doesn't know," Sterne said.

Holy crap!

At long last, the veil lifted from Cass's eyes.

For four years, he'd been blaming Sadie for an affair she'd never had. He'd walked away from her in Dodge because he'd thought she'd been playing him for a fool. Sadie hadn't been lying about Sterne back in Dodge. Sterne had been lying to *her!*

Cass clenched his fists. He had half a mind to smash Sterne's face. "God aw'mighty! Why haven't you told her?"

Sterne's hand shook as he poured himself another dram.

"I tried, once."

"Once?"

"She kept fingering that damned button."

Cass knew exactly what Sterne meant. Sadie fondled her pendant whenever she was nervous or afraid. She'd confided to him, once, that the button's cap hid a secret latch. She liked to fantasize that Michelson had used the tiny compartment to hide ciphers. Or maybe to carry quinine in case he got shot. Sadie used the compartment to store a lock of her father's hair. She'd doted on Roarke Michelson. His murder had shattered her life.

Cass folded his arms across his chest. "Trying once isn't good enough."

"Michelson was a decent father. I won't take that away from her."

"Michelson didn't know?"

"Not until the end."

Cass cursed. "So help me God, if you were one of those Terry's Rangers who lynched him—"

"I wasn't." Eyes like granite-colored ice collided with his. "A few years after the war, Meg figured out Michelson betrayed the Confederacy. That he was working as a Pinkerton. Knowing she would be ostracized if the secret leaked, she flew into a rage. She told Michelson he was despicable. She threw our affair in his face. The window was open, and one of their neighbors overheard the argument. That same night, the Klan went gunning for Michelson. Meg never forgave herself."

"Where were *you?*"

"Corsicana. Meg and I parted ways in '54—at her request. I never suspected she was pregnant. Not until the spring of '79, when Ranger business led me to work with Allan Pinkerton, did I learn about the lynching. When Pinkerton discovered I'd been assigned to patrol Grayson County for a spell, he asked if I'd ever met one of his operatives, a Roarke Michelson. I began piecing the story together then."

Cass's head was spinning. He sat heavily in the chair

across from the man whom he'd hated for so long. A man who clearly thought he was doing the right thing by protecting Sadie from the truth. A man who didn't know his daughter *at all.*

"You can't keep sitting on this powder keg, Sterne. Sadie has the right to know you're her father. She'd want to know."

"Sadie has the right to be *happy,*" Sterne corrected him. "That's why I'm counting on you to keep this matter a secret, William. You owe Sadie that much after riding out on her in Dodge. She never betrayed you. All my girl ever did was try to protect you—and mostly from me.

"That's why she asked me to accompany her to Chicago," Sterne continued in that same grim tone, "to get the restitution Pinkerton owed Michelson's heir. She figured if she got me on a northbound train, I couldn't track you. But once Pinkerton saw her grit and resourcefulness, he offered her a commission. It was Pinkerton who bought out her brothel contract. I didn't have that kind of money on a Ranger's pay."

Cass dropped his gaze from the lawman's. Now he felt lower than a snake's belly. Never once had he suspected these outlandish circumstances. Who would have? If he hadn't found Sadie's Pinkerton badge, he would have accused Sterne of telling whoppers!

Cass's hand shook as he reached for the scotch Sterne had poured him. It was the long-awaited dram of Glenmorangie he'd dreamed of sharing at his rival's expense. Only Sterne wasn't his rival. Not anymore.

But that wasn't the only reason Cass barely tasted the smooth, smoky flavor as it slid down his throat. He owed Sadie an apology of cosmic proportions! How was he supposed to make amends, if he wasn't allowed to spill the beans?

Sterne reached into the breast pocket of his vest. After rummaging around for a moment, he withdrew something metallic and tossed it Cass's way. The tin flashed in the lamplight before it landed on the table and skittered up against Cass's glass.

"What's that?" Cass bit out, staring at his lifelong dream.

"A vote of confidence."

Cass raised his eyes from that battered, old Ranger badge and locked stares with its wily owner. "I thought you were retired."

"That's what the governor wants folks to think."

Cass sucked in his breath. "Governor Ireland's been in on your charade? From the beginning?"

Sterne nodded.

Cass bit back an oath. Sterne's ruse was bigger than him and Sadie. It was bigger than Baron's election. It was even bigger than the legislature. Sterne's ruse was the whole damned state of Texas, with its fence-cutting cattlemen, vigilante sodbusters, and blood-soaked range lands!

"So why are you confiding in me?" Cass demanded warily.

"I may have misjudged you. And Sadie could use the help."

Cass's mouth salivated as he glanced once more at his tin-star dream. "You're offering me a commission?"

"That's the normal order of business when a Ranger goes undercover."

Cass's soaring spirits stalled, hitting the ground hard. He should have known there'd be a catch. "You want a man inside Baron's organization."

"Is that a problem?"

Cass's Coyote mind raced. Baron was his friend. Sadie was his woman. But no matter how many angles Cass considered, he couldn't find a way out of his predicament without betraying at least one of them.

He cursed silently. The only option he had at the moment was to play along. He knew too much. Sterne couldn't let him go running back to Baron, not without being thoroughly convinced Cass was serving the law. Cass needed time to find Collie and learn what had really transpired between Baron and Hank. He needed time to determine if Pendleton had masterminded the sniper attack on Baron.

"Count me in," Cass said grimly. "But count Sadie out. I don't want her getting caught in the crossfire when The Ventilator starts gunning for Baron again."

Sterne stiffened. "Sharpe broke out of Huntsville?"

"Looks that way. Sadie spotted him at Aquacia."

Something dark and foreboding flickered through the Ranger's eyes. "You keep that bastard away from my daughter."

"Nothing would please me more." Cass shoved back his chair.

"One other thing," Sterne said coolly. "Sadie answers to Allan Pinkerton, not the Rangers. She has her own mission. Stay out of her way."

A muscle ticked in Cass's jaw. Abruptly, he reached for Sterne's tin-star and did something he'd never once conceived of doing in his whole life: he pocketed a Ranger badge under false pretenses.

In the final analysis, Cass didn't give a rat's ass about Pinkerton or his secret army of nameless, faceless minions. If Cass had to use his Ranger badge to keep Baron alive and Sadie safe, then by God, he would.

CHAPTER 16

Devil's Eve was the time when ghosts and goblins went bump in the night.

Or so the scaredy-cats said.

Collie snickered at his humor and took another swig from his half-empty bourbon bottle. He was more than a little roostered. After escorting Baron to his hotel suite—where Poppy had been busily tying orange and black ribbons to a basket full of soul cakes—Collie had been only too happy to let the Harpy Queen shoo him out the door. The thought of spending Devil's Eve with the Westerfields had given him the heebie-jeebies. He'd seen for himself what kind of vermin Baron rendezvoused with in lonesome bathhouses.

Collie wasn't eager to continue his employment with Baron. He hoped Sadie would convince Cass to quit, too. Ever since Collie had learned Cass wanted revenge against Sterne, Collie had had a bad feeling. The kind of feeling a fella got when he was staring down the wrong end of a loaded gun. Collie wasn't worried so much about his own safety; he could disappear faster than a six-legged jackrabbit. But it did occur to him that Sadie and Wilma were vulnerable. If anything happened to either of them, Cass was just hotheaded enough to turn vigilante again.

And that worried Collie.

Nobody knew better than Collie what Cass was capable

of doing with a gun. Two summers ago, Collie had watched in astonishment as a half-dead Cass had managed to fire off one shot—*one shot!*—with a Winchester rifle to saw through the rope lynching his Injun friend, Lynx.

At other times, Collie had seen Cass cock his .45 *with his heel* and drill a knothole at 50 paces while aiming over his shoulder! Whether Cass was firing his guns stupid-drunk, blinded by rain, or shaking with cold, he never missed.

The trouble was, even Cass couldn't survive a bullet in the back.

"Dead is dead," Collie explained to his furry sidekick. "It doesn't matter whether you're a Ranger, a vigilante, or an outlaw."

Vandy ignored him. The coon was busy gorging himself on the sugar skulls some Mexican family had arranged beside potted chrysanthemums and a colorful skeleton doll, draped in a sombrero and serape.

With nothing better to do than wait for Cass and Sadie to get tired rutting, Collie had gone prowling. He'd sneaked inside Wilma's so-called "secret" cave and helped himself to his favorite Halloween spirits. He'd found the cave several days ago, along with the Wild Turkey Wilma had hidden inside a crate marked, "Ripy Brothers Distillery, Tyrone, Kentucky."

Which just proves that reading leads to drink. And sin. And that anybody who forces book-learning on a boy is an unholy influence.

"If I didn't know how to read, I wouldn't have been tempted to jimmy open that liquor crate with a crowbar," he told Vandy righteously.

The coon *whuffed.* He was sniffing a papier-mâché coffin at the Garcias' gravesite.

In this part of the world, Devil's Eve, Halloween, and the Mexican Day of the Dead all collided at the Witching Hour. After chugging enough bourbon, Collie had gotten the bright idea to ride out to the boneyard to see what all the *Día de los Muertes* hoopla was about. To the best of his knowledge, folks in Kentucky didn't paint sugar skulls or go singing for soul cakes. At least, not in Blue Thunder Valley.

That's why Collie was crouching behind a Lampasas tombstone on the spookiest night of the year. About 20 yards away, a band of shrieking, ash-smeared urchins was dancing, singing, and feeding the bonfire they'd rigged in the granite belly of a dried-up water fountain.

Collie watched wistfully. His boy's heart yearned to join in the fun, to wear a mask, smash pumpkins, and spread creepy gossip about evil property owners, who liked to turn their scatterguns on stray dogs and trespassing kids. God knew, he could share plenty of hair-raising tales on *that* subject.

But Collie had never been much good at making friends.

At least, not Human friends.

His brow furrowed with his effort to understand the sing-song taunts. Ring-leaders, who were dressed like tramps in patched gingham and garish skull masks, were ribbing the younger boys. Although the *Tejanos* spoke in Spanish, Collie intuited that the shortest gang member was supposed to earn his stripes by tugging the bell pull of the eerie old caretaker's cottage, huddling in the shadow of a lightning-sheared oak. The tree's leafless limbs resembled giant claws, whose twig talons kept rubbing together, scratching and grasping at the wind.

The shack itself was supposed to be haunted by the soul of an outlaw, who'd been lynched from that oak. No one lived in the house anymore. The limestone ruins sported jagged panes of glass, which glittered like fangs each time a lightning spear flashed. Even Collie's heart skipped a beat to think of pranking *La Bestia*—or The Beast—with nothing but rotten eggs and flour pellets as defense.

His hand edged toward his six-shooter as the sky growled at the noisy mortals, cavorting below.

"Why is it," he muttered to Vandy, "that no storms have threatened this region for six months, and yet one is brewing on Devil's Eve?"

The coon flopped on his back and kicked up his paws.

"Oh, so now you're calling me a yellow belly?"

Grunting with pleasure, Vandy rolled across the gravesite, his ringed tail upsetting the skeleton doll.

"You want whupped?" Collie threatened in an exasperated undertone. "'Cause that's what *Señor* Garcia's going to do when he wakes from the dead!"

The cheeky coon whickered, a sound reminiscent of Human snickering. Then his beady eyes—or maybe his twitching nose—noticed how Collie was unfolding an orange linen napkin. Vandy heaved himself to his paws with interest.

"Don't bring any angry ghosts over here," Collie scolded. "I got enough problems with the live folks."

Vandy ignored this order, trampling skeleton dolls and paper coffins in his eagerness to sniff the treat up close.

Collie scowled, imagining some angry spook's retribution. It was a good thing he had so many dead kin watching over him, thanks to those trigger-happy Hatfields from Virginia. Of course, whenever folks back home got suspicious about his family origins, he'd swear up and down on Bibles, crosses, rosaries, and a couple of other sacred relics, too, that he wasn't related to any Kentucky-born McCoys. He'd even fooled Sera, and that was saying a lot. Sera had a spooky way of knowing the events of the past, by touching something metallic, like a brass button, Peacemaker, or whittling knife.

"You can't be too careful when you've got the wrong blood in a blood feud," Collie told Vandy with all the amassed wisdom of his 17 years. "Luckily for you, my ghosts could probably wallop any ghosts in this cemetery. Ghouls, too. And that includes Mrs. Westerfield."

Collie snickered at his churlish humor. "I mean, *something* scared that woman into being nice tonight. And it wasn't you, Fur Face."

Collie suspected that to Poppy, Devil's Eve must be like Christmas to nice folks. After all, he'd found her humming and decorating a Halloween basket. At the time, she'd described the soul cakes as a *"token of appreciation"* for certain hotel staff, who'd gone *"beyond the call of duty to serve my husband's needs."*

Collie figured he'd gone *way* beyond the call of duty to serve Senator Rat-fink Scum-bucket, so he'd helped himself to a couple of tasty treats. Caching food was an old habit; even when his Pa had been alive, Collie had never known where the next meal would come from. But all his city living must have dulled his instincts, because Poppy had caught him thieving.

"Take another cake, dear boy," she'd encouraged with a beatific smile. *"I have plenty more."*

"To tell the truth," Collie confided to his coon, "she kind of freaked me out. I kept expecting her head to spin around. Or her eyes to pop out. Or black spiders to crawl out of her nose. Every time I pinched myself, I never woke up. So I reckon there really must be gingerbread inside this napkin."

As Collie unfolded the linen corners from his loot, Vandy frisked with all his rascally charm. He wuffed. He reared up on his hind legs. He put a little black hand on Collie's heart.

But Collie kept his snack well out of the reach of those clever paws.

Vandy whined.

"What, you want one?"

The coon licked his chops, his black eyes bright with hope as he stared at the prize. The cakes looked like little round cookies, except they were plumper and decorated with raisins in the shape of a cross.

"Too bad," Collie taunted, shoving a cake into his mouth.

The coon whimpered.

Collie grimaced.

"A little heavy on the molasses," he choked, reaching for his bourbon. He washed down the confection with a hearty swig. "Reminds me of something Sera used to bake, before her sister-in-law gave her cooking lessons."

Vandy pricked his ears. He knew all about Sera. She was the preacher's daughter, whom Collie had worshiped from afar. Before the coon grew too fat, he used to hide out in the copper kettle hanging over Sera's kitchen sink. He would wait there for his chance to steal the hickory nuts—better known as "hiccurs" to Kentucky folk—that Sera liked to chop for her bake-off recipes.

Sera Jones (now Mrs. Jesse "Lynx" Quaid, Collie thought a tad enviously) had been aptly named Seraphina, after angels. She and her doctor brother had taken Collie in, treated him like kin, and made him feel like being born hadn't been the revenge of a vindictive God. Until he'd met the Jones family, Collie had been a wild thing. He'd spent most of his childhood hiding in the woods outside of Blue Thunder—at first to elude the heavy-fisted moonshiner who'd been his Pa, and then to avoid the Orphanage Committee.

Of course, he'd also had to disappear for weeks on end from lazy-ass tin-stars, who'd preferred to blame him for every runaway dog and broken window in the town, rather than conduct a real investigation into the complaints.

"It's better to wear a tin star than to be arrested by one," Collie advised Vandy. "Or in your case, it's better to be a coon than a hat. So I reckon I should stop letting you steal food. Even from dead folks," he added grudgingly. "Here."

He offered the gingerbread to the coon.

Eagerly, Vandy rose on his haunches. He wrapped a paw around Collie's forefinger. His whiskers twitched. He sniffed the confection.

Then the strangest thing happened. Vandy, who ate everything from tarantulas and rattle snakes, to scented soap and rotting melons, turned up his nose at Poppy's soul cake.

Collie hiked an eyebrow. "The cake wasn't *that* bad, churnhead."

Vandy shuffled over to *Señor* Garcia's burned-out luminarias. Hunkering down, the coon began to gnaw a candle in a saucer of sand.

"Seriously? You'd rather eat wax?" Collie frowned. "Hey. You aren't sick from all those sugar skulls, are you?"

Shouts rose from the revelers, distracting Collie.

Apparently, the ring-leaders had bullied three of the youngest boys into pranking The Beast. Clutching their sacks of flour in one hand and their eggs in the other, the trio was creeping with great trepidation onto the porch of the house. Lightning sizzled over the chimney in great, purple spears. The oak tree moaned like some wounded soul. In the filtered moonlight, Collie recognized Joaquin, the shoeshine boy, leading his companions to their ultimate goal: the bell pull by the door.

Five feet.

Three feet.

An arm's length away.

Joaquin stretched shaking fingers.

A sudden light flashed behind the house's jagged windows. A deafening boom shook the panes even as splinters spewed from the hole that materialized in the door's rotted wood.

Holy crap!

Miraculously, Joaquin wasn't hit by the rifle blast. Bleating like a lamb, the kid dropped his flour and eggs and bolted off the porch. His companions followed in hot pursuit, shrieking, *"La Bestia!"* The rest of the revelers took up the cry. Soon all the *Tejano* children were bounding around like moonstruck jackrabbits, while rifle cartridges chipped tombstones, splintered fence rails, and cracked through tree branches. When a rotted old oak bough tumbled from the sky, it nearly crushed Collie's skull.

Sonuvabitch!

"Beggarticks!" he hissed at his well-trained coon, and Vandy dived under the bush where Collie had stashed his Winchester and saddlebag. But when Collie tried to grab his rifle, he nearly got his hand blown off.

Grabbing his bourbon, Collie ran in the opposite direction. Bullets were whining over his head. He felt like a metal duck in a shooting gallery. When he dodged right, the sniper drilled a cartridge into the dirt by his boots. When he ran left, a potshot zoomed past his shoulder.

"I owe you a slug, boy!" a Midwestern accent bellowed from the cottage. "For putting a hole in my bowler!"

Even as Collie recognized Hank's voice—and realized The Ventilator had been the sniper on the grocer's roof— the bourbon bottle shattered in his fist. Collie swore. There wasn't a damned thing he could do to retaliate. His .45 was out of firing range.

Why would Hank try to plug Baron if Baron's paying him hush money?

Maybe Tito was the real target in the Square...

But why finger me for Tito's murder? Hank doesn't know me—at least, not well enough to hate me...

Wait a minute. Hank must have an accomplice. An accomplice who doesn't like me.

I'll bet it's Pendleton!

His mind racing with allegations, Collie ran for the cover of a mausoleum. He had some half-formed plan to pick the lock and hide inside. But he'd barely charged through the porch's skeleton dolls and marigolds when his gut started burning. The pain came out of nowhere; he thought a shell had hit him. He clutched his stomach. He doubled over. When he didn't feel blood, he realized he was sick.

The churning in his gut reached volcanic proportions. Helpless to stop the fiery surge to his throat, he spewed gingerbread, blood, and other chunky matter that he dimly recognized as dinner. He had a moment to be mortified; another to realize he'd been poisoned.

Pendleton isn't Hank's accomplice.

Poppy is!

Then the second wave of nausea hit. Collie's retching sounded like the roar of a locomotive to his ears. Even though the rifle blasts had stopped, he figured he was doomed. Hank was probably listening, enjoying the sound of a stomach turning inside-out in a graveyard on Devil's Eve.

Feeling like his innards were exploding, Collie toppled face down beside his vomit. His tongue had swollen. He was struggling to breathe. By the time stars started spinning inside his head, his toes and fingers had grown numb. He was completely helpless. He couldn't hold onto his .45. It bounced down the mausoleum's steps.

The squeal of an opening door was the last thing he remembered before the vortex claimed him.

CHAPTER 17

Halloween dawned beneath ominous, gray clouds pierced by jagged spears of light. In Lampasas, most people rejoiced to see the thunderheads and prayed the drought had finally come to an end.

Jazi was among the contrary folks, who prayed for another dry rain. As she watched Sadie apply her make-up in Wilma's cave, Jazi confided, between coughs, that she wanted to dress as a Mambo, go trick-or-treating, and maybe even sing for soul cakes with Joaquin, the shoe-shine boy, who'd told her about *Tejano* traditions. Jazi had set her heart on getting twice as much candy by celebrating both Halloween and the Day of the Dead.

"I thought you were afraid of witches," Sadie teased. Her whiskey alto was raspier than usual after standing in the woods last night—with wet hair—and arguing with Cass.

"Not any more. Cass said he'd save me from the witch," Jazi confided with an impish grin. She broke the seal on a fresh tin of Serenata's pastilles and offered one to Sadie.

Shaking her head at this newest evidence of her lover's Coyote Charm, Sadie politely refused a lozenge. When her singing voice became strained, she favored a brand called *Fishmerman's Friend*. Its base ingredients of menthol and eucalyptus were rare, because most modern-day nostrums relied upon cocaine to relieve discomfort. Sadie shunned opiates. In the immortal words of her field agent manual, *"A Pinkerton must keep her wits about her."*

"Are you still going to sing in the Halloween show?" Jazi asked wistfully, propping her derriere on the vanity. "Even with a sore throat?"

"You know what they say, 'The show must go on,'" Sadie said, dusting powder over her freckled nose. "As a matter of fact, I need you to run upstairs and remind Cotton to hail me a hack. I'm due at rehearsal in half an hour."

Jazi's brow knitted. She was triple-wrapping the cord of her *gris-gris* around her fingers. "I wish you and Mama could be friends. Then you could visit us in New Orleans."

Sadie fixed a pleasant smile on her face. An act of God would be required to make her and Randie friends. However, Jazi didn't need to know that. On impulse, Sadie dragged off her pearl necklace and draped it over the child's sausage-style curls.

"For me?" Jazi breathed. "To *keep?"*

"Forever and ever."

The child squealed, jumping up to admire her reflection. She looked flushed and glassy-eyed, and Sadie hoped that excitement, not another bout of sickness, was the cause.

"I'm beautiful!"

"I *told* you you were, silly."

Jazi threw her arms around Sadie's neck and sniffed back tears. "Thanks for being my friend, Maisy."

Sadie's heart warmed as she watched Jazi dash for the stairs on her errand. As much as Sadie hated to admit it, Randie couldn't be all bad. She'd raised a darling child.

With a furtive glance to make sure the trap door was closed, Sadie concentrated on arming herself—a task that Jazi's visit had forced her to delay. She fastened a pistol to her thigh and slipped a stiletto into the sheath sewn beneath her collar. She snapped plump caps onto the buttons of her bodice; they were easily detached when she needed a smoke bomb. Her cameo could do all kinds of damage, not the least of which was spray ink into an assailant's eyes, and her belt buckle could be "unsheathed" as a knife.

Like her daddy's pendant, her Pinkerton ring hid a secret compartment. Today, she'd chosen a sapphire cabochon. Depending on the color of her gown, the stone could be exchanged for a ruby, emerald, or topaz, all of which snapped closed over a tiny needle that injected a powerful sleeping draught.

But Sadie's handiest weapon, when she was forced to wear a skirt, was her .32. It was attached to the sliding mechanism beneath the right sleeve of her jaunty, bolero jacket.

Satisfied her arsenal was in good working order, she gathered her hat and reticule and headed upstairs.

As her private hack rolled down Third Street, Sadie could see pedestrians in trousers and petticoats shopping up a storm, no doubt hoping to avoid the merciless heat as the sun crept higher. The bargain hunters were haggling with street vendors over last-minute purchases, primarily sugar skulls, although crosses, candles, and ritual toys were also flying off handcarts bedecked with orange marigolds and yellow chrysanthemums.

The Day of the Dead was actually a 72-hour period, from All Hallows' Eve through All Souls' Day. A popular time to build altars, decorate gravesites, and honor departed loved ones, the tradition was dear to *Tejanos* and Mexican immigrants. But *Día de los Muertos* had also been heartily embraced by Lampasas rowdies, who wanted nothing more than an excuse to wear a mask and make mischief for three days.

This notion caused an image of Cass to flash through her mind. Last night, after she'd ended their argument, he'd initiated another round. The fracas had started when he'd insisted she ride Pancake with him to fetch her mare.

"Mount up." Blocking her path, he'd shoved the buckskin's leads into her hand. "I'm taking you back to town."

"I prefer my own horse."

"Quit being so mulish. You don't know what's waiting out there in those dark woods. Or who."

"I can fire a gun as well as any man."

He snorted. "Except me, and Hank, and Collie and Sterne—"

"I can fend for myself!"

"Tell that to Collie after he saved your ass."

Incensed to hear him use her confidence against her, she snapped, "I think you're forgetting who wears the badge around here!"

He backed her into his horse's flank. She sucked in her breath. His eyes were fairly smoking.

Facing Cass, when he took on the Lucifire persona, was an unnerving challenge. At six feet, two-inches, and dressed entirely in black, he towered over her like an Olympian-sized spike, forged on some fire god's anvil. The shadows cast by his hat brim only seemed to make the sapphire flames of his soul burn brighter in that unyielding glare. She had to square her shoulders and ball her fists to keep from cringing.

"Either you mount up willingly," he said in a low, fierce undertone, "or I'll truss you up like a turkey and throw you over that saddle."

Tyrant.

To add to his growing list of sins, Cass had somehow found Rex before she had. The Ranger had been waiting for her, pacing Wilma's boudoir like a caged wolf. Rex had fired the opening shot by demanding to know why she hadn't hidden her Pinkerton badge better. The debriefing had gone downhill from there. She'd been too angry to spare Cass by hiding the truth about his snooping, and Rex had turned florid at her description of the Bowie knife stuck through her handbill's nose.

Wilma hadn't taken the news much better. She'd quickly deduced that her "secret" tunnel wasn't so secret and that Collie was responsible for her missing bottles of Wild Turkey. To keep Collie in Wilma's good graces, Sadie had been forced to describe how the boy had saved her from Hank—or rather, from The Ventilator. Apparently, Cass had already guessed Hank's alter ego. Rex was the one who'd enlightened her.

Then Rex dropped another bomb: he'd recruited Cass.

"Wait a minute. You sent him after *Hank?*" Sadie quailed at this news.

"He'd already made up his mind. I just made sure he wouldn't get arrested for it."

Sadie didn't like this plan, mostly because she was afraid Cass would come back in a pine box. But how could she protest? He was finally living his Ranger dream. She'd thought she would feel better, knowing he was on the right side of the law. Now she wondered how she would cope with the fear.

As if sensing her turmoil, Rex raised an eyebrow. "You have a problem with Cassidy going undercover?"

She steeled herself against a show of womanly weakness. "Of course not. We need a mole in Baron's organization. Cass can follow him back to the Rocking W. I can't."

Rex grunted. She didn't like the way those keen, gray eyes were assessing her, probing for the truth.

"The badge is a probationary measure. He'll have to prove himself."

"He will."

"You're that sure, eh?"

"Being a Ranger is all Cass ever cared about. You just made his life complete."

"What about you? And what you care about?"

A slow heat rolled up her neck. She felt betrayed by it. She didn't want Rex or anyone else know how she used to keep the fragile dream of marriage locked in the deepest, darkest chambers of her heart. Every now and then, during an especially maudlin bout of sentiment, she would drag out that cherished fantasy, polish it, admire it, and try it on for size—rather like a glass slipper.

But Sadie was a realist. Cass was a Ranger now. He couldn't marry her, and no other man could possibly want her as the mother of his child. Not after he learned how she'd lived 11 years of her life as a whore. Or how she'd let her five-year-old, twin sister drown.

"I'm a businesswoman," she answered coolly. "Money is my freedom. It lets me live the way I choose. *That's* what I've always wanted."

Rex darted a speculative glance at Wilma, who was careful to avoid Sadie's eyes. Annoyed with them both, she stalked from the room to pour a stiff drink.

Recalling that restless, sleepless night, with no one to hold except José Cuervo, Sadie was grateful when her hack finally rolled beneath the elaborate, wrought-iron gateway to Hancock Park. She was looking forward to dress rehearsal. She needed the diversion.

Unfortunately, when she reported to the Grand Park's stage, she learned her accompanist was running behind schedule. A quarter of an hour later, she was still pacing her dressing room floor, waiting for the slacker to show up. Since the chamber was small and cluttered with furniture, her bustle and cumbersome skirts left little space to work off her annoyance.

She glared at her unabashedly feminine surroundings: a butter-cream wardrobe and folding screen, painted with blush-colored roses; a matching vanity with a pink marble top; a velvet chaise lounge with swan fabric; and the inevitable vases. *Dozens* of vases. Each emerald-and-ruby-colored vessel was stuffed to overflowing with last night's tribute-bouquets.

When space had run out on the furniture, the floor had become the next logical place to sow her garden. Some enterprising hotel worker had even arranged her posies by color. Her chaise looked like a boat, floating in an orange-gold sea of hellenium, dahlias, and witch hazel. The assault of fragrances was making her nose itch.

Suddenly, she noticed the festive orange and black basket, brimming with Halloween goodies. Some knucklehead had put it on the floor instead of making space for it on the vanity.

Great. It'll probably be swarming with ants.

But it wasn't.

Her curiosity piqued, she reached for the attached card. *"Chantelle O'Leary"* had been etched across the envelope in Cass's sloping scrawl.

Interesting. When did Cass have time to send me an apology basket?

Torn between annoyance and delight, she broke the seal on the flap. The message read:

> *'Destined' to be a perfect ending! Brava, show-*
> *stopper!*
> *~ Cass*

Her eyebrows knitted.

"Brava?" That was it? Not, *"You were right about Hank, and I'm a dog for ever doubting you?"*

Or *"I was wrong to think Baron could be trusted."*

Or *"Can you ever forgive me for being so bossy, ornery, and cussid?"*

Now she really was pissed. Didn't Cass remember *anything* she'd told him over the years? He should at least know better than to send her dessert. Back in Dodge, she'd blistered his tender, 21-year-old ears about the realities of fishtail skirts and how they showed every ripple of unsightly fat in the stage lights.

"No sweets!" she'd bellowed, throwing a strawberry shortcake at his head. The scapegrace had been nimble enough to dodge it, and for the next 20 minutes, they'd had loads of fun scraping whipping cream off the wall and smearing it all over each other's private parts.

Sadie grinned at the memory.

Then she pouted.

Didn't he at least remember *that?*

Snot head. She had half a mind to shove a caramel apple up his nose.

She scowled at the arrangement of delectable edibles.

Wait a minute. Is that a soul cake?

Suspicion flurried through her mind. *When did Cass start celebrating* Día de los Muertos?

She reached once more for the card.

And frowned.

Never, in the 13 years that she'd known him, had she seen him sign a document, *Cass.* For contracts, he always wrote *William A. Cassidy.* For a love letter, he scrawled, *Billy,* his pet name from childhood. Sometimes, when he was feeling his wild oats, he signed a love letter, *Reb.* But never Cass.

And good God! She sniffed the paper. *Is that violet perfume?!*

She was just about to start examining the food, when a sharp rap rattled her door.

"Finally," she groused, stalking to the door to throw it wide. "I thought you'd never get here—"

Only her visitor wasn't her accompanist.

Baron stood on the threshold, dressed in impeccable gray-silk morning attire. In his case, the clothes didn't make the man. As wide and brawny as a bull, he used his breadth and his walking stick to force his way inside, ignoring her sputtered attempts to greet him civilly. His size seemed monstrous in such cramped quarters. His bloodshot eyes and gray complexion didn't radiate health. Or lust. All she could sense in Baron's manner was hostility.

She backed up three steps.

He slammed the door behind him.

"What's the matter, Sweet Pea?" His lip curled, part leer, part sneer. "I heard you wanted some company."

Sadie rallied her wits, despite the pounding of her heart, which even a deaf man would have heard slamming against her ribs. After the incident at the bathhouse, she worried Baron intended something violent.

Fortunately, she was wearing an arsenal of Pinkerton gadgets. She consoled herself that she'd handled more than one barn-sized bully in her life.

"I'm honored," she purred. "What kept you so long?"

"Trouble on the shooting range. Bo Bodine's dead. His rifle backfired."

Sadie felt the blood drain from her face. "Th-that's awful."

Baron grunted. "It just proves what I've been saying for years: Bodine was a moron. His inane rhetoric used to stall my bills in committee. Now I'll finally be able to get some agricultural legislation passed."

Sadie gaped. Was Baron actually *bragging?* Was the sick bastard plotting to arrange a "lethal accident" for every prominent sodbuster in the senate?

Meanwhile, Baron's canny gaze was sweeping the room. When his eyes lighted on the Halloween basket, he reached for a chocolate and popped it in his mouth.

"Anyone else here?" he demanded between chomps.

Sadie had to fight nausea to muster a come-hither smile. "Why? Do you prefer threesomes?"

"You do get around, don't you?" He popped another chocolate in his mouth.

"I aim to please."

"That's what I hear. And speaking of Cassidy—" Baron stooped to pick up the gift card, which had fluttered to the floor. Munching on a soul cake, he scanned the note. His brow furrowed, and accusatory eyes bored into hers. "Where's Cass?"

Sadie had trouble hiding her anger when she snatched the paper from his hand. "Don't know."

"I find that hard to believe. Especially since you and he are such close friends."

"Don't let the basket fool you. Cass is friends with lots of women."

"Mostly redheads." Baron's chuckle wasn't reassuring. "Tell me. Are you acquainted with my wife?"

"Can't say I've had the pleasure."

He snorted. "You sure?"

"I think I'd remember."

"Uh-huh." He didn't look convinced. "Let me tell you a little something about my Popsicle. Pleasure is the least of her talents. She's far better at revenge. Turns out, the talent runs in her family."

"Just hers?"

"I suppose every man has his share." An ominous glint

entered his eyes. Reaching into his coat pocket, he produced a linen handkerchief. When he unfolded the corners, he revealed a strand of red hair—one that looked alarmingly like hers.

"Your calling card," he jeered. "My wife found it in my underwear drawer. Needless to say, she raised quite a ruckus."

Sadie didn't have to feign surprise. "Senator, I do confess to being one of your biggest fans. But I assure you. I draw the line at pinching underwear."

"You think I was born yesterday?" He stalked closer, his breadth squeezing out the light from the open window. "You put on a wig and a maid's uniform and searched my suite for Sterne! Your stunt caused a great deal of trouble for a lady friend of mine, and if anything happens to her or her child, so help me God, I'll take every ounce of their pain out on your flesh!"

Sadie struggled with her composure. He'd leaped to the right conclusion—for the wrong reasons. He hadn't yet guessed she was a Pinkerton. But then, what man in his right mind suspected a woman of being an undercover detective?

"Senator, I enjoy pleasure games as much as the next woman, but I'm not sure I understand what role you're asking me to play in this fantasy you've dreamed up."

"You think you're the only floozy who ever tried to blackmail me?"

"By stealing your underwear? Come now, Senator. Even you have to admit that's—"

Baron's fist lashed out. She hadn't anticipated the blow, so she didn't duck fast enough. Ears ringing, eyes stinging, she staggered backward, her hips striking the vanity.

But Sadie wasn't 13 and defenseless any more. With the fury of a wounded tiger, she snapped her wrist to draw her pistol.

"Touch me again," she spat, "and your wife will find *lead* in your underwear next time."

Baron's fist tightened over his walking stick. "Seems like you need a little lesson in firearms, Sugar Plum. Even my wife knows you don't draw a gun on a man unless you have the balls to pull the trigger."

Sadie drew a shuddering breath. She was a crack shot, but she'd never aimed to kill a man, and the tip of Baron's walking stick was only inches from her pistol's muzzle. If her bullet caused a wound that wasn't immediately mortal...Well, Baron's cane could do a lot of damage before she fired a second shot.

"Get out," she snapped.

His smile was far from pleasant. "Whatcha gonna do if I don't, Sweet Pea? You're all alone out here. Ain't nobody around to hear you—"

Another knock rattled her door.

"Miss O'Leary," an authoritative voice boomed. "Open up. It's Marshal Wright. I have questions about Tito Ferraro."

Her gun hand quaked with relief. She hated her show of weakness. But she hated even more that she'd given Baron a reason to silence her. Permanently.

"Come in, marshal," she called hoarsely. "Senator Westerfield was just leaving."

Baron's vengeful glare stabbed through her before he pasted on a horsey smile for the opening door. Wright doffed his hat. While the lawman's eyes were momentarily averted, Sadie hid her gun beneath her skirts.

That's when the strangest thing happened.

Baron began to wheeze.

He clutched his abdomen.

He staggered.

Alarm darkened Wright's craggy features as the senator abruptly crashed to his knees, puking all over Sadie's dahlias.

"What the—"

Before Wright could finish his sentence, Baron toppled like felled timber. Gurgling, he flailed on his back, blood-flecked drool dribbling down his chin. His chest heaved in great, labored gasps.

Wright muttered an oath, ripping open Baron's coat, vest and shirt. "Don't just stand there, woman! Fetch a doctor!"

CHAPTER 18

Devil's Eve. That's what Cass used to call the night before Halloween. In his youth, he'd looked forward to making a nuisance of himself, mostly as vengeance on Townie Folk, who'd treated him like dirt throughout the year. Cass had fond memories of pranking the high-and-mighty planter class back in Pilot Grove. He'd lopped off the heads of scarecrows, unhinged garden gates, overturned wagons, and painted picket fences a nauseating shade of pink.

Unfortunately, he hadn't had time to amuse himself this year, and not just because of his manhunt. Cass's mind kept straying to Collie. He was beginning to fear the kid had finally mouthed off to the wrong bully—namely, Hank. Collie hadn't returned to the hotel room last night, and the stable boy hadn't seen Rhubarb since 1 a.m.

Cass tried to tell himself he was wasting brain space to worry about the kid. Collie was notorious for disappearing acts that could rival any ghost's. On a night like Devil's Eve, what dyed-in-the-wool troublemaker wouldn't want to blow off a little steam? When Cass spied a surrey on the jail's roof, he imagined he saw Collie's influence in the mischief, especially after Sid yelled out the door:

"You can't hide that kid forever! You'd best get your loyalties straight, Cassidy, or you'll go down with him!"

Cass hid his smirk. Apparently, Collie was still at-large,

rather than cooling his heels in the hoosegow.

But as the morning wore on, Cass's worry grew. Nobody had seen hide nor hair of Collie at the Commercial Saloon, the Barleycorn, or even Odd Fellow Hall. However, some craps players in an alley were buzzing with gossip—*unbelievable* gossip—about another person near and dear to Cass's heart. When he remained skeptical, one of the gamblers shoved a special noon edition of the *Dispatch* into his hands. The headline read:

Baron Poisoned by Chantelle:
Jilted Floozy Ambushes Senator in Hotel Dressing Room

Cass was pretty sure his jaw hit the dirt.

The article read:

"According to Dr. Berger, Senator Westerfield swallowed an overdose of arsenic by eating tainted soul cakes from a basket in Miss O'Leary's dressing room. Miss O'Leary declined to comment..."

Eight minutes later, Cass was kicking aside jack o'lanterns and sprinting up Wilma's porch steps. But the cagey madam had been expecting him. She cracked open the door before he could reach for the knocker.

"It's still too early for trick-or-treat, *cher,*" Wilma greeted in her usual, unperturbed manner. She was dressed in some ceremonial Mambo costume, including a white robe and indigo apron that reeked of a pungent incense. Her dark curls were completely swathed in a silk scarf, patterned with amethyst, sapphire, and aquamarine swirls. Her ears were pierced by enormous gold rings, and when she cocked her head, another set of rings jingled from the long ends of her headdress.

"But it's not too early for costumes, I see." Cass pressed forward, but she wouldn't budge. He scowled. "Don't tell me you're still pissed about last night."

"I don't get mad; I get even." She flashed her Cheshire-cat smile. "And while I'm deciding on your comeuppance, you should know that Rexford Sterne stopped by. He left word he wants you to report to his campaign office. *Double pronto."*

"Sterne's not the boss of me."

"You're a newly minted Ranger, are you not?"

Cass scowled. He didn't think he would ever get used to taking orders. Especially from Sterne.

"Sterne can wait. I read the newspaper. I know you're hiding Sadie."

As if on cue, Cottonmouth and Gator stepped out of the shadows, flanking Wilma like a pair of copper-skinned gorillas.

"Sadie isn't receiving visitors at the moment."

"She'll receive me!"

Gator grinned, cracking his knuckles in a menacing manner. Cotton flicked the tip of his pigsticker with his thumb.

"Cher, be reasonable," Wilma soothed above her gorillas' posturing. "Sadie had a rough morning."

"I had a rough morning! I've been tracking an outlaw since 2 a.m., without a goddamned thing in my belly except the gnat I swallowed by accident!"

Wilma had the good grace not to smirk. "So you caught the outlaw, then."

Cass's jaw twitched with annoyance. *Not exactly.* But he did know Hank was hiding in town.

"I'm in no mood for a quarrel, Wilma."

"Then get some food, *cher.* And some sleep. In a couple of days, I'm sure Sadie will be feeling better."

Cass's heart stalled. *"Feeling* better? Did she get sick too?"

A dark flush rolled up Wilma's cheeks. "Of course not. But you threatened to truss her up like a turkey. After that nonsense in the *Dispatch,* Sadie's not in a forgiving mood right now. Give her some time. A week should do." Wilma blew him a kiss.

Then she closed the door in his face.

Cass blinked. If he hadn't been so shocked to see his reflection gaping back at him in the glass panes, he might have smashed his fist through her window.

So Sadie was still angry with him, was she?

Well, there's more than one way to skin a cat, like Baron said!

His spurs chinking a harsh little tattoo, Cass stalked down the porch stairs and stepped out beneath purple thunderheads, none of which had unleashed yet. Kicking up a dust storm in the street, he made a great show of heading for Sterne's campaign office.

But the moment Cass was sure he was out of sight of Wilma's picture window, he backtracked, creeping along her 10-foot fence, climbing a handy cottonwood tree, and sneaking through an open casement on the second story.

Sadie nearly jumped a foot off the vanity stool when she heard a fist hammering on the door of Wilma's boudoir.

"Sadie!" It was Cass's voice. "Open up! I know you're in there."

She muttered an oath, casting a desperate glance at her reflection in the elaborately carved, serpentine mirror. Next she gazed at the hopelessly melting ice in the washrag in her fist.

Dear God. Not Cass. Not now!

No one was supposed to know she was hiding out in Wilma's bedroom—well, except for Rex. Wilma had insisted on delivering Sadie's report about Bodine's "accidental death," minus the embarrassing detail that she'd let Baron smash her face, of course.

At the time, Sadie had been too exhausted to argue with Wilma's wisdom when she'd urged, *"Lay low and plead a woman's complaint."* Wilma had seemed to think Rex would do something violently illegal if he spied Sadie's black eye and the one-inch gash marring her cheekbone, thanks to Baron's wedding ring.

The good news was, the cut wouldn't scar and her vision was as sharp as ever. The bad news was, she looked like she'd collided with a locomotive. Even so, Sadie couldn't imagine Rex getting violently illegal about a shiner.

Cass, however, was another matter.

"Go away!" she shouted, darting on bare, catlike feet around Wilma's love lair so she could turn down the gas lamps. *Where the hell are Cotton and Gator? What good are twin bouncers if neither of them can barricade a street door?*

"Are you poisoned?"

"No!"

"Then we need to talk," Cass called.

"I don't want to talk!"

Sadie clutched Wilma's black, satin robe around her throat and backed as far as possible from the bombazine keeping the noonday sun from pouring through the windows. Light was not her friend right now.

"This isn't a social call, woman!"

"Yeah? Well, I'm not open for business."

"What the devil's the matter with you?"

"You! You know better than to send me a basket full of pastries!"

"I didn't send you any pastries!"

She blew out her breath. She didn't know whether to be relieved or alarmed to have her suspicion confirmed about his forged signature. "Well, someone did. And signed *your name* to the card."

"What?" He rattled the brass door handle. "You think *I* tried to poison you?"

"No, I think you're a cockroach! Last night, total strangers showered me with roses, but you couldn't give me one stinking daisy! Or a bottle of champagne. Or that forged card, apparently! You didn't even stay for my second solo! You were too busy ransacking my vanity and sticking a knife through my nose!"

"Served you right! You showed up on Sterne's arm. And as I recall, I gave you a gold chain for your button!"

"Yeah? Well, who asked you to? Get lost!"

A heartbeat passed. Then another. She curled nervous toes through the plush, shag pile of Persian wool. She knew Cass too well to think he'd tucked his tail and slinked away just because she'd turned diva on him.

And then she heard it. The dreaded scraping of a widdy in the lock.

"Cass, so help me God, I'll brain you with a candle stick if you come busting through that—"

But he was a lot faster with a lock pick than she remembered. She'd barely had time to grab the brass implement of his destruction before the door banged open, and he towered on the threshold, scowling.

"Why is it so dark in here?"

"I was sleeping!"

"The bed's made."

She cursed her stupidity. *"On the chaise!"* she fired back. "What the hell kind of man breaks into an unwilling woman's bedroom?"

He cocked his head. She could tell by the flicker of his emotions, his anger was rapidly dissolving into suspicion. "It's not like you to hide in the corner, Tiger."

She swallowed hard. Damn his Coyote instincts. "I want you out of this room! *Now!*"

His wary gaze flitted over the ebonized furnishings. The boudoir's showpiece was a towering half-tester bed in the Rococo style. The mahogany posters gleamed like dark flames in the flickering storm-light, pouring through the doorway. Sensual furs and silky comforters enticed male visitors for a sumptuous romp beneath a gold-and-burgundy canopy, crowned with a medallion of Wilma's monogram.

Cass didn't look impressed. He was too busy hunting for threats. At least, that was Sadie's guess, since he barely glanced at the lovers writhing on the scarlet silk of the hand-painted dressing screen. Nor did he pay attention to the tinkling crystal in the chandelier; the wicked sleigh-chaise that could be cranked up or down to accentuate pleasure; the boxy, chintz-draped chiffonier (whose deceptively staid drawers hid Wilma's most imaginative tools;) or any of the ruby vases, sporting blood-red poppies mingled with the fluffy plumes of albino peacocks (Sadie's favorite love toy.)

Cass did, however, focus on shadows, especially around the bottom of the dressing screen, draperies, wardrobe, and mattress. He tossed her a questioning look and patted his holster.

"Of course I'm alone! And safe."

"No lover hiding under the bed, eh?"

"Why must you always leap to the most sordid conclusion? Can't a woman just *sleep*, for God's sake?"

He was watching her now as if she were a confidence man playing three-card Monte. "Sure you can sleep. But first, step into the light."

Panic threatened what little composure she had left. "Cass, I'll scream this house down around your head if you don't leave! Now!"

"Truce?"

"No!"

"How come?"

"Because!"

He closed the door and advanced.

"Cass, I'm warning you! Not another step!"

His eyes narrowed, and his strides grew more determined.

"Cass, *please...*" She was cornered—literally. She strangled on a sob. The candlestick slipped from her fingertips.

Then he was standing before her, staring at her shiner. His breath sucked in on a hissing rush of outrage. In that moment, his expression was truly terrible: an unholy mask of vengeance. Satan himself would have fled for the hills.

"Who?" he demanded in guttural tones.

Tears were streaming down her cheeks. She hated herself for that show of weakness; she knew what it would cost. Her shiner didn't hurt nearly as much as the realization she would lose him—in a heartbeat—if he gunned down a senator in her defense.

"Don't leave me!" she sobbed, desperately flinging

herself into his arms.

Cass staggered, clasping her shuddering length protectively to his chest. It was bad enough that some bastard had struck a woman—*his* woman—in the face. But what really rocked his world was the sight of Sadie, shedding tears. Never, in the 13 years that he'd known her, had he seen the Devil's Daughter weep. Sadie was more of the pounce-and-claw-your-eyes-out kind of female.

"Sadie," he rasped, "I'll make this right for you. I swear. On my mother's grave, I will!"

His vow didn't elicit the desired effect. She buried her face in his throat and wept harder.

Now he was worried some of her bruises weren't visible. He struggled to rein in his fury as he searched for other damage. Anxiously, he smoothed her flaming curls away from the creamy column of her neck. Gingerly, he pushed ebony silk from her alabaster shoulders. The sight of all those darling freckles, dancing with such carefree abandon over her pouty breasts, made his heart hurt. He couldn't bear to know he'd failed to protect her in Galveston, and now in Lampasas. He would kill the sniveling coward who'd cut her face and caused her pain!

"Sadie," he begged, his throat aching, "please don't cry. I won't let anyone hurt you. Not ever again."

"How can you do that if you leave me?"

"I'm not going to leave you."

"You *always* leave me! Like you did in Pilot Grove!"

"But sweetheart, I had to. The law was hot on my trail—"

"You left me in *Dodge* because of the law, too!"

He winced, guilt searing his gut. "I was an uncurried fool. I should have believed you—"

"And then you left me in *Galveston!*"

"Oh God," he groaned, burying his face in her curls. "I'll *never* forgive myself for that. Never."

She sniffled.

A moment passed.

"Well, I did tell you to leave that time," she conceded grudgingly. "For your own good. Before you got recognized at the Satin Siren."

"Doesn't matter."

She fidgeted, wiping her cheek against his bandanna.

"But you couldn't have known there'd be a fire in my bedroom," she said, her voice muffled and contrite against his shirt collar. "No one could have known. And I really was glad to see you alive and healthy. And looking so fine. After Wyatt Earp ran you out of Dodge, I had no way of knowing how you were. Or where you were. Or if I'd ever see you again!"

Cass's heart swelled at her confession. He knew how much Sadie deplored "icky, sappy, girly feelings," as her 15-year-old self had once described them. Unless Sadie was singing to a hundred adoring men from the safety of a stage, sentiment rarely crossed her lips. In private, Sadie preferred to joke. Or throw things.

"Sadie," he murmured, "do you remember what I promised you that last night we were together in Dodge?"

Gently, insistently, he raised her head. Spiky, tear-drenched lashes quivered over luminous jewels. Sparkles of topaz, citrine, and amber flashed like sunshine in her eyes. She was his dawn. The power to light his whole world.

"I promised that someday, I would teach you how to love," he said huskily. "And I promised, too, you would like it." He ran the pad of his thumb along her bottom lip. "That time has come, darlin'."

As Cass lowered his head, Sadie trembled. How could she have forgotten a promise like that? Four years ago, she had dared to fantasize, picturing what life might have been like, if she could be free of her brothel contract and he could be free of the bounty on his head. But less than an hour later, Cass had ridden out of town, and she'd been painfully reminded her lover was a master of pretty words and ardent declarations. Never the truth.

Now Cass was a Ranger. That meant he couldn't be hers today any more than he'd been hers as an outlaw. But as lightning sizzled beyond the windows of their love lair, Sadie kissed him anyway. It was a way of keeping him close. Of distracting him. Of saving him from Hank and the hangman. In the harsh, clear light of dawn, when she had to face the tyranny of her conscience, she knew she could let Cass go, if he wouldn't be happy to stay in her arms. What she couldn't do was go on living, if she knew he'd never wake up to see the sunrise.

His tongue tangled with hers, the heady taste of spiced ardor. His clothes smelled of tobacco, leather, and horse, but the fragrance of sandalwood clung to his skin, making her long to lick the brine from his chest—and lap up the flavors beckoning much lower.

Slyly, he slipped the tie of her robe. Silk slithered in a puddle to her ankles. Her nakedness flushed, brazed by the promise of his caress. When he swept her up in his arms, his mouth was still feasting on hers. He carried her to the bed, pausing only long enough to unbuckle his guns and kick off his boots. Then he was sinking with her into the soft pelage of wolf and puma.

With a hungry little growl, she made short work of the buttons on his fly while his muscular shoulders shrugged off his shirt. She enjoyed sliding her palms over the tawny fur of his chest, tracing the golden down over rock-ribbed planes. Wickedly, she buried her fingers in the springy little curls that cradled his virility. When she squeezed, dragging her thumbnail along his ridged trigger, he growled in return.

But he wouldn't let her stroke that princely shaft. Instead, he insisted on her pleasure. After enduring years of groping from drunken, belching clods, Sadie craved a lighter, more creative touch. Instinctively, Cass understood this. His sensitivity to her tiniest tremor, her softest sigh, was a wet dream come true.

Her eyelashes fluttered closed. A dreamy languor weighted her limbs. Oh, the things the Rebel Rutter could do with his tongue! His sly, persistent kisses could make her forget who she was. Where she was. Whether heaven was up or down. He could coax tremors of ecstasy with just that clever, mobile mouth! His ability was a rare, advanced skill—and a point of pride with him.

She smiled a little at the memories.

But today he took another, more leisurely route to her satisfaction. As thunder shook the walls, he worshipped her body, every inch—every freckle. She squirmed in helpless delight as he sucked her ticklish navel; she laughed as his tongue flicked, serpent-like, between her toes. She trembled with anticipation as his stubbled chin gently scraped the quivering, inner flesh of her thigh. At last, moist little gusts of heat were tantalizing her cleft.

"Cass," she breathed, half plea, half sigh.

The pad of his thumb was calloused—devastating to her restraint. He knew that. He plied it anyway.

She arched helplessly, and he feasted.

It wasn't just his tender nipping or the wicked thrusting of his fingers that drove her wild. It was the deep, guttural growl of his satisfaction. Like some great, predatory beast, he was intent on devouring his fill. The slurping and the panting made her ooze with shameless wanting. She grabbed a fistful of his hair to encourage his feeding.

Contrary as usual, he caught her wrists and stretched them over her head.

"But Cass—"

"Silence, wench. I'll please you any damned way I want."

"Like hell."

He chuckled wolfishly.

It was the old game, and she loved it—especially when he entered her with a juicy sound.

His fingers twined with hers. "Ever fly to the moon?" he taunted huskily.

She bit back a moan. "Not with you."

"Liar." Sharp little teeth prickled her earlobe. "I think I'll stop."

"I'll kill you!"

"That's my angel."

Her breaths were ripping now. Every fiber of her being threatened to splinter with sensation. Like some crazy, chaotic kaleidoscope, he had her spinning out of control.

Fire and ice, silence and thunder—her senses were imploding. And then, just when she didn't think she could bear another exquisite second of his love-making, she shattered into a hundred-million prism pieces, careening through rainbows like a wild, shooting star.

His hands gripped hers hard as she rocketed through that blizzard of sparkles.

"Through all time, you and me: born for you," he crooned the lyrics in her ear.

Tears streamed down her cheeks. One by one, he kissed them away. With infinite tenderness, he smoothed the tangle of curls from her swollen cheek. Then he folded her against his chest. She clung to his neck, afraid to speak the words that ached to be freed.

I love you, Cass.

The sweet, steady thrumming of his heart was like a lullaby. Feeling safe for the first time since Galveston, she closed her eyes and slept.

CHAPTER 19

As shadows lengthened across the bed, Cass lay beside Sadie, watching her breathe. His throat ached to spy the glistening trace of a tear; his blood boiled to see the gash and the puffy, green-black bruise that marred her perfect beauty. If he used his imagination, he could picture the outline of knuckles and the wedding ring that had raised that shiner.

His lips twisted in a silent snarl.

After those headlines in the *Dispatch,* he didn't need a crystal ball to know Baron was responsible. Cass now understood why Sadie had hidden in the shadows—and why Wilma had tried to send him away. Their efforts had only delayed the inevitable. Cass didn't give a rat's ass if Baron was sick. Or a senator. The bastard was *not* going to get away with hitting his woman!

With the stealth of his canine namesake, Cass slipped from the bed and gathered his clothes. In a brothel, nobody cared about the proprieties, so he dressed in the hall and buckled on his guns. The familiar weight of his six-shooters brought to mind another problem.

Hank.

Cass muttered an oath as the name rolled through his mind. He'd almost forgotten his vow to determine what had really happened between Baron and The Ventilator at

Aquacia Bathhouse.

Well, Baron can tell me himself when I drag him out of that hospital bed.

Retrieving one of his three widdies—in this case, the decoy he liked to let lawmen find in his hatband—Cass relocked Sadie's door. Grimacing with the effort, he bent the slender pick and snapped off its tip in the keyhole.

That should keep the spitfire from tracking killers by her lonesome.

As he descended to the first landing, he glanced out the vaulted windows. Shafts of light punched through pewter storm clouds. He figured the hour was after four o'clock. Sundown was about 90 minutes away. Across the street, candle flames flickered in the jack o' lanterns, smiling so gruesomely from a neighbor's porch steps. Silhouetted by the setting sun, a man in a chocolate Stetson loitered in that yard. He perched on a hay bale like some reckless scarecrow, tapping cigarette ash and blowing rings of smoke into the breeze.

Other than daring the devil by smoking on a flammable seat, the man wasn't remarkable. He had a brown duster. Brown boots. Brown hair. Nevertheless, prickles of warning sprinkled Cass's scalp.

Hank?

Cass couldn't see the man's face, but his instincts had never failed him. Determined to confront his nemesis, Cass crawled out the parlor window to avoid Cotton.

But when Cass rounded the building, a buckboard of whooping, dark-skinned children rolled down the center of Third Street. The boys were throwing straw at each other. The girls were eating soul cakes and sugar skulls. Cass guessed the black-robed padre was driving the orphans to a Halloween fandango.

Only a few seconds ticked by as the church wagon trundled past, but when the dust settled, Cass realized the man on the hay bale had vanished.

Muttering an oath, Cass checked the bullets in his guns

and headed for the livery. He hoped to challenge Hank there, but when he reached the stable yard, he realized he'd followed a dead trail, at least where The Ventilator was concerned. Cass did find a roan tethered next to Pancake; however, the gelding wasn't Rhubarb.

A fresh wave of worry plagued Cass's gut. Where the hell was Collie? And why hadn't he stopped Baron from hitting Sadie? Collie could be a surly cuss, but he had his priorities straight. If he'd thought Baron was in a fist-swinging mood, the kid would have protected Sadie, not abandoned her.

Mounting up, Cass turned Pancake toward the town's hospital. But he hadn't cantered more than a block when he spied a commotion near the Public Square. A small but noisy crowd of *Tejanos* had gathered beside the red-and-white pole of Boomer's Barbershop. By the time Cass had ridden the distance, Sid had arrived on the scene.

"All right, all right, simmer down," the marshal boomed. *"Silencio!"* he added, wading through the anxious *Tejanos*. "There are no such things as goblins. Not even in cemeteries."

"But little Pedro saw a monster!" cried a chubby *señora*.

"And evil fire magic!" a youthful voice chimed in.

"The monster called down thunder," shouted another boy from the rear. "He blasted a hole in the old caretaker's door!"

"Sí!" shouted several *niños*.

Sid snorted, folding brawny arms across his chest. "And just what were you boys doing on Mr. Oldham's property? *After dark?"*

A guilty hush settled over the younger members of the audience.

Sid drilled his gunfighter's glare into one of the shorter hecklers. "Well, Joaquin?"

The boy fidgeted, averting his eyes. "Er…I think I was lost, *señor*. On my way home from church."

Amusement vied with the authoritative scowl on Sid's face. "You *think* you were lost?"

Somebody snickered.

"I'm not going to find any rotten eggs or flour residue if I ride out to that cottage. *Am* I, Luis?"

"Oh no, *señor*," the older, taller rascal lied. "Flour bombs are for babies."

"Yeah?" Sid lowered bristling, black eyebrows. "Then what do you know about the surrey on my roof?"

Luis gulped and bolted. So did a half-dozen other adolescents, scattering in every direction.

"I'll lock you up and throw away the key!" Sid hollered after the mischief-makers. "Don't think I won't!"

Cass snickered behind his hand.

Sid caught his eye and reddened. "Shut up." Hiking his trousers, the marshal bellowed to the rest of the crowd, "All right, folks! The show's over! Move along, or you'll be doing all your trick-or-treating from jail!"

Well, *that* lit a fire under the macabrely curious. Before Cass could count to ten, the sidewalk beside Boomer's barber pole looked like a ghost town.

Sid chuckled. "Works every time," he confided to no one in particular.

Cass swung from the saddle.

"What're you doing here?" Sid demanded, hooking his thumbs over his gun belt.

"I came to get my boots shined. Is that a crime?"

"Maybe," the marshal said ominously. "I can sure make it one."

"Hey!" Joaquin protested.

"Aren't you just a little curious about what those boys saw at the cemetery last night?" Cass demanded.

"You telling me how to do my job?"

"Nope. Just asking a civil question of a peace officer."

Sid grunted. He didn't look convinced. "Well, seeing as how you're a stranger to these parts, I reckon you wouldn't know about local Halloween traditions," he said. "The fact is, I hear the same cock-n-bull story every year. Ghosts dancing 'round the lynching tree. Goblin faces peeking out the windows.

"'Course, I might be troubled to investigate further for a

good reason," he added grimly. "Like, you think McAffee was causing mischief at the Oldham place. Or maybe you got wind he was poisoning folks."

"Aw, c'mon, Sid. Who put a bug in your ear about that boy? Collie's a good kid."

"Not according to your boss's wife."

"Poppy?"

"That's right. I couldn't say anything last night 'cause she swore me to secrecy. She was afraid for her life."

Cass frowned.

"Look, Cass. I should be keeping my mouth shut, but we go back a long way. So I'll tell it to you straight. About two days ago, Mrs. Westerfield came to me in a hand-wringing tizzy. Said she'd sent Tito on an errand. He was supposed to walk to the post office and mail her correspondence. He should have been gone 20 minutes, but he never came back. He missed his appointment to drive her to a Suffragette meeting. He missed lunch and dinner, too, which she claimed was unlike him. She was deeply worried. She said she doted on that boy."

Ignoring the skepticism on Cass's face, Sid continued, "Mrs. Westerfield checked the livery. Tito's horse was missing, and he'd cleared his carpetbag from the hotel room. At first, she thought he'd quit his job. But then she remembered how he and Collie had argued. How the boy had threatened to make him pay. And then she noticed that Collie was whittling with Tito's knife."

"What?"

"I know you think the kid's reformed. So I did a little investigating. Sent out wires to marshals in surrounding towns. Tito's horse showed up in Belton yesterday. The circuit preacher, who was riding the nag, claimed he bought it in Lampasas for $100. From a fella named McAffee."

"That's ridiculous!"

Sid hiked an eyebrow. "Are you saying a *senator's wife* is telling whoppers?"

"No," Cass ground out reluctantly. "I'm saying there has

to be another explanation."

"Well, I've got a poisoned corpse on my hands, a sworn testimony from a senator's wife, a missing suspect, and a sick senator—whom Collie had plenty of time to poison last night," Sid added grimly. "The longer McAffee hides, the more suspicious he looks. If you care about that kid, then convince him to pay me a call. With an alibi."

The marshal's tin star flashed as he swung up into the saddle. Pinching his hat brim, he gave Cass a grim nod before he spurred his gelding.

Cass stood scowling after Sid's cloud of dust. None of Poppy's story made sense. First of all, why would she go to Sid? She had no faith in him as a lawman.

Secondly, Collie had his own whittling knife, one of the few gifts his Pa had given him. Collie wasn't likely to covet someone else's blade.

Third, the kid wasn't any horse trader, but if he'd been trying to raise cash fast, he sure as hell wouldn't have sold a sweet-tempered, reliable mare for a measly $100!

Cass felt a tentative tug on his sleeve. Joaquin stood beside him, a dab of bootblack on his nose. A small cross, make of bone, peeked from the open laces of his orange and green *serape.* He was crumpling the brim of his *sombrero* as he turned the hat nervously in his hands.

"*Señor* Cass, Collie is *mi amigo.* Did he really do all those bad things the gringo lawman said?"

"No, *niño.* " Cass forced a smile for the youngster, whose butternut face was creased with worry. "Sometimes, lawmen have to sort through a lot of gossip and misunderstandings to find the truth. Kind of like Marshal Wright did today, when you were too afraid to tell him what you really saw at the cemetery."

Joaquin's chin jutted. "You saw how he was! He thinks I'm a baby! He wouldn't believe anything I said!"

Cass dropped to one knee and squeezed the boy's shoulder. "*I* think you're man enough to tell me the truth."

Joaquin fidgeted. He averted his eyes.

"Marshal Wright's gone now, son. You can speak your

piece. Tell me about this fire and thunder that blasted a hole through the door at the Oldham place. Was it a rifle shot?"

Joaquin nodded reluctantly. "I saw a shadowy figure, wearing a Stetson. He was inside the house. He was a mean *hombre.* He kept laughing and shooting at us *niños!"*

Cass's jaw hardened. "Did he hit anyone?"

"Only Collie."

Cass must have blanched, because Joaquin added hastily, "I mean, he hit Collie's liquor bottle when he was running past the fountain."

"What else can you tell me?"

"He kept shouting at Collie. Something like, 'I owe you a slug for putting a hole in my bowler!' Then Collie got kind of squeamish. He lost his dinner."

Squeamish? Cass frowned. That wasn't a word he would normally use to describe Collie. "Where?"

"On the steps of the Villarreal tomb. About a 100 yards southeast of the central fountain," Joaquin added helpfully.

"Did Collie come back to town with you?"

Tears glistened in the boy's eyes. He shook his head.

Something cold settled in the pit of Cass's stomach. He would have bet his badge that Hank was the sniper in the cemetery.

"Joaquin," he said grimly, pressing a nickel into the youngster's palm, "I want you to do me a favor."

Joaquin nodded eagerly.

"Go and find General Sterne. Tell him *Señor* Cass sent you with an urgent message. Tell him everything you saw and heard at the cottage. Tell him the truth, just like you told me. Then tell the general I'll be at the boneyard, scouting around. Can you remember all that?"

"Si, señor!"

"Gracias, niño."

Sheet lightning illuminated swollen thunderheads as Cass cantered toward the cemetery. The wind was picking up, tearing red and brown leaves from thrashing trees. Along the road, he encountered several *Tejano* families. Huddled for warmth in their mule-drawn carts, they were headed back to town after their ritual grave-decorating. He waved them to a halt so he could question them in Spanish.

None of the *Tejanos* remembered seeing a youth of Collie's description, much less a sniper trespassing on the Oldham property. The general consensus was that the cemetery had emptied of all revelers, because preparations must be made for the Feast of the Dead, which *Tejanos* typically served in their homes at sundown.

His uneasiness mounting, Cass thanked them for their help and rode on.

Judging by the disc of brilliance that tried, unsuccessfully, to burn through the overhead gloom, Cass guessed he reached the cemetery's gate around half-past four. Orange marigolds and rusty leaves tumbled across his path as he hid Pancake in a shrubby area, partly to protect the buckskin from the brewing storm, and partly to avoid discovery. His *Tejano* informants might not have seen Hank, but that didn't mean the bastard had abandoned the premises.

A quick scan of the main path allowed Cass to find Collie's tracks. They were easy to recognize, thanks to the coon prints accompanying them. Unlike the vast majority of foot traffic, Collie's trail traveled south, following the fence and its hedgerows. For some reason, the boy had skirted the central fountain, which still smoldered with the pungent aroma of burnt cedar. Cass guessed the kid had wanted to avoid Joaquin's gang of *Tejano* revelers. Until Cass had gotten the boy interested in Texas and Rangerhood, Collie used to shun most human company.

Straining his senses for bushwhackers, Cass followed Collie's trail to a lightning-sheared oak. Or maybe the tree's limbs had been sheared by gunfire, Cass mused, spying a slug in the trunk about a foot above his head. A large, rotted limb had crashed across a tombstone, where coon prints abounded, suggesting Vandy had frisked for treats. A crushed patch of grass told where Collie had parked his rear; broken marigold planters marked where Hank's potshots had struck pay dirt.

Tamping down a surge of rage, Cass continued tracking. He spotted an orange napkin fluttering in a bush; the scattered shards of a bourbon bottle; and long, running strides where Collie had dodged bullets. Then Cass found the vomit on the mausoleum stoop.

About three feet further south, twin gouges told the story of boot heels being dragged off the stoop onto the lawn.

Five yards further, Hank had heaved Collie onto his shoulder.

Sick with dread, Cass picked up his pace, loping through the rain-starved grasses. He soon realized Hank's tracks weren't heading toward the caretaker's cottage; instead, they were leading toward a park-like area, dominated by a ponderous, granite structure.

Good God. Was Collie locked inside that mausoleum?

As if in answer, a ring-tailed wraith lumbered back and forth along the building's stoop. Every so often, Vandy would rise on his haunches, scratch the door, and whine in a pitiful manner.

Cass's heart wrenched.

The rustic little house of death looked as gloomy as the lowering thunderheads. Mildew-colored lichen dotted the weathered stone and the twin colonnades that flanked the entry; the weeping angel topping the roof was missing several fingers and toes. Unlike most Victorian mausoleums, which incorporated light to uplift the spirits within, this tomb had no windows. Nor was it engraved with a family name, although Cass suspected the bones inside belonged to White men. He found himself missing the colorful skeleton dolls that lent a festive, almost *friendly* feel to the *Tejano* tombs.

He forced his feet forward.

To approach a mausoleum—with the intention of entering it—would have been spooky on any day of the year. On Halloween, the proposition was downright ghoulish. Cass's palms grew damp as he removed the trigger guards from his guns.

Suddenly, Vandy grew excited. The door was beginning to move; its rusted hinges squealed in protest. The eager coon galloped into the shaft of candlelight that pierced the cemetery's gloom. Scratching and wriggling, he squeezed his girth past the door.

Cass held his breath. He expected to hear Collie's muffled greeting.

Instead, the sound that reverberated through the ruddy interior was Vandy's growl.

"Quit playing around," a female voice snapped. "And hurry! We have preparations to make at the house."

Cass slowed his strides. His hands flexed instinctively over his holsters.

Within moments, Poppy pushed her way onto the lawn. She was dressed in a peculiar fashion: a black monk's robe with bell-shaped sleeves. Cass hiked an eyebrow. Why was she wearing a Halloween costume in a mausoleum? Why wasn't she at the hospital with Baron?

He halted a judicious 20 yards from the tomb's doorway. When she turned and saw him, she shrieked, making a great show of clutching her heart and fanning her face.

"Good heavens, Cass! You gave me such a fright!"

"Did I?" he countered in gravelly tones. He had no patience for her theatrics today, not after the whoppers she'd been telling Sid about Collie. Part of Cass wanted to believe she was prone to hysterics, that she'd merely leaped to some unflattering conclusions about an insolent young man, whom she considered backwards and crass.

Another part of him feared she had deliberately implicated Collie in Tito's murder.

"Where's Collie?" he demanded.

She raised her chin a notch. "Honestly. You don't have to bite my head off. He's inside."

"Doing what?"

"Helping me arrange the memorial flowers, of course."

Cass's eyes narrowed as he considered her response. He supposed it could be true. But then, why hadn't Collie greeted Vandy?

"Aren't you jumping the gun?" Warily, he began to close the distance between them. "Baron isn't dead yet."

She blew out her breath. "The flowers aren't for Baron; they're to commemorate the Day of the Dead—*a church holiday.*"

Lightning spat above the angel on the roof. Undaunted, Poppy held her ground, blocking the door and toying with the emerald ring below her scarlet fingernails. The flickering glow that emanated from the mausoleum limned her head and shoulders in orange. For some reason, Cass was reminded of Jazi's vision: the witch with the bloody claws and flaming hair.

He pushed the absurdity aside.

"I wasn't aware you had kinfolk in Lampasas," he probed in dubious tones.

"I don't like to speak of him."

"Because he's dead?"

"Because he's a bastard."

Cass halted before her. Whether she'd meant her kinsman was illegitimate or unscrupulous wasn't clear. "So that's why there's no surname over the keystone?"

She nodded. An oddly intense glow had kindled in her stare.

Suddenly, the utter silence in the mausoleum registered on Cass's senses. If Collie was really arranging pots of marigolds behind that door, wouldn't he be grumbling to Vandy about the task? Wouldn't Cass hear scraping and rustling? Footsteps and coon snuffling?

"I'm glad we ran into each other," Poppy said, distracting him with her husky tone. "I'm glad we'll have this opportunity to put last night behind us." She pasted on a smile—one that looked a tad ghoulish beneath the color-leeching flash of sky fire. "I'd hate for Baron to get the wrong idea."

"Me, too."

"So it'll be our secret. Forever."

"Uh-huh." He was only half listening. In fact, he was

trying to see past her shoulder into the tomb.

Maybe that's why he was so surprised when she sprang at him like a sex-starved alley cat. Their chests collided, and he *oomphed,* staggering. She threw her arms around his neck, and something sharp pricked his skin. He thought it must have been her ring, but he was too busy muttering oaths and disentangling himself from her headlock to give the matter much thought.

"Dammit, woman! Enough!" He shoved her aside.

"My sentiments exactly." A vicious little smile curved her lips. "Good-bye, Cass."

He crossed the lawn toward the tomb. Dizziness assailed him by the third step. With his fourth step, pinwheels of light were spinning in his brain. His heart was speeding. His lungs were wheezing. His mouth tasted like sand.

Against the backdrop of candlelight, a shadowy figure in a brown Stetson swam into focus. The silhouette shoved the tomb's door wider. Instinctively, Cass reached for a Colt, but his knees were buckling. The ground was speeding upward at an alarming rate.

He never felt the bone-jarring jolt of that collision. He was unconscious before he hit the dirt.

CHAPTER 20

Sadie woke with a start. Dark purple shadows were creeping across the bed. She was cold, and her heart was pounding harder than usual. For a moment, she wasn't sure why.

Then she realized she was clutching a pillow, not her lover. Cass had left her. *Again!*

Fighting off an inexplicable sense of dread, she threw back the quilt and turned up the gas lamp by the bed. According to the timepiece on the mantel, the hour was after 5 p.m. Masked revelers were probably prowling the streets, demanding candy and singing for soul cakes.

Turning her back on her battered reflection, she threw on a shirt and trousers. Since Wilma was two inches shorter—and enviably rounder in the hips—the Cajun had ordered Gator to haul Sadie's traveling trunk from the cave to the boudoir. That meant Sadie had mostly men's clothing to choose from. However, the wardrobe suited her. No lady walked the streets, looking like she'd brawled in a saloon. Even whores didn't show their faces in public after a beating, since damaged goods raised less money.

She returned to the vanity, where she encountered Wilma's ritual implements. Before Cass's arrival, the Mambo had insisted on chanting a healing spell for Sadie's eye and imploring Loa Eshu to protect her from evil. Sadie hadn't dared to protest, although she had cracked a few nervous jokes. Needless to say, Wilma hadn't considered them funny.

Confronted once more by the evidence of the Cajun's spooky side—a side which Sadie didn't understand, and wasn't sure she wanted to—she glanced over her shoulder like a guilty child. Satisfied the door was closed, she wrinkled her nose and gingerly pushed aside dried rosemary and peony root, guttered candles and etched bones, and a cotton poppet with red hair and a black eye. The doll looked alarmingly like her.

Remind me never to piss off Wilma.

At last feeling safe enough to reach for her brush, Sadie perched on the vanity stool and began working the snarls from her curls. She'd just about finished the process when she heard voices arguing in the hall.

"Thanks to some pranking kids and their ghost stories, the uncurried fool decided to play hero," Rex growled. "He rode off to a potential hostage situation. *Without backup.* Now no one knows where he is."

"If you didn't think Cass was ready to ride alone," Wilma retorted, "you shouldn't have made him a Ranger."

Sadie lowered her hair brush.

Cass is missing?

She stomped on boots, all the while straining her ears to hear the escalating argument.

"I pinned Cassidy to give him immunity in case he had to draw his gun," Rex said, "*not* so he could run half-cocked through the streets on a personal vendetta. You were supposed to keep him out of the brothel."

"I did send him away, *cher*, but—"

"You didn't stop to think he might sneak back? To flap his jaw?"

"Cass is a braggart," Wilma conceded. "But he's not malicious. He won't break a pact just to cause pain."

"That's easy for you to say."

"Non, cher. In truth, it is not. Cass discovered a long time ago I am not what I pretend to be. He has kept his silence

on my account with great nobility."

Sadie frowned. Wilma was talking about her Octoroon ancestry, right?

"Dammit!" Rex said. "I wanted to tell her in my own time. In my own way."

"And so you shall, *cher.* Sadie's not the type to fume in silence. Don't you think she would have confronted you by now?"

Wait a minute. They're talking about me?

"Wilma!" Sadie bellowed, proving her old friend right about the fuming part. "What are you two yammering about?"

Dead silence came from the hallway.

Sadie stormed to the door and grabbed the handle.

It wouldn't budge.

She frowned. She tugged. She twisted the lock. Her mind flashed back to that horrific night in Galveston, and panic welled inside her. She half expected a bomb to crash through the window at any moment.

"Rex!" She started pounding on the door. "I can't get out!"

She heard the rumble of masculine ire. Then came the jingle of spurs. Someone jiggled the handle—to no avail.

"The lock is jammed. Looks like it was broken. From the outside."

Sadie sputtered an oath at Rex's assessment. This time the vision flashing through her mind was of one thoroughly dead Coyote.

"Cass did it!" She kicked the brass housing of the keyhole. "*On purpose!"*

"Why would Cassidy lock her inside?" Rex murmured.

"Love games," Wilma answered breezily. "The *chirens* are always playing dungeon prisoner and pleasure slave—"

"I am *not* playing, dammit!" Sadie was banging both fists on the door now. "Let me out! So I can *kill* him!"

"No one's killing anybody," Rex snapped. "You got a screwdriver?" he asked Wilma.

"I have many things for screwing, but—"

"Why do I get the feeling you're stalling?"

Wilma made an exasperated sound. "Must you read treachery into every single—"

"And now you're hiding something."

"Impossible man! Don't you have a killer to hunt? Not to mention a rogue Ranger? Cotton is perfectly capable of removing a door from its hinges—"

"So am I."

A Colt cylinder clicked. Sadie bit her lip. She'd suddenly remembered why Wilma had cautioned her to keep out of Rex's sight.

"Don't you *dare* put a dent in my brass!" Wilma flared. "I just polished—"

"Are you clear, Sadie?" Rex demanded in gravelly tones.

She cursed herself. Maybe if her shiner had hurt worse, she wouldn't have forgotten about it!

"Wilma's right," she said sheepishly. "You should be hunting Hank. And Cass is probably playing Halloween drinking games with Collie…"

"Step back," Rex commanded. "Now."

Sadie gulped. Desperately glad she wasn't the target of Rex's bullets, she fled to the corner, covering her ears. Sparks spit through the keyhole. A heartbeat later, he was kicking in the door. She glimpsed Wilma behind his shoulder, shaking her head in exasperation. Sadie actually considered diving under the bed.

Instead, she somehow managed to straighten her spine. She mustered the courage to face the man who'd been like a father to her for four years. Wintry-gray eyes raked her for damage, but they didn't have to look far.

The icy hellbroth darkening that gaze made Cass's outrage seem tame.

"It wasn't Cass!" she blurted. "It was Baron!"

Rex's chest heaved at this news.

"Come into the light."

The thread of iron underlying that deceptively calm voice would not be disobeyed. Sadie dragged her feet a few steps.

She couldn't bring herself to meet his eyes.

"Sadie," he said in a soft, grim tone. "We have a great deal to discuss. Not the least of which is…" He gestured toward her cheek. "I should never have allowed you to masquerade as my lover."

"No!" Sadie hurried toward him then, afraid of what he might do. "Bruises heal. I knew the risks. I took them anyway. For God's sake, Rex, don't do anything rash! I could never forgive myself if harm came to you or Cass because of some stupid shiner! I'm a Pinkerton! I was doing my job."

His jaw hardened. "And I'm a Ranger. It's time I did mine."

He released her from that vise-like stare. Nodding curtly, he turned on his heel, his spurs chinking as he headed down the hall. The glance he tossed at Wilma was raw with accusation.

The Cajun's dark eyes grew bright with tears.

Burning with remorse, Sadie joined her friend in the hall. "I'm sorry, Wilma. I was so upset about the lock, I didn't stop to think."

"You're more like him than you know, *chere.*" Wilma's lips curved wistfully as she watched her lover's brawny shoulders descend out of sight. "Now we must trust our men to do their jobs, so we can do ours."

Sadie frowned. "What do you mean?"

"Boo was playing hide-and-seek with Gator this afternoon, and no one has seen her since. Was she in the bedroom with you?"

"No." Sadie's face heated to think what an eyeful Jazi would have gotten if she'd been hiding under the bed. "Thank heaven for small miracles, eh?"

But Wilma didn't look amused. In fact, she looked downright disturbed. "It is strange, *non?* Just last night, the child couldn't stop talking about trick-or-treating and singing for soul cakes. She pestered the devil out of me to help her stitch a Mambo headdress and apron. Now the time has come for apple-bobbing and candlestick-jumping, but she cannot be found."

"Did you search the cave? If I were Jazi, I'd be hiding in your contraband and playing pirate-princess."

Wilma sighed. "Mira has turned this house upside-down. But I shall search myself. Perhaps Boo has fallen asleep in a wardrobe."

"Where *is* Mira?"

"Questioning the cook." Wilma shot Sadie a suspicious glance. "Why?"

"No reason."

"Bien." Wilma didn't look fooled. "Just to be clear: you are forbidden to scratch out any eyes or bite off any ears until further notice."

"You really know how to take all the fun out of a full moon," Sadie said dryly.

"Coming?" Wilma was walking to the staircase.

"Sure. Just as soon as I find a suitably ghoulish mask to cover what's left of my face."

"Bottom drawer of the chiffonier," Wilma called as her head descended out of sight.

Sadie waited until the creaking of the stairs faded into the buzz of gruff male voices and husky female laughter in the parlor, below. Then she hurried to the far end of the hall and lowered the staircase to the attic.

Time to see if Miranda Reynolds sent me that basket of poison.

The more Sadie thought about Randie's presence in Lampasas, the more she thought it was suspicious. Why was the bawd hiding in the brothel's attic? Why wasn't she earning her keep like the rest of Wilma's girls? Surely there was more to the mystery than Jazi's childhood innocence.

Sadie thought back to all the investigative reports she'd read about the Galveston blaze: Mace's, the fire marshal's, the police chief's, the insurance adjuster's. An important fact stood out in her mind: in every document, Baron had vouched for Randie's character. So just how well did Baron and Randie know each other?

To answer that question, Sadie began to search through the meager belongings Randie and Jazi had shoved into carpetbags for their trip to Lampasas. Despite Randie's claim she had brought her daughter to convalesce in the baths, Sadie could find no bathing gown anywhere in the cramped and stifling quarters.

What she did find on Jazi's cot were a toy pony with Baron's ranching brand embroidered on its flank; colorful satin hair ribbons, much like those that had decorated Poppy's hotel altar; and a dog-eared edition of *Little Women*, which had been inscribed, *"Happy Birthday, Sugar Plum...Papa B."*

Sadie's eyes narrowed as she recalled how Baron used "Sugar Plum" as an endearment.

Then she remembered something Jazi had said in the cave:

"I never told anyone who really paid for my medicine when I was sick."

So Randie must be the mysterious mistress who'd been "competing" with Chantelle O'Leary for Baron. But just how far would Randie go to eliminate a female rival?

Sadie crossed to Randie's side of the room. The elder Reynolds had arranged her prized bottles of perfume on a whitewashed, pine vanity. Grimly, Sadie began the methodical task of tugging stoppers to inhale three scent-aphrodisiacs known to bawds: cinnamon-vanilla, jasmine-rose, and patchouli.

No violets.

Sadie released a ragged breath. So Randie hadn't forged Cass's signature. But some woman had. The question was, why?

She turned back toward the center of the room. A small yellow sphere on the floor caught her attention. Then another. Frowning, she crossed to a trunk, where she found a toppled tin of Serenata's nostrums, along with a few crushed throat lozenges in the shape of a man's boot heel. Uneasily, she crouched. Floorboards creaked beneath her feet as she stretched a finger and tasted some pastille powder with her tongue.

The residue had a cloyingly sweet taste. More like molasses than lemon. She spit it out.

"Boo? *Tu'est ce que tu fais?*"

Sadie nearly jumped out of her skin to hear Randie's hopeful voice calling from the second floor.

"Boo?" Randie called more insistently. "Are you up there?"

Now the attic's ladder was shaking. Sadie muttered an oath as Randie climbed to the third story. Caught in the act of snooping, there was nothing Sadie could do except straighten her spine, hike her chin, and fire the first bullet.

"Is Senator Westerfield Jazi's real father?" she demanded the minute Randie's dyed curls bobbed into view.

The older bawd grew pale, despite her exertion.

"You!"

"In the flesh."

"What are you doing in my private quarters?"

"Searching for Boo. Like everyone else."

Randie didn't look convinced. Her eyes narrowed as she gestured toward the shiner. "Did Cass give you that?"

"Don't be absurd. Cass doesn't slap women, unless they're naked and begging for it. But then, I don't have to tell *you* what Cass is like in the bedroom."

Randie blew out her breath and climbed the remaining rungs of the ladder. "Honestly, Cassie. Or Maisy. Or Sadie. Or *whatever* your name is today. Cass is the last person on my mind. So kindly slink back to your dungeon. I've got my own problems."

"You mean like Papa B?"

Randie's cheeks mottled. She snatched *Little Women* from Sadie's hands. "You have no right to pry into my daughter's affairs!"

"I think you mean your affairs."

Randie's chest heaved. Her usually perfect coiffure was slipping from its French braid, and the powder on her face had smeared, as if she'd recently shed tears. "I don't have time to argue. My daughter is missing!"

"And yet, *chere,*" Wilma interceded, her voice floating up from the second story, "you will answer the question. For I, too, am curious. Especially about this patron, who insists you hide your face by day and rendezvous with him after midnight—in some establishment other than mine."

Randie looked like she might like to crawl under a bed.

"I told you," Randie whined as Wilma climbed to the attic. "He swore me to silence. If I break his confidence, he'll be angry—"

"*I'm* angry," Wilma snapped. "You've broken *my* confidence. And I deserve to know why you've been lying to me."

"But Wilma, I didn't have a choice—"

"*C'est n'importe quoi!*"

Even Sadie winced to hear the thunder in the Mambo's voice. Randie looked on the verge of tears.

"You don't understand! He's trying to protect me and Boo!"

Sadie frowned. She remembered Baron's talk of Poppy's "talent" for revenge. She remembered his outrage when he'd described how his wife had found a strand of red hair in his underwear drawer. Then she remembered how Poppy had tried to hide her tins of lemon lozenges behind her back.

Maybe Baron really *was* trying to protect Randie!

Uneasiness flurried through Sadie's gut.

"Neither Wilma nor I want harm to come to you," she told Randie. "We want to help."

"*You* want to help?"

"Enough," Wilma interceded. "You will answer questions. *Now.* When did Senator Westerfield learn about Boo?"

Randie fidgeted, averting her eyes. "Last spring. When Boo was sick. I was desperate! I couldn't afford her medicine! I begged Baron for a loan. We rekindled our affair. Then he got it into his head Boo might be his daughter…"

"So you let him believe the lie," Wilma accused.

Randie's chin quivered. She hiked it. "You know what a whore's life is like. I want more for my daughter. Boo *deserves* more. But I never dreamed Baron would take matters as far as he did. I never dreamed he'd add her to his will!"

Wilma's eyes locked with Sadie's.

"When did Mrs. Westerfield learn about the change in Baron's will?" Sadie asked, beginning to piece together a new motive for several unsolved crimes.

Randie shrugged. "About two weeks later, I suppose. Baron was pretty shaken up about the fire. He leaped to the conclusion that some granger faction or political rival wanted him dead. No amount of rationales could dissuade him otherwise.

"But I didn't know anything about the will until Tito met me at the train depot. When I reached Lampasas, he confided he and Cass had witnessed the signing in private, while Mrs. Westerfield was out of town."

Which explains why someone might want to steal Tito's and Cass's signatures from a hotel register. "So you followed Baron to Lampasas," Sadie said. "A rather rash move for a mistress, when the patron's wife is in tow."

Randie's eyes flashed like emerald lightning. "I was *invited* to Lampasas. I received a letter from Baron, encouraging me to bring Boo for the mineral baths. But when I sent word we'd arrived, Baron flew into a rage! He said he'd never written a letter! He accused us of trying to sabotage his re-election campaign. So naturally, I showed him the page with his signature."

"And what did Baron say?" Wilma demanded.

"He…he said he'd get to the bottom of the matter."

"And has he?"

Randie winced. "I don't know. I've been afraid to ask. He's been on edge. Especially about that sniper. And Tito's death…"

"Understandably so." Sadie folded her arms across her chest. "Apparently, someone has been forging his signature.

This 'someone' stands to lose a great deal of money if Baron gets any sicker and Jazi remains in his will. My guess is that 'someone' is Poppy."

"Tito *was* poisoned," Wilma interjected thoughtfully. "And poison is a woman's weapon."

"And Poppy favors violet perfume," Sadie said, recalling the gift card inside the Halloween basket. "The scent of violets accompanied at least one document that I can prove was forged."

Randie's complexion turned ashen. "But surely you don't think Poppy would hurt Boo! She loves children. She has always wanted children!"

"Oui. Children of her own," Wilma said grimly. "Not the child of her husband's mistress. What you may not realize, *chere,* is that Mrs. Westerfield used to clerk in her father's law office. She is more than capable of writing a credible will."

Randie cried out, covering her mouth with a shaking hand. "Oh God, this is all my fault." Tears were streaming down her face as she pulled a crumpled paper from a pocket in her skirt. "About 20 minutes ago, I found this letter on my pillow. I thought it was a joke. A Halloween prank."

Frowning, Sadie took the page and read it aloud for Wilma's benefit:

"If you want to find your daughter, look in the cemetery. Come alone, or you'll both become permanent residents."

Wilma plucked the paper from Sadie's hand. A moment later, she dropped the page as if she'd been burned. She was muttering invectives and making arcane gestures.

"What?" Randie cried. "What did you see?"

"Blood on the moon. There's no time to lose. I will alert Marshal Wright. Sadie will go with you."

"But the paper said—"

"Irrelevant." Wilma waved this protest away like it was smoke. "You will wear identical costumes. You will work as a team to lure the madwoman out."

"We must operate under the assumption Poppy has an accomplice," Sadie said. But she refrained from mentioning the crushed pastilles. She figured Randie would escalate from fear to hysteria if she thought Jazi had been drugged—or worse. "We should wear bullet proof vests."

Randie frowned. "There's a vest that stops bullets?"

Sadie's neck heated as she realized she'd just betrayed the true nature of her work. "Uh…yeah. Rex wears them. We can borrow a few of his."

Randie looked like she was about to question the efficacy of this plan, but Wilma interceded.

"Dépêche-toi!" The Mambo was herding them like goslings toward the ladder. "You're burning daylight, as Cass would say!"

CHAPTER 21

Cass had a roaring in his brain, a burning in his gut, and a weight on his ankles that kept trying to drag him into the darkness. Dimly, he realized he tottered on the edge of the abyss. If he let go, he could ooze into a deep dullness. No pain. No worries. No struggles. An eternity of nothingness yawned before him.

But to an adrenaline junkie like Cass, "nothingness" was the definition of Hell. So he fought his way back to the surface. Scratching and clawing at shreds of shadow, he embraced the pain. He welcomed the nausea. He opened to the flashing cyclone of light, funneling through his brain.

"Damnation," he groaned as pinpricks of sensation became screaming nerves. He was lying on his side, staring at a lumpy, stinking puddle that he suspected was vomit. Maybe even his vomit. None of his limbs worked.

"Did you have a nice nap, Snake Bait?"

"You're *alive?!"* Cass had never been so happy to hear a wisecracking pain-in-the-ass in his life.

"Of course, I'm alive," Collie retorted. "God hates me, and Satan fears me."

Cass laughed—or rather, he tried. The sound came out more like a wheeze. The boy was somewhere behind him in the gloom. Cass hadn't yet figured out how to turn his body so he could see more than the vomit, and five inches beyond that, the black expanse that looked like a marble wall.

"Just for the record," Collie said. "That wasn't much of a rescue."

"You're welcome." Cass grunted. He was wrestling the hemp that bound his wrists behind his back. "Where are we?"

"Judging by the lack of windows, the R.I.P., and the coffin—"

"We're in a *tomb?!*"

"I was going to say a really lame Halloween party, but yeah. 'Tomb' works, too."

Cass cursed again, this time succeeding in rolling to his haunches. Now he could see the light source that cast a dim, ruddy glow on the walls. A candle sputtered inside a canvas sack, which was lined with sand. The luminaria sat on the coffin. Judging by the low level of the flame, the wick would soon gutter.

"How long have I been out?" Cass demanded.

"Long enough for Vandy to chew through my ankle ropes."

"Good. Get your butt over here."

Pressing the sides of his feet together, Cass triggered a special mechanism in his right boot heel. A knife sprang from the toe.

Collie grunted with satisfaction. Apparently, he'd been looking forward to this moment. Plopping down on his buttocks, he started the tedious task of cutting his wrist bonds on the blade.

Meanwhile, Cass craned his neck to the side and spied a ray of light. It came from the outside, piercing a keyhole. "Can you pick the door's lock?"

"It's got a keyhole, don't it?"

"Doesn't it."

"Doesn't it what?"

"Your *grammar,* boy."

"You think I give a rat's ass about book-learning right now?"

"Do you ever?"

"Nope."

Cass sighed. At this rate, he'd be edifying the kid for the rest of his life. "So how did you wind up in here?"

"I was stupid."

"You?"

"It happens."

The ghost of a smile touched Cass's lips. Considering the nightmare Collie had lived through, the kid was remarkably calm.

"*It happens?* That's all you're going to tell me?"

Collie shrugged. His hands were free, so he started working the knots that bound Cass's wrists. "Poppy gave me some soul cakes. Vandy took one whiff and refused to eat them. That's when I suspected something was wrong with the cakes. Unfortunately, I'd already washed one down with bourbon."

"You think she used bad eggs?" Cass asked cautiously, remembering the suspicious stinging sensation on his neck moments before he'd passed out.

Collie snorted. "I think *Poppy* is a bad egg. That woman's so crazy twisted up inside, her brain's rotting out. I heard her talking to Hank. They're in cahoots. They arranged for Bodine's rifle to backfire. And the Satin Siren to burn down. And a half dozen sodbusters to have 'fatal accidents.' They even arranged for some sugar planter back in Galveston to drown, after he jilted Poppy and asked some other woman to marry him. Apparently, Hank is Poppy's nephew. He knocks off folks she doesn't like, and she keeps him out of jail."

Well, that certainly explains a few things.

"So you're saying Poppy doesn't like me?" Cass asked dryly.

"Well, you did help Baron make a new will," Collie deadpanned. "Apparently, she got Hank paroled so he could plug you and Tito from the grocer's roof. Only in your case, she had a change of heart 'cause she wants babies."

Cass's neck heated as he realized just how close he'd come to being buzzard bait that day. Apparently, when Poppy had bailed him out of jail, she'd intended to lure him into an ambush. Her "change of heart" would explain why she'd kept throwing herself between him and a hail of bullets.

"So when Hank failed to gun down Tito," Cass theorized, "Poppy tried to poison him—and you and Sadie, too, because she decided you were threats. When Baron visited Sadie in her dressing room, he ate the soul cakes Poppy sent. Now Baron's in the hospital. That proves he didn't know about the poison."

Collie grunted. "I don't think Baron pays enough attention to Poppy to know *what* the hell she's doing—whether it's forging his name or tampering with his medicine."

Cass muttered an oath at this revelation.

At last, the ropes fell away from his wrists.

Collie climbed to his feet. "I don't blame you for staying clear of Poppy's bed," the boy said grimly. "But since you refused to give her babies, she ain't feeling so forgiving anymore. She told Hank to fetch some kerosene. My guess is, she doesn't want our bodies—or Jazi's, either—to be identified when this tomb gets re-opened on All Souls Day."

"Jazi?"

"Hank kidnapped her and took her to the cottage."

Cass cursed vehemently. So Jazi was the "Miss Reynolds" whom Baron had written into his will.

Since Cass's gun belt and Bowie knife were missing—and no doubt in Hank's possession—Cass drew a stiletto from his shirt collar and started sawing his ankle bonds. "When did you hear Hank and Poppy talking?"

"Hard to tell. A minute feels like a day in this place."

"Then we're burning daylight."

"Got ya covered, pard." Collie pulled a lock pick from his cuff.

By the time Cass had sawed through the last loop of hemp, thunder was concealing the sound of the opening door and its squealing hinges.

"Nice timing, kid."

"That was *planned,*" Collie said loftily.

Cass didn't doubt the kid's word. Collie's survival instincts were downright uncanny.

As Cass joined the boy on the threshold, wind kicked up brown, crackling leaves and whisked them inside the mausoleum.

"Hand me the Remington in your boot."

Collie didn't argue for once. But then, he wasn't the deadeye Cass was.

"You'll find a Winchester in Pancake's saddleboot," Cass said.

"Assuming Hank didn't get to Pancake first."

"Good point. You got some other plan?"

Collie's smile was grim. "I stashed my Winchester and my ammo under a bush."

Cass nodded, snapping open the Remington to check for bullets. "Once you get your rifle, circle through the woods to the front of the house. Create a diversion. I'll take the back."

With a terse nod, the boy set off with his coon for the treeline. Cass covered them until they were out of the .38's range. Then he turned his attention to the house. He'd sent Collie on the safer route—the landscaped route—because little more than tombstones stretched between the mausoleum and the back porch. The last grave marker was positioned some 20 yards below the wall of limestone ringing the yard.

Even if a sniper wasn't the best of marksmen, all he'd have to do is sit in an upper window—or behind the chimney—to pick off anyone who approached the wall from Cass's direction. Under those circumstances, running up the hill would be suicide.

Cass hoped Hank had reached this conclusion, too, and therefore, was focusing his rifle on the front of the house.

Grimly, Cass waited for Collie to fetch his Winchester and get in position.

Daylight was fading fast.

* * *

Boiling black thunderheads obscured the setting sun as Randie and Sadie crouched in a thicket about 50 yards below the front of the caretaker's cottage. For ease of movement, they'd donned white linen tunics and denim trousers, which they'd rolled to their knees. Only their boot toes could be seen beneath woolen mantles of forest-green and chocolate-brown plaid, which Wilma had hoped would be hard to spot against the backdrop of autumn trees.

To complete their disguises, they'd styled their hair in similar fashions and tied on black velvet masks. Under the gloom of a thunderstorm, Sadie felt confident she could pass for Randie—as long as Poppy didn't get too close. If her mask was challenged, Sadie would say she had come directly from a Halloween party.

As for Randie, the plan was to use her as a diversion, mostly because Randie had insisted on galloping heroically, if futilely, into hell to save her daughter. Sadie had the devil of a time convincing the older woman to wait in the woods for Marshal Wright. God only knew where Rex and Cass were.

"Now. *Promise me* you'll stick to the plan," Sadie told her avenging-angel-of-a-cohort. "Poppy's dangerous."

Randie snorted. "To children."

"That kind of thinking can get you killed."

Randie's jaw hardened. She gazed dubiously down her voluptuous figure, which was now swathed in 14 layers of silk and cotton batting. "I thought you trusted these vests."

"Like I said, Rex swears by them." Actually, Sadie had entrusted her life to the vest on several Pinkerton assignments, but she couldn't very well tell Randie that. "The gambler, Luke Short, practically invented these vests. He was an acquaintance of mine, back in Dodge City. He once survived an assassination attempt because the silk handkerchief in his breast pocket stopped the bullet. I don't know why silk stops slugs, but it does. The batting is extra protection."

"So if the vest works, then I'm safe. Quit hen-pecking."

"The vest will protect your vital organs, but it won't protect you from a bullet in the head. Or anywhere else."

"I think you're forgetting Boo is *my* daughter. I should be the one to rescue her!"

Sadie was hard-pressed not to shake the woman. "Boo needs a live mother to tuck her in tonight, not a corpse to mourn on All Saints Day.

"Here, take these," Sadie added gruffly, pressing two of her detachable buttons into Randie's hand. "When one hits the ground, it makes a black cloud of smoke. It will give you camouflage if you need to run."

"What about you?"

"Oh, I have a few tricks up my sleeve. Don't worry about me." Sadie spun the wheel on her Smith & Wesson. "I can hold off Poppy's hired gun until reinforcements arrive."

Randie slid a sideways glance her way. "You're not what you pretend to be, are you…Sadie?"

"Is that a crack about my sharpshooting or my singing?"

Randie's pale lips carved out a tense smile. "Let's just say, I still think you're a bitch. But I'm glad you're a bitch on my side."

"Back at ya, sister." Sadie winked. Then she drew a sobering breath. "All right. Sit tight. Marshal Wright will be here soon."

Randie nodded fretfully.

Giving the soprano's hand a fortifying squeeze, Sadie tugged her mask over her face and began slinking through the thirsty, crackling underbrush in the woods. Because the cottage sat on a hill, it would be hard to approach unseen. Nevertheless, Sadie did her best to time her movements through the open spaces to coincide with the thunder, not the lightning. Every time sky fire spat, it rent her shadow-cover and lit up the woods. Ghostly shimmers danced over leafless pecans and ancient elms; evergreens soughed mournfully in the rising wind.

Sadie gritted her teeth, tightening her fist over her gun. Halloween—in a thunderstorm—was one hell of a night to be in a cemetery. But Cass had always called her the Devil's Red-haired Daughter, hadn't he? She took comfort in that.

No lanterns or candles burned in the dilapidated shell of the caretaker's cottage. Sadie crouched for many long moments behind a crooked tombstone, studying the ruins, trying to guess where Jazi might be hidden. What looked like a smokehouse, toolshed, and root cellar were still part of the property. Heavy wood rot—or maybe termite damage—was apparent on all of the structures. Sadie suspected that anyone who dared to step foot inside the auxiliary buildings would splinter a floorboard and bust an ankle.

The main house didn't look much safer. Through narrowed eyes, she scanned the roof, then nearby trees, for signs of a sniper. If Poppy's accomplice was lying in wait with a rifle, he'd done a masterful job of hiding himself. Streaks of lightning failed to illuminate the brass receiver of a Winchester anywhere overhead.

But they did illuminate something small, round, and shimmery in the sun-cracked dirt of the drive.

Sadie caught her breath.

A pearl!

No. *Three* pearls. And there was a fourth! The gems and been dropped at irregular intervals as if someone had been marking a trail!

Her heart thudded against her ribs as she adjusted her eyes to the dancing sheets of light. Every time the sky brightened, she lost track of the shimmer that heralded the pearls. She gritted her teeth. Patience had never been her strong suit, and her nerves were already stretched as tight as fiddle strings. She squinted into the flickers. The pearls appeared to be heading toward…

Dear God. They were heading toward an open grave!

Cursing under her breath, Sadie crept from tree to tree, shadow to shadow. It was nerve-wracking work. She kept imagining she'd be shot in the back—or she'd find Jazi's severed head. The gruesome vision was due to the ax, jutting from the mound of dirt beside the grave. Sadie guessed the ax had been used to dig the pit, since the ground was as hard as granite, and no shovel would have cracked it.

Thirty yards.

Twenty yards.

Ten feet.

Gulping a bolstering breath, Sadie dashed for the cover of the dirt pile, which stood between her and the house. Muttering a prayer, she dared to peer around the crumbling mound to the hole. Her heart wrenched when she spied Jazi huddled in a ball inside the pit. She'd twined the cord of her *gris-gris* so many times through her fingers, her nails looked slightly blue. An ugly, purple bruise marred her temple.

Bastards. Goddamned bastards!

"Jazi," Sadie whispered urgently.

No response.

"Jazi!"

The feeble flutter of Jazi's shirt assured Sadie the child was alive—barely. She fought back tears of rage. She had to get Jazi out of there. But how? She couldn't lift an unconscious nine-year-old out of a six-foot trench. Not without help. She glanced wildly around the yard for some sort of ladder. Or rope.

That's when she heard the ominous hiss and rattle.

Sucking in her breath, she gazed in growing horror at the diamondback emerging from a hole in the trench. The snake was winding its way toward Jazi's inert form. In the fading light, with the viper so close to Jazi's stomach, Sadie was terrified a bullet would hit the child.

Merciful God.

She tightened her fist over the .32. Her hand trembled as she worried that a shot would alert Poppy and her accomplice. Under the circumstances, Sadie figured she didn't have much choice. She had to shoot that snake!

Clamping both hands over her gun grip, she prepared to fire.

A nerve-jangling growl rumbled from the bushes.

Startled, Sadie swung her gun toward the sound. A roly-poly, ring-tailed varmint appeared, galloping toward the pit. A flash of lightning glanced off a leather collar.

Vandy!

The coon scrambled into the grave.

Sadie held her breath. Raccoons ate almost anything; she knew that much. But with Jazi's life in the balance, Sadie worried Vandy had met his match. The rattlesnake was about three feet long—a baby, by Texas standards—but the coon didn't have a lot of room to maneuver. Not with Jazi's body lying diagonally across the gravebed.

The snake lunged and missed.

Vandy proved to be as wild and canny as his forbears, despite the civilizing influence of leather collars and trout almondine. He feinted.

The snake lunged again.

The coon retreated.

Sadie's heart hammered in her ears. Vandy was luring the snake away from Jazi's body!

As the growling and hissing crescendoed, Sadie gritted her teeth and dashed sweat from her eyes. She hoped the thunder was drowning out the dance of death so Poppy wouldn't hear.

Fangs flashing, Vandy snarled and pounced.

The pit grew ominously quiet.

Her heart crawling to her throat, Sadie strained desperately to see past the inky shadows that crowded the grave. All manner of horrific visions plagued her mind.

But in the next flicker of light, she spied a long, limp form dangling from Vandy's jaws.

Air rushed from her lungs.

"Good boy," she whispered.

Vandy's ears flicked. Bright, inquisitive eyes stared up at her.

Then the coon tossed aside his meal. Hunkering down beside Jazi, Vandy rested his head on the child's heart. He whimpered.

Sadie's eyelids prickled. Snakes were one thing. But Vandy couldn't defend Jazi from poison.

Suddenly, she noticed a blond head in the woods near Randie's hiding place. Collie was waving his rifle at her. He seemed to want her to leave the yard, to run to safety.

Hardening her jaw, Sadie shook her head. The boy was a civilian. She was a Pinkerton. Jazi's safety wasn't her only responsibility. Sadie still needed to solve her case. The time had come for her performance as Miranda Reynolds.

Drawing a fortifying breath, Sadie shoved her gun into her waistband, covered it with her vest, and stepped away from the shelter of the dirt pile. She didn't honestly believe Poppy would shoot Randie on sight. A mind as warped as Poppy's would want a verbal showdown. An opportunity to brag.

"Poppy Westerfield," she bellowed at the top of her lungs, "so help me God, if you've harmed a hair on my child's head, I'll rip out your heart and feed it to the buzzards!"

Seconds dragged by.

"Show yourself, Poppy!"

Spears of light rent the gloom. Thunder rolled, rattling the jagged panes of the cottage's windows.

That's when Sadie spied the hangman's noose, dangling from a leafless cottonwood.

CHAPTER 22

Every hair on Sadie's neck stood on end.

The wind was knocking the bare branches of the hanging tree together. Beneath that unsettling noose, eerie fingers of shadow splayed over a black-robed figure in a voluminous cowl.

Goosebumps scuttled down Sadie's spine.

She could see no features in the black, shadowy oval that should have been a face. But a human female lurked in there somewhere. A flesh-colored hand with red-lacquered nails gripped a gun.

Sadie rallied her nerve. "And who are you supposed to be this Halloween? My confessor?"

"Oh, it's much too late for that."

"You have a flare for the melodramatic, ghoul friend. I'll give you that."

"Impertinent whore! I am Asrael, the Angel of Death! The Regulator of God! And you shall hang for your crimes!"

"Uh-huh." *Looks like Poppy needs to have a few screws tightened.* "Well, I have news for you, Asrael. Angels don't poison people or abduct children."

"I do as God commands."

"Yeah?" Sadie tried to remember a passage—any passage—from her Pinkerton field manual that addressed an agent's conduct, should she be confronted by a lunatic with a gun. Sadie was pretty sure putting Poppy out of her misery wasn't legal. Or ethical. But it sure would have been well-deserved.

"I hear God says to turn the other cheek," Sadie said carefully. "To let bygones be bygones. So I'll make you a deal. Let my baby go, and we'll disappear into the wilderness like we never existed."

"Your baby?" Poppy spat. "Baron's seed belongs to me! By divine right! By all that's legal and holy! I am his *wife*, you blood-sucking whore!"

Right. And your brain would have to be as twisted as a pretzel to want the bastard. But Sadie figured Randie wouldn't say that—which was too bad.

"Then you must love all of Baron's children," Sadie said in her best beast-soothing voice. "That is why you celebrate the return of the *angelitos* tonight."

"The spirits of my babies will return tonight," Poppy conceded grudgingly. "But they won't be leaving here alone!"

"So…you poisoned Jazi?" Sadie recalled the dead plants in the Westerfield's hotel suite. Understanding dawned. "And you poisoned Baron's medicines?"

"I was careful! *Chantelle* poisoned Baron! Don't you read?" Poppy snapped.

"But you put *something* in his medicines. Something that made him sick."

"He deserved it. He was fornicating with you and half the house staff. I wanted his infidelity to stop, but I didn't want him dead."

"So you could make babies?"

"So I could live in the governor's mansion, you moron!"

Interesting.

Sadie suspected the article in the *Dispatch* had pushed Poppy over the edge. All these months, while using tainted medicines to keep her bull in the pasture, Poppy had never anticipated that Baron might snack on a poisoned confection, intended for his mistress.

Just another reason to question Poppy's sanity.

"I have to agree, you'd make the perfect governor's wife," Sadie lied in velvet tones. "Too bad all your plans revolve around Baron. And his health is failing."

"Baron was as healthy as a bull until *you* started sucking the life out of him!"

So Poppy felt spurned and decided it was payback time? Sadie was beginning to feel sorry for Randie, who'd actually had to live this nightmare. "Let me guess. You hired a henchman—somebody who doesn't have half your brains—to get rid of me at the Siren."

"I wouldn't say *that*," taunted a cold, cruel Midwestern accent.

Sadie sucked in her breath. *Hank!*

Shrouded by shadow, the outlaw leaned his shoulder against a porch pillar, a can of kerosene waiting by his boots. A match flared in the darkness. His cigarette tip brightened. When the tiny flame plummeted from his fingertips, Sadie's eyes widened. The match landed dangerously close to the kerosene…only to be rubbed out by the killer's boot toe.

She loosed a ragged breath. It was gratifying to know Hank didn't intend to torch the whole yard.

"So you're the one who hurled Greek Fire through my window," she deduced grimly. "Now *that* was a brilliant plan.

Too bad it went awry," she added for Poppy's benefit. "Despite all your efforts, someone found out you've been forging Baron's signature. *Someone* knows you've been paying assassins to get rid of his rivals. All this time, Baron has been turning a blind eye, pretending not to see—until he started getting blackmailed. Until he started fearing for his *life*. That's the real reason why Baron hired Cass, isn't it? To protect you and him from Hank?"

"Ridiculous," Poppy snapped. "Hank's family. Not that it's any business of yours."

"I can fend for myself, auntie."

"Of course you can, dear boy. Don't you have some corpses to cremate?"

"I thought I'd torch them all at once." Hank grinned. "Saves matches."

Sadie's scalp prickled. "Anyone I know?" she demanded with less asperity than she'd intended.

"You might say that."

He thrust his hips forward. Lightning illuminated the pair of walnut-inlaid gun butts, strapped to his hip.

Sadie's heart iced. She would have recognized that double-holstered rig anywhere.

"I don't believe it! Where's Cass?"

"They don't call me The Ventilator for nothing."

No! Sadie choked back tears. She wanted to scream. Or vomit. Or better yet, send Hank to hell.

Keep your wits about you, Sadie. You're not out of this mess yet. Think of Jazi. Save Jazi. Then you can rip off the bastard's balls...

Sadie steeled herself against her fury. Every nerve felt like it was being licked by demon fire, but she kept her teeth firmly clenched to silence the primal roar of grief. Sucking down breath after shuddering breath, she furtively touched the mechanism that operated the pistol under her cuff. The yard was nearly dark. Collie probably couldn't see Poppy in her black robe, and he didn't have a good angle to shoot Hank. Sadie couldn't count on the boy for help. That meant she would have to be smart enough, fast enough, to take out two gunmen.

She let a smoke bomb roll into her other palm.

What the hell is keeping Wright and his posse?

"What I still don't understand," she said hoarsely, stalling for time, "is why you've waited so long to teach Baron his lesson. After all, he's had other women. *Lots* of women."

"But you're his favorite."

"Me?" Sadie did her best to look surprised.

"Don't play dumb with me, whore. You talked him into

re-writing his will. You tricked him into naming your spawn as his heir!"

Sadie supposed this wouldn't be a good time to spill the beans that Jazi wasn't really Baron's daughter.

"Baron has been on edge, that's all." Sadie struggled to put a soothing note in her voice. "He thinks someone's trying to kill him." *And with good reason, apparently!* "I'm sure if you sat down with him and had a heart-to-heart talk—"

"How dare *you* give me marriage advice, bitch! For 20 years, I've stood beside my husband! He was nothing until I taught him how to read and write the law. But then he threatened to put me in an asylum. *Me!* When I was finally in the family way. When I was going to have our little Barry…"

Poppy's voice broke.

Sadie tasted bile as she guessed the outcome of that confrontation. "He hit you, didn't he?" she prompted more gently. "And you miscarried."

Poppy made a small inhuman sound, like the whimper of a whipped puppy. "He never shared my bed again…"

The more agitated Poppy got, the more her gun hand quaked.

"…He wouldn't let me have another baby."

Now the six-shooter's muzzle was bobbing erratically in her fist.

"He didn't want my babies, because *you* gave him one, strumpet! It's all *your* fault that Baron doesn't love me anymore!"

Holy crap, Sadie thought. *She's going to fire!*

"Poppy Westerfield!" It was Randie's voice, pitched high in nigh hysteria. She'd emerged from the woods and was waving her white sleeves like a windmill. The tactic was a crazy, brazen, *courageous* thing to do—the best diversion she could possibly create while her .38 was out of firing range. "Satan himself couldn't keep me from you!"

Sadie took full advantage of the distraction. She threw the smoke bomb at Poppy's feet and drilled a bullet into

Hank's right arm—hopefully, his gun arm.

"Run, Sadie!" she shouted at Randie in an effort to confuse Poppy further.

Poppy staggered backwards, blinded by black, sulfurous plumes. "Hank!" she screamed between coughs. "*Hank, there are two of them!*"

Above the outlaw's blood-curdling howls of pain, a gunshot rang out. Sadie had barely taken three steps when Poppy's bullet hit her in the back. She "*oomphed,*" pitching forward onto rock-hard earth. Her momentum sent her somersaulting down the hill. She crashed hip-first into a tombstone, her temples pounding, her face pointed at the sky. For an endless moment, she couldn't move. She couldn't breathe.

That's when all hell broke loose.

"Randie!" The cry of anguish was masculine.

Sadie's ears were ringing. A full moon was spinning through the storm over her head. As if she were peering through a fuzzy telescope, she watched horses gallop past. She heard bullets whining through the air. A man with waxed mustachios was wrestling a woman with a black hood and poppy-colored hair for a gun. Further away, like a tiny speck on rippled glass, she saw a blond man in a pitch-colored Stetson charging up the hill.

Then some helpful person was hauling her to her feet. Dragging her up by her collar. Clamping an arm as bendable as steel over her breasts.

Still too winded to speak, she wheezed in protest as iron fingers bit into her scalp, yanking her head backwards against a granite shoulder. Pinpricks of light danced inside her brain. She thought she might pass out. Then the stench of sulfur jolted her senses. A red-hot gun muzzle jammed into the tender flesh beneath her chin. She yelped.

"Think you can beat me, Cassidy?" a sneering, Midwestern accent panted in her ear.

An ominous click reverberated through the bones of her jaw.

"Let's see how fast you can *really* draw, Lucifire."

CHAPTER 23

———◆———

Cass forced himself to halt his charge up the hill, his muscles screaming, his heart in an uproar.

When a gunman used a woman as a shield, it was worse than a crime. It was an abomination. But the stakes in this showdown had risen astronomically the moment Cass realized the gunman was The Ventilator.

And the woman was Sadie.

Kill or be killed. That was the law of the gun. No one knew that law better than Cass. Over the years, he'd been accused of being a showboater. A braggart. A pretty-boy with a fancy set of pistols. Because he talked nice and acted polite, tough characters often mistook him for a mealy-mouthed weakling.

Hank had been one of those tough characters. For seven long years, Cass had been haunted by his choice to flee the Rocking W rather than face Hank at high noon. To make the guilt worse, Hank had used those years to terrorize decent folks. His Wanted Posters accused him of extortion, rustling, arson, smuggling, armed robbery, kidnapping, rape, manslaughter, and capital murder. But thanks to Poppy, the charges never stuck. Hank always got paroled.

Cass's breaths shuddered from barely controlled rage. He gazed into the glazing, tawny eyes of the woman he loved. The woman who was the reason he still aspired to do good deeds in the world. Her temple was bruised. Her throat had blistered from the gun metal. Cass reasoned that if he'd shot Hank seven years ago, Sadie would be safe.

The thought made something inside Cass go dangerously dark and cold.

So help me God, if Hank spills a single drop of her blood, all the torments of hell won't keep me from doling out my own brand of justice.

Hank's right sleeve was soaked with blood. Sadie had tried to disable him rather than kill him. Cass knew this because he'd watched her do it while he'd been running up the hill and his .38 had been out of firing range. In Hank's adrenalized state, his pain wasn't great enough to drop the six-shooter he'd cocked under her chin.

"Let Randie go." Cass didn't know why Sadie was pretending to be Randie, but the matter was moot. He played along. "Your quarrel's with me."

"Always the ladies' man," the outlaw jeered. "You know she's screwing Baron, right?"

Sadie whimpered.

Cass's jaw hardened. "Relax, sweetheart. This will all be over in a minute. I promise."

Hank laughed. "Rebel Rutter, my ass. You're more like Cuckold Cass."

"Yeah. You got me there, pal. You're superior in every way. You want me to stroke your dick, too?"

"Naw. I think I'll let your woman do it. After you're dead."

Cass smiled pleasantly. Hank had no idea what type of vengeance he'd just bargained for at Sadie's hands. "Now that would be a sight to watch from hell."

"Your sass ain't helping her, smartass."

"Aw, c'mon, Hank. You don't want to kill a woman. You want to test me. See how fast I can really draw."

"Well now, let's see. Since I'm already wearing your gun belt—" Hank's lip curled "—it looks like you've failed that test, grasshopper. Toss aside the piece."

Cass was holding Collie's gun in his right hand. His *weak* hand.

So he obeyed.

Not even Lynx knew Cass was a southpaw. He'd perfected the ruse by the age of 12, practicing long and hard to become proficient with both hands. He picked up his fork with his right hand. He brushed his teeth with his right hand. He even pumped bullets into his six-shooter with his right hand.

But when it came to close encounters, Cass's salvation, an 18-ounce Smith & Wesson, was strapped to his left forearm.

"Spread 'em," Hank snapped.

The magic words, Cass thought darkly.

Now Sadie's life—and his, too—relied on split-second timing. He raised his hands over his head. He puckered his brow. He made sure he looked worried enough to keep Hank from getting suspicious.

On the inside, Cass was iced steel.

"This isn't going to go well for you, Hank. You'll never leave Lampasas County alive."

Hank laughed at the warning, as Cass knew he would. Guns had a way of inflating a coward's confidence.

"That's brave talk for a dead man. Or maybe I should say, a dead *boy*. S'long, sucker."

Hank leered. He started to turn his gun muzzle away from Sadie's throat.

With the speed of a striking rattler, Cass triggered his .38 and fired. The bullet drilled through the center of Hank's forehead.

The outlaw blinked.

His jaw went slack.

A heartbeat later, he was toppling like felled timber.

"S'long, Hank." Cass flexed his wrist to hide his pistol beneath his sleeve once more. "See ya in hell."

Sadie hit the dirt. Now she was flailing in her mantle, which had tangled around her legs. Cass stepped forward, extending a hand to help her up.

"Are you all right?"

"No!" she snapped, slapping his hand away.

"Well, let me—"

"Don't you *dare* touch me!"

"Good God, woman, what's eating you now?"

"I'm not *Randie*, you insufferable, pig-headed—"

"I knew that!"

"You did not!"

"C'mere," he growled, grabbing her left arm and hauling her to her feet.

"I hate you!"

"No, you don't—"

Her right fist plowed into his gut, and he *oomphed,* doubling over. *Okay. Maybe she does.*

"I just saved your life," he wheezed.

"You just saved *Randie's* life. And you called her *sweetheart!"*

He refused to release the wrist she kept twisting in his fist. "That was for show!"

"Like crooning *Destiny* in my ear was for show!" She tried to punch him again.

He caught her other arm and spun her against his chest. "You need a paddling something fierce!"

"And you need a restraining order for your pecker!"

Suddenly, a gunshot drowned out the thunder. They gasped, hugging each other tight. Hearts hammered in syncopated rhythms; lungs wheezed like squeezeboxes.

A wail of grief shattered the night.

"Baron," Cass choked, shoving Sadie toward the tombstone. He lunged for his fallen six-shooter. "Take cover!"

"Like hell!" She grabbed the .32 from her waistband. "I'm going with you!"

Together, they sprinted through lightning and shadow, around the corner of the house, toward the dirt mound by the grave. Sadie ignored the pounding in her head and the pain in her chest every time she dragged air into her lungs. She thought she might have bruised a rib when she'd rolled down the hill. But she couldn't worry about that—she *wouldn't* worry about that—as long as Jazi was in danger.

Beneath a ghostly moon, she spied Randie wrapping her mantle around her child's slender shoulders. Jazi was hugging a raccoon that was trying to eat her *gris-gris*. Sadie figured all must be right again in the Reynolds's world.

Near the lip of the pit, Sadie noticed Collie, covered with dirt. He stood with a Winchester at the side of a grim-faced Sid Wright, whose kneecaps were stained with grass. Younger and more agile than the other members of the posse, Collie and Sid had undoubtedly been the heroes who'd hauled Jazi from her grave.

The third man on the scene was Rex. Still pretending to be retired as a Ranger, he sported a Lampasas deputy badge, which suggested he'd been spontaneously sworn-in by Sid. At any other time, Sadie might have ribbed Rex about his demotion. But today, his wolfish features were grim and his gun-metal gray eyes were stark. He was gazing at the tragedy that had transpired some 10 feet away.

"What happened?" Sadie whispered, halting at his side.

A muscle ticked in Rex's jaw. "When Baron heard about the posse, nothing short of leather straps could keep him in that hospital bed. He begged us to let him reason with Poppy.

"But when we arrived, she was like a woman possessed. She told him if she couldn't have his babies, no woman would. She tried to shoot Randie. Baron struggled with her for the gun, and it went off."

Jesus. Sadie sickened to see the senator convulsed with grief. He was cradling a limp, black-robed figure against his heart.

Sadie turned her head away. She knew it wasn't her fault that Poppy had mistaken her strand of red hair for Randie's. Poppy had declared war on Miranda Reynolds long before Sadie had ever searched Baron's underwear drawer. Even so, it was hard to take satisfaction in solving a case that had closed so tragically.

When Sadie forced herself to look once more, she saw Cass squatting to clasp his weeping boss's shoulder. Jazi had wrapped her arms around Baron's neck. Randie, who was kneeling beside Cass, clutched the handsome young gunslinger's arm.

Pain lanced Sadie's heart. She drew a bolstering breath.

"You all right?" Rex demanded, darting a much too perceptive glance her way.

"Sure. Why wouldn't I be?"

"Well, for one thing, you're bleeding."

"Yeah," she murmured, "on the inside."

"What?" Rex demanded.

She gave him a wan smile.

Suddenly, she felt tired. More tired than she'd ever felt in her life.

"Nothing. It's getting late. I have a report to write."

She turned on her heel and headed for her mare. Rex fell into step beside her.

Charcoal clouds boiled over a full moon. Thunder boomed a final warning. Before Sadie could untether her mare, the rain finally started pouring down.

In a special, morning edition of the *Lampasas Dispatch,* Poppy Westerfield was memorialized as a model citizen, a big-hearted philanthropist, a tireless devotee to women's rights, and a loving wife.

With mixed feelings, Sadie snipped the article and included it in her Pinkerton report, along with Bo Bodine's obituary, and a third clipping that announced the date of the legislative hearing to determine Baron's fate in the senate.

Sadie was sure Baron's attorneys would find some way of convincing the court that any illegal correspondence that had ever come from the senator's pen had been forged by his wife. Personally, Sadie couldn't believe that Baron didn't know *something* about Poppy's crimes. Just like Sadie couldn't believe that Pendleton hadn't worked to cover up her conspiracy with Hank. After all, Pendleton had faithfully served the Westerfields for two decades. He'd managed their business accounts. He'd lived in their house!

Then again, neither Pendleton nor Baron had ever guessed that Poppy was poisoning her husband.

Sadie sighed. *It's all out of my hands now.*

Shaking her head at the convoluted nightmare her investigation had uncovered, she pasted down the flap of her plain brown mailing envelope. She was glad to be done with Baron's case. She was in a hurry to get her package to the post office and her portmanteau to the train station before the whole household woke to learn she was leaving. Fortunately, the residents of Wilma's boardinghouse didn't begin stirring until noon.

"Are you sure you won't reconsider, *chere?*"

Wilma had joined her in the solarium, where they could bask in glorious streams of November sunshine. The madam was sipping a fragrant cup of chamomile tea, laced with anise, cloves, honey and—judging by the silver flask sitting by her elbow—a dollop of bourbon. Wilma looked especially refined in her gray-satin day dress, with its demure lace bodice and pinstriped skirt.

Sadie looked more like an underfed muleskinner. She sported a scruffy beard and a stringy, shoulder-length wig that could easily have served as a bird's nest. As for her clothes, she'd traded her sodbuster's sack suit for a miner's overalls.

"You saw the telegraph, Wilma. *'Agent missing.'* Delta Belle hasn't wired headquarters for six days. And that's two days longer than a Code Red."

Like Sadie's own code name, *Scarlet Diva,* Delta Belle was an alias for a Pinkie. The agent's real name was Araminta "Minx" Merripen, a Saint-Louis native, who'd been assigned to a mission in Denver. The wire from headquarters hadn't revealed any additional details. All Sadie knew was she'd been summoned to the Denver office for a debriefing.

"Allan Pinkerton is a reasonable man, *chere.* You need several days to heal. Wire him about your black eye—"

Sadie snorted. She hadn't worked four years to earn the Agency Chief's respect, only to concede now that she was soft—too soft to do a job when the Master Detective had ordered her to report to Denver.

"I'm traveling as a man. The shiner will give me a brutish look. Nobody wants to quarrel with a brute. And that means I'll get plenty of sleep on the train."

Wilma was careful to keep her gaze on her toddy as she lowered the dainty, rose-patterned cup to her saucer. "Are you sure you're not running away?"

Sadie stiffened. "Are you sure you're not trying to piss me off?"

Wilma was never daunted by Sadie's temper. *"Talk* to Cass. Wouldn't you want the same courtesy?"

Sure. Talk to Coyote Cass. The man could make any lie, any absurdity, sound plausible.

Last night, after the doctor had announced Jazi would soon be feeling as good as new, Sadie had crept upstairs to visit the child. Approaching the sickroom's open door, she'd heard Cass's merry laughter; she'd spied him sitting on the bed, his golden head close to Jazi's cheek. The child had snuggled in her nightgown against his chest. Randie had perched on the mattress beside his knee. The threesome had looked like the perfect, wholesome family—the ideal portrait for *Ladies Home Journal.*

Sadie had wanted to cry.

"Cass needs his sleep," Sadie said briskly. "He's the worst patient ever, although I hear Collie ranks a close second."

Wilma tossed her one of her incredibly annoying, insightful glances. "I think you're making a mistake."

"The *mistake* would be to wait around here, wasting time. Cass is a Ranger now. He's confined to Texas. I've been called to Colorado."

"Did I mention that Mace is in Denver? And he recommended you for this mission?"

Ugh. Sadie wrinkled her nose. "Don't we have any other male operatives in the west?"

"Of course we do. But Mace pulled rank. Apparently,

he's looking forward to working with you again."

"Right. Like he's looking forward to a toothache. Did he really request me for this assignment?"

"Apparently, he considers you the lesser of two evils."

"Now that's disappointing. Who's more evil than I am?"

"Pinkerton's mistress."

Sadie smirked. That actually made sense. Mace would have to tow the line with the Agency Chief's woman. "Then I'll consider that a compliment." She plunked her miner's hat on her head and tucked her envelope under her arm.

"What should I tell Rex?" Wilma demanded.

Sadie winced. She hated long good-byes. Mustering a devil-may-care grin and a breezy tone, she quipped: "Tell him I'll see him the next time I'm in Texas."

"And you think he'll be satisfied by that?"

"Honestly, Wilma." Sadie stooped to buss the Cajun's cheek. "It's not like he's my father."

With a cheerful wave, Sadie swept past potted palms and baskets of trailing poppymallow. She was so intent on getting to the door, she didn't bother to glance out the window. If she had, she might have noticed a tow-headed youth under the sill, whittling an image of his raccoon.

Feeling like a cotton pod had exploded in his brain, Cass dragged himself out of bed and splashed water on his face. He didn't like that he still felt groggy after his encounter with Poppy's stinger ring. No liquor of his acquaintance had ever packed that kind of wallop, and that was saying a lot, because he was pretty sure he'd cozied up to every liquor ever distilled from grapes, juniper berries, agaves, sugar cane, potatoes, corn, rye, and wheat. Hell, if spirits were distilled from turpentine, he'd probably drunk them too. And mostly in Dodge.

Wilma's doctor had said Cass was drugged, not poisoned—which had sounded like a bit of hair-splitting to his mind. Dr. Berger had hypothesized that Poppy must have pricked Cass's jugular vein with a super-powered jolt of opium. That's why he'd fallen asleep so fast.

Well, whatever that stuff had been, Cass didn't want to be pricked by it again. The stinger ring had given him a hangover with none of the feel-good benefits that made a headache worthwhile.

Grimacing into the stream of daylight pouring past his curtains, Cass yawned, stretched, and scratched his chest. Glancing south of his navel, he realized for the first time he'd been shucked.

Imagine that. Me butt-naked in a whorehouse, without a single redhead in sight. Where's Sadie?

He reached for his trousers. At about the same time, a commotion started in the hall. He recognized Collie's gruff, backwoods grumble.

"Where'd you hide my coon? He'd better not be in your travel bag. No coon of *mine* is sailing to New Orleans! You got that, Freckles?"

A tiny foot stomped in indignation. "I am *not* Freckles! Just for that, you're going to have to give me your harmonica."

"What?"

"You heard me," Jazi said imperiously.

"I don't have a harmonica!"

"Oh yes, you do. You stole Gator's."

"Shh!" Collie hissed. "Vandy dropped it in the tub of mudbugs."

Jazi giggled. "Serves you right."

"Listen here, you rotten girl. You said you'd give Vandy back if I whittled you a coon. Well, I whittled you a coon."

"Rotten girl, am I?"

Biting his tongue to keep from laughing, Cass cracked open his door. Jazi and Vandy had been inseparable last night, much to Collie's annoyance. Nevermind that Collie had hoisted the child from a would-be grave. Jazi had declared Vandy was her hero. To her mind, the coon had braved witches, snakes, and bullets to run to her rescue.

Collie had argued that Vandy heard a rattler, decided it

was dinnertime, and did what comes naturally to coons. Judging by the stand-off this morning, Cass guessed that Collie was no closer to winning the argument. Jazi, who smelled like a strawberry patch, stood toe-to-toe with her red-faced opponent. Even though Collie towered two feet above her, Jazi wasn't the least bit intimidated.

"Just for calling me names, you owe me a whistle," she scolded. "And a shoe shine. *And* some salt-water taffy. Better make it orange-flavored, if you want your coon back."

"That's blackmail!"

Cass donned his poker face and stepped into the hall. "Is there a problem, folks??"

"Jazi stole my coon! You're a tin-star. Arrest her!"

"Good morning, Cass," Jazi chimed in brightly. "Collie's being an ogre again. Can you blame Vandy for preferring to be with me?"

"Not in the least."

"Hey!"

Cass chuckled. "Don't you two ever get divorced. It'll be hard on the cubs."

"Huh?"

Jazi grinned. "Cass knows all about grown-up things. Would you like an invitation to my tea party, Cass? I baked some lovely gingerbread."

"It's pretend," Collie warned.

Jazi sniffed. "Shows you how much you know. Vandy thinks it's divine."

"Well, *that* explains everything," Collie grumbled. "Vandy! Get your ring-tailed fanny out here!"

"Mon dieu," Wilma scolded, hiking her skirt as she hurried up the stairs. *"Qu'est-ce qui se passe?* Do you want to wake the dead, *chirens?"*

Jazi quailed, edging closer to Cass. "Does she mean the witch?"

"No, sweetheart." He wrapped an arm around her shoulders. "Wilma was just worried about…er, folks who need their beauty rest. Like your mama."

"Speak for yourself, churl," Randie teased with a yawn. Appealingly rumpled, she was strolling out of Jazi's room in a flowing aqua gown, which couldn't quite hide the sweet little bulge in her womb.

Randie had confessed last night that she was pregnant with Baron's child. Apparently, she'd told Baron the news when he—or rather, Poppy—had invited her to Lampasas. Despite how Randie had misled him, she had high hopes that Baron would marry her, or at least provide for the child. Since he would no longer be taking Poppy's "medicines," his doctor expected him to make a full recovery. And Baron's attorney expected him to be fully exonerated.

Knowing Baron as well as he did, Cass didn't share the Pinkertons' belief that Baron had ordered the murder of innocents. But Cass did believe that a horrified, guilt-ridden Baron had tried to protect his wife from the law. For 20 years, Baron had been living a private hell, married to a mentally unbalanced woman—a woman whom, deep down, he had never stopped loving.

Cass hoped that Baron could finally be happy with Randie.

"Has anyone seen Sadie?" Randie asked. "I think Gator may have mistaken my traveling trunk for hers. They're practically identical, and mine's missing."

Jazi sucked in her breath. "Oh no! I put the gingerbread in Mama's trunk."

Collie blanched. "You did *what?!*"

Muttering a hair-raising oath, the boy turned and bolted down the hall.

As Collie's noisy clomping echoed in the stairwell, Cass hiked an eyebrow at Wilma. "What was that all about?"

The madam chuckled, shaking her head. "It appears that Vandy may be on the next train to Denver. With Sadie."

CHAPTER 24

———————◆———————

Sadie checked her pocket watch and frowned. The time was 12 minutes past the hour. The train whistle should have blown by now. Two short toots would have signified the locomotive was chugging forward.

Opening her stateroom door, she looked up and down the Pullman's corridor. Passengers in sack suits and calico skirts were milling around the sleeper car, shoving battered portmanteaus into overhead berths or soothing cranky toddlers.

Finally, she saw what she'd been searching for: a chubby, huffing man in a black frockcoat, whose cap was wrapped with gold braid and affixed with a brass plate that had been engraved with the initials of the Gulf, Colorado, and Santa Fe Railroad.

"Conductor," she called, waving him to her door. "I have a connection to make in Fort Worth. What's the delay? Are the tracks flooded from last night's storm?"

"Oh no, Mr. Jones," the conductor said, pushing his spectacles up his perspiring nose. "It's the Rangers."

"The *Rangers?*"

"Yes, sir. The station master received a wire about twenty minutes ago. A couple of Rangers have been ordered to search the train for contraband."

"You mean, like firearms?"

"No, sir. Like gingerbread."

Gingerbread?

Sadie's eyes narrowed suspiciously. Before she could ask her next question, a cheer rose from the depot's porch. In response, the sodbusters and their children rushed eagerly to the east side of the car and peered out the windows. Their whistles and "Huzzahs" began rattling the walls.

Irritably, Sadie elbowed a spot for herself at a window. It didn't take long to spy the two rangy roughriders at the station. The sea of bowlers, bonnets, and parasols were parting to give them access to the train.

The younger of the men wore a chocolate-brown Stetson and a fringed buckskin coat that flapped open to reveal denim breeches. He balanced a Winchester on his shoulder and a .45 on his hip.

The older man was sheathed from head to toe in black. His Stetson was tilted at a rakish angle to allow a pale gold curl to blow across his brow. When he unleashed his dazzling smile, every female over the age of 13 giggled or fanned their cheeks.

"No reason to be alarmed, folks," Cass called, hooking his thumb under the lapel of his vest and showing off his tin star. "Just some routine, Ranger business."

"Is it Hawkeye Jenkins?" one eager adolescent called from the crowd. "The mean-eyed, ornery varmint who robbed the bank in Belton?"

"No, son. We've got our sights set on another varmint. One who's more of a kitchen thief."

A kitchen thief?

Suspicion flurried through Sadie's mind. She noticed the ever-faithful Vandy wasn't trotting at his boy's heels.

Damn.

Ducking her head inside the train, she hurried back to her stateroom and closed the door. Surely Vandy hadn't stowed away in her portmanteau. She hadn't packed anything remotely tasty!

Except maybe lip paint.

Groaning to envision red, oily stains all over her white unmentionables, she knelt, digging the trunk's key from her overalls' pocket and wrestling with the lock.

It wouldn't open.

Now she was beginning to see the dilemma. Gator had grabbed the wrong portmanteau.

A sleepy snuffling reached her ears. It was followed by muffled scratching.

"Yes, yes, I brought my widdy," she grumbled, tugging the lock pick from a secret pocket beneath her shoulder strap. "You should be more careful. You could have gone to Hatsville. That's right. *Suffocated!* And who would Collie have blamed? *Me!* That's who."

Vandy whined to hear his boy's name.

Poor little coon.

At last, the locking mechanism clicked, and the lid popped open. Fifty pounds of wriggling varmint leaped into her arms.

Ugh. Sadie turned her face away from Vandy's eager, slurping tongue. *Not so little after all.*

"Don't you *dare* chew my beard, you tubby menace!"

Suddenly, the door crashed open. Cass loomed on the threshold, one great scowling mass of mischief.

"Hands up!"

"Oh, you're a real crack-up, wise-guy."

Her arms were completely encumbered by Vandy, who was now trying to eat her hat brim.

"That's Ranger Wise-Guy to you," Cass retorted, holstering his gun. *"Deputy!"*

Collie's scowling face bobbed behind Cass's shoulder. "Yeah, yeah. Put a sock in it."

He pushed his way into the room. Vandy squirmed with excitement, reaching a paw for his boy. Suddenly, the flinty gray of Collie's eyes warmed, and a dimpled grin softened the harsh angles of his jaw.

"Dang coon," he said gruffly, stooping to lift Vandy out of Sadie's lap. "Didn't I warn you about lids with locks?

And strawberry smells that ain't nothing but perfume?"

Like a toddler, the coon clasped his paws around Collie's neck and *whuffed* with affection.

Sadie's heart turned over. She sneaked a peek at Cass. The deep blue of his eyes danced like sunshine on water. He was fighting a lopsided grin.

Collie shot them both dagger glares.

Cass cleared his throat, looking official and grave once more. "Lock up the bandit, deputy. I don't want to be hearing any more tales of gingerbread theft. Not for a coon's age!"

Some eavesdropper snickered. A few others guffawed.

Turning beet-red, Collie tugged his hat lower and stalked into the corridor, where he was greeted by whoops, whistles and lively applause. Children wanted to pet his coon. Old-timers thumped him on the shoulder. Even Collie couldn't keep a straight face under that onslaught of adulation.

Sadie suspected Cass had just turned the Kentucky-born thief into a life-long Ranger.

Bracing his weight against the jamb, Cass stuck his head out the door. "Conductor! Find me a stateroom for those trunks I brought along. Then tell the rapper to rattle her hocks! We're burning daylight!"

Sadie arched an eyebrow. Since when had Cass learned to speak railroad slang?

"Yessir, Ranger Cassidy, sir!"

Cass preened.

But the moment he slammed the door and turned to confront her, he wiped the barn-sized grin off his face. "As for you, hotfoot, you're under arrest!"

"Is that a fact?" Pleased that he'd dragged her portmanteau all the way from Wilma's house, Sadie decided to play along. "And what, pray tell, is the charge?"

"Disturbing my piece!"

"Uh…did you just say what I think you said?"

"Damned straight." Merriment lurked in his gaze. "Legs spread, hands over your head. Prepare for a strip search."

"Dog." Her lips twitched. "I think this Ranger business has gone to your head."

"Ranger Cassidy does have a nice ring to it."

"Yes." Wistfulness crept into her tone. "Yes, it does. But I should probably warn you, Rangers don't have deputies."

"Collie will be wearing his own badge soon enough." He cocked his head. Nothing got past those coyote instincts of his. "You have a problem with that?"

"Not me. But a couple of tribal reservations might object after we cross the Oklahoma border."

"Not to worry. My best friend—er, I mean, my *other* best friend—is a Cherokee."

The long-awaited toots came from the train whistle. Steam hissed. Wheels whined. Sadie braced herself as the sleeper car jolted. The long string of Pullmans began inching their way north like a monstrous black caterpillar.

"Uh…Cass?"

"Yeah, sweets?"

"The train's leaving."

"I can see that."

Donkey butt.

"Don't you have somewhere else to be?"

"Now you're talking." He dragged down her bed, flipped back the blankets, and bounced on the mattress to test the springs. "Not bad. 'Course, anything would beat a bedroll with a tree root jabbing your back." With a wink, he sailed his Stetson onto a hook by the door.

She hid her smile. *Always the showboater.*

"Come over here, detective."

"I like where I am, thank you."

"Aw. Do beards make you shy?"

She snorted. "Apparently, we're not communicating."

"I noticed that too." Shrugging out of his vest, he tossed it on a chair.

"What I meant," she said dryly, "is that you should be on your way to Ranger Headquarters. To get your next assignment."

"You are my next assignment." He started unbuttoning his shirt cuffs. "Sterne said he'd have my neck in a noose if I let you disappear like that other Pinkie did."

Sadie hiked an eyebrow. "You talked with Rex?"

"In a matter of speaking. You know, that telegraph under Wilma's Voodoo altar sure comes in handy. She wired Sterne, and the station master, and burned some herbs against evil spirits too."

Sadie suspected Wilma would never live down that incident.

"Cass," she said more sternly. "Ranger jurisdiction is limited to Texas. Didn't you rob a stage coach in Denver?"

He removed the .38 from his forearm. "As I recollect, I robbed three."

"Three?!"

"Those were the glory days, eh?" He tossed a stiletto and a Bowie knife onto his growing arsenal.

"You have a bounty on your head! You can't disembark in Denver!"

"Sure I can. The police chief runs the racquets. Besides. I stole the silver for him." With a cheeky grin, he popped off a boot.

She wanted to box his ears.

"Not to rain on your parade, hotshot, but I have news for you. *My* chief isn't so lax about the law. And since I'm supposed to be meeting with him in four days, I suggest we part ways in Fort Worth."

"Naw. Hell's Half Acre would seem a tad too tame after Dodge." He popped off the other boot. "'Sides. I've got a hankering to meet your chief. I'd like to ask the all-mighty Allan Pinkerton why he sends womenfolk to war."

Uh-oh. Sadie was pretty sure she'd blanched. "Please tell me you're not going to shoot my boss."

"Okay." He indulged her with a fallen angel's smile. "I'm not going to shoot your boss."

She groaned. She was definitely going to have to ditch Cass before they reached Denver.

Rising from the mattress, he unbuckled his gun belt. Then he sauntered toward her, all sizzle and sin in his gaping black shirt and adorably darned socks. Tufts of golden hair curled past his sagging placards. Sunlight glanced off the thigh-hugging leather that sheathed his legs. Tawny stubble roughened his chin, allowing the roguish cleft to play hide and seek with her fingertips.

As she smiled into his eyes, mischief flared anew in their sapphire depths.

"You know," he drawled, stroking a knuckle along her chestnut sideburn, "I've been a Ranger for a whole damned day, and I still haven't put a man in handcuffs."

"Poor darling. I can see how that might distress a big, brazen tin-star like yourself."

"Wanna get arrested?"

She hid her smirk. "Well now. That all depends on how you negotiate my surrender."

Chuckling wolfishly, he dragged her forward for his kiss. Her beard didn't slow him in the least. He plundered her mouth with velvet thrusts; he teased her lips with toe-curling nibbles. He tasted like salt and cinnamon; he smelled of sandalwood, leather, and cloves. The erotic mingling of flavors and scents made her pulse quicken and her skin flush.

Luxuriating in all his chiseled planes and angles, she shimmied closer, and he rewarded her submission, kneading her buttocks. She reveled in the shower of sparks, heating her belly. His expert petting promised the kind of pleasure a saint would have sinned for.

And she had never been a saint.

Abruptly, he raised his head. He licked his lips. Flames danced in the dark centers of his midnight-blue eyes.

"Well? You want to be my prisoner?"

"Hot damn." She didn't mind that she was panting. Not one little bit. "I think I'm tempted. But consider yourself warned, Lucifire. A tricky She-devil like me usually winds up on top."

"I'm counting on it, Tiger."

He loved her like a firecracker. A rocket. A shooting star.

He prolonged her ecstasies, taking her to exquisite pinnacles that even she'd never climbed to before. The fortress of her heart cracked open, and sentiment began to flow. She confided that she'd missed him over the years. That *Lucifire* and *Destiny* were songs about him. That writing lyrics and singing their melodies were ways of remembering all the good times they'd shared. She confessed how she wanted to see him happy, but that it was hard to let him go.

"Hell, I'm not going anywhere, woman," he growled against her ear, "except to Denver. With you."

She smiled a little at his promise and snuggled closer, resting her check on the downy fur of his chest. "I'm glad," she admitted.

"You are?"

"Didn't I just prove it?"

He chuckled. "I reckon you did."

Tucking the blanket around her shoulders, he began to stroke her hair. The steady thrumming of his heart lulled her. Wooed her. She was beginning to slip into a nice, fuzzy doze when his voice rumbled once more beneath her ear.

"You think we should get ourselves a coon?"

She started awake, imagining stolen jewelry. Gnawed beards. Lip paint trampled into her bloomers. She grimaced.

"No."

"But what if Vandy meets a lady coon and—"

"No."

"You know, having folks to love isn't a bad thing."

She bit her lip, relieved for the cloaking shadows of cedar trees, limestone bluffs, and cumulus clouds as they sped past her window. "What…um…do you mean?"

He kissed her hand. "Ask me again. After we get home from Denver."

He twined his fingers through hers. They were strong and thick, warm and callused. He squeezed. She squeezed back.

Denver. She closed her eyes and sighed. In four more days, she would have to report to Allan Pinkerton.

Until that time, she supposed she could dream.

Turn the page for an

excerpt from

DANCE
TO THE
DEVIL'S TUNE

Lady Law & The Gunslinger Series
Book Two

◆

Adrienne deWolfe

Denver, CO
November 1883

Cass swept up the limp, unconscious form of the woman he loved and carried her to the bed. He paused only long enough to fling aside a corner of the quilt. As he tugged off Sadie's boots and smoothed her chemise around her ankles, she smiled softly, oblivious to his betrayal.

At least for the moment.

Hardening his heart, Cass reached behind her neck with the light touch of a veteran thief and slipped the hooks that latched her necklace. A river of diamonds, emeralds, and gold-platinum spilled into his palm. He shoved this bait into his bag of loot. Pinkerton had gone to great lengths to accumulate the precious gems appropriate for Sadie's *contessa* disguise—gems that were supposed to lure the master thief, Maestro, to her side. The emeralds would fetch an especially handsome price from Cass's criminal contacts in the Underground.

"Whether you like it or not," he chided her softly, tucking the quilt around her voluptuous curves, "a female tin-star has limitations. And I'd rather you learned that lesson from me than a Pinkie Killer."

He inhaled deeply, filling his lungs with the musky scent of woman, patchouli, and lavender-scented linen. He couldn't resist brushing a silken curl from her breasts.

Wistfully, he watched the dance of darling, rose-gold freckles each time she took a breath.

His throat worked. He forced himself to look away.

Retrieving his Stetson, he turned down the lamp and slipped into the hotel's hall.

"Is it done?" Collie demanded, never missing a stroke with his whittling knife.

Cass nodded curtly at his 17-year-old sidekick and tugged the penthouse door closed.

Collie's raccoon snorted awake. Spying nothing out of the ordinary, Vandy flopped over, waved his paws in the air, and promptly fell back to sleep.

"Some watch dog," Cass muttered.

"Don't go busting your spleen on Vandy. Pinkerton's the one you're pissed at for putting your woman at risk."

"I got plenty of spleen to go around," Cass growled, envisioning the moment when he got his hands on the bastard who'd killed a Lady Pinkerton. *So help me God, Sadie will* not *suffer the same fate.*

"I'll take these rocks to the fence," Cass said. "Don't let Sadie out of your sight."

"I ain't the push-over you are, Snake Bait."

Cass glared at his sidekick.

"Aw, lighten up," Collie said sheepishly. "You're Coyote Cass. Maestro's no match for you. You'll bait him. You'll trap him. He'll hang, and we'll all go home in plenty of time for Thanksgiving."

Cass nodded grimly. Turning on his heel, he stepped over Vandy and headed for the elevator. He hoped Collie was right.

Because Thanksgiving or no, Cass wasn't sure Sadie would ever forgive him.

LADY LAW & THE GUNSLINGER SERIES

Devil in Texas
Dance to the Devil's Tune
Devil Plays With Fire

Adrienne deWolfe is a national bestselling author and the recipient of 48 writing awards, including the Best Historical Romance of the Year. She consistently delights readers with sexy, action-packed Romances, including her *Wild Texas Nights* series and her *Velvet Lies* series. In addition, she is the author of the bestselling non-fiction ebook series, *The Secrets to Getting Your Romance Novel Published*.

A fiction-writing instructor who has taught at the college level, Adrienne continues to mentor aspiring authors. She offers fiction coaching and story critiques through her website, www.WritingNovelsThatSell.com. For information about her books, visit www.WildTexasNights.com.